DEAD BUT ONCE

By Auston Habershaw

The Saga of the Redeemed
The Oldest Trick
Consisting of: *The Iron Ring*
Iron and Blood

No Good Deed
Dead But Once

DEAD BUT ONCE

Saga of the Redeemed: Book III

AUSTON HABERSHAW

HARPER

VOYAGER

IMPULSE

An Imprint of HarperCollinsPublishers

DEAD BUT ONCE. Copyright © 2018 by Auston Habershaw. All rights reserved. Printed in the United States of America. No part of this book may be used or reproduced in any manner whatsoever without written permission except in the case of brief quotations embodied in critical articles and reviews. For information, address HarperCollins Publishers, 195 Broadway, New York, NY 10007.

Digital Edition APRIL 2018 ISBN: 978-0-06-267701-3

Print Edition ISBN: 978-0-06-267702-0

Cover photographs: © MirasWonderland / Getty Images (mask); © Volodymyr Baleha / Shutterstock (background)

Harper Voyager, the Harper Voyager logo, and Harper Voyager Impulse are trademarks of HarperCollins Publishers.

HarperCollins is a registered trademark of HarperCollins Publishers in the United States of America and other countries.

FIRST EDITION

17 18 19 20 21   HDC   10 9 8 7 6 5 4 3 2 1

*This book is dedicated to this ugly world of ours,
and to those who fight to make it better, no matter what
and no matter how*

"A man's character always takes its hue, more or less, from the form and color of things about him."

—FREDERICK DOUGLASS

PROLOGUE

The tax man carried a mace—a two-foot shaft with a two-pound steel ball at one end—and where it swung, bones broke and men crumpled. This was just the beginning of the problem. The tax man wore mail, of course, and rode atop a solidly built mare—a Benethoran Red—barded in mail down its flanks and across its chest. The tax man was not alone either. Two men, also armored, their tabards bearing the white tower and red rose of House Ayventry, kept a keen eye on the alleys and dark corners of Eretheria's back streets, crossbows loaded and drawn. Thusly guarded, the tax man proceeded on his rounds, a kind of mobile fortress of steel and horseflesh, his satchels jingling with the coppers of peasants unlucky enough to be listed in his fat, leather-bound ledger.

It was dawn in the Ayventry District. The narrow

street markets had yet to come alive, the bustle of livestock and guild members on their errands was still an hour or two in coming. The peasantry was waking up to the sound of chickens clucking and the smell of wet thatching over their heads, and just starting to wonder about eating breakfast, if indeed they were so blessed as to have enough food for the luxury. This was the best time to catch a man at home, and so this was the time the tax man made his rounds.

People who could afford chickens and breakfast were often first on his list.

Outside, the last breath of winter had filled the air with a fine mist of icy damp—a kind of rain that did not fall so much as pervade the air. In an alley beside a bakery, from her post behind the rain barrel, Bree Newsome clutched her shawl tightly around her head and shoulders and tried not to shiver. She failed. *Not much longer*, she thought.

She drew back into the shadows for a moment and stretched out her fingers, trying to remember the warming spell she had been taught. She recited the energies to herself, *Dweomer for ice, Fey for fire, Dweomer for calm, Fey for desire; Ether for darkness, Lumen for light, Ether for dead things, Lumen for life . . .*

The warming spell called for the Fey, and anger, as it happened, was something Bree had in abundance. She found that little knot of rage she had kept in her stomach since her father and brother had been levied into the Count of Ayventry's armies, clenched her fists, and let its fire soak her with a few grunts and fierce expressions. The warmth filled her, banishing the penetrating cold and damp, at least for a moment. Then the ley of the world reasserted itself against her feeble efforts and, once again, the cold seeped in.

Bree shivered anew. For the thousandth time in her short life, Bree wished she were a real sorceress.

Somewhere nearby, Bree heard the jingle of a horse's harness. She took a deep breath and whistled, soft and low. She caught a glimpse of Gilvey Wilcar, the cooper's boy, darting across the street. Not part of the plan. What in the name of Hann was he doing? This was supposed to be *her* plan—they had agreed on it. He'd sworn and spat.

Fear tightened Bree's stomach like a harp string. She'd seen someone try to roll a tax man and fail before. That mace had crushed the man's face like a ripe melon. In a few minutes, that could be her face. Could be Gilvey's. She tried to take a calming breath, but having channeled the Fey just a moment ago made that hard.

Don't mess this up, Gil.

Please.

Somewhere close by, an old woman began to sing. It was an old tune—Bree had heard it since she was a little girl:

> *Go march to war, my darling,*
> *The Levy calls your name.*

> *Go march to war, my darling,*
> *For Spring has come again!*
>
> *And I will be awaiting*
> *The sound of victory's bell.*
> *And I will be awaiting*
> *The stories you will tell.*
>
> *Go march to war, my father,*
> *The Lord must earn his fame.*
> *Go march to war, my father,*
> *For Spring has come again.*
>
> *And all thy little children*
> *Shall crowd about thy door.*
> *And all thy little children*
> *Will love their father more.*

There were probably a dozen more verses—every time Bree thought she knew them all, her mother would sing a new one she'd never heard. It was meant as a salve, the song—it was bereft of heartache, of loss, of the struggle to survive when your father was levied into the campaigns. Instead it focused on the joy of reunion and the grand times that would come when your man returned with the lord's pay in his purse, jingling happily. It was crap, but it was inspiring crap.

But that wasn't why the old woman was singing it now. Rather, she sang it as a warning:

"Where the tax man goes, the press-gang follows."

The levies had been the way of things for all of Bree's life—and of her father's life, too. The people of Eretheria were used to them, but times had changed for the worse of late. It was all well and good to sing pretty ballads when only one man in ten or twenty was levied off. Quite another when it was one in five. One in four.

Quite another when the cap was lifted to two men per household instead of one.

Quite another when the campaigns lasted months instead of weeks.

Quite another when the tax man came around *twice* in the same year.

Bree's father had been pressed into service a week ago. Gilvey's father had been hiding in the eaves of his own workshop for two days. Nearly every family Bree could name had been paying the tax man by selling their own livelihoods—horses, tools, pigs, ducks, chickens—in the hopes that a black mark in the tax man's ledger would mean a pass-by when the press-gang came around.

They were usually wrong.

Bree wondered what her mother would do if they hit her house again and her family still couldn't pay. Maybe stick *her* in a pot-helm and make her march? Maybe levy her baby brother? *Did the world just become this crazy,* she wondered, sneaking deeper into the darkness of the alley, *or did I just get old enough to notice how it's always been?*

The tax man's horse passed by the mouth of the alley. Bree pressed herself against the wall and worked the camouflage spell she'd been taught. The Ether was so thick in the shadows that it went off with barely a hiccup. When the crossbowman peered down the alley, he seemed to look right through her. *So far, so good.*

Gil's turn. She heard a crash and a shout. "Look out!" The tax man's horse neighed with displeasure.

"Clear the road, by Hann!" the tax man roared. "Ugh! Gods, man, what *is* that?"

Gil's voice was bright and clear. "Fertilizer, milord! Best for sale anywhere."

The tax man looked unimpressed. "Just get it out of my way."

The crossbowman stepped away from the alley and moved out of sight. Holding her breath, Bree crept to the entrance of the alley, causing the camouflage spell to slip off her.

An oxcart had been tipped over, its contents—a stack of barrels, cheaply made—strewn across the narrow street. Some had broken open, spilling manure across the cobblestones. Of course, manure on a city street was hardly unusual and the smell ought to have been easily concealed by the potent odors of a thousand other animals and people living in close proximity. This manure, though, had been enchanted. A little thing, of course—a little bit of the Ether infused to create a stench of almost physical density. The manure to end all manure.

Gil had a rag tied under his nose and hood pulled over his head, both to conceal his identity and to keep the smell from overpowering him. He made a show of fumbling with the heavy barrels. "Right you are, sir. I'll . . . *ugh* . . . I'll have this out of Your Lordship's way in . . . *ummmph* . . . a twinkling . . ."

The tax man clapped his gauntlet over his nose. He motioned to his two guards. "Go and help him, dammit. We're going to get off schedule."

The crossbowmen set their weapons down and approached the pile of manure barrels with all the enthusiasm the task warranted. One of them tipped one barrel upright and immediately began to wretch.

The tax man groaned beneath his gauntlet. "Come on, man—it can't be that bad."

Gil tried to lift a barrel, only to fumble and drop it again. The barrel broke open. "Oops! I . . . uhhh . . . I'll get a shovel." He darted down an alley.

"Wait! Don't . . ." the tax man called after him, but Gil was gone. He heaved a sigh. "Bloody imbecile. What fool packs manure in barrels anyway?"

The tax man watched another moment or two as his men struggled with the odor and the barrels and the overturned oxcart and then, sighing heavily, deigned to dismount. "Come on, now—let's at least get it so the horse can get by."

Bree saw her moment. As the tax man and his guards put their backs into rolling barrels through sticky manure, all of them focused on not vomiting in the street, she slipped out of the alley and to the side of the tax man's horse, which had been executing a slow and subtle retreat from the enchanted manure since it had been spilled.

The collected taxes were held in saddle-bags enchanted so that only the tax man could open them. Bree, though, had no interest in opening the bags. She drew out a knife and cut the straps holding them in place with a few precise cuts and then slipped back into the alley. Then, under the cover of relative darkness, she ran for all she was worth.

After making sure she wasn't followed, she met Gil three streets away in the yard behind a blacksmith's shop. Maybe no more than a year older than she, the cooper's boy was tall and broad of shoulder with a shy little smile and kind eyes—none of which Bree would ever admit to noticing.

"I was beginning to think they caught you," Gil said.

Bree snorted. "What was with you running across the street like that? They might have seen you!"

Gil shrugged. "The oxcart was stuck. I needed a lever to knock her over. Saw a piece of wood across the street, so . . ."

"Sloppy." Bree frowned. "What would Ramper say?"

"I don't care much what that no-good cutpurse says." Gil scowled and offered to take the heavy saddlebags from Bree. She let him.

"Gil," Bree said, "we're *all* cutpurses now."

Gil looked at his feet as he mulled it over. "Yeah, well, let's get this to the Gray Lady."

Ramper could usually be found wherever men played t'suul where their wives couldn't find them. Today he was in an abandoned barbershop, both barbers having been levied into the armies of House Davram a week or so before. Planks had been laid over the big brass basins where leeches were kept and blood was drained, making a pair of tables on which the multi-colored tiles were slapped and money was exchanged. The players were laborers, mostly, gambling their copper commons with clay pipes clenched between their teeth, their eyes bloodshot from the cheap Verisi tobacco smoke that lay yellow and heavy in the room.

Bree remained in the doorway as Gil went and whispered in Ramper's ear. Ramper was probably a man in his thirties, but he looked older—his face was creased in deep wrinkles that seemed to run from his forehead to his chin in complex webs of worry and pain. He had few teeth, and so spoke with his lips pursed close together. "Another success? She'll be cheered by that, my ducks, and no mistake."

The men at their game looked up. "Who? The Gray Lady?"

Ramper grinned despite himself, the gaps in his teeth showing gums stained purple by smoky rooms and conjured booze. "Mind your tiles, gentlemen, lest the Lady lay a curse on curious ears."

A few of the men made the Hannite cross and bent back to their game, but Bree knew they were listening just the same. The Gray Lady wanted it that way. Her reputation was as much a tool as the spells she had taught the likes of Bree, Gil, and Ramper.

Ramper pressed a stone into Gil's hand. "Follow the light."

Gil nodded and the two youths left out the back, where a sewer entrance had already been pried open by a crowbar.

Gil hopped down into the darkness. He held his hands up. "C'mon! I'll catch you."

Bree might have climbed down by herself, but she let herself be caught and lowered into the dark stink below Eretheria. A globular clutch of sewer demons scattered as she was set down, sending shivers from her toes to her hair. "Quick," she hissed. "The stone!"

Gil fumbled in his purse for a moment as Bree held her breath. She could sense the oily little sewer demons closing in as they stood there, the creatures' eyeless, formless bodies ready to drag them away into the darkness. She could swear she smelled their breaths, could hear their rimless mouths calling her name. She closed her eyes and said a prayer to Hann . . .

And then the stone flared to life and they were bathed in a white glow. Adjusting to the light, the two teenagers saw that they were alone, the demons having fled. Bree let a little sigh escape her.

They held hands and delved into the labyrinth of the sewer, the enchanted stone held as high as they could manage beneath the low stone arches. Bree fought back a low, rolling panic as they got farther and farther from where they had come in. She hadn't done this as often as Gil, and getting lost was a constant terror of hers. She remembered all the stories about the restless dead wandering beneath the streets of the city, ready to snatch the unwary. She could sense the wriggling darkness of the sewer demons, always lurking just beyond the small sphere of light the stone made.

Gil kept his eyes trained on the stone, sometimes pausing at cross tunnels and swinging it back and forth. The false paths caused the stone to dim, the right one made it glow bright, and so they continued, on and on. Gil guided Bree past streams of foul black water and around piles of rotting garbage with all the grace of a prince.

And then, finally, there was a light ahead—candles flickering by the dozens and dozens in some large, domed chamber. "Damn," Gilvey muttered. "We're late."

The chamber was perhaps thirty feet across and filled with people—mostly young people like themselves, but also some grown men and women and even a few elders. Each of them was holding a candle, and all of them had their eyes fixated on the woman at the center of the room.

She wore a dark green cloak of fine quality and tall riding boots caked with grime. She was tall—taller even than some of the men—and had a face out of a storybook. Her skin was pale and unblemished, her golden hair clean and shiny, and her gray eyes seemed to encompass them all at once.

The Gray Lady. The Dark Mage.

She was speaking, her voice forceful like a priest's. "You—all of you—have been lied to."

"Good," Gilvey whispered in her ear. "We didn't miss much."

"Shhh!" Bree said, elbowing him.

The woman went on, "The people who rule you, who control you—the people who rule and control the whole world—have convinced you that mastery of the High Arts is the result of innate talent. That magi are born and not made." She smiled; her perfect white teeth seemed to light the room all by themselves. "This simply isn't true."

A mutter rippled through the audience—those who were new, those who hadn't come before, voiced their doubts.

The woman held her staff high and made it flash with light and hum with power. The crowd fell silent. "Bree Newsome!" she said, pointing her hand straight at Bree. "Step forward!"

The people parted. Bree felt a flutter in her stomach; she nearly wilted before the dozens of eyes fixed upon her. Still she stepped forward, straightening her dress and curtseying. "Yes, Magus?"

The mage smiled warmly at her. "Bree has been coming here for a week or two, haven't you, Bree?"

Bree curtsied again. "If it pleases, Your Grace."

"You all know this girl?" The woman asked the crowd, "You recognize her as one of your own?"

Some nods. One man—a friend of Bree's father—shouted out that he would vouch for her.

"Bree," the mage said. "Show these people what you've learned."

Bree curtsied again as best as she could manage. Then she took the saddlebags from Gil and held them up for all to see. Then, she examined the runes etched into the leather—the Dweomeric enchantment that kept them closed.

She forced her body to be loose, twiddled her fingers, and gathered the Fey energy in the room by focusing on that knot in her stomach, that fire in her heart, the *anger* she felt at the levy men, at Count Andluss, at the world in general. She spoke the words she had been taught, but remembered the mage's advice: *Fey spells are not known, at least not conventionally. They must be felt, practiced—they are more like physical exercises than precise recitations. Think of them like a dance performance—you might make mistakes, but grace and the ability to improvise can transform errors into advantages. Just remember this, whatever you do: once you start a Fey spell, don't dare stop until it is done.*

The power flowed through her suddenly, like a burst of adrenaline, and Bree directed it at the enchantment. There was a soft pop and then the saddlebag sprang open with a whiff of brymmstone. Bree upended the saddlebag and a shower of copper coins hit the floor with a crash.

The people cheered and dropped to their knees, gathering up as much money as they could. The Gray Lady smiled at them. "Take as much as you need— take it for your families, for your friends, for yourselves. But remember who gave it to you—not me, but one of your own."

Bree wrapped her arms around the mage's stomach—she could feel the woman was strong, solid, tall. Like her father. She wept openly, her face buried in the green cloak.

At length, the mage caught her by the chin and lifted her face to look at her. To her shock, Bree saw that the Gray Lady, too, had tears in her eyes. "The Fey is always so hard on the heart, isn't it? I'm sorry, Bree. Maybe I should have asked Gil."

"It's okay," Bree said, sniffling. "Thank you, Magus."

The Gray Lady smiled. "Please," she said, "call me Myreon."

CHAPTER 1

MIDNIGHT IN THE HOUSE OF EDDON

Bored, rich Eretherian adolescents comprised a unique economic opportunity for certain entrepreneurs who had the resources and connections to entertain them. Though a few of the young lords and ladies liked to slum it among the commoners and guild members in city taprooms and bars, most preferred to visit a variety of private estates that clustered around the outskirts of the capital. These were private clubs and gaming houses of the highest quality, where the young and the adventurous could come and gamble their parents' money among their own class with all the comforts they were seldom allowed at home and all the discretion their vast purses could afford. Chief among these "evening clubs" was the House of Eddon, the estate of Lady Hool and her mysterious brother-in-law, Waymar.

The game that night was t'suul, but then again, the game was *always* t'suul in the House of Eddon. There, in a hall of dark wood, leather, and bearskin rugs, the air filled with the scent of wood smoke and fine tobacco, the sons of earls and nieces of viscounts slapped down ivory tiles into the wee hours of morning before the blazing fire of two massive hearths. The place was packed—every settee had a lady and every chair had a gentleman. Every table was crowded round by powdered wigs and lace-trimmed sleeves; the air hummed with conversation and the clack of the t'suul tiles.

Artus drew a Rhondian cigarillo from a pewter case he kept in his sleeve pocket and lit it on a match in that effortlessly cool way he'd seen Tyvian do a thousand times—flicking the head off a ring so the flame flared up in front of his face and then cupping it so the cigarillo would light.

He burned his hand. To his delight, nobody saw. He affected a confident swagger as he strode across the room, doing his level, sixteen-year-old best to look intimidating. In the presence of these coddled, highborn teens, it worked wonderfully. Where he walked, younger boys moved aside and the older ones—those who wore swords and knew how to use them— gave him polite nods. Artus of Eddon, concierge of the house Lady Hool built from nothing, rubbed his pencil-thin moustache and scanned the crowd.

Sir Damon Pirenne, tall, wigless, and clad in a shade of gray that made him look like a rock seal, tapped Artus on the shoulder. "Pardon me, Sir Artus."

"Just Artus."

Sir Damon's pate shone with perspiration in the crowded room. "Yes, of course—Artus. There are four gentlemen at the front door requesting entry."

More? Artus frowned. "House?"

"Davram."

"We're up to our bloody noses in Davram right now. I see so much green and gold, I'm starting to think Lady Hool was just made Countess." Artus shook his head—too much of any one house, and the other houses would start to think the House of Eddon was starting to play politics, and Tyvian had been *very* specific that was never supposed to happen. "Did you suggest Madame Borgio's?"

Sir Damon nodded. "I did. I suggested Kasim's as well, but they were insistent. They claim some relation to the Earl of Leventry."

Artus closed his eyes and took a deep breath. *Kroth-spawned rich boys, I swear.* "You didn't invite them in, did you?"

Damon shook his head. "Of course not, milord."

"Artus," Artus reminded him.

Sir Damon blushed. "Yes. Sorry. Habit, you know."

"Look, if you didn't invite them in, then they can't

pass by our wards, which means you can just slam the door in their faces and they'll leave."

Sir Damon grimaced. "They are . . . well, they *seem* well connected. It doesn't seem *genteel* of me to—"

"Would you rather I get Lady Hool to do it?"

The color drained from Sir Damon's face. "I see your point, sir . . . errr . . . Artus. Door slamming it is."

The knight made an about-face and headed back toward the door. Artus watched him go and shook his head. He was a good sort, Sir Damon, but in his life before he'd acquired a sizable debt to Hool, he'd been a landless hedge knight who only ate on the sufferance of his betters. Talking back to the landed nobility did not come naturally to him, even if they *were* teenagers.

There was a commotion at one of the tables. Artus wandered over to have a look at the action. Valen Hesswyn—grandson of Velia Hesswyn, the Countess Davram—was sliding a hand-high stack of gold marks in front of him. Artus took a glance at the table—a lot of gray tiles, a lot of stacks left afield. Somebody had been running up the tally, meaning they hoped to win big or lose bigger. Artus did his best not to shudder at the board. For the young nobility, the loss of thirty gold marks in a single clutch was barely enough to cause hurt feelings, but among the people who *really* knew how to play the game—dark-eyed Illini mercenaries and foulmouthed Verisi pirates—that kind of board meant somebody was about to get stabbed.

As it stood, the current loser of the clutch—some thick-necked Vora squire—was looking fairly sore about the loss. "Burning the stack is bad form," he growled.

Valen Hesswyn's eyes narrowed. One of his flunkies—a squat bruiser of a young knight named Ethick—put a hand on Valen's shoulder. "You accusing His Lordship of something?"

The Vora boy rose halfway from his seat. "I'm accusing him of having bad manners, that's what." The conversation at the table stopped. While nobody actually touched the hilt of a rapier, it was only a matter of time before someone did.

Which, of course, was what Artus was here to prevent.

He slid between a few spectators, slipped a dagger from his wrist sheath, and slammed it into the table. It got everyone's attention. "No duels, declared or fought. You gentlemen know the rules—want to stab each other, take it outside."

The Vora squire stuck out his bottom lip. "But he . . ."

"Burned the stack on you, did he? Sore about that? Fine—nobody likes losing. But it's not bad form." Artus fished a tile out of the sakkidio—the bag in which the tiles were kept. "Do you know what *dailiki* is?"

The Vora squire shook his head.

Artus nodded. "Of course you don't—*dailiki* is

Verisi for 'good form.'" Artus held up the tile, slipped a gold mark on top of it, and slapped it on the table with a sharp *crack*. "*That* is good dailiki. I've seen you and Lord Valen here play—you *both* have bad form."

The Vora squire sank back into his chair, his expression sour. The tension, though, had gone out of the table. At length, he looked at Valen Hesswyn and nodded.

Valen Hesswyn, though, was looking at Artus. Not just looking at him, but making eye contact. And smiling. *What the hell?*

"A game later!" Valen flashed his gleaming white teeth from behind his lips. "We must play, you and I!"

Artus bowed, which hopefully concealed his confused expression. "Perhaps later, Your Lordship."

"Lordship?" Valen smiled and his flunkies smiled, too. "Don't you mean *cousin?*"

If someone had stuck Artus with a pin, he probably wouldn't have flinched as much. The noble-born did *not* call him cousin by accident. "I . . . I beg your pardon?"

Ethick laughed. "Don't worry, milord—your secret's safe with us."

Artus nodded, a smile pinned to his face. "Thanks."

Then he turned and got the hell out of there. Cousin? Secret?

A rumor. Gotta be.

Suddenly an avalanche of Tyvian's old warnings about Eretherian politics came thundering into his thoughts. What was the rumor? Who could he ask without making things worse?

He looked around for Brana—there, by the fireplace, entertaining a host of young ladies by cracking walnuts in his mouth and doing handstands. Artus grimaced.

If they only knew . . .

Of course none of them did—to the insular world that knew of their bizarre little "family," Brana was merely Artus's idiot brother. Tall, handsome, and guileless as a puppy, but most assuredly human. In reality, Brana (and his mother, Hool) were gnolls—great hairy beasts from the distant prairies of the Taqar. A kind of human/lion/dog creature—fierce nomadic hunters and warriors. Their appearance tended to, well, *excite* the more genteel at parties, hence the illusory shrouds that disguised them. Artus was endlessly thankful that truthlenses—magical devices that could see through illusions—were considered rude to use in public.

Artus started in Brana's direction, only to be intercepted by two young women, one of whom had the boldness to grab him by the sleeve. He froze. "Yes?"

They were each about his age. One tall and graceful, but with cheekbones so sharp they could be bladed weapons; the other petite, with chestnut hair and amber eyes and burgundy lips . . .

He abruptly realized he was staring. So he decided to bow, hoping it wasn't too obvious a cover.

The girls giggled. The petite one spoke first. "Sir Artus, is it?"

Artus fought back a blush. "Just Artus, milady."

She pointed to the balcony that overlooked the gaming hall, where Tyvian sometimes stood to oversee things. The doors were currently closed and the curtains drawn. "We were wondering . . . does your father receive company?"

"Master Waymar isn't my father, milady—he's my uncle. And no, he doesn't."

"Told you," the tall girl said. "See?"

Artus looked from one to the other. "I'm afraid I don't follow. My uncle is a private man, so he doesn't—"

The tall girl rolled her eyes. "Come now, Artus—everybody *knows*."

A shiver passed down Artus's spine. *Kroth—what's the rumor?* "I'm afraid you ladies got me at a disadvantage."

The tall girl crinkled her nose. "Got? *Got?*"

The petite girl curtsied. "I am Lady Elora Carran and this is Lady Michelle Orly. Pleased to meet you."

Artus bowed again. "Nice to meet you. Now, if you'll excuse me, I gotta . . ."

Michelle snorted. "Gotta?" She gave Elora a significant glare. "*See?*"

Elora offered Artus her hand. "I hope we'll see you again tonight."

Artus, his mouth suddenly dry, took her hand and

kissed it. She smelled like vanilla, and her hand was cold and soft in his own.

"Oooh," Elora said softly, "your hands are so warm."

Artus found himself grinning like an idiot and rooted to the spot. Elora and Michelle spotted some other friends and took their leave, but not before Elora gave him a long look over her shoulder that was about as powerful a sedative as any drink Artus had ever imbibed. It took Artus the better part of a minute to remember what he was trying to do.

Right—Brana. Ask about the rumor.

He moved more quickly, trying not to make eye contact. Even so, Artus knew that people were looking at him. A number of strategically placed fans concealed lips in midwhisper—what were they saying?

Finally, Artus was at the end of the hall. The north fireplace was wide enough to admit four men standing abreast and it blazed with the most expensive firewood money could buy—enchanted to last all night and englamoured to smell more pleasant. Tyvian had insisted upon it, even though it cost one hundred times more than regular old logs. And even then it still burned up.

Before the fire, Brana had his tongue hanging out the side of his mouth as he caught the walnut tossed to him by the gaggle of young ladies. Brana cracked it between his teeth and delivered the meat to the hand of some blushing young woman who, were all sense of propriety lost to her, would probably have her tongue hanging out as well. All of them were giggling entirely too much. Artus found the whole display perverse.

He was about to interrupt when Sir Damon showed up again. "More at the door, milord."

Artus groaned and pulled Sir Damon aside. "Seriously? Who?"

Sir Damon shrugged. "House Hadda this time."

Artus rubbed his moustache. He noticed that his cigarillo had gone missing. What had he done with it, anyway? "Hey, have you heard any rumors about me recently?"

Sir Damon stiffened. "I do my best not to gossip, milord."

Artus rolled his eyes. "And I'm a griffon. Out with it. What did you tell people?"

Sir Damon blinked. "Sir, I am offended—I hold the doings of this house in the utmost confidence." He paused. "But I have *heard* something."

Artus looked around. People were watching. Lots of people. *Well, too late to be subtle.* "What did you hear?"

Sir Damon shrugged. "Well, just that your uncle Waymar is the heir. Everybody's talking about it. Been the talk for days."

Artus grabbed Damon by the arm. "Heir to *what*?"

Sir Damon frowned. "Why, the Falcon Throne. The heir to all the counties of Eretheria."

Artus's mouth fell open. As rumors went, that was a big one. A really, really big one. "Nobody . . . I mean, nobody *believes* it, right?"

Sir Damon's own mouth fell open as he read the shock on Artus's face. "Well . . . I mean, it's certainly *possible*. Your uncle and your mother are rather mysterious, wouldn't you say? And wealthy. And nobody knows where you came from. So . . ."

Artus backed away from Pirenne and looked once more through the hall. Again, he found himself meeting the gaze of a dozen other young peers, most of them female. They smiled or waved or beckoned him closer—these people who, just a few nights ago, wouldn't have given him more than a passing glance. The realization struck him like a slap: *They think I'm a* prince. *Great gods, they think Tyvian is secretly* king.

Moving quickly, Artus grabbed Brana by the collar and yanked him from his admirers. "Where's Tyvian?"

Brana grinned. "Wanna walnut?" He held out his hand. "No drool on it. Promise."

Artus slapped his hand away. "Tyvian! Where is he?"

Brana snorted. "His rooms. Locked the doors. Nobody's supposed to bother him. You go up there, he'll get mad."

"Trust me—he's going to want to hear this."

CHAPTER 2

HOW TO ENTERTAIN A KILLER

Over the years, Tyvian Reldamar had developed a sort of sixth sense about whether or not somebody was planning to kill him. Though he could not express how this worked exactly, he could always tell, much in the same way he could tell when it was going to rain or whether a particular pastry was going to be tasty or not.

It was a very useful skill to have. Especially now, as the woman across the table from him was plotting to kill him. No doubt about it.

Her name was Adatha Voth. She was petite, with delicate bone structure and porcelain skin. Midnight curls fell on either side of her cherubic face, her lips were heart-shaped and luscious pink in color, and her left eye was a warm, chocolate brown. Her right eye was blind—milky white—the effect, no doubt, of whatever bladed instrument had left the dark scar running down her face from her temple to her cheekbone. The scar was a reminder to all who looked: this woman was no stranger to violence. Still, she affected an air of daintiness.

It was a ruse.

Voth's apparent delicacy was only skin-deep. Tyvian had noted the muscles in her forearms—taut, cable-thick—that bespoke someone who worked with her hands. What threw him, though, was that her hands were manicured, refined. They were not the hands of a laborer or a craftswoman, where thick calluses would be evident and nails would be chipped. What kind of person had forearms like those, but hands relatively unblemished?

A killer, that was who—somebody who did a lot of strangling or, perhaps, fenced with gauntlets on.

Tyvian found her intoxicating.

She smiled at him. Tyvian smiled back, wondering just who was paying her and what the angle was. This was their third meeting and Voth was getting progressively friendlier. That inclined him to suspect poison. She was learning his habits, his mannerisms. She was enticing him closer. Even now, she toyed with a lace of her shirt with one burgundy-lacquered fingernail, just above her cleavage—drawing the eye.

"You have me in quite a spot." Tyvian smirked, devoting his attention to the game board.

They were alone and, of course, it was late. Tyvian's private sitting room was on the second floor in the southeast corner of the House of Eddon, his—well, no, *Hool's*—private manse. One balcony was closed and its curtains drawn, and through it trickled the muted din of the gaming tables below. On the opposite side of the room the other balcony stood open, the stars spread out to the horizon, a sparkling accompaniment to a full moon. The city of Eretheria lay beneath, its steeples and spires gleaming with the silvery glow of starlight. No more than two miles distant, the Empty Tower of the Peregrine Palace pierced the sky like an ivory horn, dwarfing everything around it. It presented a phallic symbol that was difficult to ignore.

If she were going to kill him, Tyvian thought, this would be the perfect time. His bedchamber was only steps away, the mood was right, the wine was good . . .

"Do you resign?" Voth asked, her good eye sparkling. A smile tugged at the edge of her mouth. "I had expected a better match from a man of your *supposed* gifts."

Tyvian considered his wineglass. Not poisoned. He'd just poured it himself, from his own—no, *Hool's* own—private stores. Voth never had the chance to put anything in it. He'd had both her hands in sight the whole time. He picked it up and sipped. The heady flavor of a fine Akrallian white, still cool, washed over his tongue, tingling all the right spots. "If I *were* to resign, would we talk business then?"

"What *else* would we discuss, hmmm?" Voth tossed her hair and leaned forward against the table, giving Tyvian a thrilling view—should he choose to take it.

Tyvian chose to. "I can think of a handful of topics."

One burgundy-nailed finger twirled a single ringlet of her hair. "Really? Do elaborate."

She might have a knife, Tyvian thought. Were *he* trying to kill himself, though, a knife wouldn't be his first choice. Tyvian had a deserved reputation of being a good knife-fighter, and any bladed contest would constitute a risk for the assassin. Assassins hated risk.

Voth sipped her wine. "You seem lost in thought, Tyvian. I hope I'm not distracting you." She smiled, knowing full well she was. That hand kept twirling her curls. Tyvian could imagine his own hands doing much the same thing. He could imagine taking a great, big handful of that beautiful black hair and running his fingers through it.

Poisoned hair? It was possible. She probably wouldn't be playing with it so much, though. Even if sorcerously abjured against the poison herself, the risk would be pointless. She didn't need to toy with her hair to seduce him.

Wait, was he *actually* being seduced? Tyvian cocked his head to one side. "Miss Voth, are you trying to seduce me?"

She produced a sultry laugh—the deep-throated kind that made men's hearts feel like dice in a tumbler. One finger traced the rim of her wineglass in a slow circle. "I thought you already had a woman in your life."

Tyvian glanced at the spirit clock behind Voth—two in the morning. Myreon usually didn't get back until after dawn. Plenty of time. "Who says I can have only one at a time?"

Voth grinned and rose, then walked around the table toward him. "How nice to hear."

This was it. Probably. Tyvian got up as well, then backed away. "So I take it you want to table our negotiations on the price of bladecrystals for another time?"

She wrapped her fingers into the lace of his collar and pushed him back against the wall. "Very much so."

Her perfume was faint, but expensive—a subtle scent, making her closeness all the more inviting. She leaned against him, hands snaking up his sides to his shoulders, and pulled him down so she could kiss him.

Tyvian decided to kiss her back. If she had poison lips, it was too damned late anyway—he may as well enjoy his last few moments alive. Her tongue darted between his lips and she pressed against him even more tightly, moaning softly. Her hands crawled higher on his shoulders, tore off his lace collar and moved toward his bare neck.

"Ah!" Tyvian felt a sharp jolt of pain and he leapt away from Voth. *A needle! A poison needle!*

"What?" Voth blinked.

Tyvian examined himself—no needle. No injury. Then what . . . Oh. It was that stupid ring—the plain iron band he could not remove and which had very particular opinions on his moral conduct. He glared down at his hand. "Dammit all!"

"Is something wrong?" Voth came closer, extending her arms to embrace him. "Are you hurt?"

"No, I'm fine, I just—" He stopped himself. Voth moved to cup his face in her hands, lips again parted for a kiss. Her hands. Those nails. Long, pointed, burgundy-lacquered nails. *Of course.*

Tyvian grabbed one of her hands by the wrist and quickly wrapped it behind her back, pinning her arm. She yelped with shock. "Tyvian!"

He piloted her across the room and pushed her onto the sofa. "Very clever, Adatha! You almost had me, too."

Voth sat up. "What are you talking about?"

Tyvian kept his distance, ready to slip the stiletto from his sleeve at the slightest sign of Voth coiling to attack. "Bloodroot poison can be made into a lacquer and layered under the tips of fingernails—blends in perfectly with exactly that shade of nail polish, too.

One scratch on the throat and I would be as good as dead. Very clever."

Voth blinked. "You . . . you think I'm trying to *kill* you?"

Tyvian rolled his eyes. "Oh, here we go with the feigned-innocence act—spare me, I beg you. You're about as innocent as a pit viper and we both know it."

"I wasn't planning to kill you!"

Tyvian pulled over a chair, reversed it, and straddled it. "That's exactly what you would say if you *were* planning to kill me!"

Voth folded her arms. "And what if I *weren't* planning to kill you? What would I say then?"

Tyvian scowled. "Prove it!"

"Prove what?"

Tyvian pointed to her throat. "Scratch your own damned throat—let's see if you die."

"No!"

"Ha!"

"I am not going to claw my own throat because you're paranoid!" Voth put on a very convincing pout.

"Oh, what, and I'm supposed to comfort you now? I suppose you'll whip up some tears next." Tyvian affected a high-pitched voice. "'Oh, woe is me. Tyvian Reldamar insulted my honor, boo-hoo!'"

Voth looked away, her arms still folded. Tears did, in fact, well up beneath her good eye. She didn't say anything, though. She only sat there, mutely weeping. "I . . . I thought you *liked* me."

The ring gave Tyvian a pinch. He snarled at it, "Don't *you* start."

Voth glared at him with her glassy good eye. Her whole face colored red. "Do you know how hard it is being a woman in the smuggling trade? When . . ." She snuffled. "When am I supposed to meet a man who will accept me? Hmmm?"

The ring pinched harder. Tyvian clenched his teeth, but said nothing.

"I mean, *look at my face*, Tyvian!" Voth pointed to her scar, her dead eye. "Do you think I have many romantic prospects? I have to keep the walls up all the time, you know—always on guard, always ready for betrayal . . ."

The ring was like a vise on his hand. Tyvian growled under his breath, "Not on your life, you stupid thing."

"And . . . and then I meet *you*, and you're handsome and charming and kind to me. I . . . I thought we were kindred spirits, you and I!" Voth was openly crying now, wiping tears away with a corner of a throw pillow. She hunched her shoulders, letting the sobs wrack her compact frame. "I . . . I thought we were in *love*, dammit, and . . . and it was just another *game* to you, wasn't it?"

Tyvian sighed. "No. It wasn't a game. I . . . I promise." The ring blazed at the lie.

Voth pressed her face into the pillow. "Go away! I won't have you see me like this! Just . . . just go away!"

Tyvian looked around. "But these are *my* chambers."

Voth pointed to the door and kept crying into the pillow. Her voice was muffled. "I've never been so embarrassed in my life!"

Tyvian stood up, the ring still digging into his hand. He knew it would do that all night, too. He moved to leave, but it pinched him still harder. "Hang it all," he grumbled.

Slowly, reluctantly, he came to sit on the couch beside Voth. He pulled out his pocket handkerchief. He nudged her shoulder. "Here."

Voth dropped the pillow and, with a precise slash, raked her fingernails across Tyvian's left cheek. Fiery pain blossomed all through the side of his face. "Gotcha!" She winked.

Tyvian lunged for her, but she was too quick. She ran to the open balcony and jumped. Hand clutched to his face, he chased after her, but the poison was already making him dizzy, and he tripped over a chair leg. "Dammit!" he growled.

"Stupid . . . stupid Krothing *RING!*"

CHAPTER 3

A VERY PUBLIC MURDER

Artus had just about resolved to go upstairs and kick in Tyvian's door when there was a crash above him. He looked up to see the doors to Tyvian's balcony burst open and Tyvian himself stagger out, hands clutching his face, blood running down his arms and staining his sleeves crimson. "Hrrr . . . Artus!" he shouted, his voice garbled, as though his face were swollen. "P-P-Poison!"

People pointed and screamed.

Tyvian staggered, evidently trying to stumble back into his room, but lost his balance and tipped over the balcony railing and plummeted toward the floor.

Brana was already in motion. He flew across the room in one stupendous leap and caught Tyvian before he bashed his brains out on the hardwood floor. In the wake of Brana's superhuman feat, a dozen people lay dazed on the floor, knocked over like ninepins.

Artus found himself fighting the press of the crowd to get to Tyvian. "Out of the way! Out of the way, dammit!"

He needn't have bothered. Brana hoisted Tyvian on one shoulder and barked, "Danger!" He then plowed through the press of concerned nobility in Artus's direction. Brana had grown in strength and size in the time since they'd moved here, but the shroud stayed more or less the same, so Artus had forgotten that, beneath the illusion, his "little" brother was now six feet and over two hundred pounds of pure, fuzzy gnollish muscle.

"Make room, people! Make some room!" Artus shouted, and Sir Damon cleared off a t'suul table so that Tyvian could be laid down. His legs dangled off the edge, but his body fit, so it was good enough. Tyvian's face was swollen to twice its normal size and his whole body was some strange combination of twitchy and limp. "Tyv . . ." Artus stopped himself. "Waymar! Waymar! Wake up!"

Brana was sniffing the wound on Tyvian's face. He got some strange looks, but nobody said anything. "Poison!"

Sir Damon took Tyvian's pulse, his face grim. "Bloodroot, looks like. Seen it before. Very fast acting."

Artus looked at Brana. "Tyvian's room—get the wands!" Brana charged away, running on all fours even though he still wore his shroud.

Sir Damon shook his head. "He's going to die, lad."

"The hell he is!" Artus shouted. He looked around at all the people standing there, staring. "What are all you people looking at? Huh? Either help or get the hell out!"

One of the nobles—the Vora squire from earlier—blinked. "I . . . I beg your pardon?"

From the back of the crowd, Hool's voice penetrated the furor. "You heard him! All of you people get out of my house!"

She was standing just inside the main entrance, her shroud depicting her as wearing a gown of silver and white that bloomed out from her hips like the petals of some rare flower. She did not look happy.

No one, it turned out, was quite willing to meet Lady Hool's eerie copper gaze—her true eye color, though everyone assumed it was a glamour intended to unnerve others. The guests began filing out immediately, with Sir Damon helping in calling their coaches around to pick them up. Artus was only loosely aware of this—most of his attention was on Tyvian, lying there on the table, his skin turning a deeper shade of gray with every passing moment.

Brana came back and dumped a half-dozen wands on the table. "Got them!"

Artus looked at them. "Dammit! Which one's the purification wand?"

Brana shrugged. "Dunno."

Artus picked up one wand and then the next—they all looked more or less the same, with only faint variations. *Dammit, where the hell is Myreon?* "Which one did you get from Tyvian's wine closet?"

Brana cocked his head. "Ummm . . ."

Artus felt a lace of pure panic trace its way across his back. Gods, Tyvian could *die!* All the times Tyvian had saved him, and now here he was, and . . .

"Kroth take it!" Artus covered his eyes and tapped his fingers on random wands. "Handras, Udent, Varner, too, Ezeliar, please be true!"

It was a slender one of some kind of rosewood with a tip like the bud of a tulip. Artus waved it over Tyvian, wondering what the trigger word was.

Hool loomed over him. "Is he dead yet?"

"No!" Artus shouted at her. "He's not going to die! He can't die!"

Hool sniffed at Tyvian's face. Tyvian was now completely still and all color had drained from his face. "He seems pretty dead."

Artus shook the wand. "Dammit, come on!"

There was a glow at the tip of the wand and then Tyvian convulsed once, every muscle contracting in one body-wide seizure. Then, as quickly as it started, it stopped and Tyvian fell limp again. He rolled off the table. Artus caught him and held him on the ground. He felt stiff and cold.

He wasn't breathing.

Tears crept into Artus's eyes. "No . . . no . . . it . . . it ain't fair."

Hool laid a hand on Artus's head. "I will eat whoever killed him. I promise." She sighed. "It was probably one of the people who owes me money. That's a lot of people to eat." She looked at Artus. "It might take me a few weeks to eat them all."

Brana bowed his head and whined.

Tyvian coughed. Once. Twice. A ragged breath was drawn in, let out. He groaned. "Krrrrroooooth . . ."

Artus leapt up. "He's . . . he's alive!"

Hool took a deep breath. "Good. I'm not hungry."

Artus stared down at the smuggler, who was beginning to get color back in his cheeks. "But . . . but he was totally dead. You all saw that, right? How . . . how did that happen?"

Hool snorted. "With him, who knows? Maybe he did this on purpose for some stupid reason. Just get him into bed."

Brana helped Artus lift Tyvian up. "Maybe the wand fixed him!"

Artus shook his head. "I don't think so. I'm . . . I'm just not that lucky."

"No," Hool said, pointing at the unconscious Tyvian, "but he *is*."

Tyvian opened his eyes to see the early dawn light chasing shadows across the ivory moldings of his bedroom ceiling. It definitely *was* his bedroom, too. He was alive. Artus actually managed to save his life after all. *I'm going to have to raise his allowance after this.*

Correction: *Hool* would have to raise his allowance.

Tyvian tried to sit up. Except he didn't move. Not one bit. His whole body, as it turned out, was numb and stiff as a fencing dummy.

Idiot boy! He must have used the wrong antidote or something. Maybe snickerbark extract—that never worked properly. Tyvian wanted to scowl, but his face was currently opposed to much in the way of expression. Or, at least, it was so numb he had very little idea what kinds of expressions he was making.

Second correction: Hool would have to *dock* his allowance, the idiot.

He was probably drunk, Tyvian thought. *This is just the kind of botched job a drunk teenager would pull.*

The house was utterly quiet; another late night in the House of Eddon, this one probably later than usual. Tyvian was alone and would be for hours, so he laid there, a prisoner in his own flesh, trying to work the feeling back into his face. After a while, everything started to tingle and burn. He took it as a good sign.

As he did this, he brooded over his situation. Adatha

Voth had tried to *kill* him. That wasn't terribly upsetting in and of itself, but what *was* upsetting was just how close she'd come to pulling it off. He was getting sloppy. Losing his edge. But for the damned ring, he might have killed her before she had the chance to scratch him. He could have held a knife to her throat, maybe broken her hand. But no. The ring, stupid dunce that it was, had fallen for her wounded-lover bit like a heartsick imbecile and dragged him along with it.

There was more to it than that, though. When last he saw her, his mother—the retired Archmage of the Ether—had told him that the ring operated by collecting those parts of him that were good and noble. Though she lied about most things, for some reason Tyvian felt inclined to believe her in this, as it was the only way he figured the ring could have that much power over him. The ring was a reflection of his better self—an artificially applied conscience—so, on some level, he *had* felt badly for hurting Voth's "feelings" and he *had* wanted her to feel better. The thing that bothered him was *why* that might be. Voth was just a bit of fun—a bit of a thrill, that was all.

Right?

Gradually, Tyvian found he could use his neck a bit. He tried lifting his head, and it was as though he were lighting his shoulders on fire. He kept trying. If nothing else, it was a bit of variety.

He thought about Voth and what she had meant

to him. She was a hard woman, deadly and ruthless. A woman who worked in the shadows but was no stranger to the halls of power. In short, the woman reminded Tyvian of himself—his *old* self. The self he'd lost the day he'd leapt out of that burning spirit engine over three years ago.

Now look at me, he told himself, glaring at nothing in particular. *Almost murdered in my own home, lying in bed like an invalid. Pretty soon Brana will probably trot in and bring me something to eat. Probably feed me like a child.* The thought was enough of a jolt that he was, at last, able to lift his head enough to see the whole of his room . . .

. . . only to discover Lyrelle Reldamar, his mother, sitting at the foot of his bed. She was dressed in a riding dress of maroon and gold, a cream silk scarf wrapped around her neck, her hair pulled up. She was reading a book, her gloves still on.

Tyvian's head thunked back onto his pillow, striking the headboard. His voice croaked like a rusty hinge. "What in hell are you doing here?"

Invisible specters stuffed feather pillows under the small of Tyvian's back and under his arms to prop him into a sitting position. Tyvian desperately hoped he was scowling.

It was then that Lyrelle Reldamar deigned to recognize him. She closed the book and slipped it . . . somewhere. She looked him over. "Good morning, Tyvian. How is Myreon?"

"Seriously?" Tyvian rolled his eyes. "Let's dispense with the niceties, Mother—get to the point. Why are you sitting in my bedroom at the break of dawn? Surely not to check up on my romantic escapades."

Lyrelle's steel-blue glare sharpened. "Is that what Myreon is? An *escapade*?"

Tyvian *knew* he was scowling now—he didn't need to feel it. He remained silent.

Lyrelle reached over to the half-finished bottle of wine Tyvian and Voth had been sharing the night before and poured some into a mageglass goblet she conjured with a gesture. "And what about this Adatha Voth? I must say, your behavior with her is disappointing."

"Voth seduced me, Mother. I . . . It didn't mean anything." Tyvian felt like he was babbling, so he stopped. "It was only a kiss."

Lyrelle shrugged and took a sniff of the wine. The corners of her mouth tugged, though the expression was too vague to read. "Hmmm . . . I rather doubt Myreon will see it that way, don't you?"

"Stop it! Just . . . just stop it! This is excruciating! Are you aware, Mother, of how perverse this whole thing is? You break into my home, unannounced, and sit there drinking my wine and interrogating me about my love life while I lie here paralyzed from the neck down!"

Lyrelle chuckled. "Always so dramatic."

"Says the woman who manipulated half the people

in the West just so she could get a magic ring stuck on her son's finger." Tyvian was sliding lower in the bed. At this point, he wasn't so much looking at Lyrelle as at the ceiling just above her head. "Will you please just present me with whatever lie you've crafted to make me dance like a puppet and then be gone? I'm having a very bad morning."

Lyrelle grinned. "You know, I don't think I've ever told you how much you remind me of your father."

The observation was like a thunderclap in Tyvian's heart. He felt, for a moment, that he had forgotten how to breathe. "Wh . . . What?"

Lyrelle nodded. "He would have liked you, I suspect. Yes, very much so."

Tyvian nailed a tight lid on the monstrous swell of emotions seeking to crowd out his rational thought. "No."

"I beg your pardon?" Lyrelle blinked at him.

Tyvian snarled through clenched teeth. "No. No you don't. You may *not* have this conversation with me, do you understand?" He slid down all the way—now he *was* looking up at the ceiling.

The invisible hands of specters dragged him back to an upright position. Lyrelle sighed. "I didn't think you'd be emotionally prepared for this conversation, and I see that I was right."

"You think I care?" Tyvian forced a snorting laugh. "All those years when I was a boy, when I would ask you *every Ozdai's Eve* who my father was, when I would write the man Krothing *letters* that you said you'd *send* to him—*that* was the time to have this conversation. Now? Kill me, stab out my eyes, slash my face—I couldn't give a rat's coffin over my father." Tyvian was surprised to find that there was a tear building in the corner of his eye. Had he functional hands, he might have wiped it away. Instead, the lousy little traitor rolled down one cheek. Its presence only made Tyvian angrier. "As far as I'm concerned, the man never existed. He's a phantom. A childhood dream. I've moved past him."

Lyrelle frowned at him and, for a fleeting moment, Tyvian thought he saw genuine empathy there—perhaps even guilt. Not for long, though. "That may be, Tyvian. But pretending your father never existed is a luxury that you will not have for long." She stood up and, with a single finger, wiped his tear away. Tyvian considered trying to bite her. But her words drew him up short.

"What are you talking about?" Tyvian found all the fingers on his left hand were able to twitch, but with no coordination.

"The rumor is that you, Waymar of Eddon, are the lost heir to the Falcon Throne."

Tyvian blinked, but refused to let the shock set in. "That is the stupidest rumor I've ever heard! Nobody will believe it. Even if they did, nobody would dare act upon it—Eretheria's nobility want no kings pushing them around. That's why Perwynnon died."

Lyrelle shrugged. "You have been ensconced in your little hideaway too long, Tyvian. Times are difficult in Eretheria. Thanks to your brother crashing the Saldorian Markets—which you failed to stop, I might add—a significant portion of the Eretherian peerage have too much debt and not enough ways to pay it off. They are frightened. The future looks uncertain. If the harvest isn't a good one—and things don't look especially promising at the moment, given how many farmers they had to levy before planting season—well, they'll be doomed. They need money and to get money they need influence—more influence than they can garner with coalition building." Lyrelle set her goblet down. "They need *unilateral* influence."

"What? Like a *king*?"

Lyrelle shrugged. "Or Sahand."

If Tyvian could have leapt to his feet, he would have. "What?"

"Sahand may no longer be a major military player, but the Crash has worked very much to his advantage. Sitting as he is atop a pile of gold in a private treasury, he's started to bail out various lords of their debts. Of course—"

"The Mad Prince's money comes with strings attached." Tyvian groaned. "Sweet merciful Hann, woman—what is Saldor even doing, anyway? Can't they . . . can't *you* do something about that? Sahand owning Eretherian fiefs is *exactly* how he managed to conquer Galaspin last time!"

Lyrelle smiled. "But Tyvian, I *am* doing something about it—I'm talking to *you*."

Tyvian froze, midscowl. "What? What could you possibly mean by that?"

Lyrelle kept smiling at him.

"No. No no no!" Tyvian tried shaking his head, but nothing much happened.

"I've made certain the rumors about your parentage are widespread, but nobody was going to give them much credence. At first." Lyrelle shrugged. "But now a top-quality assassin—the kind a Great House like Camis or Hadda would likely employ—has poisoned you in front of a host of gossipy nobles. Now, who would do that for some nobody, hmmm?"

"You're mad, woman!" Tyvian gaped at his mother. "Are you saying *you* sent Voth? Are you trying to get me *killed*?"

Lyrelle rolled her eyes. "Don't be so angry! I didn't send Voth—I swear, that was someone else's doing. But I didn't try to prevent it, mostly because I knewVoth's attempts to poison you would fail."

Tyvian snorted. "How could you *possibly* have known that? I almost bloody died!"

Lyrelle pointed at his ring hand. "An act of kindness is no mere trifle to that 'trinket,' as you so dismissively term it. An act of compassion led you to be poisoned, and therefore the ring was powerful enough to *reverse* the effects of the poison. I've learned this through my studies of Eddereon."

Tyvian swiveled his eyeballs to look at the ring. *Interesting.* "You're trying to change the subject now. Why the hell would you let on that I might *actually* be heir?"

Lyrelle folded her hands in her lap, the picture of graceful poise. "I'm doing you a favor. You're miserable, cooped up in this luxurious little prison you've designed for yourself—you just can't admit it. Do you really intend to spend the rest of your life sipping wine and playing t'suul with empty-headed Eretherian nobles? Do you really think Hool can take much more of this life? Or Myreon? Don't make me laugh."

"I have an idea," Tyvian said, snarling. "Why don't you, for once, let other people make their *own* choices in their lives? Eh? Ever tried that?"

Lyrelle smiled then, but her eyes were distant for a moment. "Yes, I did. Once."

"Really? With who?"

"Your father."

The question *Who is he?* threatened to spring to his lips, but Tyvian pushed it away with a string of colorful profanity.

Lyrelle tsked him and ticked off her fingers. "You are the right age, you have the right breeding, you have the right kind of money. Gods, you even *look* a bit like the man. Everyone, my son, is going to think you are the long-lost heir apparent to the Falcon Throne."

"That . . . this is *madness*! What do you expect me

to do? Rule bloody Eretheria? They'll never let me."
Tyvian scowled, "No—*I* won't let me! I won't do it! It
could never work!"

Lyrelle shrugged. "Who said it needed to work?
You would make a terrible king, Tyvian. All *you* need
to do is make everybody *think* you'd be a good one.
Give everybody an alternative to Sahand. Rally the
Congress of Peers, as it were."

"In other words, *be king*." Tyvian rolled his eyes.
"And if they ask for proof? What happens if I sit in
the throne and the wards burn me to ash because
I'm not the blood of the Falco . . ." Tyvian trailed off.
Something—something horrible—just occurred to
him. "Wait—I'm not, am I?"

Lyrelle pretended she hadn't been listening. "Not
what, dear?"

Tyvian glared at her. "Is Perwynnon my father?
Am I the heir?"

His mother seemed to consider the question in the
same spirit one tried to remember the birthday of a
distant cousin. "Hmmm . . . you know, I'd prefer not
to say."

"You . . . you Kroth-spawned *bitch*!"

"Language, young man." Lyrelle's eyes flashed. "I
might not be your favorite person, but I'm *still* your
mother."

"Who has no problem manipulating and brow-
beating her own son into near-suicidal political ven-
tures for her own gain."

Lyrelle shrugged once more. "Be that as it may, there is no reason to tell you your father's identity at this juncture. Besides, I thought he was a phantom. I thought you had moved on." She sighed at the flash of anger that heated Tyvian's face. "If I tell you, and Perwynnon is *not* your father, you won't be effective in the role I'm setting for you. If I tell you, and he *is* your father, you'll flee the country rather than wind up as king."

"Wind up dead, you mean—that's where this all ends, you know."

Lyrelle nodded. "Yes. I know."

Tyvian gasped. "Really? That's all you have to say?"

"I'm sure it will be a very spectacular death, Tyvian. Not everybody gets one of those—you should feel blessed."

Tyvian was sliding down in the bed again. "You'll pardon me if I don't jump for joy. Bloodroot poisoning, you know."

Lyrelle rose. "Well, that about settles things for me. I must take my leave." She caught up a silk shawl from the back of the chair and wrapped it around her shoulders. "If my auguries are accurate, Myreon should be on her way back very soon. You may want to brush up on your groveling and excuses and such."

"Always a pleasure to see you, Mother." Tyvian snarled as he began to slide sideways on the bed. "Give my regards to brother Xahlven."

Lyrelle smiled at him and patted his cheek. "Oh! I almost forgot." With a flourish of her hand, she produced a very familiar rapier hilt with a single crystal at one end, its mageglass blade not, as yet, conjured into being—*Chance*, Tyvian's sword, lost when he had been arrested in Saldor. "You'll be needing this. For your brother, I expect. Remember: in the end, this is a battle between him and me. And you, Tyvian, are my champion. Don't fail me."

Tyvian looked at the hilt as she laid it in his lap. It looked . . . different somehow, though he couldn't put his finger on it. "What did you do . . ." But he didn't finish his sentence.

Lyrelle was gone. Indeed, he realized he might never have been speaking to her at all. His mother had more simulacra than she had pairs of shoes. As he was thinking about this, he finally slid off the bed entirely and hit the floor with a thump. "Dammit all."

He supposed, in the end, it was good news that the fall hurt—the numbness and the paralysis had faded a little bit. The bad news was he was stuck on the floor until Brana came in with breakfast.

CHAPTER 4

A SEWER OF WISDOM

The main advantage of Eretheria's extensive sewer network was, of course, that Eretheria had a reputation for being one of the cleanest cities in the West. The secondary advantage, and the one most relevant to Myreon's purposes, was that the Defenders of the Balance—the "mirror-men," the militant order of Saldor's Arcanostrum—could not easily scry into them, as the Etheric ley provided for many false readings and dead ends. This meant that the sewers made for an excellent place to conduct illegal activities. *Especially* the kind of illegal activities Myreon had been engaged in for the last year.

As she pried up a sewer grate in an alley off Lake Street and slipped into the impenetrable darkness, she wondered for the hundredth time what Tyvian, the career criminal and scofflaw, would think if he knew Myreon Alafarr, faultless champion of justice, was slipping into dark corners to do mischief. She grunted to herself as she pulled a shard of illumite from her cloak and made her way down a narrow, low-ceilinged passage to the main storm drain, where she'd be able to stand upright. *Tyvian would probably assume I'm trying to make a quick copper.*

But she wasn't. Not at all.

Myreon was training sorcerers.

The little globular shadows of the sewer demons scurried out of the light as she headed toward that day's meeting place. The little *creatures*—though the term barely applied to the formless blobs—were part of the reason the Etheric ley here was so prominent. The sorcerers who had constructed these sewers had conjured the demons to eat the trash and refuse dumped in them and, at night the things would even wriggle out of drains and venture into the unlit corners of the city streets to eat whatever garbage was left lying around. They weren't dangerous, but they *were* disgusting, and superstitions surrounding them were numerous—they were bad omens, punishers of the unrighteous, and bearers of pestilence. None of it was true, but it was sufficient to keep all but the stoutest souls from nosing around the sewers. For all her intrinsic distaste for the things, she had come to think of them as another security feature.

The third security feature was the fact that the "classroom" moved day by day, and Myreon took care not to hold lessons in the same place twice. Today, they were working in a large, cylindrical chamber—a cistern where four water mains would empty in the case of a hurricane. Starlight trickled from a large grate fifteen feet above, looking up at a part of the city neither Myreon nor her students were aware of. The place smelled of faintly rotten eggs and rust, but unlike most of the sewers, the ley was a bit more even here, meaning all the energies would be easier to draw.

There were a few stools, carried in by some of her students, and a table made from an old door laid across two sawhorses. Tonight, there were almost thirty people crowded into the tight, dank space, each holding a candle and waiting for her to appear. They were mostly young and all of common birth, hailing from a dozen different professions. There were farmers' daughters and thick-necked porters, there were an array of shy house servants, an apprentice smith, two grooms, a girl who sold flowers in the Border Street Market, another girl or two who sold less legal goods, and so on and so forth. Myreon tried to know them all—it was another important security protocol, actually—but the faces kept changing each and every class. Some would come just once—just to see what it was like—and never return. Some others had been coming every day for a year. And practicing on their own, besides, despite Myreon's warnings.

She heard their whispers echoing up the tunnels long before she saw them, and she was among them long before they saw her—a legacy of her training as a field operative more than a sorceress. To their eyes, however, she appeared in their midst as if by magic. *A sense of theatrics*, Lyrelle Reldamar had once told her, *is a sorceress's best defense.*

It didn't hurt that it was a bit fun, too.

"Apprentices!" Myreon announced holding her arms up. She wore a dark green cloak, smeared with sewer grime, and beneath it a bodice of burgundy with gold embroidery, men's breeches, and knee-high riding boots. She worked a little glamour into her hair and person, so she looked taller and her hair more golden than it was in truth. It had the desired effect. Her students fell silent and drew back from her. A few of them knelt.

"The Gray Lady," they whispered.

She waved them up. "An apprentice does not kneel, save when begging forgiveness. How have you offended me?"

One girl who knelt—one of the servants—shook her head. "In no way, Magus."

"Then get up, and let's have the report." She smiled—the smiling, she had found, worked wonders. It was as if nobody ever smiled at these people or, at least, nobody of her station.

The apprentices began to talk, timidly at first, and then with more and more energy as they got worked up.

"Used that eavesdropping spell you taught, Magus. Heard the Earl of Menthay's sister saying His Grace needs another levy. Folk in Laketown best keep a top eye open."

"That camouflage spell saved my da. He's worried the mirror-men will come down on us, but every time the press-gang comes round, they can't find him, and off they go again!"

"Got my hands on a tax man's ledger and changed the figures all around with the scribble spell. Won't *he* be surprised!"

There was some money, too—boosted from the backs of supply wagons or from the saddlebags of tax collectors. Myreon always had them dump the money quickly and then incinerated the containers. Scrying might not work down here, but seekwands definitely did, and it paid to be careful. If the soldiers in the service to the nobility ever realized they were being duped by sorcery, the Defenders would come down on them like thunder.

When they'd finished the report, she walked to the makeshift table and leapt on top of it. "Apprentices, first Etheric position! Go!"

Myreon walked them through their exercises. What

few people understood was just how physical a discipline sorcery was. Channeling the Great Energies took as much control of the body as it did of the mind. The popular image of the wizened old sorcerer, decrepit and brittle, showed only half the truth: sorcerers who lived long enough to become old, usually aged so poorly thanks to the physical toll of their art. Furthermore, sorcerers who grew old also, through long experience, had become so attuned to the Energies that channeling them took less effort. What took these young people all their bodies to achieve, Myreon could accomplish with a quick gesture of the hand. What Myreon could accomplish with a quick gesture of the hand, Lyrelle Reldamar could do with a thought.

"When are we going to learn to throw fireballs or something?" Bree, a round-faced milkmaid of barely sixteen asked, her tongue sticking out the side of her mouth as she tried to build a competent Dweomeric ward around herself.

Myreon couldn't help but grin—Bree was what her father might have called a "real sparker."

"Focus on wards first, Bree. We aren't starting a war here."

"Hey! Hey, Magus!" She turned to see Gilvey Wilcar—a cooper's son with a big, honest face and stickout ears—standing with his arms crossed in front of himself. "I think it worked!"

"Hmmm . . ." Myreon extended a finger and shot a little ray of cold at him.

It flash-froze some of the hair on his arms and made him flinch. "Ow!"

She tapped his leg with one foot. "You're locking your knees again, Gil. Keep them loose—keep everything in your body loose and also focused."

Bree rolled her eyes. "That's impossible."

"Why would I waste my time teaching you impossible things, Bree?" Myreon said coolly. "Again, please. You're almost getting it."

Ramper slipped into the chamber, late as usual. Ramper was one of her more important contacts and one of her more talented students. Back in her days as a Mage Defender, he would have been the person she would want to catch to bring this whole enterprise down—he was the face of her organization. He vetted new potential students, he was given the enchanted stones to lead the apprentices to the new location each day, and he kept his ear to the ground for trouble.

He was wearing a patched cloak and mismatched clothing. He bowed to her. "Magus."

Myreon waved him up, and she saw the twinkle in his green eyes. "What is it?"

Ramper waved her over to a shadowy spot in the room. Myreon could see all the students following them with their eyes. "Mind your lessons!" she said, and then wove a ward against eavesdropping around them. "Well?"

Ramper opened his cloak to reveal a half dozen finger-thin rods stuffed into various pockets. Wands.

Myreon closed his cloak. "Where did you get those? Are they stolen?"

"Easy, Magus. Easy." Ramper smiled with his mouth closed. "I weren't born yesterday. Met a talismonger, sympathetic to the cause, as it were. Willing to sell to you for a discount." He reached inside his cloak, pulled out a wand, and held it out to her. "Have a look."

Myreon didn't touch it, but did work a few auguries around it. She got an image of the talismonger—an old man, living alone in Westercity, in the shadow of the big artifactories there. He worked and slept in a shop with two extra beds. *His sons have been levied*, she realized.

The reading could be a plant—maybe—but Myreon had no indication the Defenders even knew she was down here. Certainly they'd heard the rumors of the Gray Lady by now, but that's just what they were—rumors. The Eretherian nobility might treat rumors as fact, but the Defenders adhered to a slightly higher standard of evidence. Slowly, she let a breath out. "They look clean. Sparkwands?"

"Shoot a bit of lightning, yeah." Ramper nodded. "Give a few of us these here and we could knock over a press-gang. Let all them poor souls free and singing your praises, no doubt."

Myreon shook her head. "Use those and the Defenders are down on us."

"They'll be down on us soon enough," Ramper countered.

"You don't know what you're talking about." Myreon stuffed the wand back inside his cloak. "I do."

Ramper ran a broken fingernail along his uneven stubble. "When you started this here, you promised me—promised *us*—a change."

"And change is what you're getting. How many people have we fed, Ramper? How many people have dodged the tax man and avoided the press-gang?"

Ramper shrugged. "Tax men come back, Magus. Press-gangs take somebody else. We save a couple, and a score more get levied. Seems to me we ought to see about making *fewer* tax men. Seems we oughta make the press-gangs think twice."

Myreon scowled. "I said *no*, Ramper!"

"But, Magus—"

"No!" Myreon's voice echoed off the walls, well beyond the capacity of any eavesdropping ward to contain. Her apprentices stared at her.

Myreon sighed. When she spoke, it was to all of them as much as to Ramper. "You have to understand: what you're talking about isn't a real solution, Ramper. Killing will only make things worse."

Ramper closed his cloak, concealing the wands. "Everywhere I go, all I see is empty shops, untended houses. How much worse can it really get, Magus? That's what I'd like to know."

Myreon didn't have anything to say to that. She shook her head. "Throwing lightning and fire around will only get you killed. Back to your places, everybody. Our time together grows short."

Class resumed, but everyone had seen the wands and that sight, it seemed, weighed on everyone's thoughts. Even Myreon's. Comparatively cheap as they were, the wands were a mark of power—a kind of power these people had been intentionally, systematically denied. Her refusal smacked of just one more such denial, and she knew it.

It made her feel terrible.

As the night sky began to pale and dawn approached, the class broke up. The apprentices thanked her, clutching her hand and kissing it, touching the hem of her robe, pressing little gifts into her palm—a Hannite cross carved from wood, an old tin ring, a small sweetapple, a faux talisman against sewer demons. She tried to give them back, but they wouldn't have it.

Ramper was last. He looked at her, his eyes green like the sea—they were the clearest, cleanest part of him, burning as though with witchfire. "Folks everywhere know the Gray Lady is there to help them. We thank you kindly, Magus. Not a one of us don't understand the risk you take teaching us your secrets. I ask Hann to bless your name every night." Murmurs of assent rippled through the group. Gilvey gave her a shallow bow. A couple of the girls blew her kisses and made the sign of Hann on their hearts. But she knew

Ramper wanted to say more—to do more—and she was afraid for him.

Myreon gripped his forearm. The muscles were iron hard and wiry—a laborer's arm. "A few wands can't change the world, Ramper. Remember that."

Ramper nodded slowly. "That may be. But a fella can't be too careful, can he?"

The look on Ramper's face was a look she'd seen before, just not on Ramper. It was the same look Tyvian got anytime he was about to reveal some ridiculous plan. "Don't do anything rash, Ramper. You should just go home."

Ramper laughed. "Funny thing to say, as I ain't got one." He scampered to the storm drain and Gil helped him up. In the shadows beyond, Myreon could see a candle flickering—Bree, waiting for them.

After they had gone, Myreon scoured the cistern of any sign they had been there—every drop of wax, every scuff mark, every thread or hair—to protect them should the Defenders find the place. While she worked, she turned over the specter of the wands in her head. Who was she to criticize them? Wasn't she the one who had spurred her apprentices on, given them the confidence to stand up for themselves, taught them that they were worth far more than they had ever been told? How could the bladesmith abhor violence, when she was the one passing out the blades?

A voice, cold and flat as a lake in winter, came from behind her, although not to answer her question. *"Well met, Magus. I trust thy efforts this night were not in vain."*

Myreon felt a chill go up her spine, but she resolved not to overreact. She turned to see an animated corpse—little more than dusty bones and a few scraps of fabric—standing at the center of the cistern. It was not what had done the speaking, of course; it was merely the vessel. "What do you want?"

"I want what is due, Magus. Your gratitude. Your respect. It is my realm you use, is it not?"

"And what of your respect for *me*? Must I always speak with you through an animated corpse?"

"For now, yes. One day, perhaps, we will meet. When you are ready." Myreon sighed. The sewer's advantages against the scrying of the Defenders meant, of course, that she was by no means the first or only such sorcerer to use them. The necromancer, whoever he was, had been here far, far longer than she had and he styled himself some kind of "king of the underworld." She knew the type well; back when she was a Mage Defender and not a rogue sorceress, she'd tracked down and arrested a number of them. They invariably had large egos, poor hygiene, and questionable morals.

"Can I assume I and my students have your indulgence to use another cistern the next time we meet?"

The skeleton produced a thin, rasping laugh. *"So*

presumptuous. You wound me, Magus. A year hath passed, and still I am paid no tribute, no respect. We are allies. Peers. We should work more closely. There is much I could teach you."

Myreon snorted. "I told you—no. You are to stay away from my students and keep out of my business. In exchange, I will stay out of yours. Understood?"

The skeleton stood silent for a moment. Finally, the voice came back, slow and hard. "*As you wish.*"

Myreon nodded. "Good." With a wave of her hand, the skeleton's enchantment was dispelled and the bones collapsed onto the floor. Only after the "presence" of the necromancer had left her did she realize how tired she was.

"Home," she muttered to herself, climbing into a water main. "A bath. A long sleep. A good meal." She couldn't wait.

CHAPTER 5

COMPLICATIONS OF A POISONING

Breakfast had been porridge. Tasteless, lukewarm, beige porridge fed to Tyvian with a wooden spoon by Brana, whose practice using spoons was not extensive. Brana was not wearing his shroud, and he crouched by the side of the bed in all his huge, furry glory—haystack gold fur, big gold eyes, and tufted ears laid flat against his skull with concentration. Every time the gnoll shoveled a puddle of the abhorrent wheat paste from the bowl, he stuck his huge pink tongue out, the tip curled up toward his nostrils, as he maneuvered the spoon toward Tyvian's lips. This visual did not improve the dining experience.

At first it had struck Tyvian as unseemly to fight

the act of being fed. He was not a child and, indeed, he was hungry. But at some point enough was enough. The spoon was coming for him again, and Brana was basically licking the inside of his own nose and humming to himself in concentration. "Brana, stop please."

The spoon came closer.

"Brana, I don't want anymore."

"Just a little more," Brana countered.

"I said no!" Tyvian rolled his head away and closed his mouth. This caused the spoon to make contact with his cheek instead of his mouth. The slimy sensation of his breakfast sliding down his neck was, thankfully, largely deadened by the aftereffects of the poison. Not deadened enough, though, for Tyvian not to know it was there, pooling in his bedclothes.

"Oops." Brana's ears stood up straight and his tongue relaxed. "Sorry."

Tyvian scowled. "Well, what are you staring at? Go and get something to clean me up!"

"Okay!" Brana trotted out of the room on two legs. The young gnoll was walking less and less on all fours lately, even when not wearing his shroud.

Tyvian sighed and looked out the window. It was still early. *Chance* rested on the bedside table, taunting him. *Gods know how long it will be before I can pick up another sword.*

In his regular life of late, not being able to fight would have been a concern, but not a deadly urgency—life had been quiet this past year or so, once they'd gotten settled here. Now, though, with this blasted rumor running around . . . well, the odds Tyvian would have to fight a duel or two in the next few weeks was very, very high. One did not threaten the status quo of the Eretherian Counties without making enemies. Lots and lots of enemies. He scowled, potential plots and scenarios to extricate himself from his mother's elaborately woven cage running through his mind, tracing the threads of probability to their likely ends.

Very few of them ended well.

Kroth take that damned sorceress!

The door opened, and he opened his mouth to tell Brana to go away, but then his mouth closed like a trap. It wasn't Brana. It was Myreon.

She came to the edge of the bed and stood over him, her golden hair braided tightly around her head. The damp of the early morning mist still clung to her dark green cloak—she must have come directly to him upon her return. She did not look sympathetic at all considering Tyvian's bedridden state. "Who poisoned you?"

Tyvian chuckled, in spite of himself. "No 'How are you my dear?' or 'Are you all right?' We're just jumping right to the poisoning part?"

Myreon did not seem amused. "I want to hear you lie to me. I want to hear you tell me it wasn't that Voth hussy."

Great . . . just great, Tyvian groaned inwardly. "Who told you?"

"Brana. Just now."

He rolled his eyes. "Damned gnoll. Asking him to keep a secret is like asking a fish to stay dry."

Myreon jabbed him in the chest—enough that he actually felt it. "No changing the subject—Brana *should* have told me, because this is something I *ought* to know, you miserable, lying louse!"

"She tried to kill *me,* Myreon! Why am *I* getting in trouble for this? Shouldn't you be out seeking revenge for your wounded lover?"

Myreon scowled and ran a finger along the scratches on his cheek. "You kissed her, didn't you?"

Tyvian groaned—there was no point in lying to her. Myreon, with her Defender's arts, could read his private chamber like an open book. She could just flip back a few pages and see the whole damned thing. She probably already had. "She seduced me. You must have noticed that in your auguries, Myreon—I wasn't exactly a *willing* participant."

Myreon lips pressed together. "Don't even start that. Don't you lie to me like that!" She stepped away from the bed and turned her back to him. Outside, the sun was burning off the morning clouds, pouring through the big windows and reflecting off the spring green wallpaper. In this light, Tyvian could see the dirt on her cloak—black and oily, in streaks near the hem.

"Myreon, I've known she was planning to kill me

for a while. I was trying to lure her in. I wanted to figure out who she—"

"Maybe I'm too tall for you! Maybe if I had bigger breasts and one eye, you'd be more faithful, is that it?"

Tyvian grimaced. This was about to get unpleasant. "Myreon, you are an elegant—"

Myreon's eyes flashed. "*Elegant* is a word men use to describe furniture and sailing ships, not *women*, you consummate jackass!"

"Beautiful, then! You are beautiful! Satisfied? Is that sufficient?"

Myreon wheeled on him. "It's not about being *sufficient*, Tyvian! It's about being loved. About being *faithful*!"

"I *was*—"

"*YOU KISSED HER!*"

"I stopped! Right away, too!" Tyvian tried to remember, exactly. "Well, nearly so anyway!"

"*You* stopped?"

"Well—"

"Exactly—the ring did it! The ring made you stop—if not for it, the two of you would be wrapped up in each other's arms!"

"She. Tried. To. Kill. Me!" Tyvian spat. "I wouldn't be wrapped up in her bloody arms, I'd be dead! Gods, woman!"

Myreon waggled a finger at him. "No! I have a *right* to be mad at you, and mad at you I will bloody well stay! When we began our . . . whatever this is—you and me. When that began, what did you promise?"

Tyvian groaned and closed his eyes. *This again.*

"Yes! This again, Tyvian! What did you promise? I want to hear you say it!"

Tyvian kept his eyes shut and let the words stumble out. "That I would never lie to you."

"That's *right!* 'Never lie to you'—your exact bloody words! And now here we are!"

Tyvian opened his eyes. Myreon had her hands on her hips, her chin jutting out, her eyes flashing—just like she used to look when she was trying to arrest him. "Here we are where? With me *not* lying to you? You realize I have *yet* to tell you a lie during this entire conversation, correct? I *admitted* to kissing her, I *told* you she poisoned me, I—"

"You might have mentioned she planned to assassinate you *before* the attempt was made!" Myreon rolled her eyes. "Or does that not count? How bloody quibbling are you going to get with me about telling the truth?" Tyvian searched for the words, but Myreon kept going. "Never mind! It's you! *Of course* you're going to quibble and *of course* you're going to keep secrets from me!"

"And what about you?" Tyvian wished he could point—he wished he could do *anything* other than be forced to lie there and get scolded like a naughty puppy. "You've been keeping *lots* of secrets from me, haven't you? I can tell—your cloak is dirty, but not just any dirt. You've been in the city sewers, right? All these midnight outings, only back at dawn? Do I ask *you* about them? Do I?"

Myreon frowned, but her indignation morphed into mute defensiveness. "They're none of your business."

"Oh, really? How am I to know that? You could be having an affair!"

Myreon raised an eyebrow. "In the sewer?"

"Now who's being evasive?" Tyvian asked. "And that's beside the point! I don't ask you, Myreon, because I trust you! Why can't you offer me the same courtesy?"

Myreon's eyes flashed. "Experience, Tyvian. Experience."

Tyvian sighed. He let his head drop back on his pillow. He let the fight drop as well. There was no way it could be won and little point in continuing it. She was angry, and nothing was going to change for the better until she was no longer angry. His task, as always, would lie in finding a way to make that happen. He started to catalogue the kinds of rare flowers he had yet to give her.

It was a rather short list.

Myreon sat on the edge of the bed. She also looked tired. "From what Brana told me, you were very lucky. He's convinced you came back to life."

Tyvian grunted. "I more or less did. Side effect of the ring, apparently."

Myreon frowned. "How? How do you know?"

Tyvian closed his eyes. "I am not, just now, in the mood to discuss it."

Myreon scowled and looked away. When she spoke again, her tone made clear her intent to change the subject again. "Who hired her? The Sorcerous League? Sahand? The Kalsaaris?"

Tyvian considered the list of his enemies, all of them earned in the years since the Iron Ring had been permanently affixed to his hand, forcing him into a life of *relative* morality. "This wasn't the League's style nor Sahand's—not enough sorcery for the former and not enough physical brutality for the latter to be satisfied. As for the Kalsaaris, we haven't had a sniff of them in over two years."

"Your brother, then?"

Tyvian snorted. "If Xahlven wanted me dead, I would be dead. As I am alive, I assume he has other plans for me."

Myreon's face darkened, as it did anytime Xahlven Reldamar came up in conversation. As she was already angry, her face became dark indeed. She looked ready to spit lightning. "One day. One day we'll get even with him. We only need to find him."

"Find him? He's probably within arm's reach, shrouded to look like someone we know." Tyvian chuckled. "Hell, he's probably Sir Damon."

Myreon rolled her eyes. "That isn't funny."

Tyvian tried a smile, just to see where it got him. "But it *did* make you laugh, correct?"

Myeon glared at him. "Very well. I'll take my leave. From what I can see, you're making a full recovery."

"You make that sound like a bad thing." Tyvian offered her another smile.

Myreon answered with another glare—this one sharp enough that it might have killed Tyvian all over again. She opened her mouth and Tyvian readied for the fight to begin anew, but there was a knock on the door and Artus poked his head in. The boy had grown up a lot in the past year—something Tyvian sometimes forgot. He was getting broad in the shoulders and sporting a moustache and patchy goatee.

Tyvian welcomed the diversion. "Artus, do you think perhaps choosing a public place in which to fret over my impending demise was a bad idea? Do you have any idea the mess you caused?"

Artus shrugged. "Well maybe next time you shouldn't jump off a damned balcony into the middle of the room."

Tyvian scowled—the young man had him there. Though in truth he did not *remember* jumping off any balcony.

Artus held out a towel to Myreon. "Just drawn you a bath—Hool's orders."

A thin smile crept onto Myreon's face. "She probably smelled me coming a mile off. Thank you, Artus."

"Just remember it weren't me that said you stank, milady." Artus bowed slightly—good form, too. The boy was finally learning. Well, apart from implying that a woman smelled bad.

Myreon gave Tyvian one last glare and left for her chambers. When she'd gone, Artus softly closed the door. "Boy, you're in it now, Reldamar."

Tyvian snorted. "You, too? Dammit, boy, you *saw* Voth—you want to tell me you wouldn't let her kiss *you?*"

Artus laughed. "Well yeah, but I ain't courting no bloody mage, now am I?"

"We aren't courting."

An eyebrow shot up. "Then what the hell *are* you doing with her?"

"I . . . we're . . ." Tyvian sighed. "Damned if I know." He took a deep breath. "Do you know what Myreon's been up to lately? Where she goes, what she does—does she tell you?"

Artus held up his hands. "Hey now, don't put me in the middle here."

Tyvian pressed his lips together. "I don't need you to pry. But . . . but if you should happen to see her out sometime . . ."

"Well . . ." Artus rubbed his hands on his doublet, which made Tyvian wince. "All right. Been curious myself." He stood in the doorway for a few moments more, evidently searching for the proper words.

"Out with it," Tyvian snapped.

"Hool got a bunch of letters this morning, from all over. All five houses."

Tyvian frowned. Letters weren't, in and of themselves, unusual. "By 'a bunch,' how many do you mean?"

"Twelve. And courier djinns have started showing up outside—three so far."

Tyvian felt his stomach sink. "And?"

"They're addressed to Waymar of Eddon—you."

"Kroth." Tyvian closed his eyes. "This can't be good."

"That's what I thought."

"Well, you might as well bring me to them."

CHAPTER 6

INVITATIONS

By midday, Tyvian had received twelve additional letters and nine actual gifts, all of these via courier djinn. That made twenty-four letters overall, all of which were addressed to Waymar of Eddon and not Lady Hool nor to the House of Eddon in general. Tyvian took some solace in the fact that his alias seemed to be holding—the Defenders wouldn't come beating down his door, at a minimum—but he had gone overnight from a figure of idle curiosity to one of absolute focused obsession. Whereas before the peerage might have asked themselves, in their idle moments, who the mysterious brother-in-law of famed gaming house mistress Lady Hool was, *now* they all thought they knew—he was the supposed heir to the Falcon Throne.

Or, put another way, he was a threat to their very way of life.

The letters and gifts had all been moved to the study—a room on the first floor that really only Myreon and Tyvian ever used and, as such, was probably the neatest room in the house. Artus sorted the letters into little piles on the writing desk. The packages were set on the floor. Everything was still sealed within its envelope or wrapping, each of them marked with an enchanted wax seal that prevented anyone but the addressee from opening them. Given Tyvian's mostly paralyzed state, this meant that Artus and Brana had to carry Tyvian downstairs like a besotted drunk and help him wave his hands roughly over all the seals. Then Brana nestled Tyvian into a wingback chair and propped him up with cushions.

Though greatly improved since breakfast, Tyvian's hands still barely functioned, and so he asked Artus to read aloud for him. It was slow going, as Artus's grasp of the written word was still tenuous. Over the next three hours, Tyvian listened as Artus hacked his way, syllable by syllable, through the flowery prose of the Eretherian noble class. A finer form of torture Tyvian could never have devised for himself.

When all was said and done, there were ten letters of condolence and solidarity—all sent on the assumption he had survived the attack last night, which, given his access to sorcery, was entirely possible. Besides these, there were another fourteen invitations to various costume balls, parties, salons, and one wedding. All the letters were addressed to him from an even distribution of vassals of the five Great Houses—Davram, Camis, Ayventry, Vora, and Hadda—though the ranks of the authors varied widely, ranging from a couple of lowly peers who owed Hool money to a letter from the Countess of Davram herself. At least one letter was from a member of each Count's immediate household, with the lone exception of House Hadda, as Countess Ousienne did not *have* any living immediate family and the old spider wasn't terribly likely to go writing love letters to some nobody who got himself poisoned, not when she was sitting on a pile of gold bigger than all the other houses combined.

As for the gifts, they were mostly jewels, objets d'art, or rare books—some poetry by the immortal Casca of Rhond, a small bust of Perwynnon carved from alabaster, a variety of women's jewelry (evidently for Hool), and a small silver chest stuffed with gemstones.

The implications of all this were, frankly, shocking. Tyvian had Artus pour him a glass of Vingili '28 to steady himself. Brana had to help him drink it. Artus stood by and poured himself a glass, too. "So, what's it all about?"

Tyvian motioned with his chin to the letters

stacked neatly on the desk. "This, Artus, represents a declaration of war upon our household."

Artus frowned. "Do you mean, like, real war with armies and knights and such, or some kinda stupid war of manners or something?"

"When you put it that way, it underscores the danger we're all in, and I'd rather we didn't do that." He sighed. "But yes, this is a 'stupid' war, Artus. Yet stupid wars can kill you just as horribly as the real kind. All of Eretheria seems to think—or suspect—I'm the heir to the Falcon Throne."

Artus frowned, "How do they know you're alive? Last most folks saw was you . . . well . . . was you being dead."

"They're hedging their bets," Tyvian said, licking some stray wine off his lips. "If I'm dead, then *my* heir might be favorably inclined toward their show of sympathy."

Artus snorted. "Your heir? Who's that? You got a kid you ain't told us about?"

Brana laughed. "Secret kids! Ha!"

Tyvian gave Artus a hard look. "My heir is *you*, Artus."

The laughter died. Artus took a moment to process this and then shook his head. "But . . . but why do they even believe all of this? It's just a rumor! I'm not a prince!"

Tyvian motioned to his scratched face, registering the not inconsequential fact that he could more or less move his arms. "In their world, Artus, the only reason I might be the target of assassination is if I were politically important somehow. Suddenly, all those rumors look true. They think I'm the heir, which either means they need us as an ally or need us dead as soon as possible."

Artus pointed at Brana, who was holding Tyvian's wineglass to the smuggler's lips so he could get a drink. "What about Brana? Or Hool? Are they on the hook?"

Tyvian swallowed and licked his lips again. "Hool is supposedly my half sister by marriage—we aren't blood relations. Brana is the supposed product of another marriage between her and some unnamed father we haven't bothered to delineate, and so isn't either. As you are, again supposedly, the progeny of Hool and my fictionally deceased brother, only you have the supposed Perwynnon blood."

Artus squinted, trying to keep track of the lines of genealogy in his head. "That's . . . complicated."

Tyvian sighed. "To the Eretherian peerage, it is as simple as breathing. Every damned one of them has already figured this out, so you better get your head wrapped around it, too, or we'll never survive this."

"But they're just inviting you to parties, not challenging you to duels or nothing."

Tyvian smiled. "Yes, Artus, but where is it, do you suppose, that a fellow *gets* challenged to a duel, eh? It isn't done by djinn, you know."

"Well . . ." Artus frowned, thinking. "What are we gonna do?"

"Burn the letters!" Brana said, starting to gather them off the desk.

"No!" Tyvian moved to intercept him and fell out of the chair, winding up facedown on the expensive Illini rug. When he spoke again, it was out of the half of his mouth that wasn't pressed against the ground. "I need to answer the letters! Once . . ." He groaned, trying to roll himself over and failing. ". . . once I can write again."

Artus frowned. "I dunno. Hool won't like this— this sounds an awful lot like one of your crazy plots."

"Yes . . . or no . . . not exactly." Tyvian flailed his arm in the air. "Artus, if you *please!*"

Artus hoisted Tyvian to his feet and helped him back to the wingback chair. "I guess *I* could write the letters, right?"

"With your handwriting?" Tyvian shuddered. "I . . . I need to think. Alone. And I could use something to eat."

"More porridge?" Brana asked, his rear end wiggling.

"No! Gods, no—never mind, I'll starve." Tyvian waved his arm toward the study entrance. "Just . . . leave me in peace. At dinner I'll have something worked out. I promise."

They left him. Tyvian caught a glimpse of Hool, wearing her shroud, watching from the hallway. He assumed she'd heard everything he'd just said. Very well then.

He closed his eyes and tried to think like an Eretherian count.

By early evening, Tyvian felt he had regained enough movement in his hands to try writing responses to a few letters. He was wrong. Granted, he could make legible letters, but they lacked any kind of elegance, any kind of flair, and the last thing he wanted to do was appear a useless rube. Nothing would put him in a coffin sooner than looking like a country bumpkin trying to play prince. Nobody liked an upstart.

Letter writing in Eretherian noble circles was no minor matter. Every letter Tyvian might send would be scrutinized to the point of obsession, searching for any implied insults, compliments, threats, or promises. The way he dotted his *i*'s could be misconstrued as anything from a confession of carnal desire to the orthographic equivalent of a kick in the shins. Each letter would need three drafts—one for content, one for diction, and one for calligraphy. He simply didn't have it in him. He would have to fall upon his backup plan: fewer letters, more social engagements.

And, therefore, the implied risk of duels. But, of course, if he couldn't stand, he couldn't be expected to duel. Someone would have to stand for him, and that someone would almost certainly be Artus. Artus, though a more than competent brawler for his age, was no duelist.

Every which way I turn, there lies another bad end.

At dinner, Brana carried Tyvian into the dining room. Everyone was there, and the serving specters were laying plates upon the table. As hungry as he was, Tyvian found he couldn't think about eating. There was too much to do.

Brana installed Tyvian in another high-backed chair and propped him up like a fragile dowager. Artus tended the fire in the broad hearth to get it roaring against the chill of the evening. The sun had set about an hour ago, the gates had been locked, and Sir Damon had been sent home. The five of them were alone in the House of Eddon, and the dining room table had been warded to prevent eavesdropping, sorcerous or otherwise.

Nobody ate. They waited for Tyvian to speak.

Tyvian cleared his throat. "Friends," he said, "it seems we've gotten too comfortable."

"We?" Myreon arched an eyebrow. "Don't you mean *you*?"

Tyvian didn't rise to the bait. "We've been living in the lap of luxury this past year, pleasantly incognito, and have forgotten just how big the world and how numerous our enemies."

Artus sipped some wine. "Well, mostly *your* enemies."

Tyvian closed his eyes. "Please stop interrupting. You're interfering with my . . . my . . ."

"Careful wording designed to trick us without overtly lying?" Myreon offered, batting her eyes sweetly.

"Everybody shut up," Hool growled. She was unshrouded and curled up in her huge chair like a lioness on a rock, her mane blazing red-gold in the firelight. "Get to the point, Tyvian."

"The *point*," Tyvian said, "is that somebody is working to destroy me. Those invitations . . ." Tyvian gestured vaguely in the direction of the study. ". . . are opening salvoes in what is bound to become a massive political battle fought over yours truly. They should be considered what they are: clear and obvious warnings that, if we don't act fast, we will likely end up dead."

Silence. Hool had her ears back—she had something to say, but she was waiting for Tyvian to finish. Artus poked at his food. Myreon seemed lost in thought, her eyes distant. Brana was eating.

Tyvian sighed. "All of you, with the exception of the lovely Myreon . . ." He cast a quick glance to see if the word *lovely* had scored any points. It had not— she glared at him as though intending to set him on fire. He cleared his throat. ". . . are implicated and involved in this. We can't sit back and let this pass. Besides . . ." He shrugged. ". . . I'm assuming you'd all rather not see me dead, in any case."

Myreon frowned. "Well, not *dead*. Is tortured an option? Castrated, perhaps?"

"I don't get it," Hool said. "Why would they care if you're supposed to be king? I thought they never had kings here."

Tyvian shook his head. "Not exactly—they've had *two*. One, Perwyn the Noble, who founded Eretheria about sixteen-hundred years ago and another, Perwynnon, the Falcon King, who ruled Eretheria for about three years in the final years of Keeper Astrian X. That was just under thirty years ago."

"What happened to him?" Brana was alert, ears up. He always loved a good story.

"Perwynnon was found dead in his chambers in the Peregrine Palace, evidently poisoned, though the exact cause of death has never been determined." Tyvian shrugged—which he was pleased to realize had returned to his physical repertoire. "The method scarcely matters, though—the fact is that the ruling families of Eretheria, the five Great Houses who dictate most policy and custom here—didn't want a king telling them what to do and one or all of them had him killed. They needed Perwynnon to defeat Sahand, but once Sahand was sent back to Dellor with his tail between his legs, they quickly wanted to get rid of anyone wearing a crown."

"Which brings us back to you," Myreon said. "There are always rumors about this or that person being the heir. What's different about you? Besides your ego, of course."

"Ha. Ha." Tyvian scowled at Myreon, who smiled

sweetly back at him. "Anyway, what's different is that the economy has changed. Somebody has decided that I need to be seen as a serious candidate for heir because the spring campaigns are shaping up to be the most chaotic since the *last* time they had a king. A powerful central ruler could possibly stabilize the country—for better or for worse—and then, once the status quo is achieved again, they can just bump me off just like they did my alleged father."

Artus sat forward. "Soooo . . . is he?"

"Is who what?" Tyvian frowned.

"Is Perwynnon your dad?"

"What do *you* Krothing think?" Tyvian was surprised by the venom in his voice. He shook it off. "No . . . of course not. No."

Artus frowned. "Sorry. Touchy subject, I guess."

Tyvian took a deep breath. "It's all right. It doesn't matter. Even if I wanted to *act* the heir, I'd eventually be proven a fraud. *Only* the blood of Perwyn can sit on the Falcon Throne, you see—it's a very old, very powerful abjuration set into the stones of the palace itself. If I were to try, I'd be burned to ash or something. Likewise if I try to touch the crown, wield the royal sword, enter the royal chambers—you name it."

"That doesn't matter, though," Myreon said. "Even if you can't do those things, that doesn't mean everybody *knows* that you can't. Perwynnon himself didn't try to sit in the throne until his ascension was more or less guaranteed politically."

"Wouldn't somebody just ask him to?" Hool said.

"No." Myreon shook her head. "There's no advantage in it—if you *want* a king, and Tyvian is incinerated by trying to sit on the throne, you lose; if you want *no* king and Tyvian *can* sit on the throne, you also lose. It's too big a gamble. Nobody will risk it until they absolutely have to."

Tyvian nodded. "Myreon's right—as long as people *think* I'm the heir, I am going to be treated like the heir whether I want to be or not. Hence the invitations to parties and salons in town. Hence that box full of jewels that Vora girl sent me."

"*Us*," Hool corrected. "They sent that to us. Those jewels are mine."

Brana seemed excited by this. "What are we gonna do?"

"Well . . ." Tyvian rubbed his stubble against the back of his hand. "I'm going to have to formally renounce the throne, of course."

Artus blinked. "Oh . . . that's . . . that's *it*? I thought it was gonna be another one of your complicated plots."

Myreon shook her head. "Renouncing isn't simple."

Tyvian nodded. "To formally renounce means going to the Congress of Peers—the Eretherian governing body—and being recognized as having standing to speak."

"But you're the heir," Artus countered. "Shouldn't that give you standing?"

"But if I'm the heir, what's to keep me from ascending the throne, which happens to be in the *exact same room* as the Congress of Peers?" Tyvian said.

"And if he's the heir," Myreon added, "then nobody is going to want him anywhere near that throne."

"Except the people who want a king, and then they don't want me to renounce." Tyvian sighed once more. "So, yes—complicated."

Brana nodded slowly. "Soooo . . . what we gonna do?"

"Run away," Hool said. "Right now. Nobody will find us."

Tyvian motioned vaguely at the opulent dining room. "And give up all this for a life on the road? Gods, Hool, do you remember what we went through to get all this?"

Hool put her ears back. "Yes. I traded a bunch of stupid pieces of paper with fools and then they paid me lots and lots of money and you made me sail on a boat."

Tyvian sighed—she would never let him live the "boat" part down, would she? "We don't have to run away, Hool. I have a plan."

Hool curled one lip just high enough to show a row of jagged white teeth. "You said no more crazy plots. You said no more trouble."

"The trouble found us this time, Hool." Tyvian shook his head. "I'm sorry."

Hool folded her arms. "I say we run away. And I have the most money, so I'm in charge."

Myreon shook her head. "Actually, I think Tyvian should stay."

Artus blinked. "What?"

So did Tyvian. "Wait . . . what?"

Myreon looked at him. "Think of what you could accomplish, even as heir, even for a short time."

Tyvian frowned. "Myreon, we already have all the money we could *possibly* want."

Myreon rolled her eyes. "Gods, Tyvian—I don't mean *money*. I mean *this country*. The *people*. You could help them—you really could!"

Tyvian laughed, but tried hard to stop from laughing. He largely failed. Finally he was able to say, "Me? A philanthropist? You must be confusing me with some kind of dolt."

Myreon stood up. "You selfish, self-absorbed, preening—"

Artus waved his hands around. "Hey! Hey! Will *somebody* just tell me how the hell we can get Tyvian to renounce without getting Tyvian killed?"

Myreon slowly sat down, her mind once again distant, but her face clouded with thought.

Gradually, Tyvian tore his eyes away from her and fixed them on Artus. "It's actually simple—we just need to get invited to the party."

"We've already *been* invited to a party," Hool said. "Lots of parties."

"Not just any party—the Blue Party. The party that concludes the Winter Season and marks the formal beginning of the spring campaigns. It is held at the palace, which contains both the throne room *and* the Congress of Peers *and* will have in attendance every major player of every house. All we need is an invitation from somebody willing to sponsor me and recognize me on the floor of the Congress."

"And how do we get that?" Hool asked.

"We are, at this juncture, playing a very delicate balancing game." Tyvian searched all of their faces to make sure they were paying attention—he didn't want to have to explain this twice. Everyone but Brana was looking at him expectantly. Brana was sniffing his own armpit.

Close enough.

He cleared his throat. "On the one hand, if I appear to be too dangerous a political threat, someone is going to hire a mercenary company to lay siege to this place and kill us all before I amass too much power."

"And," Myreon chimed in, "if you appear to be too weak, somebody will hire a team of assassins to kill you off before you can be used as a pawn."

"Exactly."

Brana emerged from the depths of his own body odor, looking confused. "Soooo . . . what we gonna do?"

"Well . . ." Tyvian rubbed his stubble against the back of his hand. ". . . the short answer is that we—as a household—need to appear strong enough to resist anyone's influence, but bad enough at politics to fail to amass any power. Assuming we can do that, it will render us nonthreatening enough to earn an invitation to the Blue Party and support when I renounce. Then we can all return to obscurity here in our little gaming house."

Hool's copper eyes bored into Tyvian. "That is the stupidest plan I have ever heard. How can we even *do* that?"

Tyvian shrugged. "By throwing a party of our own, of course."

CHAPTER 7

THE HOUSEGUEST

Count Andluss of Ayventry, partly out of courtesy and partly out of sheer terror, had offered Prince Banric Sahand the whole of his city estate's west wing, even though he had brought with him no retainers, no servants—nothing but himself. From the great windows of his private chambers, Sahand could see the soaring Empty Tower of the Peregrine Palace piercing the twilit sky like the ivory horn of some fabled beast. He remembered a day when he thought he might rule from that palace—a day in his youth, now long past. It made him angry to think of it. He felt taunted by it; it dared him to violent acts.

A servant cleared his throat behind him. Sahand

turned to see a skinny, powder-wigged boy in Ayventry livery bowing to him. "Begging your pardon, Your Highness, but Their Graces have sent me to inform you they are ready to attend you at your earliest convenience."

"Go and tell them I will receive them presently," Sahand said, waving the stooge away. These Eretherians—all so delicate and polite and manicured. He felt like a bear among peacocks. *But I need them*, he reminded himself. The thought stung.

He pulled on his heavy fur cloak and strapped a longsword to his hip, its familiar weight tugging against the baldric—an unfashionable weapon in these mageglass obsessed days, but possessing a few tricks these fops were likely unaware of. In addition to this, he slipped a thunder-orb up one sleeve and a stiletto up the other, all this in addition to the knives he already wore openly on his hip and leg. Thusly armed, he planted himself in a great chair fashioned entirely of antlers and waited to receive his guests.

The Count of Ayventry, Andluss Urweel, was the fat indolent son of a fat indolent father. Sahand remembered his father well—the blubbering especially. At the end, when Perwynnon was shattering the cream of Ayventry's knighthood in battle after battle, Sahand was glad to be rid of him. And now, here he was again, sitting in what was probably the same exact room in the same exact chair ready to have almost the same exact conversation with the same exact idiot. Come to think of it, Sahand was reasonably certain this chair had been a gift from him to the Urweels, just so he would have something suitable to sit in when these conversations were destined to take place.

Gods.

To make the meeting somewhat more interesting, Andluss was joined by Velia Hesswyn, the Countess of Davram. She was visibly ancient in an age when youthful appearance was a purchasable commodity, which said something about her and, by extension, the entire miserable line of Davrams—they were conservatives, stuck in the old ways. Rumor had it that, in order for Perwynnon to get Velia's sons to join the Grand Army of Eretheria, he had bested each and every one of them in a duel with a weapon of their choice. It made for a very dashing tale, of course, but Sahand had really no interest in repeating the feat. The woman would do as she was told or he'd cut her in half and feed her dusty entrails to the dogs.

Ordinarily two Counts of Eretheria would hardly be found in the same room together without an entourage of a dozen people, but as a prince of a sovereign nation, Sahand outranked them, meaning they couldn't bring a larger entourage than himself without offering insult. So the only people present besides Sahand and the two counts was a servant and Countess Velia's grandson, some square-jawed oaf cut from the same cloth as a thousand Eretherian knights—a pretention born of power without the slightest idea of what power actually was or required of you—who was there to help the old woman stand up, sit down, walk, and so on.

After the necessary bows, the Countess introduced the oaf on whose arm she clung. "This is my grandson, Sir Valen Hesswyn."

"So this is the young man who informed you that Waymar of Eddon is dead?" Sahand asked, smiling.

Valen bowed deeply. "Yes, Your Highness. I saw it with my own eyes—bloodroot poisoning. Our assassin—"

Sahand cut him off with a sharp gesture. "Failed. The word you want is *failed*. Waymar of Eddon *lives*."

Valen's mouth fell open. His grandmother was better able to handle the shock. She nudged him backward with the top of her cane. "My grandson tells the truth, as he saw it. I am curious how you came to know he survived. He has not been seen."

Count Andluss cleared his throat. "Well, it seems Lady Hool spent the morning calling in the debts of those she suspected of colluding with the assassin. Some of those are . . ." He cleared his throat, clearly unwilling to admit that his own vassals had debts they could not pay without a loan from some glorified innkeeper. "They are known to me."

Countess Velia bowed her head. "If this is true, Your Highness, then I apologize. I had no way of knowing that this Waymar would have the resources to—"

"Stop blubbering." Sahand ran a hand through his short, iron-gray beard and gave Valen a hard stare. "Your lack of imagination is now clear to me, Sir Valen. The question becomes this: what am I to do with an unimaginative boy from a failing house who cannot even have a gutter-dwelling gaming house master killed?"

Valen stiffened. "But I didn't—"

"Shut up," Sahand barked. The force of the Prince's voice was sufficient to make old Velia jump. "I am sick of excuses—it is about all you worthless Eretherians produce. At least when you had money, you were tolerable. Now that you're all scrabbling to maintain your pathetic households and begging at the door, I feel as though I have suddenly become an orphan-master doling out gruel to the urchins."

Velia pulled herself to her full height—which wasn't saying much. "I beg your pardon, Your Highness!"

Her protest was to be expected. As was Valen's hand moving to his rapier, but he froze when a ball of yellow fire formed in Sahand's left hand. Sahand rolled it over his knuckles as he spoke. "Yes, you *are* begging my pardon, aren't you, Hesswyn? And since you are here *begging*, I should make it clear that you do not have the luxury of taking offense to the things I say to you, you fleshy waste of a human being." Sahand's eyes fell to Valen's sword. "Now, sir, if you wish to die at this precise moment, by all means draw that sword of yours. I will wait."

Slowly, his mouth closed tightly, Valen let his hand drop away from the hilt.

Sahand let the ball of fire extinguish in a *whupp* of air. He beckoned a servant in the livery of Ayventry. "Oggra—strongest you have. In a goblet or flagon—not those skinny little glasses you all like so much."

The servant bowed deeply. "A . . . a whole goblet of oggra, Your Highness?"

Sahand slapped the armrest of his chair. "Yes, Kroth take you!" The servant vanished.

Velia cleared her throat. "Count Andluss, I was given to understand that this would be a civilized meeting. The behavior of your guest reflects poorly upon you."

Sahand laughed at this, long and hard, while the counts watched, aghast. At last he controlled himself. "Ah! Is that an Eretherian threat I hear? How typical—I threaten to burn your grandson to ashes where he stands, and *you* respond by threatening Andluss here with nasty stories. Gods, what a stupid country this is!"

Count Andluss, who had been furiously minding his own business, flapped his jewel-studded hands, "Be reasonable, Velia. These are trying times for all of us."

Sahand nodded. "Yes—let's all be reasonable, shall we? Let us talk about what *I* want and what *you* want. The both of you are just about out of money, and Ousienne of Hadda is *not*. She has hired or will hire all the best mercenary companies for the spring campaigns, whereas all you have is a couple two-bit Verisi pirates playing soldier and all the sullen peasants you can slap a pot-helm on and get to march. Does this sound like a fair assessment?"

Nobody spoke. Velia looked ready to slap him. Good. A little fire under her arse would do her well.

"So, my offer. I will provide you, Count Andluss, with all the mercenaries you require from Dellor, sufficient to fight off House Hadda. And you . . ." He looked at Velia. ". . . are invited to join in an alliance, if and when you are able to kill Waymar of Eddon. This was the deal. It has not changed, except in one detail: you, House Davram, have failed."

"We will continue to employ the assassin," Velia said. "She will be successful next time."

"The hell she will," Sahand said, shaking his head. "If she didn't get him the first time, there is no way she will get close enough for a second try. I know the man too well."

Andluss looked puzzled. "He will never ascend the Falcon Throne, Your Highness. Why is he such a threat?"

Sahand reached out to take his goblet of oggra from the returning servant. "Who said anything about the man being a threat? I merely said I wanted him dead and that you should employ the finest assassin your money can buy. You either did not take my advice or could not afford to, and in either case, our arrangement is dissolved."

The Countess of Davram looked like she might explode. "You *cannot*. We had an agreement. The money we spent . . . the time it took . . ."

"We'll expose you!" Valen shouted, probably at a louder volume than he intended. Everyone stared at him. "We'll tell everyone you're marching into Ayventry! The counties will rise against you!"

Count Andluss shook his head. "Velia, control your boy, will you?"

"Valen!" Velia snapped.

Valen's face was red. "They can't treat us this way! This is . . . is . . . unconscionable!"

Sahand laughed. "Boy, if you reveal that Andluss here is colluding with me, then Andluss there will reveal you as the source of the assassin that nearly killed Waymar. And then, while the other three houses are raising their banners behind their new king, *you* will be left out in the cold as traitors and collaborators." Sahand took a quick drink, but then spat—somebody had watered it down. Gods, this country.

Velia Hesswyn planted her cane between her feet and leaned on it. "Well then, Your *Highness*, if you have no further *use* for us, we will be on our way."

Sahand waved them away. "Yes, do. I am through doing you favors. Begone. Take the boy with you, too—I am not just now in the mood to kill fools."

Valen turned on his heel and grabbed Velia by the elbow. "Come, grandmother."

The Countess of Davram had more to say, though. "You, sir," she said, glaring at Sahand, "You, sir, are *no* Prince!"

Sahand laughed. "There *are* no princes, Velia Hesswyn. There are just costumes worn by brutal men—something you would do well to remember."

Valen dragged his grandmother away a pace, but she swatted him with her cane and turned back to the Mad Prince. "Why did you summon us here, then? To mock us? To revel in our misery?"

Sahand drank his oggra and smiled at her. "Other people's misery is the best salve for one's own failures, don't you think?"

That did it. The two of them left in a hurry, or the closest semblance of a hurry a woman in her eighties could manage.

Andluss was still there. "I beg your pardon, Your Highness, but was that wise?"

Sahand grunted. "What do you care? You're getting what you wanted out of it, yes?"

Andluss nodded slowly, twiddling his pudgy fingers, "Yes, but Velia Hesswyn isn't one to surrender to fate. You've only driven her toward this Waymar. She may seek common cause with him."

Sahand laughed. "I can think of no richer fate for Waymar of Eddon than to be entangled in that old woman's bitter scheming. I know exactly what she will do, too: she will seek to subvert Waymar's nephew to her cause—she has grandchildren enough to do it, too. A boy like that is easy to snare with a pretty smile. He will be beset on all sides. Then, when she has controlled the boy, she will eliminate the man. Even if Hesswyn does make common cause, she will serve as our diversion. Waymar and his allies will have all their attention pointing in the wrong direction."

Andluss steepled his fingers beneath a double chin. "So . . . it was intentional, then? You *knew* the assassin would fail. How?"

Sahand shrugged. "Let's just say I had a reasonable suspicion. And now, let us discuss the business of my men moving through your fief."

Andluss held up a hand. "Under disguise, of course?"

Sahand grinned. *Oh, Lyrelle, how well you have trained me. If only you knew.* "Yes. Of course."

CHAPTER 8

GUEST LISTS

No." Hool snatched the invitation card out of Tyvian's hand and tore it up. Then she ate the pieces.

Tyvian did his best to keep his smile pinned in place. He was thankful, at least, that they were alone in the study. "Hool. Darling. You are being unreasonable."

"No."

Tyvian arched his back, which hurt like hell, but it was a special kind of pain—the pain that let him know the thousand tiny muscles in his back were gradually returning to service. "Hool, if we don't invite the Viscountess of Pontiverre-Nord, then we can't invite the Earl of Forêt-Blanc, which means half the lesser peers of Camien County won't show, which means we'll be throwing a bloody Vora victory party, which will make everybody *assume* we're friends with Vora, when the letters we received indicate that Count Duren of Vora wants nothing to do with us."

Hool folded her arms and fixed Tyvian with a coppery glare. "That woman smells bad."

Tyvian threw up his hands. "No one else notices! Not everybody has your nose, Hool!"

"It is *my* party."

"*Our* party."

Hool growled a little, causing the crystal goblets on the desk to shudder. "My money. My party. That's what you said."

Tyvian rolled his eyes. "You wouldn't even *have* that money if it weren't for me."

Hool nodded. "That's why you can live here."

Tyvian took a deep breath, which made his abdomen tingle a little—various oblique muscles waking up, too. He had spent all morning gathering up as many chamber orchestras and horticulturalists and gourmet chefs as possible on short notice, and Hool hadn't agreed to anything yet. "The invitations must go out today, Hool. We are at the very *limit* of polite notice for a party."

"Then we do not invite any of those terrible people." Hool flopped in very gnoll-like fashion on the couch. As she was still wearing her shroud, it looked like she had just fainted or possibly tripped on something. "There," she muttered into the pillows, "the problem is solved."

Tyvian looked at the stacks of invitation cards. At the moment, they were all made out in Artus's blocky handwriting, which meant all of them would have to be redone before going out. Doing some social calculus, Tyvian determined that if they did not invite all the people Hool *actively* disliked (rather than those she merely *potentially* disliked), the resulting cascade of subtle insults and corresponding no-shows would put their likely attendance at or below forty persons. Which, of course, was entirely too small for anything to be defined as a party. It would barely qualify as an Akrallian-style soiree.

Tyvian stroked his growing goatee. "What if we threw a salon instead of a party?"

"I do not know what that is." Hool put a pillow over her head.

"It's a more intimate gathering. No music or entertainers. No meal. It's meant to be an exchange of thought and talent—a gathering of keen minds to discuss the issues of the day." As he spoke, Tyvian got up—something he'd found he could do upon waking up, even if he was a little unstable. "Yes. That's it!"

Hool lifted the pillow and peered at him with one eye. "Explain your stupid plan."

Tyvian grabbed her by the hands and guided her to her feet. Hool went along with it, but her expression was sheer suspicion. "The salon is all about the cachet of the hostess." He guided Hool before a full-length mirror in the corner. He stepped back and gestured to the elegance of Hool's shroud, clad today in a gown of gold and cream, her illusory auburn hair done up in a pile pinned in place by a golden tiara. "You, my dearest Hool, are a woman of mystery. A woman of secret power. A woman who may one day be princess."

Hool arched an eyebrow. "But I'm not going to be a princess. You said so."

Tyvian nodded. "I know, I know—but *they* don't know that, do they? Everyone in the city knows of your wealth—gods, Hool, that vault in the cellar has enough gold to buy Bramble House out from under old Velia Hesswyn! That isn't even counting our—"

"*My.*"

"I beg your pardon—*your* overseas holdings. Your mercantile investments. Your accounts at the guild banks."

Hool looked at "herself" in the mirror, still frowning. "I know all of these things already. So what?"

"Hool, if you were to hold a party, people might stay home because they would expect it to be gauche."

Hool glared at him. "I know what *gauche* means. It isn't good."

Tyvian kept rolling. "But, Hool, darling—the thing that *makes* you a great hostess is not the table you set or the meals you have prepared or the orchestra you pay to perform—it's *you*. You are the draw."

Hool was quiet for a moment. "So I can send the orchestras home now?"

Tyvian grinned. "Who needs music when guests have your *presence* to inspire them?"

"And we don't need to have all those chefs in my kitchen?"

Tyvian placed a hand on her shoulder. "The food at a salon is for the mind, not the stomach."

Hool stared at him in that way that meant she was thinking about something very hard. Then she nodded. "Okay. Let's do it. I will be great at this."

Tyvian smiled. "You will."

"I will," Hool repeated. She turned and swept out of the study and into the hall. Tyvian heard the sound of instruments being brought to bear by several dozen performers. Hool roared over them all. "No! No more! Everybody get out before I eat you! Go! Scat!"

The door swung closed.

Tyvian closed his eyes and let the ring apply a long, slow pressure to his hand. It hurt, but not as badly as his back. Besides, it needn't have bothered—he already felt bad about the party and what it would do to Hool. *Correction—what the* salon *would do to Hool*.

He needed Hool to plan it, because he needed it to be a failure. Granted, it would be a failure even if *he* planned it—Hool was so ill-equipped to be in sophisticated circles, she'd have the peerage in an uproar the moment she opened her mouth. However, with her actively doing her best to make the party work, Tyvian was reasonably confident the salon would be more awkward than a complete and total catastrophe.

And for the purposes of his plan, it would be perfect. Hool, he suspected, would forgive him eventually.

Well, probably.

Tyvian sat down in a cozy high-backed chair by the smoldering embers of the fireplace, his muscles still screaming with stiffness. Out the window, gardeners could be seen trimming hedges and planting flowers. They were overseen by an alchemist who specialized in horticulture—an old woman in a ridiculous conical hat that went about pushing a wheeled rack of potions that, with a few drops, could enhance growth or change color or shape or render a plant resistant to wild shifts in temperature. If memory served, Tyvian was paying her and her gardeners one gold mark an hour for their services. He wondered what the split was. He rather doubted all those strong-backed young men in their soil-stained hose were pulling down more than a pair of silvers apiece for the whole day, and even that was a good wage.

Gods . . . He scowled. *Myreon's gotten into my damned head.*

Myreon hadn't been at breakfast—sleeping off another long night, it seemed. She still wasn't talking to him. She was also very clearly up to something and had been for some time.

Tyvian couldn't quite imagine what it was. Myreon had no underworld contacts to speak of—being an ex-Defender was something of a fatal flaw in that regard—and she had no obvious vices. When he thought about what she had been doing in the sewers all these nights, the best he could come up with was "forbidden sorcery."

At times he mused that she might have joined the Sorcerous League, but there was no evidence of it. Not that there would be, of course. That didn't stop him from searching her chambers several times or running a mage-compass in her room to see if anything was out of the ordinary.

He found nothing.

There were some nights he thought to follow her—tail her through the streets until he came upon her little secret—but he hadn't. Partly it was the ring; it didn't object much to him rummaging around her room (as he could easily justify that to himself as being cautious for her safety as well as his own), but tailing her caused it to pinch and sting. It had a point: following her was something of a violation of their oaths of trust.

That *was* what he had promised her, too, in that cabin aboard Gethrey's odious ship the *Argent Wind*. They had whispered it in the dark, wrapped in each other's arms. *"I, Tyvian Reldamar, promise to never lie to you, to give you my trust, and to be your ally in all endeavors. With Hann as my witness . . ."*

She had said the same. He never doubted she would keep her word; she always had, even when they were mortal enemies. In following her, Tyvian knew he was only trying to prove that he wasn't the bad one in the relationship. That she was, in the end, just like him. In his most honest moments, which were rare, he knew her failure would confirm that he really deserved her.

For some reason, though, he didn't want to know. *Maybe Artus will find nothing. Maybe he'll never look.* He had half a mind to call the boy in and reverse what he had told him yesterday morning. But he didn't.

He took a deep breath and reached for a glass of wine that wasn't there. All the serving specters were off cleaning, he guessed. Hool had been adamant about the cleaning. Tyvian looked at the writing desk across the room and weighed the merits of getting up and going over there against the merits of sitting here and warming his stiff body before the dying heat of the fire. It was a difficult debate but, eventually, he dragged himself to his feet and limped to the desk.

These invitations weren't going to write themselves. Only the middle class employed specters to write their correspondence and, for the moment, Tyvian had to pretend to be royalty.

The House of Eddon was quiet in the midmorning, especially now that all the odious cooks and people with musical instruments had been sent away. No coaches were pulling up beneath the portico and dumping their perfumed, wigged cargo on Hool's doorstep. No music was wheedling its way through the corridors as various dandies tried to woo various women. No lordlings were strutting and preening for each other over the t'suul tables. The entire place was, in a word, empty.

Hool thought it was wonderful.

After watching the plant wizard alter bushes and things in the garden for a while, she retreated to the room she referred to as her "den." One side of the room had been fashioned into terraces decorated with animal pelts. The walls were fixed with racks of weapons and the heads of other animals. There was a bear, a griffon, and a big stag. In one corner, a stuffed cliff drake stood, wings spread and claws outstretched, as though in midpounce. The whole room smelled of stale hide and dander, which Tyvian had pointed out would go a long way to masking her natural odor from the average human visitor.

She dozed with the windows open so the cool spring breeze could blow through her fur, just as it would have on the endless grasslands of her home, so far away. Brana dozed with her for a bit, but he was restless—he constantly was getting up, practicing with weapons, yipping and snarling to himself—so Hool kicked him out. At some point Artus brought up lunch—a hock of ham, raw, and a bowl of hard-boiled eggs. Artus lingered after he brought it—he wanted to talk about something. Hool didn't, so she ignored him until he went away. She ate the eggs first, popping them into her mouth like grapes. She lingered over the ham hock, licking it thoroughly before stripping the meat off the bone and then cracking it in her jaws. The best part was that she didn't need to worry about anybody seeing her, judging her, or wondering if she were some kind of monster. This was becoming the best day ever.

There was a knock on the door.

Hool sniffed the air, her ears alert—not Brana, not Artus. *Damon Pirenne.*

Grumbling, Hool rolled off the couch and snatched up the shroud and belted it on by the time Sir Damon chanced a second knock. *"My lad . . . ah . . . Hool? Are you there?"*

Hool straightened her posture and did her best human stride over to the door and opened it. "What do you want?"

Hool had a difficult time figuring out human body language at the best of times, but Sir Damon was a complete mystery. He always seemed tense around her, as though he might run, or pounce or weep or something. She assumed it had something to do with the fact that he owed her money, but despite that, he always seemed to want to be around her. She was reasonably certain he was insane.

Hool watched as he adjusted his clothes and

sucked in a deep breath and held it for some reason. He was always doing that. "I have completed my investigation, milady."

"What are you talking about?"

Sir Damon's face reddened and he mopped the top of his head with a handkerchief. "I . . . uhhh . . . the investigation into the assassin, of course."

"Who told you to do that?"

Sir Damon grimaced. "I had assumed, of course, that as part of my duties here, I was to act as protection for the house, and so I—"

Hool just wanted this social interaction to be over, so she decided to skip the next ten minutes of posturing, bowing, and him calling her "his lady," which she felt was presumptuous. "Tell me what you found in as few words as possible."

Sir Damon froze, his mouth halfway open.

Hool cocked her head. Had she broken him? "Begin."

"The assassin was let in by Lord Waymar, she poisoned him in the room, escaped via the balcony, and fled back into the city, where she hired a coach and there the trail becomes cold. I've tried to find the coachman all morning, but no luck." He smiled.

Hool nodded. "Thank you. Good-bye."

Sir Damon bowed. "As you wish, my lady."

Hool was about to slam the door in his face when she stopped. "I'm not yours."

"Your what?"

"Your lady. I'm not yours."

Sir Damon's face flushed pink. "Of course . . . I merely . . . I just didn't have a . . ."

"Just call me Hool."

Sir Damon brightened, smiling broadly. Hool had no idea why. "Of course, my . . . Hool."

Hool slammed the door in his face.

As soon as the door closed, she slipped off her shroud and let her body fall out of the stiff upright posture of a human, yawning wide. It felt good.

She flopped on a pile of furs, wanting to sleep but was wound too tightly to do so now. She hated the sensation; before she had come here, she had never had trouble sleeping. Not even when her pups were missing. Not even in that wretched cage Sahand had put her in.

Though unpleasant, living among humans was, in actuality, rather simple. All somebody needed, it turned out, was lots of money and you could do pretty much whatever you wanted—except "be a gnoll," apparently. Still, Hool *had* lots of money. And because she had lots of money, people were always asking if they could borrow it, because everybody in Eretheria had lost a lot of money at the same time she had gained hers. This was when she learned about "interest" and "liens" and things like that—basically elaborate ways somebody with a lot of money could take money from people who didn't have as much. It was a stupid and abhorrent system to Hool, but she had equated it with physical prowess in her mind, and that made it more palatable. Having money, to humans, was basically equivalent to having enormous strength to gnolls—they ruled because they had the power. If the weak didn't like it, they were welcome to die or go off and start their own pack or country or whatever.

She looked out the vast bay windows that made up one wall of her den. The outskirts of the city, punctuated by small estates and manicured tracts of land, eventually gave way to the rolling green pastures and rocky buttes of southern Eretheria, their limestone faces gleaming brightly in the midday sun. A smattering of rain from a sunshower speckled the windowpanes beneath the mottled blue sky. It was pretty, in its way.

She took a deep breath and let it out as a sigh. *But it isn't home.*

She missed the endless, unbroken horizon of the Taqar. She missed the trumpet of the manticore herd as it marched. She missed the scent of the infinite wildflowers, the oceanic roar of the tall grass in the wind, the dead quiet of the still summer afternoons, the world coated in golden light. She missed the press of the pack in the dark of winter, huddled beneath the great yurt, singing songs over firelight.

Don't be stupid, she told herself. *Only fools throw away food for dreams.* The Taqar was far away—so very far, far away—and she was here, safe and powerful and *fed*. Even if it was among humans and even if it depended on something stupid like money.

But . . . what if money could buy a little piece of home and bring it here? Hool's ears perked up. Yes. That was it. She sprung up and slipped back on her shroud. She had to find that plant wizard woman.

She had an idea.

CHAPTER 9

THE HEIR'S DAY OUT

By lunch, Tyvian discovered he could walk. Dressing himself was still a bit beyond him, but with the assistance of a cane and Artus or Brana's guiding hand, he could make his way down the stairs, eat his own food, and drink his own tea. Well, after a fashion—he still needed to wear a napkin tied around his neck like some dockworker at a fish fry, but as recoveries from the door of certain death went, things were going quite well.

The cane, he felt, would also be a fairly useful prop over the coming days. Appearing physically unsound could be advantageous—he couldn't very well lead an army from the back of a white charger if he couldn't even mount a horse. He determined to cultivate the image, authentic or otherwise. With any luck, by the time another assassin came for him, they wouldn't be expecting a healthy man as a target.

Not that being healthy had helped that much the first time around, but nevertheless . . .

After lunch, Tyvian got dressed in his best clothes—a burgundy doublet, a black cape of the softest wool, *Chance* with blade conjured and belted at his side in a jeweled scabbard, and a half dozen of his most ostentatious rings. The flarewood cane, likewise, had a diamond-encrusted lion's-head topper and a gold tip at the opposite end. Even with his rigid, injured posture, he cut a fine figure.

With the invitations handled, today's plan was to meet with the Countess Ousienne of House Hadda, ruler of the Lake Country and probably the wealthiest single person in Eretheria outside of Hool herself. Myreon would accompany him as his house enchanter—another needed sign of prestige—and he would seek to ostensibly ingratiate himself into the countess's good graces.

The Countess Ousienne, unlike her cousins, had not directly expressed any great sympathy toward Tyvian's plight. This of course made her the one least interested in seeing Tyvian on the throne, which made her an ideal candidate for Tyvian's plan. By lamely attempting to suck up to Ousienne and getting slighted—something Tyvian felt was basically inevitable—he would show himself an apparent fool and make himself more attractive to the attentions of Ousienne's primary rival, the Countess of Davram.

Tyvian had also hoped the hour-long coach ride through city traffic to the Countess of Hadda's estate would give him ample time to mend fences with Myreon.

He was wrong.

Myreon seemed determined to do nothing but look out the window. She didn't even acknowledge his existence. The Silent Treatment—the oldest weapon in the arsenal of romantic warfare. Tyvian imagined the many Brides of Hann had used it on the very God of Men Himself during the Great Trek. Numerous times, probably.

After about fifteen minutes, Tyvian decided he had had enough. "Myreon, there's a stain on your sleeve. Honey, I think."

Myreon held up her arm to look. "Really? Where?"

Tyvian pointed under her arm. "There."

She twisted her arm around. "I don't see it anywhere. Are you sure?"

"No," Tyvian admitted. "I just wanted to see if you had gone mute."

Myreon scowled at him. "You are a giant child."

"At least I'm not sulking like one."

"I'm not sulking, Tyvian. I'm being diplomatic."

"Diplomatic?" Tyvian snorted. "Diplomacy usually involves discussion."

Myreon glared at him. "Not when there's war brewing."

"That would be the *most* important time to discuss things, wouldn't you think?"

She folded her arms and looked back out the window. "I'm tired of the metaphor. I don't want to talk to you, Tyvian, because if I do, I will probably wind up killing you."

Tyvian sighed. "Are you still mad about Adatha Voth? Or that I laughed at your idea that I use my position to help the poor?"

"Both!" she snapped. "Now shut up."

Tyvian took a deep breath and swallowed his ready rejoinder. She was being ridiculous. One errant kiss and it was all over? After everything they'd been through? Tyvian decided to look out the window, too. Two could play the silent game. Well, at least in *theory*.

The outskirts of the city gave way to rows and rows of peasant houses planted on small plots of land—usually no more than an acre. Then thatched roofs cropped up in rows and winding streets, usually clustered around a well. Then the city itself began. Eretheria was built upon several hills surrounding the mile-wide Lake Elren and the slender, ivory spire of the Empty Tower of Peregrine Palace, which dwarfed the surrounding city like a mountain in a flat plain. Though it was not as populous as Saldor, Eretheria spread itself out. The roads were wider, the houses larger, and the plots of land more generous. Rising among the roofs and domes and steeples were nearly innumerable trees—Eretheria was a city of lush gardens and plentiful shade.

It was also just as fragmented as the rest of the country, with individual districts of the city falling under the influence of the various houses. Laketown, for instance, was under the control of House Hadda and its vassals; Davram Heights by Davram; Ayventry District by Ayventry, and so on. Each of these districts featured broad, tree-lined avenues upon which rested the finely appointed homes and city estates of the peerage. Off these avenues were narrower side streets, where the wealthier guild merchants kept their homes; off these were the winding, narrow lanes and twisting alleys of the peasant slums, where the regular people of Eretheria lived safely out of sight and out of mind.

At one point, Tyvian peered down one of those crooked roads as the coach was about to turn. In it, an old peddler struggled with a massive cart stuck in a pothole. Hung with beat-up and secondhand pots and pans, Tyvian could see that he wasn't selling—he was buying. People were so desperate, they were actually selling their pots and pans.

Myreon scowled and pulled back the curtain in the coach. "I hate this miserable city."

Tyvian grunted. "I'm sure life in Ihyn is far more pleasant. I understand they have the flesh-eating slime problem under control now. Oh, and I bet Illin is fairly nice this time of year, once you get by the fact that half the city is rubble and it only receives sunlight for three hours a day or so."

Myreon glared at him. "What's your point?"

Tyvian shrugged and tried not to sound bitter. "Life is tough all over. These people have it better than you think."

Myreon kept glaring.

House Hadda's city estate was a sprawling piece of property in the heart of the Laketown District known as Rose Hall. The main house was aptly named—a long single hall with a domed rotunda at its center in the shape of a massive rosebud, and uncluttered with architecturally awkward wings or outbuildings. Built into the ridge of a steep hill, the servants' quarters, kitchens, stables and other such were actually built underground beneath the main building and were accessible from without through various man-made cave entrances that opened out of Rose Hall's south side like the holes of a rabbit warren.

The front was mostly polished granite stairs rising up the slope of the front hill and flanked on either side by glorious bushes swarming with red and yellow roses, even though it was far too early in the spring for any such thing to be in bloom. Of course, Tyvian well knew that there were few natural phenomena that could not be brought to heel, assuming one had the money.

They waited in their coach at the foot of these stairs while Tyvian's note was transported up into the house by a powder-wigged servant in the red-and-yellow livery of his mistress. The countess left Myreon and him waiting a full hour before inviting them inside, which Tyvian had expected—they were arriving unannounced and his claims to an audience were primarily founded on rumors, after all. What he hadn't expected was just how painful climbing all those stairs would be, and he found more than once that he needed Myreon's assistance to steady himself. *So much for the cane being mostly an act.*

At the front door, they were met by additional servants who ushered them into the central rotunda. Here, the true size of Rose Hall became evident; the dome soared a full eighty feet into the air, its peak consisting of transparent mageglass made into the pattern of a red rose that cast its light down on the very center of the floor. It was a vast space into which had been set a small collection of wicker furniture at the exact center. Tyvian and Myreon were asked to wait here, and Tyvian lowered himself onto one end of a wicker sofa, the down-stuffed cushion hugging his sore body warmly. Myreon sat in a chair across from him. "This isn't exactly welcoming."

Tyvian shrugged. "She's being cautious. Our arrival is unexpected, and she likely doesn't quite know what to make of it yet." He cocked an eyebrow at her. "I assume you're warding us against eavesdropping?

A dome like this can have a number of very interesting acoustical properties."

Myreon frowned. "I know my job."

They were brought refreshments—tea, some cakes—and left to wait almost another entire hour. During all that time, they saw almost no one except for a spare handful of servants who were on hand to answer their needs.

"Does anybody even live here?" Myreon adjusted her robes as though she were cold. "Why live in a place this huge if it's going to be mostly empty?"

"The countess has not been blessed with many children, and many of those children have already died. Two were killed by Sahand, one by Perwynnon, and a fourth was assassinated by parties unknown. This house was originally built by Ousienne's father to house his vast family of twenty-seven children and their families."

Myreon looked around at the great hallways and rooms that branched off the rotunda. "What happened to them?"

Tyvian considered just how far he should explain, but decided to settle for the concise answer. "Politics. Ousienne is a suspicious woman and relatively vain; she wields her wealth like a weapon, and her family has caught the brunt of it." He shrugged. "And a big place like this can host a hell of a party."

Myreon frowned. "You seem to know a lot about her."

Tyvian grinned. "I had to. I robbed her once."

"What?" Myreon stiffened and rechecked her wards. "Tyvian!"

Tyvian laughed and waved his hands to calm her. "She never saw me, I promise. She'll never recognize me." He winked at her. "Trust me."

Myreon folded her arms and glowered.

At long last a servant—a rather more important-looking servant bearing the house's warding staff—came striding across the vastness of the dome's floor and stopped when he was halfway to Tyvian and Myreon's little island of furniture at the center. "Ousienne Tushael, the Lady of Hadburg, Guardian of the Lakes, and Countess of Hadda."

Tyvian and Myreon rose as the countess appeared. She wore a formal gown supported by mageglass spokes and hoops so that it was as wide as the woman was tall. In keeping with her house's tradition, she was wearing primarily yellow and red—colors which Tyvian felt did not suit her, though they may have in her youth. Her hair was clearly glamoured to appear as rust-red as it once had and a steady diet of *cherille* had kept age largely from her face, but not from her bones. She walked as though she might break. Tyvian could sympathize.

Beside her was a man also dressed in impressive style and wearing his own rapier of mageglass. He had one of her gloved hands in his own and was assisting the countess in her trek to meet her guests. He was much younger—perhaps no more than a handful of years Tyvian's senior. This, Tyvian guessed, was Ousienne's current husband—her third. He couldn't remember the man's name, but he seriously doubted that it would come up.

When she was a polite distance away, Tyvian bowed and Myreon curtsied. Ousienne looked down on them through a pair of crystal spectacles, probably a truthlens, looking for any illusion. A rude gesture, but the richest woman in Eretheria could get away with a certain amount of indiscretion. Tyvian certainly wasn't going to challenge her husband over it.

Her voice was sharp, but thinned with age. "Perhaps I ought to be the one to curtsey to you, Waymar of Eddon."

Tyvian rose and tried to gauge the woman's tone. He felt he saw a twinkle in her dark little eyes, so he chuckled along with the joke. "My reputation precedes me, Your Grace. Allow me to present my house enchantress, Myreon Laybreth."

Ousienne nodded and then managed somehow to sit down on the other couch. Her dress consumed the entire piece of furniture so that her husband, whatever his name was, took up a position behind her, like a servant. The crazy thing was the man didn't seem to mind in the least. *Just how much money would it take for you to sell* your *pride, Tyvian Reldamar?*

Tyvian grunted internally. The answer was "a hell of a lot more then Ousienne of Hadda could offer."

Maybe that was what made him stupid.

Ousienne was watching him carefully. "Are you feeling quite well, Master Waymar? I understand you had a dreadful encounter recently."

Tyvian pushed away his musings and focused on the task at hand. "My recovery may take some time, Your Grace, but I am on the whole rather well. Thank you very much for the inquiry."

"One of my cousins was laid low to bloodroot poisoning. Dreadful thing. No sense of honor in some people, I am afraid to say." The countess flipped open a fan and began to use it for its intended purpose.

Of course, the air was in no way hot, which meant the fan was enchanted. Before he could really wonder what manner of sorcery was in play, he felt the room brighten a bit and saw the fan's colorful vanes darken and molder somewhat. With a barely audible sniff, the countess put it away.

Myreon.

Ousienne did not look pleased. "I am a very busy woman, Master Waymar. Thank you for your visit."

She held her hand out and her husband took it so that she could begin to rise. Before she was halfway up, however, Tyvian met her eyes. "One of your fellow Counts tried to have me killed two nights ago."

Ousienne froze. "A forceful accusation, Master Waymar. Have you proof?"

"This assassin was expensive. A professional. Not the kind of thing an earl or viscount is likely to afford."

"That sounds like a no." Ousienne moved to use her fan again, but then remembered its depleted state.

"You don't want a king, do you?" Tyvian grinned. His directness had Ousienne off-balance—she wasn't used to this kind of bluntness, certainly not in her own home.

Ousienne slowly sank back onto the couch. "I was a loyal subject of the crown before—why not again?"

"Because kings make war with other kings, and nobody profits. Because kings seek their own ambition, and stifle those of their vassals."

Ousienne nodded. "A king sounds like a lovely thing to be."

Tyvian pointed to the livid scrapes on his face. "My experiences tell me otherwise."

"You are asking for standing." Ousienne laughed lightly. Her husband joined her. "I cannot give it to you without improving your claim, and that I won't do. You are right—Eretheria needs no king."

"But so long as I live, Eretheria may have one."

Ousienne nodded. "There will be other assassins."

"Then you see why I have come." Tyvian sank to one knee. "To swear fealty."

Ousienne's penciled-in eyebrows shot up. "Ah . . . clever. And if I turn you down?"

"Davram or Ayventry may think differently. They may have greater use for me—against you."

"Andluss? Never." Ousienne frowned. "But yes, I could see a Davram doing it. It isn't beneath Velia."

Tyvian smiled. "Accept me, and I can renounce at the Blue Party."

Ousienne said nothing for a short time, but only stared at Tyvian. Then, at last, she said, "Forgive me, Master Waymar, but . . . have we met before?"

Tyvian chose not to answer. Let her stew over it—she would either realize the truth or not, but no matter what, he was planning to make an enemy here. "Do we have an understanding?"

Ousienne smiled, but without any warmth. "I'm terribly sorry, Master Waymar, but I must be going. I have just remembered I have an engagement for which I am already unacceptably late. Please, call on us again."

Tyvian and Myreon rose as she did and they genuflected as appropriate to their station as she left. In a few minutes, they found themselves once again on the front steps. Their coach was being brought around even as they descended.

Tyvian took a deep breath of the bright, spring air. "Well, it's a start."

Myreon snorted. "That woman wants very much never to see you again. Did you see how she was looking at you? It was like you were selling apples at her door in your bare feet."

Tyvian nodded. "She smells a trap—she's not a fool. The thing is, the trap isn't for her. This is all to influence what happens at the salon. If we show ourselves to be an acceptable risk to House Davram, we're in."

"And then what, just go back to the way things were?" Myreon shook her head.

Tyvian didn't rise to the bait.

When they were halfway down the stairs, they paused beside a great fountain between the great staircases leading to the front door. Golden cherubs blew water out of golden horns into a great golden pool. Tyvian leaned against the balustrade to rest. Myreon looked at the ostentation and shook her head. "How can you stand it?"

"What?"

Myreon motioned to the estate that surrounded them—twelve acres in the middle of a city, grand gardens and a house large enough to keep an army. "This! This whole place! That woman!" She pointed beyond the front gates to the city that clustered around it. "People are suffering out there. You could *do* something about that."

Tyvian scowled. The ring began to throb. "I don't want to have this conversation."

"Why not? Because you're afraid of what the ring might make you do?"

Tyvian started down the stairs with uneven steps. The coach was waiting.

Myreon said nothing else. The silence descended again. Tyvian didn't have a way of banishing it, so he let it persist. It was the worst kind of silence—one heavy with thought, with brooding.

Tyvian fiddled with the ring. It, at least, had no

opinion about the day's events—Myreon was wrong about that. The ring did not much deal in indirect morality—the morality of distant effects. He supposed that meant *he* didn't either. What fault of his could it be if he threw away half an apple that might feed a child halfway across the world? Was he supposed to carry the world on his shoulders, only for him to crumble beneath the weight?

He looked at Myreon. She was looking out the coach windows, her posture stiff, the graceful curve of her neck catching the light in just that way that made him want to touch her. But the set of her jaw and the frame of her shoulders were clear—she most certainly did not want that. She was too busy carrying too much weight. From somewhere. *For* someone.

At the border between Davram Heights and Laketown, the road was blocked by a toll house. They had to roll to a stop and wait their turn as men in the livery of a Davram vassal inspected each conveyance and levied the appropriate toll.

There was a short line of wagons and carriages ahead of them, and so Tyvian resolved to get himself out of the silent prison of his coach and see about stretching his stiff legs a bit. He opened his door and was about to leave, when he stopped short.

There was a little girl—perhaps seven years old—in a moth-eaten dress, her hair messy, mud on her face from the passing coaches. She knelt beside the coach door, hands outstretched. "Alms, sir?" she squeaked. Her voice was hoarse.

Tyvian was struck dumb for a moment. At last he managed, "What did you say?"

The little girl sighed. Tyvian thought, for a moment, that she was about to run away, but something steeled her resolve. "Alms, sir. Alms for the poor?"

The ring tightened on his finger, but Tyvian barely paid attention to it. "Who's your liege?"

The girl's eyes widened as she got a good look at him and she stood up. Her eyes fell to her feet. "Your Grace?"

"Your liege—who is it? What fief do you hail from, girl?" Tyvian staggered down from the coach to stand beside her, leaning on his cane. "Tell me." He softened his voice in a way that he hoped a child might find encouraging. "It's all right. I'm not angry."

The girl managed an awkward curtsey. "The Dame Hesswyn, Countess of Davram, Your Grace. It's to her my father pays taxes."

A shadow fell over them. "There a problem here, Your Grace?" Tyvian turned to see a man wearing the livery of House Davram—thorns and boars.

"No. No problem. I was just speaking to the girl." Tyvian looked back to see the girl had run away.

The man—evidently one of the toll house's men—shook his head. "Vermin keep showing up, day in and out, begging from travellers. Sorry for the trouble, milord."

"Is this normal?" Tyvian looked to where the girl must have run—there was a stable and a small inn just down a side-road from the main boulevard. Gathered in front of it were maybe a dozen people, all disheveled to varying degrees, sitting on the front porch and passing a clay pipe around.

The toll man shrugged. "Get a few most years. Never so many as this, though. Tough times in the country, they say."

The ring was crushing his hand. Tyvian was abruptly aware of it, and of how he looked in his fine doublet and starched lace ruff, *Chance* by his side in a jewel-encrusted scabbard. He turned to tell Myreon he'd be right back, but found her staring at him already. "Go on," she said, "I'll wait."

Tyvian nodded and, legs stiff, limped off the road and down a little incline into the inn-yard. He spotted the girl, clinging to the leg of a young woman in a similarly tatty dress. Judging from the simple pattern and color, they were likely made from the same bolt of cloth. They saw him coming—they all did. Whatever conversation had been taking place stopped. The clay pipe was no longer passed; it remained in the clutches of an old, old man with a patchy beard.

Tyvian had never given alms in his life. Never. The poor were ever present, inexhaustible—charity in the form of a few silver crowns in a few tin cups was a wasted effort, a pointless gesture to assuage the giver's guilt. Tyvian had never been one to feel guilty. At least not until recently.

Something about this was different, though. These people should *not* have been poor, this he knew. Were they lazy, then? Leeches looking to score a quick copper from an unsuspecting rube of a lord? He looked at their faces, at their hands as he approached—no, these were working people. He could see the calluses on their fingers, the sun spots on their faces. Even their clothing, ragged though it was, had been sewn in better days from sturdy material by a skilled hand. He could hear Myreon's voice in his head *These people are suffering.*

When he got within easy earshot, the group curtsied or bowed as required and waited for him to say something. He cleared his throat. "What are you all doing here?"

The girl's mother spoke. "Alms, sir. We need money. It's been a hard winter."

"Last year's harvest was robust," Tyvian countered. "You should have saved."

The old man with the pipe coughed and shook his head. "Taxes went up, begging your pardon, Your Grace. Our Lords took double the share—not enough left to feed us. We need money for food."

"Food?" Tyvian frowned. "Aren't you farmers? Purchased from whom? From where?"

The old man shrugged. "Where else? From our lady's own stores. Said she'd sell at half the rate."

Tyvian could scarcely believe his ears. "At half the . . . Hann's Boots, man, she's selling you *your own crops and livestock* back to you?"

They all nodded. The little girl, emboldened by the group, added, "And she's levied my papa into the wars! Before planting, too!"

More nods. More complaints of early levies and high taxes, and from more places than just Hesswyn's fief, too—from two other lesser lords as well. Given the run-up to the spring campaigns, Tyvian realized that it likely wouldn't be much different anywhere in the area. Maybe anywhere in Eretheria at large. "Gods," he breathed.

The people stretched out their hands to him. "Alms, sir!" they cried. The girl's mother looked on the verge of tears. "Please, sir—I can tell you are of good heart! Have pity! It shames us to ask, but we must! We *must!*"

Tyvian shook his head, still in disbelief. This had to be what Myreon meant. What kind of madwoman was Velia Hesswyn, to drive her own vassals to this pass?

Tyvian dug into his purse and gathered up a few silvers. Then he stopped. "No. Not nearly enough." He took the purse from his belt and upended it on the ground. About twenty gold marks and twice that in silver hit the muddy ground. "There—take it all. Feed your families." On his finger, the ring relaxed its crushing grip.

The people exchanged looks. "But, Your Grace," the old man said quietly, almost under his breath. "If we come back with this much . . . Dame Hesswyn might . . . well . . . she might get to thinkin' we've got more to tax."

"Then tell her where you got it. Tell her I gave it to you because she's starving her own damned people and going to wind up with her head on a pike if she isn't more careful." Tyvian grimaced. *Not going to get invited to the Blue Party with that attitude, Reldamar.*

The people paled at his words. "And . . . and who are you, Your Grace?" the mother asked, curtsying as low as she could.

Tyvian groaned inwardly—he'd been hoping to avoid this part. "My name is . . ." He thought about it—should he lie? Just the thought of doing so made the ring throb. That settled it. *Go to hell, trinket.* "My name is Waymar of Eddon."

All of them—every single one—gasped as though he were Hann Returned. They knelt and bowed their heads. The old man had tears welling in his eyes. "I knew it," he said, his voice cracking. "I followed your father. I'll follow you, Your Grace." He came forward and kissed Tyvian's hand. "Only point the way."

Tyvian recoiled, his hand darting back as though bitten. Before anyone else could swear fealty, he fled back to the coach as though chased, stiff legs be damned.

He got in and slammed the door. His heart was pounding. "Let's get the hell out of here."

Myreon never took her eyes off him, her expression unreadable. She reached up and pounded on the ceiling of the coach. With a shudder, they began to roll away.

After a time, Myreon asked him one question. "Was that the ring back there, or was it you?"

Tyvian didn't answer.

CHAPTER 10

RSVP

By dinner, the responses to Tyvian's morning invitations began to flow in. Chief among the array of guests was the Countess of Davram. This was a mild surprise, as Tyvian rather doubted the woman would show up herself, but it was a welcome one—an embarrassing salon attended by a Countess would be sufficient to secure Tyvian's meager political goal of being forgotten as soon as humanly possible and never mentioned in polite company again. Of course, such an RSVP meant that Hool's salon was *absolutely* going to happen the day after tomorrow—it was official now, and vested with all the permanence the Eretherian social calendar conferred. There was no turning back. All that remained was to get their household in order so that the event would be merely awkward and not a flaming catastrophe.

Over a plate of braised pork loin in a white wine reduction with princess mushrooms, Tyvian explained the finer points of etiquette. "First rule: no hitting anyone."

Hool swallowed a slice of pork loin whole, giving Tyvian a glimpse of her white fangs. "What if they *deserve* to be hit?"

"I reiterate—no hitting anyone. This rule couldn't be clearer, really."

Dinner was attended by Brana, Hool, Artus, and himself. Myreon had again vanished into the city, claiming she had some sorcerous materials to purchase. Sir Damon had insisted on remaining that evening as added security—he had shown up wearing a smallsword and a buckler, of all things, and was solemnly pacing the grounds as sentry. Tyvian hoped the man had a bladeward, or he was likely to wind up with a knife in his kidneys.

"*Why* can't I hit people?" Hool asked.

Tyvian grimaced. "If you hit someone, you will wind up in a duel."

Hool's ears perked up. "But then I get to kill them—there, problem solved."

Tyvian pinched the bridge of his nose. "Second rule—no duels."

Brana looked up from his plate, which he was busy licking clean with his broad tongue. "Wrestling?"

"Wrestling falls under 'hitting,' so no." He looked at the two gnolls. "Incidentally, you two should be wearing your shrouds. What if Sir Damon were to come in?"

Hool snorted. "He's on the other side of the house right now. I can smell his terrible perfume."

Artus frowned. "He wore *perfume* for sentry duty?"

"He's always wearing that stuff." Hool sucked down another slice of pork. "Always."

"This reminds me of another rule for the salon: no sniffing the air."

Hool licked her fingers clean. "Why are all these rules just for me and Brana?"

"Because, as he is a human being, Artus has a distinct advantage over you two when it comes to interacting politely with other human beings."

Artus nodded. "And he also already told me this stuff."

"And I already told him this stuff. Years ago," Tyvian confirmed. He sipped his wine—a cool, fruity white from some new Saldorian vineyard. Quite good for a table wine, he supposed. He'd have to order another case.

Brana belched at a volume that caused the chandelier to shake. "What about that? Can I do that?"

Tyvian sighed. "This might be an easier way to look at things: do *I* belch?"

"Only when you drink too much," Hool said.

"Look, I'm only trying to ensure the two of you don't act like barbarians."

"I am *not* a barbarian," Hool snarled. She looked at Tyvian. "If someone says that, I will break their lying jaw!"

Tyvian grimaced. "Hool, as charming as your threats of physical violence occasionally are, might we dispense with them for the time being? Just think murderous thoughts to yourself for a change."

Hool scowled. "Then maybe don't make me invite terrible people into my house."

Artus frowned and sipped his own wine. "What's the big deal? I don't get it."

"What don't you get, Artus?" Tyvian asked.

"You keep talking as though we are in danger, but so far it's just sounds like fancy clothes, cushy chairs, and good booze. Where's the danger?"

Tyvian groaned inwardly. He wondered if he had the energy to explain. "Artus, back in your village, were there people everyone liked? People in the community that everyone envied and wanted to be like?"

"Yeah. Some." Artus nodded. "So?"

"When those people were in trouble—if they asked for help or were threatened by danger—what happened?"

Artus shrugged. "Everybody would come to help them. There was one time Brother Cork got attacked by bandits on the road. Marik and some of my brothers rounded up a posse and rode them down."

"Now, what about people *nobody* liked? People everyone thought repulsive and terrible. Any of those?"

"You mean Old Man Greeby and his mangy dogs?"

"Yes, that is precisely who I mean—did you ever help *him* out? If he was threatened, did you band together and bring his harassers to swift Northron justice?"

Artus scowled. "I'm not an idiot, you know. I know where you're going with this. You want us to come outta this salon looking like Brother Cork and not Old Man Greeby."

Tyvian motioned to the gnolls. "And his mangy dogs."

"Watch it," Hool growled. "I haven't hit anybody recently and I'm starting to miss it."

Tyvian ignored her. "Except, Artus, in this instance we aren't talking about village politics involving nothing more than who gets snubbed at the church social or whether or not somebody's prize hog is considered for a ribbon at the fair. We are talking about *very powerful* people with standing armies and lots of money and centuries of shared political history. We, as outsiders, represent a threat to their world on par with the greatest they've ever faced. We need them to *like us*, Artus, or they are going to crush us."

"Or we could just run away, like I said." Hool sniffed at the mushrooms, but let them lie.

Tyvian sighed. "I'm just trying to get everything back to normal."

"What if we don't want to go back?" Hool growled. She folded her arms and sank deep in her chair, staring at the fire.

Tyvian blinked at this, but before he could fashion a response, there was a knock at the door. He dragged his stiff body to its feet as Hool and Brana rushed to put on their shrouds—perhaps it was Myreon, home early. It wasn't. Sir Damon stepped inside, holding an envelope. "A letter for Master Artus, sir."

Tyvian extended his hand and the knight gave it to him. Artus was next to him before Sir Damon closed the door again. "Give it here!"

They all watched as Artus ripped open the envelope like a hound assaulting a duck. Brana came up to look over his shoulder, even though to Tyvian's knowledge the gnoll had never quite gotten the knack for reading. They all waited as Artus squinted at the flowery handwriting, mouthing the words to himself. From this, Tyvian had a fair approximation of what the letter said before Artus looked up, eyes alight. "It's from Elora!"

"Who is Elora?" Hool asked, still sulking in her big chair.

Tyvian shrugged. "She's a girl—a grandniece of Countess Velia. Artus is infatuated with her."

Artus clutched the letter to his chest. "I am *not!*"

Tyvian rolled his eyes. "Please—it's painted all

over your face. You can't even say her name without smiling or blushing."

Brana came around in front of Artus and peered closely at his face. Then his tongue hung out and he pointed at him. "Ha ha! Artus is in love!"

"I barely know her!"

Brana danced from one foot to the other. "Artus is in lo-ove! Artus is in lo-ove!" He did a cartwheel, huffing with gnollish laughter.

So Artus punched him in the groin. During the ensuing wrestling match, Tyvian snatched the letter from the floor and looked it over. Elora, in an impeccable and polite hand, was inviting Artus for an evening stroll through the Floating Gardens. She insisted they would be properly chaperoned (though by whom was unclear). The coach was waiting outside.

Brana threw Artus bodily across the room, breaking an end table and shattering a decanter on the floor. Artus, though, was already on his feet, even if one hand was bleeding. At this point Hool stood up. "Stop it or I will sit on your heads!"

Tyvian ignored it all and went to the window that overlooked the forecourt. Sure enough, there was a coach—bearing the Hesswyn seal, no less—standing by the portico. Seals, of course, were easily forged and, looking at the handwriting in the letter, it was awfully formal for a young girl asking a boy out for a romantic walk. The flourishes at the starts of sentences were in a diplomat's hand, for certain—staid, efficient, if still attractive. It was very possible the girl wrote the letter—the signature looked legitimate—but she had been coached. By whom, though? An older relative? A *great-aunt* perhaps?

Behind him, Hool was moving the dining room table and rolling up the carpet where the glass had broken. "If you're going to wrestle, do it in the middle of the room! No more breaking things!"

Tyvian licked his lips. What was the play, here? Not youthful infatuation, certainly—he knew who the girl was and guessed she was much less impressed with Artus than he was with her. She had all the markings of a social climber. It could be nothing more sinister than her trying to get her romantic hooks into a young man who very well might wind up a prince. Or it could be something else. Was this a trap, or was this some attempt by Countess Velia to improve relations? In any event, it might be worth sending Artus just to see what they were after.

Artus pinned Brana with an arm bar, forcing Brana to tap out. The two rolled slowly to their feet, breathing hard. Brana was grinning. "Good pin, Artus!"

They slapped hands and then hugged. "You're an arse," Artus said, smiling.

Tyvian held up the invitation. "You can go, Artus. Don't bring a sword, but definitely bring a machete or two."

Artus poured some brandy over his cut hand. "What? Why?"

"Your paramour isn't being totally straight with you—expect a surprise. Hopefully it's a pleasant one." Tyvian thought about it, then added. "Bring Brana, too."

Hool scowled. "Why? Brana is not in love with this girl!"

Tyvian nodded. "No, but Brana, against all odds, is popular with young women and is a good person to watch Artus's back."

"I don't want Brana to go!" Hool countered.

Tyvian looked at Brana. "Brana, do *you* want to go?"

Brana paused from moving back the furniture and wiggled his arse. "Yeah! I go, too!"

"Artus," Tyvian said, "do *you* want Brana to go?"

"Ummm . . . well . . ." Artus scratched his head.

Tyvian tapped the invitation. "There's going to be a chaperone, Artus—your torrid adolescent imagination is going to be disappointed anyway."

Artus looked at Brana, who was quivering all over with excitement. "Okay—fine."

"There!" Tyvian looked at Hool. "It's settled."

Hool glowered at him. Saying nothing, she rose and left for her bedchamber. She slammed the door hard enough for a painting to fall off the wall.

Tyvian grimaced. "I'm sure she'll be fine. You two get dressed. Have fun, but keep your eyes open."

Artus nodded, already pulling off his dirty shirt. "Yeah, thanks. See you later."

Tyvian snapped his fingers at him. "One more thing . . ." He paused—was he really about to say this? *Gods—I guess so.* "Keep it in your pants."

Artus's mouth hung open. "Gross!"

Brana laughed, tongue lolling out. "Pants! Ha!"

When the door closed behind them, Tyvian watched from the window until they got in the coach and rattled off. For the first time in his entire life, Tyvian felt old.

CHAPTER 11

WILD NIGHT

Elora, as it turned out, did *not* have a chaperone. She was sitting in that coach, all alone, dressed in a midnight blue and silver gown that exposed her whole shoulders and a generous quantity of her upper chest, wearing a teardrop diamond necklace that basically formed an arrow straight down her cleavage. And Artus got in with his idiot "brother" in tow. Like a chump.

As the coach rattled off, Artus was stuck sitting *across* from Elora instead of next to her, which basically meant they got to look at each other but remained safely out of each other's reach. They were, instead, forced to make polite conversation while Brana stuck his head out the window.

Elora smiled and nodded at Brana. "Does he always do that?"

"Yeah. Pretty much." Artus slapped Brana on the backside. "Stick your head back in! You look like a loon!"

Brana popped back inside, his golden eyes alight. "We're going to the lake!"

"I love that glamour on your eyes, Brana," Elora said, touching him on the knee. "It's very striking."

Brana laughed at her and then sniffed the air. "Dogs!" he shouted, and stuck his head out the window again.

Artus sighed. "Sorry about this."

Elora waved off the apology. "No, no—it's all right. I was too subtle. Maybe we can convince him to walk home, though?" She gave Artus a wink. It hit Artus like a knife to the gut, taking his breath away.

Did she really mean that? Did she really want the two of them to be alone? Well, obviously, right? She came here alone. Artus found he had to use all his willpower to avoid blushing, all while stupid Brana shook his rear end in his face.

Elora laughed. "It's all right. I think he's kind of adorable."

Artus grimaced.

They arrived, and of course Brana was immediately out the door. Shaking his head ruefully to Elora, Artus descended, then held his hand out, helping the lady down. That first touch was electric. Though improper, Elora let her hand linger in his for a moment too long. A blush overtook him and he withdrew his hand. Embarrassed at his own cowardice, he looked around . . . and his embarrassment was forgotten. The Floating Gardens had caught Artus's attention since they first arrived in the city. They seemed so other-worldly, so unnatural—floating above Lake Elren like a kind of fairy crown, serene and untouched. The mageglass bridges that connected them looked like gossamer threads, too delicate to be real. Now, at the edge of the lake, Artus got a close-up look at one of the lowest ones.

The bridge was wide enough for two people to walk abreast and slender in its construction—the single arch was no more than an inch thick in any one place, and did not thicken or broaden toward the ends, as a bridge should—so that Artus thought it improbable it could hold his weight, let alone the weight of the three of them collectively. Of course it was mageglass, and so was only half real anyway. The laws of nature did not strictly apply. Still, he was a bit nervous—as much about the bridge as he was about Elora's proximity.

They made their way across together, Brana in the lead, and after a first hesitant step—which caused Elora to give him a mocking look, causing him to blush—they made it across to the first garden. It floated only a few inches off the surface of the lake and many of the flowering vines that covered the trellises that ringed the garden's edge dipped their roots down to touch the water. The center of the garden featured a single cherry tree, already in bloom, with even more flowering vines encircling its trunk. Everything was colorful and fragrant, even in the light of the moon. The grass was lush and soft beneath the soles of his shoes.

Brana was no sooner on this garden than he was hurrying off to the next one—across another narrow bridge to another, slightly higher hunk of floating earth. As soon as he was out of sight, Elora took Artus by the hand once more—and the surge went through him again. This time he had the good sense to not let go. Her amber eyes twinkled in the moonlight, and her necklace positively sparkled. "I'm *so* glad you came tonight, Artus!"

Artus felt his whole body tingle. He felt as though he and the garden were floating into the sky. "I'm glad, too."

Should I kiss her now? The question—one he hadn't considered until exactly that moment—was enough to make his heart beat at twice the normal rate. Should he? What if he was wrong? What if he was misreading her signals? Were they, in fact, signals? Maybe she always went about with her shoulders bare like that! Maybe there was some rule of etiquette the kiss would violate. *Gods*, he thought, feeling a bead of sweat run down between his shoulder blades, *why is this suddenly so terrifying?*

Elora was still smiling up at him. "We're all so sorry about what happened to your uncle. The others are going to be so pleased you're here!"

Artus, again, felt his head spinning. "Others?"

"Oh, just my cousin, Valen, and his friend Ethick. Oh and Michelle, of course." Elora made a face, "I can't seem to do anything without that girl tagging along."

Brana ran back into view. He had a rose in his teeth and one behind his ear. "Here, Artus!" he said, handing him the spare flower.

Artus took it. The stem was slick with the gnoll's saliva. "Yeah," he said to Elora, "I know exactly what you mean."

Some more people were coming up the bridge. Artus turned to see Valen, followed by the thick-necked Ethick, and then Michelle. They were all dressed as though they were about to go on a hunt or something—high boots, thick doublets, and the willowy Michelle in a suede dress cut for riding. They were all holding mugs of what looked like beer. "I spy two lovebirds!" Valen shouted, loudly enough that it echoed off the lake. He looked to be just a trifle drunk.

Elora rolled her eyes. "You weren't slumming it, were you?"

Ethick belched. "That ale house was far from a slum. Charged us three silvers a mug!" He took a sip from the mug. "But yes. We were slumming it—we were drinking beer! Disgusting place, though—no cushions on the stools or anything."

Valen slapped Ethick on the arse. "Yes, because we all know you don't have enough cushioning back there, eh?"

"Really, Valen," Michelle groaned. "Control yourself—you only had two." She looked at Artus and gave him a shallow curtsey. "Well met, Master Artus. Pleased to see you again."

Artus smiled and shrugged. "You can just call me Artus, really. It's okay."

That earned him a smile from Michelle, who pushed a stray hair behind her ear. Then Brana trotted up and gave her the other rose, and she turned bright red from her ears to her nose—the blush was visible even in moonlight.

This sent Valen and Ethick into hysterics, though they refused to say why. Michelle, unable to banish the blush, folded her arms and scowled. The rose, though, remained in her hand.

Elora looked displeased. She took Artus's elbow. "Well, are we going to stand around looking like buffoons, or are we going to do something fun?"

Artus jerked a thumb toward the bridge leading to the higher garden. "I thought we were going to walk through the gardens?"

"Pshaw." Ethick rolled his eyes. "That might be all well and good for you Eddonish lads, with the ladies on your arms and what-not, but what about me and

Valen, here? Are we going to nuzzle each other in a gazebo or something?"

"I'm not on his arm," Michelle snarled, but then gave Brana an apologetic smile. "I mean . . . you know what I mean. No offense."

Brana grinned. "Want another flower?"

Again, Michelle turned deep red. "No. Thank you, but no."

Ethick thrust his tankard forward like it was a cavalry saber. "Back to the ale house!"

Michelle groaned. "Do we have to?" Ethick made a pleading gesture and she rolled her eyes. "Okay, fine."

Valen smiled. "Sounds fun to me." He looked at Elora and Artus. "Up for it? Can Lady Elora handle a cushion-less stool?"

Elora sniffed. "If we must, but let's not stay all night. I'd rather not go home reeking of tobacco."

Valen chuckled and then called to Brana, "Hey, flower boy! You want to come get drunk?"

Brana looked up from the chain of flowers he was weaving. "Drunk? Okay!"

And so they went, Valen leading the way. Artus noticed that Brana, on the way to the bridge, offered Michelle his arm. At this point, her blush looked permanent . . . but she did take his elbow.

This—running into Valen and Ethick and Michelle here—had to be what Tyvian had meant when he said "expect a surprise." Except it didn't seem like such a sinister surprise to Artus—they were trying to make friends with someone who might be important one day. What was so suspicious about that?

The ale house was tucked a few blocks inside a neighborhood of Westercity, or so Artus was told. The big, palatial homes of the wealthy had given way to the small houses and cottages of the poor. The ale house was mostly outdoors, actually—rows of tables and stools set up beneath a heavy canvas awning and lit by smoky tallow candles. The ale was inside the small brewery, which seemed chiefly to consist of a man squeezed behind a short counter and surrounded by massive wooden casks.

The brewer was pleased to see his mugs return, and particularly pleased to see members of the peerage drinking his brew. He had his son—a lad of maybe ten—come round with a pitcher every few minutes, just to make sure nobody's mug went empty. Valen was paying for everyone, but Artus noted the coinage being passed along. The brewer was gouging them—it was costing two gold marks for a round, which was about ten times what Artus guessed it should be. This fact never seemed to dawn on Valen, or anybody else, for that matter. Two marks wasn't enough money for Valen to care about, even if he did notice. The brewer, meanwhile, looked as though he was being blessed by the gods with every coin Valen slipped him. Artus was pretty sure the man was weeping with joy when they turned their backs.

No one else was in the alehouse—they had the place to themselves. It made Artus wonder why— the beer wasn't too bad, actually, and on a cool, clear spring evening, it should have been quite the draw for locals who had worked a long day. Maybe the nobles frightened them off. Maybe that was why they were being charged so much.

In any case, Artus didn't bring it up. There were far more interesting things to think about.

Elora, for instance.

Valen, Ethick, and Brana were at a separate table, each taking turns chugging beer to impress a completely unimpressed Michelle. This left Elora and Artus alone at their table, perched on stools, heads close together, holding hands. The crickets chirped in the untamed lawn at their feet; in the distance somewhere, a man sang an old Rhondian ballad to the tune of a squeaky concertina.

Elora smiled. "This is actually quite nice. I wasn't expecting this."

Artus smiled back. "What?"

"I wonder sometimes what it's like to be a peasant." She shrugged. "You know—no obligations, no expectations. Just go out into the world and . . . and, you know, live your own way."

Artus laughed. "*That's* what you think it's like?"

Elora rolled her eyes at him. "Oh, come on—this is unfair. You've lived among them all these years, so you obviously know better than I do, but think about it—if you and I were poor, we could come here every night, by ourselves! If we wanted to . . ." She stopped herself, blushing. "Well, you know—we'd be freer than we are now."

Artus squeezed her hand. "Assuming we could afford it."

Elora snorted. "Well obviously we'd have *jobs*. Everybody has a job—*I* have a job." Artus laughed, but she pressed on. "I do! I'm the hope for my whole family, Artus! If I don't succeed in bringing honor to House Davram, my great-aunt will have no choice but to cut us off—my father has only a small fief, and he can't protect it himself. Gods, we're one bad battle away from him being declared errant, and then we'd be homeless!"

"You wouldn't be homeless," Artus said, surprised at the bitterness in his voice. "All that means for you is you'd rent a fancy house here in the city."

"Fancy? It would have, what, seven rooms? Ha!" Elora shook her head. "You're the son of royalty. You have more money than anyone. You don't under-stand."

Artus looked around at the houses clustered to-gether on the street, most of which housed two or three families and not many of which had more than seven rooms altogether. He thought of his own home growing up, far across the mountains in the distant northern kingdoms. The little farmhouse had three rooms for ten people, assuming you didn't count the barn. He sighed. He really didn't understand. He decided to change the subject and use the single piece of romantic advice Tyvian had ever given him. "That's a nice necklace."

Elora looked down, cupping the tear-drop shaped jewel and holding it to the light. "You like it? It's my mother's. I filched it from her vanity this afternoon. I like how subtle it is."

"It goes with the dress very well," Artus added.

Elora's smile sparkled to match the diamond. "Thank you very much!" She leaned forward, batting her eyes. "I wore it for you, you know."

Artus wasn't sure which was more surprising—that he had actually taken some of Tyvian's advice, or that it had worked so spectacularly. He leaned forward, too, so close their noses were almost touching. "Now I *really* wish I hadn't brought Brana along."

Elora rolled her eyes. "Stop talking about your brother for five seconds, will you?"

Artus shut up. They stayed there, gazing into each other's eyes, nose to nose, and neither of them moved. Artus felt trapped—unable to retreat, but unable to advance. Eventually, it was Tyvian's voice in his head that jarred him from the stalemate. *Kroth's teeth, boy! Kiss her!*

So he did. He wasn't exactly sure how to go about it—the few times he'd spied on Tyvian kissing Myreon had typically been interrupted by Hool before he could get any real good idea of what to do. He puckered his lips and pressed, basically. Elora pressed back, sealing her lips around his in an airtight lock. They stayed there, sucking on each other's faces for a few seconds, which was probably the best few seconds of Artus's life to date. Then she stuck her tongue in his mouth, and he nearly gagged in surprise and broke away.

Elora's eyes were wide. "Sorry! I'm sorry! I'm so sorry!"

"No, no!" Artus shook his head. "It's okay . . . I'm . . . I didn't expect that . . . I just . . ."

Valen's hand fell on his shoulder. "All right, lovebirds—that's enough of that. Time to hear what Artus of Eddon has to say for himself." Valen's breath smelled heavily of beer. As did his doublet.

Artus looked to see Ethick and Michelle, both a bit tipsy themselves, standing behind him. "Where's Brana?"

Ethick laughed. "Your brother can't hold his liquor, that's for sure!" He pointed. Brana was curled up in a ball, sleeping under the table.

Michelle cocked her head. "Awww . . . he's so cute! He looks like a little puppy under there."

Valen laughed. "His tongue is hanging out far enough, eh?" Ethick joined him in a series of belly-shaking guffaws.

Artus frowned. "You had something you wanted to ask me?"

Valen sat on a stool next to Artus. He was drunk,

so he tipped a little. Artus righted him. "Can't hold your beer either, can you, Valen?"

Valen laughed. "Shit's so weak, you . . . you don't realize . . . how much you've had." He belched. Artus wished Tyvian were there to see it. "Anyway . . . who told you you could call me Valen and not milord?"

Michelle rolled her eyes. "He's royalty, Valen. You should call *him* milord."

Elora snorted. "Valen outranks *you*, Michelle. What's your excuse?"

Artus looked around at them all. "Are we seriously talking about this? *This* is why you interrupted us?"

Elora blushed. This caused Artus to blush, too. Then Michelle blushed for some reason. Ethick and Valen laughed.

"Okay . . ." Valen held up his hands. ". . . okay, okay—first question: how many duels have you been in?"

Artus blinked. "Duels?" He wondered what he should say. None? Would that look bad? Artus decided to be vague. "Oh, well, a couple. I guess."

"Really?" Elora asked, eyes lighting up. "Did you win?"

Artus frowned. All of them were examining him like some kind of bug in a jar. Again, what to say? If he was counting the number of times he'd been in a fight for his life, well . . . "Uh, yeah. I won. I'm still here, aren't I?"

Michelle gasped and put a hand to her mouth. "They were to the *death*?"

Artus forced a laugh. "Well, yeah, obviously. Uhhh . . . that's just how they do it in Eddon."

Michelle cocked her head like a bird. "What's Eddon like, anyway? I hear the most *awful* stories."

Artus shrugged. "I don't know. It's not that bad."

"I hear gnolls steal children in the night," Michelle said.

Elora giggled. "Oh, that sounds dreadful."

Artus did his best not to frown. "Nope. They don't do that."

Ethick snorted. Valen also looked like he was trying not to laugh.

"What?" Artus asked.

"I've heard your Uncle Waymar's had to dodge assassins before," Valen said. "That true?"

Artus snorted a laugh. "That's for sure. I'd say at least . . ." He counted in his head. It took longer than he thought. "I can't even count the number of times somebody's tried to kill him, honestly."

Valen laughed. "No, seriously."

Artus shrugged, pleased he didn't even have to lie. "Seriously. A lot of people don't like him."

Ethick frowned. "And he's survived every time?"

Michelle rolled her eyes. "Obviously. Dunce."

Valen rubbed Artus's shoulder. "So . . . what's his secret?"

Artus met Valen's eye. He noticed it was clear, sharp. *This guy's not half as drunk as he looks.* "It's a secret."

Ethick hooted with laughter. The young ladies' mouths formed perfect O's. Valen clapped him on the shoulder again and then whistled for the brewer's boy. "Another round!"

Artus frowned. *They're gonna get me more drunk, and they're gonna pump me for more information. Tyvian was right. This is just a setup.*

Even Elora . . .

The beer came around again. Artus looked at Elora as he drank it. Did she know, or was she just a pawn? Bait for a trap. She'd kissed him, hadn't she? A girl didn't stick her tongue in a boy's mouth unless she meant it, right?

The conversation went on, but Artus steered it away from Tyvian and himself. He found himself talking about t'suul. "So you've played it in Illin?" Elora asked.

"Not *in* Illin, just with some Illini . . . people." They had been pirates Tyvian knew, but Artus didn't think that was especially pertinent.

Ethick frowned. "Were they any good?"

Artus shook his head. "In Illin, you don't play t'suul to be clever. You play it to be brave."

Valen nodded. "Dailiki. Like the other night, right?"

Ethick gulped his beer. "I don't get it. Why don't you play to win?"

Artus shrugged, trying to remember how the Illinis—dark, brooding people with thick moustaches and scarred hands—had put it. "Because nobody wins in life. T'suul is like life, you know? You don't control what tiles you have in your clutch, you can't control what the sakkidio contains. You just have dailiki—bravado, courage—and that's it. You against fate."

Valen grunted. "They must lose a lot of money that way."

Artus smirked. "In Illin, they don't play t'suul for money. They play for blood."

Silence. The three young peers looked at him as though expecting a joke. Artus merely smiled and sipped his beer. "Or so I've heard."

Valen laughed and slapped Artus on the back again, but too hard. "You're all right, Artus of Eddon."

Artus smiled. "Thanks."

Brana suddenly popped up from under the table where he had been dozing. "Artus! Myreon!"

"What? Where?" Artus blinked and staggered to his feet (maybe he *had* had a bit too much).

Brana pointed. Squinting into the darkness, Artus thought he might have seen a tall woman with a staff turning down an alley. Then again, it could have been anything. Tyvian's request that he follow her came trickling back into his mind, but he stayed rooted in the spot. "Was that her?"

Elora looked in the same direction. "Was it who? Is something wrong?"

Something big passed in front of the moon—like

a huge bird of prey—that made all of them look up. A griffon. And where there were griffons riders in Eretheria, there were Defenders of the Balance.

Artus looked up into the clear night sky and saw a second griffon glide past, the man on its back wearing armor that gleamed like mirrors in the moonlight—they were looking for something. "Yeah. Something's wrong." He looked at Brana. "We should get home."

Elora caught his face in her hands and gave him a little peck on the nose. "Don't worry about that, Artus. It doesn't concern us."

Brana's ears were alert. "Gotta go. Gotta go now."

Elora slipped her arms around his waist. "Let him go. Stay with me."

Artus looked at Brana and then back into Elora's warm, amber eyes. Then back at Brana, who was on the balls of his feet, ready to run. He knew something was going on, now. A troop of mirror-men marched by, the sergeant holding a seekwand outstretched. They were tracking somebody—definitely trouble.

"Artus?" Brana whined.

But it wasn't *his* trouble, was it? They weren't tracking him or they'd have already found him. Hell, he didn't even know for sure that *was* Myreon they were after. He waved Brana off. "Go on home, Brana. It's probably nothing. Tell Waymar what happened. I'll be . . . I'll be back later."

Laughing, Valen and Ethick slapped him on the

back, said he was a good fellow, but he wasn't paying attention to that. He was looking at Elora, feeling her hands around his neck, and letting the warm glow of the beer overtake him.

It was too good a night to ruin with Tyvian's stupid plans.

CHAPTER 12

THE COST OF CONSPIRACY

That evening's meeting was arranged for another deserted cistern in another corner of the city. Myreon got there early this time, before anyone else. She needed to get out of the house anyway—away from Tyvian. She kept trying to not be angry about the whole thing; Tyvian was who he was. The ring hadn't made him any different, really. He was still the same old rakish smuggler, the same old self-absorbed duelist. Why should she be surprised he wasn't faithful to her? Why should she get angry at him for not using his power or wealth to help others? He was no different than any of a thousand selfish men of means. Why did she expect more of him?

Because he could be different.

She grimaced at this thought as she laid a few wards against eavesdropping and seekwands around the entrances to the cistern. She'd believed that. She'd believed it when he came back to rescue her in Saldor—she, disgraced and petrified in a penitentiary garden. Tyvian and she had been sworn enemies, then—she'd been his nemesis, hunting him across the West as a Mage Defender. Still, he'd come, saved her, brought her away. She'd believed in Tyvian when he risked his life to save those girls in the Cauldron—a dirty whorehouse being torn apart by Tyvian's old friend-turned-madman. She'd believed it when Tyvian had tried to stop his brother, Xahlven, from crashing the Saldorian Markets and failed. She even believed it today, when he'd given all that money to those poor farmers.

But that was the ring. That wasn't Tyvian. Sometimes Tyvian had trouble telling the difference these days—a side effect, perhaps, of wearing it all the time—but Myreon knew. She remembered the old him, back when he was a notorious smuggler and criminal. The viciousness in his eyes, the callousness of his words, the cruelty of his actions. *That* was Tyvian. She had to remember that, otherwise she'd get too angry to think, and anger was a distraction from her work—from this, her true calling.

Stirring up insurrection? Is that all I'm good for, now?

And why not? She wasn't a Defender anymore. She

wasn't even a law-abiding citizen—what other good *could* she hope to create in the world, if not this? She'd tried living Tyvian's way, at first—indulging in all the luxuries Hool's vast wealth could afford. But there was little pleasure in it, in the end. Myreon needed a higher purpose. This, she had decided, was it.

The rumors on the street that evening let her know her work was appreciated. She, the Gray Lady, was everywhere, apparently. Chickens taken as tax had magically been returned. A tax man had been unable to find the address of a poor widow. A press-gang's wagon had broken an axle out of nowhere, allowing some of the levied men to slip away in the confusion. *The Gray Lady*, they said, *answers your prayers*.

Her apprentices began to trickle in, arriving in twos and threes, as few of them liked to wander the sewers alone. She greeted them warmly, smiling all the while, and heard their reports. Another evening, another little bit of solace offered these people. *Her* people.

She heard the commotion coming from one of the tunnels before she saw who was making it. She froze, as did the rest of the class, their heads coming up like deer in a meadow. Not the Defenders, surely, and not the necromancer—both would be quieter than this. Then who?

"Ramper!" she breathed as his wiry, ragged figure hopped down from the tunnel and put his hands up. Gil was there, with someone in his arms—Bree!

Ramper took her from Gil and ran her over to the simple plank table. "Hurry, Magus! She's hurt real bad!"

Bree had blood caked around her lips, her breathing coming in ragged gasps. One eye was swollen shut with a horrid purple bruise. She looked frail and tiny, her hair plastered to her sweat-soaked forehead.

Myreon looked at her class. All of them were still and alert, like startled rabbits. "Class dismissed. Scatter, all of you."

The apprentices began to leave, but not quickly. Some gathered around, offering to help. Myreon ignored them for the time being—priorities. "What the hell happened to her?"

Ramper grimaced. "Tried to boost the same tax man twice—thought mayhap we might lose the man his post, eh?"

"Please, Magus! You've got to help her!" Gilvey cupped Bree's face. "It's all right, Bree—we're here. The Gray Lady has you. It'll be all right."

Ramper shook his head. "Bloody bastard was sneaky this time. Caught Bree here lifting the bag. Hit her with that mace a' his a few times—ribs, face. Woulda killed her."

Myreon gently touched Bree's chest. Even that light pressure made Bree choke with pain. Her ribs were shattered. "What do you mean *would have* killed her? What stopped him?"

Ramper looked up at Gil. Gil looked down at his hands. "Well . . ."

Myreon felt a spike of panic strike her lower back and spread outward. "No. Tell me you didn't."

"It weren't the boy's fault," Ramper said, shifting his weight. "That tax man, he was . . . he was a right bastard. Striking a girl like that . . ."

"Gil, did you use a wand?"

Bree moaned.

Gil pointed at the battered girl on the table. "Just save her, Magus! Please!"

Myreon shook her head. This needed answering *right now*. "Ramper! Did you give Gilvey a wand? Did he use it to kill a tax man?"

Gil flinched at the word *kill*. "I don't know he's dead. I just zapped him a few times. Just a few."

Myreon could scarcely believe she was hearing this. "Sweet Hann's mercy! How *long* ago?"

Ramper shrugged. "Before sunset. Spent the last few hours lying low, dodging the mirror-men, making sure we weren't followed."

Myreon turned to face what few of her apprentices remained. "Everybody needs to clean up any sign we have *ever* been here—every candle, every spot of wax, every mark of chalk, every splinter of wood—go. Now."

Ramper chuckled. "But Magus, we lost—"

"Every stool, every candle, every scrap of wax—we leave so much as a floor stain behind and the mirror-men will be on us all by tomorrow afternoon!"

"But . . ." Gil frowned. "We weren't followed!"

Myreon snapped her fingers. "Go, now! This is why *I'm* the mage and you are the apprentices! *Go!*" Around her she heard a flurry of activity. She glanced over to see a serving girl snatching up candlesticks and putting them in her apron. A stable hand—a kindly man with big, warm hands—scraped wax drippings off the floor with a pocket knife.

Myreon reached into her robe for some healing ointment. It wouldn't work well here, thanks to the Etheric ley, but with just the right infusion of the Lumen, she thought she might be able to heal many of Bree's injuries. She had to focus, though, and there was no time to lose. She counted back the hours since sundown—one hour to learn of the murder, one hour to track down either Gil or Bree or Ramper's home, and then the seekwands came out and they were on the trail. The Defenders could be here at any moment . . .

She managed to turn her attention back to Bree. She forced a smile for the girl. "Does it hurt?"

Bree nodded. Her eyes were red with tears. "Are . . . are we going to be okay?"

Myreon stroked Bree's hair. "I'm going to chan-nel the Lumen now. I need you to think of happy thoughts—good things. Sunlight. Laughter. Can you do that?"

"Laughter?" Bree tried to smile. Half her teeth were gone on one side. "What I got to l-laugh about?"

Myreon kept her face serene. "Close your eyes. Talk it through. What do you see?"

Bree was quiet for a moment and then, with a shallow, painful breath, she began to whisper. "Gil, last summer. Before any of this happened. He's chopping wood in his yard, his arms like tree branches themselves. He's smiling at me and I'm watching him. Then he picks this dandelion. I'm thinking he's going to give it to me—a sweet little gift. I stand up all straight and fix my particulars, and push back my hair, and . . ."

Myreon was working the augury to precisely identify her injuries—she found them. They were extensive. She began to rub the healing ointment under Bree's bodice and on her face. "And then what?"

"He . . . he *ate* it! All in one bite." Bree gave a giggle, and then coughed with pain.

There! The little bloom of Lumenal energy was there, if only for a fleeting moment. Myreon pressed both her hands to Bree's chest and chanted beneath her breath. The concentrated energy lit the little table. She and the girl were floating in a sea of sunlight, the smell of daffodils and fresh grass in their nostrils. The healing ointment burned away, doing its work. And then, as quickly as the light had come, it faded. Myreon let out a long breath, feeling the fatigue creep into her arms.

The color was back in Bree's cheeks. Her eye was just a bruise now, her face restored to its proper shape.

Her teeth hadn't returned, but one couldn't hope for miracles. The peasant girl sat up with Myreon's help. She began to relace her bodice. "I . . . I can breathe. Still hurts, but—"

Myreon nodded. "I'm . . . I'm sorry, Bree. Not very much Lumen here—not great for a true healing spell."

Around them, most of the apprentices had already fled. Only Ramper and Gil were left, still scraping up bits of chalk from the evening's lesson. *Good*, Myreon thought, *I can protect three, if it comes to it.*

"Magus!" Gilvey shouted, pointing.

Myreon looked. She was looking down a drain pipe that led into the cistern—one at exactly eye level. And from deep, deep inside it, white light was dancing, throwing shadows on some distant wall. It was getting closer.

Tattlers.

"Get behind me!" Myreon shouted, planting her staff and facing the pipe.

Ramper, Bree, and Gilvey, wands drawn, clustered behind her.

Tattlers came in from the grating above. There, in the moonlight, Myreon saw mirrored helms and the flickering tips of firepikes closing in.

Ramper made a sour face. "They're coming from everywhere."

Myreon performed an Ether-bloom spell, flooding the area with Etheric energy that caused the first wave of tattlers to wink out of existence.

Without hesitating, she turned around and pushed Bree and Gilvey into the closest water main and waited for Ramper to enter even as mirror-men emerged into the cistern, their pikes blazing. "Stop in the name of the Balance!" they roared.

Not likely.

Myreon hit them with a sunblast that caused the lead few to stumble back, temporarily blinded, but their mageglass armor protected them from the worst of the burns. This was intentional—she wasn't trying to necessarily hurt them, just create enough time to escape.

She turned her back and dove into the pipe after Ramper. She sketched a quick guard on the wall of the pipe as she crawled in—a nasty surprise for their first follower—and then hurried after the dim shadow of Ramper's backside as it wriggled through the small space.

Fortunately, the pipe soon opened onto a larger passage, where Bree and Gilvey were waiting—this, in itself, made Myreon angry. "Go, you idiots! Run! Now!"

"We want to help!" Gilvey said, his voice cracking.

Myreon caught him by his collar and shook him. "Listen to me: *You. Cannot. Help.*" She pushed him. "Run, boy! You'll make an ugly statue."

A firepike bolt sizzled out of the pipe and struck the wall between Myreon and Gil. The boy jumped like a rabbit and he and Bree shot down a side passage. Ramper was next to her, returning fire down the pipe with his sparkwand, screaming obscenities.

"Idiot!" Myreon pushed him aside just before a firepike bolt would have caught him in the chest. "You think wizard hunters care about your toy wand?"

Yet Ramper just laughed and ran after Bree and Gil. After a split second of hesitation, Myreon followed. The seekwand the Defenders were using would work particularly well down here, which meant they would catch Ramper, Gil, and Bree's trail easily—it's what brought them down on the cistern in the first place. Myreon might have escaped if she didn't go with them, but she couldn't bring herself to sacrifice those children to the Defenders for her own safety.

Head low, she ran for all she was worth, working a slight Lumenal enchantment over her eyes to allow her to see more clearly in the pitch-darkness. Light poured from her gaze and she could see the shadowy labyrinth of the sewers in stark, black-and-white relief. Ahead of her, Ramper glowed bright with a little shard of illumite in his hand, and Gil and Bree were starkly visible in its pool of light. The Defenders, of course, would be using the same basic enchantments she was—enchanted into the visors on their helmets.

"Ramper!" she shouted, "ditch the light!"

Ramper pocketed the illumite, but the damage was done. A tattler, bright and happy, zoomed past Myreon and affixed itself to Ramper. He swatted at it, but it dodged clear. A few more showed up, too, attaching themselves to Gil and Bree. The one that came for Myreon she quickly dispelled, but she couldn't afford to pause long enough to dispel the others. By Defender regulations, set out by the Gray Tower itself, tattlers preceded Defenders into unsecured locations by only twelve paces. She pushed the others forward, knowing the firepikes weren't far behind.

"Keep running!"

Her heart pounded. Routes through the labyrinth of sewers blossomed in her mind as she planned their potential escape.

Was this what it was like, Tyvian? she wondered, as she ducked around a corner to dodge a squad of mirror-helmed men who were trying to cut them off. *Is this what I put you through for all those years?*

She nearly ran into Gilvey and Bree as they had come up short at a dead end. "Kroth! Where's Ramper?"

Bree looked pale, her hands on her knees. "Don't . . . don't know . . . lost him . . . somewhere . . ."

Myreon heard the shouts of the mirror-men as they searched. Glancing behind, she caught sight of the glow of their firepikes, lighting their way in the dark. The tattlers were giving them away—they glowed like fireflies.

Gil batted at his. "Can't you get rid of these things?"

Myreon waved a hand, spoke a few words, and dispelled Bree's, but, again, time was against her. "Come on!"

They doubled back, coming so close to the Defenders that they were able to squeeze off a few firepike shots. Myreon found herself realizing just how terrifying those weapons were when aimed at you, and how thankful she was for their sheer inaccuracy.

Unfamiliar with this part of the sewers, Myreon started guiding them through turns at random, hoping to lose the mirror-men in the labyrinth, possibly even shake the damned tattler that circled around Gil's head like a halo. She had Bree by the hand, dragging her at double speed into the dark.

Rounding a corner, the height of the tunnel dropped suddenly and Myreon struck her head on a stone crossbeam. Sparks danced in her vision from the impact and she fell backward into the shallow, slimy water that pooled at the base of the tunnel. The Lumenal sight spell dropped away and the darkness closed in.

"Magus!" Bree shouted.

The sewer demons immediately attached to Myreon's arms and legs, sucking on this or that patch of foulness with their circular, cilia-lined mouths. Myreon instinctively brushed them off, a shudder running up her spine. She swayed a bit as she rose, slapping away any other of the semisolid beasts that sought to feed. To her hands, they felt like little rolling blobs of rotting fruit.

They were at a T-shaped intersection, but Myreon wasn't really sure which way she had intended to go—both directions had low ceilings. Behind them, the echoes of the Defenders still chased them, but more distantly.

Gilvey had his shirt off and was trying to catch the tattler with it, but the nimble little Lumenal construct was far too quick. "Damn . . . this stupid . . . thing!"

Myreon dispelled it. "We've only got to get onto the street and lie low for a few days. I know some safe houses. We're going to make it."

"Can't you . . . can't you fight them?" Bree asked, as she clutched her skirts and shuffled around to stay away from the little piles of sewer demons wordlessly sucking at her bare toes.

"Yes," Gil panted, "rain fire on them. Turn them to stone or something."

Myreon took a deep breath at the thought and tried not to shudder. "Hush. We might be able to escape without violence. Stealth over speed now. Follow me."

Myreon picked a direction and went, but more cautiously than before. She fumbled forward in the dark, tapping with her feet ahead of her, in case of a sudden drop.

"Can't you make light?" Bree asked, clutching at Myreon's robe. Her hands were trembling.

Myreon hushed her quiet and added in a whisper, "Sometimes the wisest sorcery is no sorcery at all."

They soon heard the faint sound of rushing water—near an aqueduct, then, or perhaps near or beneath one of the many public fountains Eretheria was famous for. The sound might muffle the sounds of their pursuers but would also muffle the sound of their own footsteps. Then it would be only the seekwand drawing the Defenders close. Myreon turned toward the sound . . .

. . . only to find herself at another dead end, an ancient iron grate blocking their path. She enchanted a bit of light onto the end of her staff. On the other side of the grate there was a large chamber where water fell from drains in the ceiling and into an aqueduct elevated above the floor of the sewer tunnels. This was the overflow of a fountain at street level—if they could get through the grate, they might find some way out.

But the grate was bolted into the stone with ancient and rusty iron screws that she could not hope to break. The grate itself was too heavy and too dense to be easily blown apart by the Shattering, and even if it were, the noise would be deafening—the Defenders would be drawn right to them.

They couldn't go back either—any attempt to retrace their steps might bring them in contact with the Defenders, and then they were done for. She knew she couldn't bring herself to seriously harm a Defender-at-arms just doing his duty. She took hold of the bars and shook, rather lamely. This didn't do much more than stain her hands orange with rust flakes.

"Kroth."

She groaned.

"We've got to get out," Gilvey said, facing back where they had come from. There was light approaching—flickering, orange light. Firepikes.

They had perhaps a minute . . .

"Doth the lady require assistance?"

The voice—that raspy whisper—was so unexpected that Myreon jumped back from the grating. There—beyond it, lying on its side in a little gully. A human skull, its sockets glowing with that faint, green light. Myreon looked over her shoulder—Bree and Gil hadn't heard it. *Is it even real?*

"An accord must be struck. The help I offer, and in exchange . . . my due."

Myreon scowled. She didn't have time for this. "I'm not haggling with you, dammit. Either help or get out of the way."

Bree's eyes were wide. "Who . . . who are you talking to?"

Myreon glared at the skull. It had gone dark. "No one. Don't worry about it." Myreon grimaced. There was one way she could do this herself, maybe. She didn't like it, though. "Stand back, both of you."

The two teenagers drew back from the rusty old grating. "What are you going to do?" Bree asked. In the dim light, her face looked . . . eager. *She wants to see what I can do.*

"This grate, this tunnel—they're corroded already.

If I can corrode them a bit more, maybe we can kick the grating out."

"What kind of spell is that?" Bree asked.

"Hurry!" Gil whispered. The pikes were coming closer. They could hear distant voices, the scrape of boots on stone.

Myreon pulled on the ample Etheric energy in the ley around them and cast a rot curse on a few likely spots around the edges of the grate. Quickly the metal began to brown and the bricks and mortar around the edges cracked and flaked. The light on Myreon's staff went out, its little flare of Lumenal energy obliterated by the concentration of the Ether.

Bree clung to Myreon's cloak. "Isn't that black magic?"

Myreon reconjured the light—it was very difficult, even for such a small bit. There was hardly any Lumen left here. She grimaced. "There's no such thing." She braced herself and gave the grate a good, firm kick. It budged a bit, its rusty edges crumbling away. She took up her staff. "I'm going to pry at it. Gil—go keep a lookout. Let me know if they get too close."

"How close is too close?" Gilvey asked.

Myreon slid her staff into the space between the wall and the grate. "If they start shooting at you or giving you orders." She looked at Bree. "Help me with this—we're going to pry it off. On three?"

Bree grabbed the end of the staff. "Okay."

"One . . . two . . . *three!*" Myreon and Bree both put all their weight onto the staff. The thick wood bent at a frightening angle, but it didn't break. Then, with a sudden groan, the ancient iron grate snapped free from its moorings and fell to the floor below.

With a whoop of joy, Bree leapt into the chamber beyond and Myreon quickly followed. "Gil, come on! Let's go!"

Gil rose from a crouch, slipping on the loose mortar covering the ground. "Coming! I . . ."

He didn't finish the sentence. There was a crack and a rumble and then, all at once, the walls of the tunnel, weakened by the disintegration spell, collapsed on Gil as he was halfway through the door.

Bree screamed. Myreon grabbed the boy by his one free hand and tried to pull, but the weight of centuries of ancient construction was crushing his body from his chest down. He lost consciousness almost immediately, his chest unable to expand, unable to breathe. He had to have broken all his ribs, his hips, his legs . . .

"Gil!" Bree patted his cheeks. *"Gilvey!"*

The voice came drifting in from the darkness, the barest whisper in her ear. *"Such a pity. But for thy pride, I might have rescued thee. This is, after all, my realm."*

The accusation stung. Myreon felt suddenly ill, but there was no time.

Bree was clinging to Gil's head. "No!"

Myreon reached forward and guided Bree back. "We've got to go."

"Go? You've got to get him out! Hurry!"

Myreon looked down at the girl and felt her own breath stolen away. "I . . . I can't. Not without killing him anyway."

Bree's mouth fell open as it all hit her. "But you can *heal* him! You can heal him like you healed *me!*"

"There is . . . there's not enough Lumenal energy here to do that, even if I could get him out. Bree, we have to go."

"No!" Gil's head lolled down, limp and covered in ancient dust.

Myreon felt tears welling in the corners of her eyes. "I'm sorry, Bree."

"*But I love him!*" Bree screamed, patting at Gilvey's cheeks. Tugging at his hair. "*No!*"

Myreon closed her eyes. It wouldn't take the mirror-men that long to find another way around . . . probably. Gods help them if a Mage Defender was on the scene by now. They would have little trouble blasting this passage open with concentrated barrages of the Shattering, cooper's boy or no cooper's boy.

"Gil," Bree cried, "wake up! Gil, it's Bree! You can't . . . you can't go!"

But we have to. "We've got to go, Bree." Myreon put a hand on her shoulder. "Cry later. Live now."

"He didn't deserve this," Bree sobbed.

"Nobody deserves this," Myreon said, her face bitter. "Come on, now. Say good-bye."

Bree stood up and laid a soft kiss on the back of

Gilvey's head. Her body still shook with sobs. "You should have been able to save him. It wasn't . . . it wasn't supposed to be like this."

Myreon took the girl by the wrist and guided her slowly away, her own steps blinded by tears. *You could have helped*, she thought to herself, *you could have, but you didn't.*

"I'll find you," Myreon whispered. "When all this is over, you and I will have words over this." But the threat had no teeth, and Myreon knew it. For all her anger, the only person she could find energy to blame was herself.

CHAPTER 13

FAMILY BUSINESS

Lyrelle Reldamar stood in the gardens of Glamourvine—the ancestral Reldamar estate in Saldor—peering down into the perfectly circular pool of water that rested at the center of a hedge maze. To the outside observer, she appeared to be a striking woman in her late forties, hair like liquid gold, dressed in a gown of ivory and violet, a delicate mageglass wand in one hand—a sorceress from a fairy story.

But she was old. And she felt it. For all the power she wielded, for all the wealth she possessed, time— that old killer—was catching up with her. Too quickly.

And there was still so much to do.

There, by the side of the garden pool, she did not feel as old as she might have. The pool, of course, was no mere pool in the same way that Lyrelle was no mere sorceress. It was a power sink—a bottomless well built along a ley line that siphoned the energies of the world into it and stored them, like a kind of bank. It had been collecting power now for many centuries, and Lyrelle found herself drawing on it more and more of late. Because of this, the garden around the pool existed in a kind of bubble in time—apart from the flow of the world around it, quiet and permanent, and yet immovably powerful. Lyrelle, if pressed, might have admitted a certain envy of it.

Sitting atop the surface of the pool was a frog on a lily pad. It was not, in fact, a real frog or a real lily pad. It was a demon—an imp—that had shrouded itself to appear as such. It was delivering its report. Its voice was in a sort of permanent half snicker, as though the world was a joke only it understood. "That is all that transpired, my queen."

As usual, the thing was likely lying. That was the way with imps. Lyrelle fixed it with a dubious frown. "Really? Are you certain?"

The false frog blinked its bulbous eyes. "Of course, my queen. As ever, I live to serve!"

Lyrelle sighed. "Because when I sent your brother, Finerax the Fulminous, to observe the same meeting, *Finerax* told me something quite different. There *was* no Defender raid. No human girl was killed. The necromancer did not contact the Gray Lady at all, and certainly not for a long conversation in the midst of a harried escape." She channeled a pure sphere of Lumenal energy to form at the tip of her wand—pure death to an Etheric creature like a demon—and pointed it toward the shrouded imp. "I wonder . . . whom should I believe?"

The frog transformed into a fuzzy kitten with big, innocent eyes. It still sat on the lily pad. "Me! Me, oh grand one! Finerax lies!"

Lyrelle extended the wand. "This is your last chance, Akta the Unspeakable. Out with it."

The kitten shivered. "Very well! It was not the girl who died, but the boy! You should have seen the girl's tears, my lady—so sweet, so numerous! Oh, and also the necromancer spoke to the Gray Lady for but a moment only. But the raid is true! I know it! Have mercy on me and fie unto my wretched brother for his lies to *you*!"

Lyrelle smiled, satisfied. That, then, was the truth. An imp could always be counted upon to tell the truth if, by doing so, it might do its own kind some disservice. "You are dismissed. Return to your surveillance. I expect updates every eight hours. Begone."

Akta muttered some servile compliments and then vanished into a pool of shadow, leaving Lyrelle alone. At least for the moment. She sat down upon a stone bench and let the sphere of Lumenal energy at the tip of her wand dissipate harmlessly back into the power sink. She shook her head. *So, Myreon has finally made her mistake.*

Waving her wand over the power sink's placid surface, she scryed visions of the future. Many she had already seen—a city in flames, death in the streets, heads on pikes. Some were new: Tyvian at the head of an army of farmers, Delloran soldiers burning the Empty Tower. Visions of her own death.

She waved them away, resolving to ponder them later. Scrying the future at one point in time was unreliable. It was a statistical science—not individual visions, but aggregates of such, observed and noted and analyzed until a likely knowledge of what was to come could be gleaned. Lyrelle was particularly good at it, but it took time. Patience.

Eddereon, her ostensible gardener, but in reality so much more, emerged from the hedge maze. His broad shoulders and thick black beard made him look fearsome in the moonlight—shades of the highwayman he had been before the ring took its hold. He bowed. "Your elder son is here."

Lyrelle nodded. This had been expected. Xahlven had need of the power sink, and so he had come to taunt and threaten his mother in hopes of distracting her as he used it. She only hoped she could play her part well. "Bring him to me, please."

Xahlven was taller than Tyvian and more handsome, in a conventional way. He had Lyrelle's golden hair and her piercing blue eyes. He had his late father's chiseled features—the face of a storybook hero. He was wearing the black robes of his office—Archmage of the Ether, Chairman of the Black College of the Arcanostrum. His staff seemed to suck the very light from the air, dimming the glow of fireflies and even causing the moon to grow dull. Such a petty enchantment was a juvenile trick—something used to intimidate lesser magi and hedge wizards. It demonstrated just how little her eldest son thought of her. This was as it should be—it was just what Lyrelle wanted him to think.

She smiled warmly at him. "Good evening, Xahlven. To what do I owe the pleasure?"

"I just received word from Mage Defender Argus Androlli of Eretheria Tower. They detected an imp during a raid operation this very night. I assume it was yours."

"Contrary to your extremely low opinion of my morals, I do not commonly traffic with demons, Xahlven. Unreliable creatures, so very prone to falsehood and deceit."

Xahlven smiled and laughed. "Spare me. You yourself taught me that anything that behaves predictably is a tool that needs only the proper application to be useful. I come only to remind you of the warning I gave you last year."

Lyrelle made a show of thinking. "Now, which warning was that, precisely? You scold your own mother on such a regular basis, my dear, it becomes difficult to keep all the threats straight."

Xahlven walked around to the other side of the power sink and planted his staff in the ground as though intending to punctuate his seriousness. Of course, in actuality he was planting it to absorb some of the power coming off the pool. Lyrelle might have stopped it, but she let it happen, knowing Xahlven was watching her keenly. Little did he know that she didn't need to lift a finger: the auguries she had enchanted into the flowerbeds earlier that evening flared to life, recording precisely what it was Xahlven was doing for later review.

"Eretheria is at a delicate junction, Mother. I realize you believe yourself permitted to meddle in any political sphere you wish, but there are forces at play here that you do not understand. Leave it to those of us whose task it is to guide the world. You are retired—it is time you remembered what that means."

"I suppose it means sitting here in my garden, reading a book, and minding my own business?" Lyrelle snorted. "It sounds dreadful. Besides, I have a stated personal interest in what transpires in Eretheria. As do you."

"Tyvian." Xahlven scowled. It never suited his face, she felt—Xahlven had a face meant to smile, and yet he did it so rarely. Lyrelle found herself again wondering where, exactly, she had gone wrong in raising him. So dreadfully, dreadfully wrong.

"He is your brother, Xahlven. It should go without saying that I care for him."

Xahlven held up a hand. "Spare me. I'm aware of how you bolstered that little rumor. It won't work. Even Tyvian knows it won't work. He won't stick his head in a noose—not for anyone. Not even that ring can make him do it."

"As ever, you underestimate your brother."

"*Half* brother!" Xahlven snapped. He pursed his lips, ready to say more—Lyrelle saw that anger flare up, usually so deeply buried. It was the same flash she had seen in Tyvian's eyes when she discussed his father. She felt a little tug of regret, deep in her stomach. *What kind of woman am I, to be hated so by her own children?*

Xahlven, though, swallowed his rage. What remained was that arrogant, sardonic expression that made him look so much like Whistreth Reldamar, his father. "This is your final warning, Mother. You have fewer friends in the Arcanostrum than you imagine, and the Keeper of the Balance will do nothing to protect you. You act on your own."

Lyrelle couldn't help but grin. "That has always been the case."

Xahlven pulled his staff up from the ground and backed away. "Let it never be said I was less than reasonable."

Lyrelle nodded. "Yes. Some things *are* best left unsaid."

Xahlven shook his head and turned away. After he left—after Lyrelle was certain he was gone and had left behind no enchantments, no little imps of his own—she checked the results of her augury to see what Xahlven had drawn from the power sink. When she found out, she sat back in surprise.

Lumenal energy. A huge amount of Lumenal energy that he'd channeled through the staff and into a series of gemstones concealed beneath his cloak. The Etheric glamour placed upon the staff—to make it suck the light—was more than just a diversion. He was *collecting*.

Interesting.

"Now, my elder son, what precisely do you intend to do with that?"

Lyrelle went back to the pool, waved her wand, and continued to parse the myriad paths of the future.

CHAPTER 14

SOME SEMBLANCE OF JUSTICE

Each of the Great Houses of Eretheria maintained a palatial estate in their respective corner of the city, and each of these estates had a grand plaza that splayed outside their gates, usually around a fountain of great architectural and sorcerous ingenuity. Most days this was a place of commerce—street vendors of every description would wheel out their carts of wares by the time the sun rose, there to hawk and sell to the steady stream of wealthy passersby that came to and from those great estates behind their impenetrable wards.

Before Dovechurch, the seat of House Ayventry and city home of Count Andluss, the plaza was formally known as Tower Plaza, so named for the device at the heart of all Ayventry-sworn coats of arms—a tall tower, resolute and proud. The broad fountain at the center of the square featured a squat turret in which stood an array of regal men and women—Counts and Countesses of old—fashioned from bronze and at whose feet issued the water that filled the fountain. It was, Myreon knew, a favorite place for children to play in the heat of the sun, as the fountain was vast and shallow.

Since the Illini Wars, Tower Plaza had earned itself a different nickname. Traitor's Plaza was what anyone outside the Ayventry District called it, because thirty years ago, House Ayventry had been the only Great House to refuse to swear fealty to Perwynnon and, instead, throw in its lot with Banric Sahand. At the time, it looked very much like Sahand was going to roll straight across Galaspin and into Saldor, so the Count of Ayventry at the time, Andluss's father, had made a political decision based on the size of the armies camped on his doorstep. It turned out he made the wrong bet, and Perwynnon had made him pay for it in blood and fire. The cream of Ayventry's young knights spilled their life on the tips of Perywnnon's lancers, and the once-powerful county and house fell into the start of a three-decade decline, now poised to reach its nadir in this year's campaigns, faced with an ascendant Hadda in the west and a desperate Davram to the south.

Such politics, though, seemed very distant to Myreon at that moment. Very distant indeed.

"Magus," Bree said. Her voice, trembling and soft, was incongruous coming from the lips of her shroud—that of a male farmhand, straw hat pulled low over stick-out ears. "What are we going to do?"

"Shhh, Bree—if you've a mind to talk, at least try to sound like a man." Myreon's own shroud was that of a farmer's wife—bonnet, dress, apron, rosy cheeks and all. The idea was to look like farmers from the countryside, come to the market from the inner fiefs surrounding the capital.

Of course, there was no market today. Today was an execution.

Myreon and Bree had heard about it that morning, from the eaves of an old windmill she kept as a safe house—warded so that the Defenders would have trouble finding it. Ayventry criers had ridden up and down the lanes and boulevards of the district, announcing that the men who had murdered a servant of the count with "magicks most foul" were to be publicly punished at noon in Tower Plaza.

Myreon hadn't wanted to come. It was an old Defender tactic—she could smell it. What better way to catch a man's accomplices than to get them to attend his sentencing? She wanted to stay in the safe house for another few days, maybe get word to Tyvian somehow.

Bree, though, could not be dissuaded. Gilvey's death last night had sharpened something in the girl.

Her eyes had lost some of their vulnerability, their openness—it was like she had pulled back into herself to harden her edges. She was a piece of red-hot iron plunged into a blacksmith's cooling tank. Myreon wasn't sure what was going to emerge yet—a lot of it might just depend on what the girl saw today. And that was why she had finally agreed to come. Bree had to see this.

They stood at the far edge of the fountain, a hundred yards or so from what would be the scene of the action. A stage had been erected just outside the gates of Dovechurch, built to be as tall as a man—everyone was to have a good view. *What* they were about to view was also abundantly clear; there, at the center of said stage, was a great wooden block with a notch cut out.

Beneath this notch was an open basket.

There were a few thousand people in the plaza, all of them crowded shoulder-to-shoulder and the press only becoming denser the closer one got to the cordon of mercenaries the count had hired to keep the peace. These were hard-nosed Galaspiners wearing mail and bearing poleaxes—not the kind of men a crowd of peasants was likely to rush. The mood, though, was still raw.

Myreon squeezed Bree's hand.

Bree yanked her hand away and climbed up on the lip of the fountain to get a better view. "It might not be them. They mighta picked up just anybody."

Myreon grimaced. There was no way everyone

had escaped from the cistern last night. The Defenders had been everywhere and there was enough left of their classroom for a seekwand to get a fix on any number of them. Even now, Myreon was confident the Defenders were combing the city for those who had eluded them.

And that included her and Bree.

Myreon scanned the crowd, trying to pick out any mirrored helms, any firepikes poking above the sea of knit caps and straw hats. Nothing. This, if anything, made her more nervous.

"We should get closer. We can't do anything this far away." Bree began to pace along the edge of the fountain, stepping past a half dozen onlookers.

"*Do anything*"? Myreon pushed her way through the crowd and caught up with her, catching her arm. "No. Stop."

Bree tried to shake herself loose. "Let go!"

A fanfare of trumpets announced the arrival of a wagon at the back of the crowd. It was flanked by a pair of Ayventry men-at-arms on either side, their shields bearing a red-and-white checkerboard pattern with a white tower in the upper right quadrant—some vassal of the count, closely related, but Myreon couldn't place it. She would have needed Tyvian there to parse the heraldry, but at the moment it didn't seem terribly important. As the crowd parted to allow the wagon to pass, Myreon got a better look at who was in the back. Bree saw before she did, and her sharp intake of breath let her know what she was going to see before she saw it.

Three people—two men and a woman—were bound by head and hands inside a trio of pillories mounted on the bed of the wagon. They were the kindly stable hand from last night, one of the serving girls who frequented Myreon's class—Shari was her name, she thought—and Ramper. They all looked roughly used, but Ramper most of all. One eye was blackened, and a great cut above his other eye had bled all over his face, drying in crusty brown-black streams. He was awake, though. Calm even.

In instances like this, it was commonly expected for the crowd to jeer, to throw things, or to otherwise taunt the condemned. Today the crowd was quiet. The unexpected mood made Myreon's body tingle. Something momentous was going on and she had missed it somehow. She stopped looking for Defenders in disguise for a moment and focused instead on the murmurs of the crowd. Their whispers came to her in disjointed pieces:

". . . *wouldn't go with the press-gang, I hear* . . ."

". . . *been learnin' magic from the Black Mage in the sewers.*"

"*Saved a man from his taxes, but the ol' Count wanted them anyhow* . . ."

". . . *tax men tried to ravish the woman, the men killed him. Same as happened to my sister in Westercity. Listen* . . ."

At the front of the crowd, a coach carried Count Andluss from his own front door and across his own front lawn to deposit him on the steps of the stage. There he was joined by a few powder-wigged, rapier-wearing retainers and a hooded executioner bearing the torturer's guild tattoo on his right pectoral muscle. Following them were an array of servants holding things the count might need—a chair, a fan, a series of scrolls, a decanter of wine, etc.

The condemned made it to the front of the grumbling crowd. Myreon turned to caution Bree against anything rash only to find that Bree had vanished into the crowd. "Dammit!" Myreon cursed and hopped up on the fountain's edge, trying to see. *There!* About ten yards away and growing—Bree's shroud was pushing past people, stomping on feet, wriggling between gaps.

Myreon dove after her.

On stage, she heard a crier reading the charges in a voice amplified by a brooch at his throat.

"It was yesterday before the coming of dusk that these three persons acted with extreme malice toward an officer of our beloved and gracious Count Andluss and, with the use of wicked and proscribed magicks, did lay him low with mortal wounds and didst also injure three others most grievously."

Myreon tried to make forward progress, but no one would move—she got as many elbows and sharp looks as she did nods and *excuse mes*. Scowling, she altered her shroud into something more forceful—a mercenary in full mail, a warhammer looped through his belt, his face a patchwork of saber scars. Then, with as little as a sneer, everyone suddenly remembered their manners.

Bree had a head start, but her farmhand shroud didn't grant her the same social leeway that Myreon's battle-scarred mercenary did, and Myreon was closing the gap. She wondered what the girl thought she could accomplish; she wondered also what foolish notions she might have put into the girl's head over these past months. Her death and the deaths of these others—these were all on Myreon, she knew. *Gods, what a horror.*

The crier kept talking. *". . . it is with a sad and heavy heart that your liege lord, Andluss Urweel, Master of the Gap, Warden of the Azure Forest, Steward of the Great Road, and Count of Ayventry, hath seen fit to condemn these killers to death by beheading. May Hann guide their spirits to the Hearth of the Father."*

Myreon reached out and grabbed Bree by the collar. "Where do you think you're going?"

Bree saw her—or, rather, Bree saw her shroud and screamed. Myreon laced some Compulsion into her voice. *"Calm down. It's me."*

Bree stopped kicking, but her farmhand face looked anything but calm. "We've got to do something! *You've* got to do something! Please!"

Myreon shook her head. "There's nothing I can do, Bree. There's nothing any of us can do."

The count's men-at-arms dragged the serving girl before the block, her arms tied behind her back. She yelled out over the crowd, her voice shrill with panic. "I didn't do it! I didn't do nothing! Hann save me, I'm innocent as lambs! Gods! Gods, *hear me*!"

"There *is* something we can do!" Bree said, clutching Myreon's illusory mail. "There are thousands of us, Magus! How could they stop us all? We could just . . . just . . . *stop* this, for once and all. It ain't fair, Magus! It's not right!"

Somewhere out of sight, a drumbeat began. The executioner picked up a massive axe and began to spin it about his body, stretching his arms, testing the weight of it. The crowd gaped in horror . . . and also in appreciation of the spectacle.

"No! Nooo!" The serving girl sobbed. The executioner's assistant bent her over the block.

Myreon didn't look. She focused, instead, on Bree. "I'm sorry, Bree. I'm so, so sorry."

The drumbeat stopped. The axe fell with a meaty *thok*. The crowd wailed.

Bree watched with wild eyes. She screamed as no farmhand ought to.

Myreon looked around, aware suddenly that they'd drawn a lot of attention. Men whispered to one another, backing away. A woman with her children tugged them behind her. Myreon scanned just above the crowd—there!

Firepikes. A whole squadron of them, coming closer.

It was Ramper's turn on the stage. Unlike the girl before him, he grinned at the mob with his gap-toothed grin. "You all know me—seen me about, no doubt. Done good by many a' you and wrong by those who earned it, eh? We all known this was where the path ended. No tears for me, I'd wager, and Hann forgive if some say otherwise."

Myreon looked at him as he scanned the crowd. *Looking for us?*

"To those out there think I done a wrong, know this: had I the moment, I'd stick this fat hog Andluss with a spike twice what I done for that tax man, and I'd get fat off the drippings. Daresay there's some out there who'd say the same."

This prompted a gasp from the retainers on the stage. Count Andluss himself summoned a fan to help keep his humors in balance. He also sat in the chair.

The executioner grabbed Ramper by the scruff and pushed him toward the block. Ramper dug in his heels. He shouted, "But thanks to the Gray Lady, friend to us all, I'll *have* my moment!"

Myreon tore her eyes from the firepikes and stared at Ramper. *What?*

Ramper's hands were free.

Bellam's Instant Release. She'd taught him that spell—a spell for cheap cuffs and poor bindings. "Oh, gods!"

The crowd shrieked. Ramper pulled a long dagger

from the executioner's belt and slashed the man across the stomach. He leapt across the stage, his ragged hair streaming behind him. Everything in the world seemed to move in slow motion.

The count's retainers stood up, seeking to draw their rapiers. The count clutched his armrests, eyes wide . . .

. . . only to have Ramper plunge his stolen dagger right into the left one. To the hilt.

A split second later, Ramper was run through by three different rapiers. In his death throes, he shrieked three words in Akrallian: *"Mort! Aux! Tyrans!"*

The executioner swung his axe, taking Ramper's head clean off, spraying Andluss's retainers with blood.

Count Andluss stood up, knife protruding from his skull. His arms flopped awkwardly, trying lamely to pull the dagger free. He fell from the stage, backward.

At first there was silence.

And then the crowd cheered.

"We *need* to get out of here." Myreon grabbed Bree.

"He's dead!" Bree screamed in Myreon's face, but it wasn't in terror. The girl was grinning like it was her wedding day.

There was bedlam on the stage. The stable hand was being muscled toward the block. One of the count's retainers, his ivory doublet stained with blood, was shouting something, his rapier drawn and still dripping crimson.

Someone in the crowd threw a rock.

Myreon pulled Bree away from the press of the crowd as they advanced toward the stage. "Get to the Wheel and Serpent in Davram Heights. Go!"

"But, Magus," Bree said, "you've got to help them! Use your magic!"

Myreon grimaced. There was no time. The Defenders were getting closer. She worked a Compulsion, drawing what little Dweomer she could through the orderly cobblestones at her feet. *"Go to the Wheel and Serpent!"*

Bree, her eyes wide with shock, fled immediately.

The mercenaries surrounding the stage locked into formation and advanced a few paces into the encroaching peasants, their poleaxes angled outward. Somebody got mouthy, and got six inches of steel in his throat. The crowd roared with disapproval.

Meanwhile, the Defenders were almost upon her. Making sure Bree was clear, Myreon now saw she had two choices—plunge into the growing riot, or fall into the hands of the mirror-men. She recognized the mage at their head, even through the press of bodies—Argus Androlli, his Rhondian-black hair and chiseled features caught the sun in just the right spots, making him look rugged and stern in all the best ways.

He saw her, too. He smiled, looking straight through

her shroud with a truthlens on a silvery chain. He had the perfectly clear, monoclelike prism pinched between his right cheekbone and his eyebrow, leaving his hands free to react to any moves she made. Myreon, bizarrely, felt herself relax. At least now the choice was made for her. She knew what came next.

She stepped away from the screaming people, from the growing hysteria of the mob. She didn't look back—couldn't. She didn't want to know what was happening.

Androlli called a halt to the column when it was just in front of her. Around them, the crowd surged and screamed and howled curses, but they dared not come within reach of the firepikes, even now. With a wave of his staff, Androlli cancelled her shroud and she didn't bother opposing it. What was the point, anyway? "Ah, Myreon—so good to see you again."

Myreon gestured around her. "People are about to get hurt! Aren't you going to do anything about this?"

Androlli's smile vanished and he pulled out some casterlocks. "I am. I'm arresting the Gray Lady."

"You don't know the whole story."

The Defenders stepped into a defensive perimeter around them. A few people threw rocks, but they bounced off invisible guards. Androlli waved the casterlocks in her face. "Come with me and I'll hear all about it. Including how you incited a group of anarchists to commit murder yesterday afternoon and a riot today."

Myreon flushed. "Oh gods, Argus—I didn't! I didn't know."

Androlli's face was grave. "Yes you did. That's what makes it so hard to believe." He extended the casterlocks. "If you please, Magus."

Myreon looked at him, at his deep, dark eyes—still warm, despite everything that had happened—and extended her hands. She couldn't fight him. She didn't have it in her to hurt him. He clipped the casterlocks over her fingers. They were cold and tight, immobilizing both hands entirely, as though they were in a vise. When she heard the lock click into place, she felt like she might faint.

Petrification again! Gods no!

The mob grew uglier, but Androlli's sorcery kept them at bay, Compelling large groups of them to step aside or flee in terror, allowing them to pass. Eventually, they were free of the riot. They were headed toward Eretheria Tower—the seat of Saldorian influence in the city. Once she passed its gates, Myreon knew she would never see the light of day again. At least not for a term of years. At that precise moment, she felt she might have deserved it.

A coach rattled to a halt beside them, bearing a coat of arms Myreon didn't recognize. The door popped open to reveal a big, bearded man in black studded leathers. He was met by the Sergeant Defender and the big man exchanged a few words with him.

Androlli, meanwhile, was reading her the charges

against her. She didn't pay attention, focusing instead on the big, hairy man—he was looking straight at her. He smiled.

Who the hell is that?

The Sergeant Defender saluted beside Androlli. "Magus, an urgent letter for you."

Androlli blinked. "For me? Here? *Now?*" He put out his hand, and the Sergeant Defender deposited in it a rolled-up scroll.

From her angle, Myreon could see inside the scroll before Androlli unfurled it—*it contained no writing.*

"Argus . . . wait . . ." she blurted.

It was too late, though. Androlli had it open and looked at the scroll and then nodded . . .

And then did nothing. At all. He just stood there, staring into space, scroll held limply in one hand. The paper furled itself up again by reflex.

Myreon blinked. "Argus? Argus!"

Nothing. She noted that the Sergeant Defender, who had sneaked a peek over Androlli's shoulder, was also standing there, staring off at nothing.

The big man walked over and pretended to whisper into Androlli's ear, but actually was looking at her. "Please, Ms. Alafarr, get into the coach. I am told the spell will not last long."

Myreon's mouth fell open. "But . . . but what spell *is* that?"

The big man took the scroll back from Androlli, who surrendered it willingly. He then slapped the

Mage Defender on the back. "Thank you very much, Magus—we've been looking for this one for a while!"

"Who *are* you?"

The man smiled. "A friend." He grabbed her by the ring set into her casterlocks and dragged her toward the coach. "Let's get going."

Myreon glanced back at the column of Defenders. They remained at attention, waiting for orders that never came. From a distance, it looked very much like Androlli and the sergeant were in some kind of private conference.

Then the big man was helping her through the door of the coach. Bewildered, she climbed up . . .

. . . only to step not into a coach, but into a library. A sense of queasiness assailed her and she sagged against the wall for a moment—it had been a long time since she'd used an anygate.

CHAPTER 15

STRONG WORDS

The library was old in the same way that grand houses and ships grow old—a permeating scent of wood polish, a certain musty familiarity. The towering bookshelves seemed to stand like sentinels, lit by narrow little skylights set into the ceiling. The whole place seemed so very familiar, but Myreon was too dizzy to make sense of it.

The big man was beside Myreon, helping her into a chair. "What . . . who are you?" she managed to say.

The man grinned again. "I am Eddereon, known in Eretheria as Eddereon the Black. I know your friend Tyvian." He held up his right hand. There, between two fearsome knots of scar tissue, was an iron ring. Just like Tyvian's.

Myreon gasped. "Oh . . . oh gods! There's *more* of you?"

Eddereon bowed. "If you'll excuse me—I've other duties to attend to in the city."

Myreon tried to grab his sleeve, but her hands were still locked in the casterlocks and the vertigo still had the world tilting to one side. She almost fell out of the chair. "Wait! Androlli and his sergeant—what will happen to them?"

Another voice, this one familiar—*very* familiar—came from the other end of the library. "The Un-Sigil of the Void, when written that small, is ultimately harmless. I imagine they will be quite frustrated when they realize you've vanished."

Myreon's head whipped toward the speaker. There, at the other end of the library, flipping her way through the yellowed pages of a thick book, stood Lyrelle Reldamar.

"Archmagus!"

Lyrelle thumped the book closed and set it on a huge desk with a few others. She pulled a pair of gold-rimmed spectacles off her nose and slipped them into some invisible pocket of her gown. Myreon hadn't seen her in person for almost seven years, but she barely looked a day older. Her golden hair had the slightest streak of gray, her eyes and mouth had the faintest wrinkles tugging at the corners, but that was it. She stood as she ever did, straight-backed and graceful, clad in a relatively simple dress of cornflower blue with white lace and pink ribbons worked through the bodice. She seemed to take Myreon in at a glance—every detail, every wrinkle, every stain—and summed it up with a, "Hmph. You are in dire need of a tailor who knows your measurements."

Myreon looked down at herself. "I'm . . . my apologies, Archmagus—I—"

Lyrelle shook her head. "Merely an observation, child, not a judgement. At least you aren't currently covered in sewage." At Myreon's gasp, Lyrelle nodded, "Yes, I know where you've been. I've been watching you quite closely." She picked another book off the shelf.

"You have?" Myreon felt a chill down her spine. "Why?"

Lyrelle smiled at her. "A mother has the right to take an interest in her son's romantic partners, no?"

Despite herself, Myreon felt herself blush. "Tyvian and I aren't seeing eye to eye at the moment."

Lyrelle thumped her book closed and put it back on the shelf. "Yes, I know. Did I not just say I have been watching you closely? Whatever do you think that means?"

Myreon felt the blush hit full force. "Of course. I'm sorry."

Lyrelle rolled her eyes. "You are far too deferential,

my dear. It's always been your failing." She snapped her fingers and the casterlocks on Myreon's hands crumbled into dust. When compared to the rot curse Myreon had used last night, the precision of the disintegration spell was startling—had it not been done by the most powerful sorceress in the world, Myreon would have thought its use incredibly reckless. She held up her hands, looking for any damage done.

Lyrelle smiled. "There you are—*that's* more like it. Suspicious of everyone; only convinced by what she sees with her own eyes—good. Tyvian needs someone like you."

Myreon looked around at the library a bit more closely. There were two other doors besides the anygate through which she had come. Both were closed. A mageglass chandelier fit with feylamps hung from the center of the ceiling, where the room widened into a rotunda. This was where the desk was situated. Myreon remembered that desk. She remembered this room. It all came rushing back. "Am I at Glamourvine?"

"Yes. I do not particularly enjoy attending public executions, as it happens. Especially those that do not go as planned." Lyrelle shook her head, as though frustrated with something that she didn't have time to explain. She gazed at the bookshelves. "My father-in-law would be aghast at my having moved the library in here, so close to the anygate—he was always expecting some monster or rival black wizard to come hopping through. I only did it, you know, to make it easier for me to lend books to people." She sighed. "That was before I decided educating people in order to improve them was a colossal waste of time."

"It worked with me!" Myreon stood up. "I was greatly improved by your tutelage, Archmagus!"

Lyrelle smiled warmly at her—there was always something magical in that smile. Something that made the depths of Myreon's soul feel good. "You are an exceptional person, Myreon Alafarr. Not everyone is so lucky. Particularly not those vicious little scamps you've been teaching in the sewers."

Myreon froze—the warm feeling fled straight through her feet. "Wait . . . you . . . you know about that? But, you can't scry down there!"

Lyrelle sighed. "Scrying, scrying—always scrying. Everybody seems to think scrying is the only way to spy." She chuckled, picking up another book and, flipping it open, planted her spectacles back on her nose. "If the only means I had to spy upon people was my scrying pool, I'd be in a fine pickle indeed. Yes, Myreon, I know all about your little tutoring sessions. I've brought you here—rescued you from the very jaws of doom—to tell you that it has to *end*."

Myreon's heart doubled its pace. "Archmagus—"

Lyrelle shook her head as she flipped pages. "Please, Myreon—I'm retired. Call me Lyrelle or, if it makes you feel better, Your Grace."

"I can't stop," Myreon blurted. She stood up a bit

straighter. "I won't. They need me. The way they're treated—"

"And now that they have murdered a Count of Eretheria and started a riot, how do you suppose they'll be treated in the future, hmmm?"

"Andluss brought it upon himself!" Myreon found herself yelling—she could scarcely believe it.

"Andluss is—pardon me, *was*—a product of his environment. It isn't as though he could *choose* to forego the levies. Not if he wanted to keep poison out of his wine. Not if he didn't want to wind up living in the streets with his former vassals. Likewise, those students of yours who assisted Ramper l'Etourneau in his murderous assault on the count's officers didn't do it because he whispered in their ears and magically made them brutal killers—they were predisposed to this behavior to begin with. Why else would they sneak out of their homes in the dead of night and go searching for you in the sewers? You are a means to an end to them, Myreon. They are using you to make their own violent little fantasies more plausible to execute."

Myreon gestured, trying to make a shape out of something formless in her mind. "The idea was to give them some means to . . . to . . ." She searched for the word.

"Fight back?" Lyrelle looked at Myreon over the top of her spectacles. "Is that it? A way for them to deny their liege lords their lawful rights over them? A way to effectively revolt?"

Myreon said nothing. The answer was yes, though—clearly yes. She knew it, Lyrelle knew it. She looked at her feet, remembering the roar of the mob, still fresh in her ears. "I thought I could temper it."

"Those people are enraged, Myreon," Lyrelle said softly, placing the open book in her hands on the desk. "Their anger cannot be tempered or focused—it is merely destructive. And chiefly to themselves and those they love."

"But—"

"When you became a Defender of the Balance, Myreon, what exactly did you take *the Balance* to mean?" Lyrelle waggled a finger at her. "The Balance is, and ever has been, the *status quo*. Eretheria has functioned as a nation happily and prosperously for centuries. It will function that way again, provided you allow your fledgling revolution to be weeded out. That is how the Balance works."

Myreon frowned. "But it won't be *just*. What about justice?"

Lyrelle looked sad for a moment. She slipped into a chair and motioned for Myreon to sit beside her. When Myreon sat, the retired archmage took her hands. "Myreon, what I'm going to say to you will be very upsetting, but I beg you to listen and remember well what I say."

Myreon nodded. "What is it?"

"Justice is the quest for what is often thought of as

a 'more perfect balance.' Saint Juro wrote of justice: 'we can, as thinking men, envision a world in which all persons' qualities and aspirations are held in perfect accord with one another, and thus see the death of suffering. As we see it, so must Hann have shown it to us, and so must it exist.'"

Myreon nodded again. "*The Kingly Meditations*. I read it here—in this very library."

Lyrelle patted her hand. "Indeed you did. But Juro is wrong, Myreon. Justice for everyone is not real—it is an idealized state, a concept more than a functional model. When we speak of 'the Balance' we use the definite article—*the* Balance, not 'a' Balance. That Balance is a balance of all things—light and dark, order and chaos, justice *and* injustice—and there is only one such Balance. To invite men and women to aspire to a state of universal justice is to invite disruption of that balance, every bit as much as a world of complete injustice would be.

"The acts of my son Xahlven to destabilize the world by crashing the markets was designed to push Eretheria to this turn—to drive them toward a point where an uprising would be inevitable." Lyrelle shook her head, gripping Myreon's hand tightly. "This must not come to pass, Myreon. If it were to succeed, true justice would not be achieved—far from it. The land would simply plunge into a wholly different and likely more violent form of injustice than currently exists.

War, unfettered from Eretherian Common Law and customs of engagement. Wholesale slaughter of the innocent. Blood in the streets."

Myreon was grave. "But you always taught me to strive for justice and truth in all things."

"I did, yes." Lyrelle smiled. "Such was your role at the time. But life asks us to change our roles from time to time, and we must bend to the whim of fate. You are no longer an agent of justice—that is the purview of magi like Argus Androlli."

"So what is my role, then?"

Lyrelle smiled. "The only chance we have of preventing disaster is to make certain a moderating voice can gain sway over both the nobility and commoners of Eretheria alike."

Myreon frowned. "How is that possible?"

"By making sure Tyvian Reldamar declares his intention to be king."

Myreon's mouth fell open.

Lyrelle patted her hand and, in the corner of the room, a bell rang. "Come, let's get you out of that atrocious clothing and get some warm tea into you. You've had a frightful day."

CHAPTER 16

THE EDDONISH SALON

The morning after kissing Elora in the ale house, Artus felt as though things ought to feel different. The world should have been up and singing along with him, but it was not. Today was the day of Hool's salon, and the House of Eddon was a collected bundle of nerves. Hool was so on edge that when it came time to dress, he was almost thankful for the respite from her glares. Almost.

Since he had taken up with Tyvian Reldamar, Artus had grown somewhat used to fancy clothing. He did not like it, per se, but he could tolerate it and allowed that, after a time, you forgot that you looked an awful lot like a petunia with arms and legs. Today, however, he felt as though some kind of line had been crossed.

The full-length mirror in Tyvian's bedchamber was framed in gold and was fashioned with women's faces at the corners that were enchanted to mutely express their appreciation for whatever you were wearing. At the moment, they were mouthing "oooh" and "ahhh" at Artus, apparently because they liked the color pink and he was wearing a lot of it.

It all began with the shoes—suede with a four-inch heel, dyed a rosy pink, emblazoned with white diamonds. Artus could barely walk in the damned things. His breeches and doublet were the same pink shade, but with gold and white incorporated as well. His doublet had six diamonds stitched down the center, flanked by a herd of galloping horses embroidered with silver and gold thread. He wore a powdered wig, too—a hot, tight-fitting thing that made him feel like his head was baking—and made him basically look like some kind of ornament meant to be stood atop a cake.

And Tyvian wasn't even done with him yet.

"Why'd it have to be *pink*?" Artus asked, twisting in the tight clothes before the mirror. One of the golden ladies of the mirror gave him a wink.

Tyvian was behind a dressing screen. He came back, stripped to the waist and carrying a small, clam-shaped object full of white powder. "What's wrong with pink?"

Artus shrugged. "I dunno. Isn't it a bit . . . well . . . girly?"

Tyvian snorted. "Don't be ridiculous—pink is a masculine color. Virile. Powerful. The color of the dawn. Here, hold still." He positioned Artus by the shoulders to face him and, taking a little brush in his hand, began to apply makeup.

Artus knew better than to move, but he did permit himself a sigh. "Why do I need makeup?"

"Artus, you have what some might call a 'peasant's complexion.' You've taken on entirely too much sun—there are freckles on your damned nose, for Hann's sake! It gives the impression that you labor with your hands."

Artus frowned. "I do labor with my hands! All the time! Hool worked me like a dog getting this whole thing ready!"

Tyvian kept dabbing the brush on Artus's cheeks and nose and then worked his way up to the forehead. "Yes, well, the Countess of Davram and her family would rather not be reminded that such a thing as manual labor exists."

"You'd think they'd do their fair share of work in the army—no escaping the sun on the march. Aren't they soldiers?"

"Only in the Eretherian sense—which is to say 'no.'" Tyvian passed a hand over the cosmetics case and the powder changed shade to a light pink. "Pucker your lips, please."

Artus recoiled. "What? No way!"

Tyvian advanced on him, makeup brush extended. "Artus, if I don't rouge your lips, you'll look like a drowning victim."

"I don't care!" Artus said, grabbing a pillow from a chaise and holding it like a shield. "You won't be making my lips pink!"

"Of course not! Do you think I'm making you up like a harlot? Pink? Gods no—I'll be making your lips *rose*." Tyvian waved Artus over. "Come now—be a man about it."

Artus tried to think of some kind of alternative, but came up with nothing. Scowling, he dropped the pillow and puckered his lips. Two quick brushes from Tyvian and a spot on each cheek, and the smuggler put away his makeup box. "There! You look almost presentable."

"What's a salon, anyway?" Artus said, extending his arms as Tyvian attached a sword belt and short rapier around his waist.

"Ostensibly it's a social gathering where ideas and concepts of import are discussed among equals. In point of fact, it is mostly a place where some vaguely academic pretense is arranged so people of quality have an excuse to gossip and plot among allies." Tyvian stepped back and looked Artus up and down as though he were a sculpture nearing completion. Two of the golden ladies of the mirror blew Artus a kiss.

Artus scowled. "Do I have to stay the whole time?"

Tyvian snorted. "Yes, you have to stay the whole time. It's being thrown in your own damned house."

"That ain't fair!"

Tyvian snapped his fingers at him. "Watch it! You let your 'ain'ts' slip out here and we're through—we may as well volunteer to be assassinated in our sleep."

Artus fell silent, looking himself over in the mirror again. The rapier clattered uncomfortably against his leg. "Don't . . . errr . . . *doesn't* this mean somebody can challenge me to a duel?"

Tyvian shrugged. "Remember rule number two: No duels. If you *are* challenged to a duel, you get to pick weapons. Just pick something grotesque and unusual and watch the other fellow implode in a puff of well-laundered fabric."

Artus blinked. "Oh. Okay."

Tyvian retreated behind the dressing screen. "Now part of your job today is to keep Hool and Brana out of trouble, understand?"

"Aren't *you* going to be there?" Artus frowned, tugging gently at his lace collar.

Tyvian poked his head around the screen and snapped his fingers at Artus. "Don't *touch* that collar, understand? You are supposed to look like you've been wearing things like that your whole damned life. It's part of you."

Artus stuck his tongue out.

"Say it!"

Artus sighed and looked up at the cathedral ceiling. "These clothes are part of me. They make me who I am. I and my clothing are one."

Tyvian nodded before vanishing back behind the screen. "To answer your question, *no*, I am not going to be there at the start of things. I am going to be delayed because I am ill—which is only partly untrue, as my back is still stiff as a headstone. The real reason I cannot go, though, is because I've received word from Myreon. She's evaded the Defenders and is in one of our safe houses—I'm going to collect her."

Artus frowned. "And you're going . . . now?"

A pair of breeches appeared over the edge of the screen. "It's only a short ways away. Don't worry, I'll be back in plenty of time to make a fashionable entrance. Besides, given the line of questioning you endured the other night, it seems likely that House Davram sent Voth to kill me. They don't understand how their assassin failed and it worries them. I want them to be worried."

"And how is this supposed to help us?"

Tyvian kept talking as he got dressed. "Let's just stick with 'it's complicated' for now and I'll explain later when you have the advantage of a piece of paper and a quill. The main thing is for you to make sure— make *certain*—that Hool doesn't assault anybody. I've tasked Sir Damon to help with this as well, but it's you I trust more."

Artus twisted in his clothing, still getting a feel

for how much range of motion he had. The answer was "not much." "So, what, I'm just gonna just hang around and talk and stuff?"

Artus heard Tyvian snort as a shirt appeared over the edge of the screen. "You say that as though it isn't monumentally important, but it is. I need you to keep your eyes open and your wits sharp. Do *not* get challenged to a duel, understand? Be polite and deferential and make sure your conversation is sparkling and witty enough to be interesting, but not so witty that people take offense."

Artus felt his stomach tighten. "Saints, is that all?"

The bell for the front door rang, echoing faintly up the stairs and down the hall to Tyvian's chambers. An icy spike of panic suddenly assailed Artus. Drinking and playing t'suul with a bunch of stuffed shirts was one thing, but a formal event? Artus felt as though he were about to ride into battle. Not that he'd ever ridden into battle, exactly.

Tyvian waved a hand at him from behind the screen, shooing him toward the door. "You can do this, Artus—you've been practicing for a year. Remember: pay attention, keep Hool and Brana out of trouble, and no duels. Our guests are waiting—off you go!"

Artus wandered toward the door, trying to think of a reason not to go downstairs, but failing. "Hey!" he asked, brightening, "What is the thing they're gonna—*going*—to be talking about? The . . . the 'vaguely academic premise'?"

Tyvian poked his head around the screen again, his devilish grin in place. "Us, Artus—the topic of discussion is *us*. You are entering enemy territory. Be ready. Stay focused. No duels. I'll be down in an hour or so."

An hour! Artus felt terror settle into his stomach like a hot coal. "Oh. Right. Yeah. No duels." He turned and left, marching down broad, carpet-lined hallways to the sound of polite laughter and gentle conversation that had begun to waft up from the garden.

Enemy territory.

Hool, with the assistance of Sir Damon, had truly outdone herself preparing the House of Eddon for the salon. Artus didn't know what, exactly, Tyvian had said to her, but Hool seemed to be taking the responsibility much more seriously that he would have thought possible. She had become a terror to be near—every dusty end table, every antique chair, every crystal trinket had been buffed and placed in a location specified by her. Artus and Brana had personally been made to beat every single carpet in the house within an inch of its woven life. After he'd returned home from being with Elora, Artus had been forced to huddle with Sir Damon in the kitchen over an eye-watering jug of some alchemical mixture, polishing spoons into the wee hours until they seemed to produce their own light.

And then there had been what happened to the gardener. Artus didn't quite know what had occurred—he was too busy beating rugs and moving furniture—but whatever it was had sent the old alchemist home looking as though she were haunted by ghosts.

Hool had declared that the salon would be held outside in the garden—tradition be damned—and so Artus descended the stairs and made a left turn toward the back of the house, trying very hard not to fall on his face in his elevated shoes. Brana was waiting at the bottom, having been "dressed" by Tyvian an hour before.

Brana's face split into his openmouthed grin as he saw Artus come down. He punched Artus in the arm. "Pink. Like a flower."

Artus scowled, raising an eyebrow at the alterations in Brana's shroud that made his clothing brown, yellow, and green. "Laugh it up. *You* look like a dandelion."

Brana looked down at his own illusory doublet and did, in fact, laugh. "This is fun."

Eretherians, as it happened, were not a punctual people, and Artus had a few minutes to himself before the guests really started arriving in earnest. With that time, he was able to truly take in what Hool, by way of one harried elderly alchemist, had done to the garden: she had changed it into something not really seen in Eretheria. The topiary bushes and beds of elegant Eretherian lilies and petunias and roses had been replaced with great bushy clumps of waist-high grass and carpets of exotic-looking wildflowers. Around the alabaster fountain at the center of it all, Hool had laid many of her hunting trophies—pelts of bears, rock panthers, wild bulls, and the like made a kind of carpet to keep the mud from the guest's shoes. Mounted on wooden poles thrust into the earth, Hool had arranged a series of torches that were burning actual manticore fat, each sending a greasy black plume of smoke into the sunny spring sky.

Artus understood at once what was going on—if the topic of the salon was to be about themselves, Hool was showing them a window into her inner self. It was all a grand display of her hunting prowess and the wild places she once called home. Understanding was one thing, but he gaped at it all nevertheless, not sure whether he ought to be impressed or worried. He spied Hool having stiff conversation with a few of the early arrivals—fops and dandies and lesser personages Tyvian had described as "useful sycophants." Hool had no drink and her hands were bunched into fists at her side. Her eyes darted around, surveilling each of the guests carefully.

She's scared.

Artus frowned, feeling some of his own unease dropping away. Of *course* she was afraid—this was even more alien to her than it was to him. Still, he could think of no way to help. They were, he decided, equally doomed without Tyvian there to guide them. He tried to figure out whether or not it had been an hour yet.

He looked, but there seemed to be no sign of Elora, and past that his ability to interact socially was limited. Aside from a polite nod of the head from the elderly Countess Velia when she was announced, Artus appeared to make no impression whatsoever on the guests, pink doublet and hat or not. They spoke among themselves and seemed to have little interest in involving him in the conversation. He wondered if they had some kind of sixth sense for somebody who was lowborn and could instinctually ignore them without thinking. He knew the type—he ran into them often enough in the streets of Ayventry during his pickpocketing days. They were actually quite easy to rob, so long as their purses weren't sorcerously sealed. A significant part of Artus suggested that he start picking pockets right there, just to make things interesting. The other part of him spoke with Tyvian's voice: *No duels.*

In the end, Artus hovered near the edge of the party, wineglass in hand, and looked at the strange wildflowers that had come to bloom in the garden. He felt like a complete and total ponce.

"Artus?"

And then there was Elora, smiling at him from over a fan painted with pink roses. She was wearing the exact same shade of pink as he was, only in the form of a hoop-skirted gown with blue accents.

He quickly executed what he hoped was a serviceable bow. "I've been looking for you!"

Elora motioned to her dress. "We seem to match. How embarrassing."

Artus felt color rush to his cheeks. "Well, it were . . . *wasn't* my idea. Sorry."

Elora shrugged. "I don't mind, really. I think you look rather dashing, actually."

Artus blinked. "Really? I feel like a petunia."

"Pink is a very masculine color. Bold, you know?"

Artus had no idea how to respond to that, so he closed his mouth and scanned the party. Hool was getting a lot of attention and she still looked displeased about it, but now more annoyed than worried. She didn't look likely to kill anybody yet, so that was something. There was, again, a gaggle of ladies surrounding Brana, chuckling at whatever he was saying. "At least he isn't breaking walnuts," Artus muttered.

"What? Your brother?" Elora giggled. "He's so funny. He tells the best jokes. He stays completely straight-faced the whole time—he never gives it away."

Artus shrugged. "I'm not sure he knows they're jokes."

Elora laughed. It was light, airy laughter—perfectly suited to the setting, he guessed. He wondered if she had to practice that kind of thing when she was growing up, or whether she was just naturally elegant. "Should we rejoin the party?" he asked.

Elora slipped a hand under his arm. "I'm bored. Let's go inside—there are some of the regular crowd in there."

Artus let her tug him toward the house. "Who?"

Elora smiled at him. "From last night? Valen? Michelle?" She sucked in her cheeks to imitate Michelle's thin, bony face.

Artus chuckled, which was something he realized he desperately needed to do. "Lead the way!"

Elora hugged his arm close. "No, no—*gentlemen* lead, Artus."

Artus found himself puffing out his chest. Elora, so close, was warm and smelled like sunshine somehow. "Oh. Right, sure." He grinned. "Here we go!"

CHAPTER 17

THE WRONG KIND OF COMPANY

The woman talking to Hool had breath that reeked of onions, though nobody but Hool seemed to notice. Hool hated onions. "My Lady Hool," the woman said, her mouth partially open, allowing the noxious fume to escape, "I must say this is the most unique garden I have ever explored. Where in the world did you acquire such interesting flora?"

Hool frowned at this woman whose name she had been told but did not remember—there were too many people here to bother remembering their names, anyway. "They are called *flowers*, not floras. I made a wizard summon them from the ground. She didn't want to, but I made her anyway."

The people around her tittered with false laughter, as though what she had said were actually funny. They all reeked of magic and wine and that stupid white powder they put on their faces. She wanted to be rid of them; she wanted to roar and chase them away, like so many squeaking birds. *But I can't*, she told herself, *these people are important. They have money and power. Tyvian says we need them to like us if he's going to not be king. Or be king. Or something.*

The woman with the onion breath fanned herself, spreading the horrible stench further. "Oh my, but you *are* a delight! Such wit! I see that your reputation for candor is—"

"You don't like the flowers, do you?" Hool broke in.

"I . . . I beg your pardon?" Onion Breath said, pressing her fan to her chest. "I was just—"

Hool pointed at the closest flower bank. "These flowers are like the ones on the Taqar. They are pretty and strong and tall and cover the land. They are wonderful flowers, because they grow back all by themselves every year, even after a cold winter. I don't care if you don't like them."

The woman tried to smile—tried turning this into a joke, Hool guessed, but she failed. "I . . . ah . . . I see, Lady Hool, but . . ."

Scowling, Hool walked away from her, even while knowing she was supposed to stay. *Supposed to pretend—everything is always pretending now.*

But there was really no escape, as Onion Breath

was simply replaced by four other fools. These ones, Hool knew, were somehow more important—they had arrived in the same procession of coaches as the withered old Countess of Davram, who at that moment was sitting in a chair at the edge of the garden, watching Hool's every move through a crystal monocle. Her wrinkled neck and bony fingers reminded Hool of a vulture. She thought the old Countess ought to have been wearing black and not green.

One of the people in front of her—a tall man with silver hair and a long silver goatee—was asking her a question. "It is my understanding that women often study the physical arts in Eddon. Pardon me, milady, but are you of that ilk?"

Hool frowned at him. "I could pick you up over my head, if that's your question."

They all laughed again. Hool had no idea why. She'd stopped trying to figure out human jokes years ago. She sniffed the air to see if she could locate Tyvian, realizing belatedly that she'd just stuck her nose in the air and sniffed audibly while surrounded by human nobility—one of Tyvian's rules. They were looking at her strangely. She stopped, inwardly cursing the twisted path that led her to this stupid place with these stupid people.

She had hoped that transforming her garden into something akin to her home would have given her confidence, but the opposite was true. The grass wasn't the same. Even the flowers weren't quite right. Perhaps it was because they were all shut in—corralled on three sides by hedges and on one side by a big stupid house full of empty, worthless things.

The long-goatee man cleared his throat. "So, if a man were to challenge you to a duel, would you fight it yourself?"

No duels, Tyvian had said. "No. Duels are stupid." Hool didn't look at him, instead craning her neck and cocking her head to listen—where was Tyvian? Didn't he know she hated this? He had to know—and that meant this was all part of his stupid plan. He was deliberately trying to embarrass her. He had talked her into this, only to sneak away at the last minute. Oh, when she got her hands on him . . .

She looked back to see the goatee-wearing man was bristling at her, his mouth locked tight. One of the women laid a hand gently over her own. Hool's instinct was to attack her, but she held perfectly still, as though the woman were a butterfly she was allowing to alight. "Sir Arving is one of the finest duelists in Eretheria, Lady Hool. He is Countess Velia's personal champion. He has bested sixteen men in duels to the death!"

Hool considered the bearded man more closely. He was old, but strong and lithe. Still, he had a big belly and his balance was off just a tad—he was sitting back on his heels, probably because of his big belly. She tried to think of a polite thing to say that wouldn't make him angrier. Tyvian said they needed friends here. "I'm sure your duels were not stupid." It didn't seem to work—the man looked somehow even more offended. She tried to come up with a compliment. "You must be very good at killing people."

"My Lady Hool!" Hool turned away from Sir Arving to see Sir Damon bowing to her. He was dressed in a powdered wig and lacy doublet like the rest of them, but his big nose and his kindly eyes were the same. "I have an urgent message for you." He nodded to Sir Arving and the two women with him. "If my lord and ladies will pardon us?"

They murmured their assent, though Sir Arving was still glowering at her as they walked away. When they reached an out-of-the-way corner of the garden, he stopped and wiped his face with a handkerchief.

"Well?" Hool put out her hand.

"Well what?" Damon looked at her hand. "Oh! Oh no, my lady—there's no message."

"So you lied to me?"

The knight blushed. "I . . . well . . . I really meant to lie to *them*." He jerked his head in the direction of Sir Arving. "Old Ironsides Arving looked about ready to run you through."

Hool glared at him and waited for a sensible explanation.

Damon stammered for a minute and then shrugged. "I just thought you needed to get away from them for a few minutes. That's all."

"Really?" Hool frowned. "How did you know?"

The knight laughed. "You really don't know, do you?" He pointed at her face. "Everything you think is written all over your face, all the time."

Hool cocked her head. "How often are you watching my face?"

Damon blushed again. "I . . . uhhh . . . not . . . well . . ."

Hool had very little idea what to make of this. She noted that the man was again holding his breath a little, as though he was trying to fit through a tight hole. His eyes kept touching upon her face and neck and sometimes her breasts and then quickly would dart away, as though he were worried about being caught. He had spent most of this conversation staring at the hedge over her left shoulder. "Are you my champion?"

Damon breathed a sigh of relief for some reason. "I have sworn myself to your service, milady, and will serve in that capacity if called."

"So when you were champion to your last master, you would do whatever he said and tell other people what he wanted them to hear?"

Damon nodded. "Well . . . yes. Mostly. That and the duels."

Hool cocked her head. "What duels?"

"As His Grace the Earl of Mollary, Hann rest him, was of advanced age, it would have been considered poor form to challenge him to a duel." Damon squared his shoulders. "However, honor needs to be satisfied from time to time, no matter how gracious the gentleman in question. When he was challenged, I stepped in to fight on his behalf."

Hool looked at him and sniffed lightly, so as not to be obvious about it. He smelled a little bit of shame, she thought. Not much, but a little. "Did you miss saying whatever you feel like saying?"

Damon laughed. "I? My lady, I daresay I have not done that in my entire life."

"You should. And you should never fight my battles for me. My enemies are mine to kill," Hool said, nodding. Sir Damon kept chuckling at her. She resisted growling. "What is so funny?"

"Nothing," he said, choking on his own laughs. "It's . . . it's just that you are . . . you are a *remarkable* woman, Lady Hool."

Hool snorted. She knew flattery when she heard it. "I told you to call me Hool."

Damon blushed. "Are all women in Eddon this . . . indiscreet?"

Hool decided to hedge her bets. "No. I am special."

Sir Damon held out his arm. "Then I feel very fortunate to be in your service, Hool. Shall we charge back into the fray?"

Hool considered the arm and then, on a whim, decided to take it. His biceps were small, but very firm. Not bad for a human. They walked back to the crowd together, and Hool noted that he grew tense as they got closer. "What are you worried about?" she asked.

"Nothing," he said and, when they arrived at the edge of the fountain, he released her arm. "Would you care for wine?"

"No. I would like water. Please."

Damon bowed deeply. "Thy wish is my command, Lady Hool!"

Hool watched him go, frowning. *What an idiot.* Though she felt compelled to add, *But he is nice.*

The salon continued around her, polite conversation masking sidelong glances her direction. They were talking about her, but whispering behind fans or with their backs turned. What they didn't realize was how good Hool's hearing was. Some of the group had some kind of magic that made their words unintelligible from a distance, but others were not so clever. She tried to ignore them, and instead spent a little time watching Brana entertain the ladies.

Brana was currently balancing two wineglasses on his nose and a lady was standing on a chair, ready to add a third, while people stood about in breathless anticipation. Humans didn't always realize how many muscles one needed to hold perfectly still, and her pup had them in spades. He was steady as a pillar. *And the humans love him, too.*

But it was the love of a pet or entertainer, not a fellow person. Brana, who was really only a pup of about six years old, had no idea how people saw him. He just liked people. He was happy and kind and loyal, and none of these withered, selfish people would ever see that. They just saw a handsome shroud over a puppy that liked to play. *He never would have been like this on the Taqar. By six, I had brought down my first gazelle myself. I was a hunter, not a pet.*

A conversation drifted to her ears from across the garden. It was Onion Breath and Sir Arving. And Countess Velia.

"She is beautiful, that I'll grant, but she is as rough and unpolished as a river pirate." Sir Arving chuckled. "And her looks are only glamour, anyway."

Onion Breath snorted. "Oh yes—oh yes, I know. She's wearing a shroud, I'd swear to it! Probably a toothless, tanned laborer under there. Probably a thief on the run."

The Countess said something from behind a fan, and some manner of socerery kept Hool from understanding what exactly was said, but the expressions and postures of her two lackeys shifted instantly. They went from amused to horrified and then disgusted—Hool knew the body language well. She had seen it every day of her life from the moment she and her pups had been captured on the Taqar to the moment Tyvian Reldamar broke open her cage all those years ago.

Velia Hesswyn, the Countess of Davram, could see through Hool's shroud.

A spike of panic shot through her. She almost bent her back and tensed her legs in a gesture natural to a gnoll but resisted and kept herself upright. No.

Remain poised. She was stronger than these people. She was a lady, even if she was a gnoll.

But they would tell other people. Rumors would spread. She already had a reputation for being a harsh creditor. There were those that said she was a cannibal, too. All that, though, was based on the assumption that she was at least *human*. That she at least, on some level, belonged here.

Hool watched the three of them whispering to each other and tried to think of what to do. Surely Tyvian had known this might happen! Why didn't he warn her? Where *was* he?

She saw Sir Arving look over at Brana, his lip curling beneath his moustache. "Great Hann," he muttered to Onion Breath, "can you believe that creature, aping the behavior of a man? Disgusting."

Onion Breath nodded, face behind her fan, and whispered back. "A thing like that belongs in the circus. In a cage."

A cage. He had been, of course. Hool's memory flew backward to that stinking dungeon in Freegate, to Brana, three years old, cold and alone and abused. Crying in the dark, blood matting his fur, whimpering for his mother.

And of Api, Brana's sister. The one who had not come back. The one Hool hadn't been able to save.

Despite herself, Hool felt her hackles rise. She looked over at Brana, who had finished his balancing trick to the applause of a few young women. He had his tongue lolling out the side of his mouth, happy as a bird in summer.

Hool threw her shoulders back, rose to her shroud's full height, and marched across the garden, knocking aside anyone who got in her way. Her eyes were fixed on Onion Breath. On her every movement, her every gesture.

They noticed her when she was about ten feet away. Sir Arving's hand darted to his rapier and he stepped partially in front of the woman. The countess still sat in her chair, her fingers clutching the crystal top of her cane, watching from one side.

Hool pointed at Onion Breath. "Say it to my face, bitch!"

The salon fell silent, completely and utterly. Even the birds in the trees held their song.

Sir Arving stiffened. "Are you, by chance, addressing my wife, my lady?"

"*Yes*, I'm addressing your smelly wife, you awful, skinny old man!" Hool drew close enough that she could have reached out and tugged off his moustache. Arving remained in place, stone still. Hool felt a hand on her upper arm.

She whirled to see Sir Damon bowing to her again. "My Lady Hool, Lord Waymar has sent a message—"

Hool waggled a finger in his face. "No! Not this time." She pointed at Onion Breath and Arving. "This stinky bitch and her mate want to put my Brana in a cage. *In a cage!*" She pushed past Arving and got in

Onion Breath's face. "Just *try* it, woman. See how long it takes me to kill you." Her teeth were bared, which of course just looked to everyone else like she was smiling. She did not care.

Color drained from the woman's face until she looked practically corpse-like. "I don't . . . I don't know what you're—"

Hool faked a lunge at Onion Breath and the woman fainted dead away. Sir Arving dropped to his wife's side, his eyes bulging.

"Are you perfectly finished, Lady Hool?" The voice was from the Countess Velia, creaking and old.

Hool turned to face her. She could hear everyone breathing around her, smell their fear, their confusion. They were tensed, ready to bolt, ready to attack—something. Hool knew she couldn't attack this old woman—who knew what kind of magic she had hidden away in the folds of her massive dress or in those half dozen rings or in that cane? Still, Hool wanted to hurt her. She wanted to hurt her more badly than she'd wanted to hurt anyone in a long time.

"Be very careful about what you say next, madam," Velia said, her sharp little eyes glittering in the sun, her thin lips twisted up into a smile. "I am not a woman lightly crossed."

"Easy now! Easy, my lady!" Sir Damon interposed himself between Hool and Sir Arving.

Hool pushed him off. "I am not *your* lady. These

titles are so stupid!" She pointed at the countess. "Her *Grace*? This old carcass is anything but *graceful*."

Sir Arving had his glove off and made to strike Hool, but Hool blocked his blow and punched him hard enough to knock him flat on his back. Blood poured from a broken nose.

And then people *really* started to get mad.

Two things became immediately apparent as soon as Tyvian stepped off the grounds of the House of Eddon. The first was that it seemed as though every single Defender of the Balance in Eretheria was marching around, firepike lit, and that every griffon in their service was cruising the air above. They were quite clearly looking for somebody, and Tyvian was fairly certain he knew who that someone was.

The second thing was that Adatha Voth was following him. Either that, or another assassin of similar skill. Again, it was his sixth sense about these things that tipped him off—an odd shadow on the roof of a barn, a flash of motion from the corner of his eye. Meeting Myreon in Davram Heights was suddenly a lot more dangerous. He probably should have turned on his heel and walked right back into the house, but then he thought of how angry Myreon would get if he didn't show and how much helping her at this moment might do to repair their relationship.

Gritting his teeth, he pressed on.

Voth couldn't risk taking a shot at him—she had to assume he had bow wards—but then again, Tyvian wasn't too keen on being shot at, bow wards or not. The first thing to do was to ditch his horse. He tethered it at a likely-looking tavern and went inside.

The place was crowded with old men and men who had disguised themselves to look old—fake beards of wool, an affected limp. *Dodging the press-gangs*, Tyvian thought. Yet, it almost certainly had the opposite effect, since places like this were probably a popular place to hit for those wagons—you could nab seventeen, eighteen men on a raid.

Tyvian drew a lot of attention, just by his dress. The press of sweating, filthy laborers parted for him as though he were on fire. A number of them knuckled their foreheads. Two men knelt. Tyvian elected to ignore them.

"The heir!" somebody whispered. "Perwynnon's own son!"

Tyvian grimaced. *How in hell can they know who I am?* He scanned the assembled rabble, trying to pick out the man closest to his size and with the least soiled shirt. It turned out to be a mathematics equation lacking a satisfying solution. He pointed his cane at an entirely too-large fellow who had, by some feat of gluttony, never spilled a spot of food on his tunic in his life. "You. We're going to exchange clothes, you and I."

The man blinked. "Beggin' your pardon, but why?"

Tyvian held up his cane. "This is worth one-hundred and eighty-five gold marks, and it is the cheapest thing I am wearing. That's why."

The man was naked inside of seven seconds. Tyvian took rather longer—he had selected this outfit specifically for the salon, and the idea that he was forced to give it up before its debut rankled. At last, though, he was clad in the overlarge tunic and the breeches that needed to be cuffed so as not to get caught beneath his boots. His boots he kept.

"Now . . ." He addressed the assembled old men from the bar, where they all clustered, hanging on his every word. "There is an assassin in the streets, hunting me as we speak. I haven't much in my purse at the moment, but any man who assists me in evading this killer can come to my house for a gold mark this evening, no questions asked."

The old men exchanged glances and muttered among themselves. Tyvian held his breath—taking on trained killers probably wasn't in these gentlemen's repertoire. If they threw him out the back door, he was no better off than before.

At last, their spokesman—the naked man who was now holding Tyvian's clothes—stepped forward. "Begging your pardon again, sire, but, well . . ." He looked back at the men, who all nodded, "you don't need to pay us a thing. For you, we fight for free."

Tyvian felt simultaneously relieved and also incredibly disturbed. He put a brave face on it. "She's a short woman, dark hair, one eye, and probably watching the front door of this place as we speak. Let's go get her."

The men raised their fists as one. "HUZZAH!"

Tyvian grimaced. He found himself hoping Voth was a talented enough professional to avoid killing any of these brave, stupid yokels.

They charged out the front door of the tavern, screaming battle cries that probably hadn't been uttered in thirty years, brandishing empty bottles, walking sticks, and knives. Voth might be good enough to pick Tyvian out of a crowd, but not if that crowd was an armed mob looking *specifically* for her.

Tyvian charged out with them and, as soon as he could, melted into the crowd in the confusion. After a few more blocks, he was confident he wasn't being followed.

But there was now no way in hell he was making it back to the salon in time. He took a deep breath. Maybe it would be fine. Maybe Artus and Hool and Brana would control themselves without his help. Besides, the whole thing was *supposed* to be a mess, anyway. Yes, it would probably be fine. Almost certainly.

Tyvian snorted.

Who am I kidding? We're doomed.

CHAPTER 18

WELL, *THAT* WENT WELL . . .

By daylight, the great game hall of the House of Eddon was a world transformed. The great windows poured sunlight on the t'suul tables, the grand hearths stood cold and empty, and all the leather furniture seemed a bit drab and careworn without the firelight to make it glow. Here, sitting around the biggest t'suul table of them all, were a variety of young gentlemen and ladies who, while not strangers to Artus, also seemed transformed.

Valen Hesswyn was the center of everyone's attention. He was sitting in one of the high-backed chairs and wearing clothing that seemed just a touch more impressive than everyone else's. His dimples and white teeth showed with every joke and jibe and, when he saw Artus, his eyes lit up and he stood. "There he is! Artus of Eddon, our esteemed host! It's about time you found your way back here!"

Artus bowed, but he wasn't sure how low he was supposed to go in this circumstance, primarily because he'd never really been in this situation before. "All thanks go to El . . . to Lady Elora, here. She rescued me from . . ." He nodded in the direction of the garden.

Elora curtsied. "Cousin."

Valen bowed. "Cousin."

The reminder of their relation immediately put Artus on guard—what was the game this time around? More attempts to learn about Tyvian? *At least*, Artus reasoned, *I'm not drunk now.*

Valen extended his hand and Artus took it. The grip was overly firm, but Artus tried not to read into it. He looked Artus in the eye, still smiling. "There is an ancient tradition—one those of our circle have participated in for generations. A rite of passage, if you will."

Artus frowned. "I'm listening."

Valen snapped his fingers and Ethick produced two buckets of rotten apples he had stashed behind a sofa. "To the stocks!"

Everyone clapped, even Elora.

Artus clapped along, too, but with less gusto. Stock baiting—they were going stock baiting.

Great.

A pillory, sometimes called only "the stocks," was the standard punishment for petty criminals in Eretheria. A thick plank of wood would have three holes cut—one for the head and one for each hand, small enough so a person couldn't slip their head through when the thing was closed around them. The feet would also be chained to the heavy stone base, and there the criminal would be left to stand for anywhere from an afternoon to a few days or even a week. Their neck and wrists would grow raw and painful, they'd get terribly thirsty and hungry, their back and legs would cramp up, the sun would burn their face, and then, to top it all off, occasionally young, rich twits would come along and chuck rotten things at them from afar. Artus knew all of this—he had been in the stocks five times by the time Tyvian fished him off the street. Now, it seemed, fate had made him the young rich twit with the rotten apple.

They didn't need to go far—the closest pillory was no more than a half mile from the gates of the House of Eddon. The procession of young lords and ladies, their swords on their hips and parasols on their shoulders, walked out the front gates and down the cobblestone streets until they were there, arrayed in a half circle, about ten paces from the pillory in question.

The stocks had two people in them. One was an old man with a beard and shock of white hair that stuck out in all directions, like a mane. Artus could smell the feces and alcohol on him from twenty feet away. The other was a boy, perhaps eleven. He was pale and skinny and he was shivering despite the midday sun. A Defender of the Balance stood watch, leaning on his firepike, but if he had any opinion about the troop of people in party clothing who'd just appeared, he kept it to himself.

"Five says the boy lasts longer than the old man," Ethick said and picked up an apple. He took aim and threw, just missing the old man and causing the apple to explode.

The old man woke up with a start. "Kroth take you, you shits! You piss-hole arse-faced mud goblins! I'll kill you! I'll rip your ears off!"

Everyone laughed. Valen picked up an apple and threw it at the boy. He hit the boy on the leg, causing him to whine. "Ow!" he said. "Please, sirs! Leave me be! Just leave me be!"

Valen shook his head and looked at Ethick. "Oh, my friend—this is a bet you're going to lose."

Others began to chime in, each taking one side or another of Ethick's bet, all of them throwing apples. A barrage of rotten fruit exploded on the old man and the boy alike.

Elora picked up an apple and batted her eyes at Artus. "I've never done this before. Artus, can I have some help?"

Artus froze. "I . . . uhhh . . . I've never done this before either."

Elora frowned. "Oh. Okay then." She then made a good throw that hit the boy right in the cheek. He immediately began crying.

Artus watched Elora's face, to see her reaction. She smiled broadly and clapped her hands. "I hit him! Gods, what a good throw!"

A collective groan came from those who had bet on the boy. "Damn." Ethick grunted, "That was barely any sport, too."

Sport?

"Pay up." Valen held out his hand. "All of you."

People dug into their purses and slapped their money into Valen's hand. When he got to Michelle, she had her arms folded. "I didn't bet."

Valen scowled. "What do you mean you didn't bet?"

"I don't like this, Valen. It's nasty."

Valen snorted. "Oh, is that so? Michelle Orly, daughter of Sir Nobody of Nowhere, is dictating propriety to me? That's rich." He held out his hand. "Pay up."

Artus looked over at the pillory. The boy was crying, his eye swelling from Elora's hit. The drunk was still ranting incoherently, which only seemed to frighten the boy more. His whole, stick-thin body was shivering. Artus knew that kind of cold—knew it deep in his bones. He still remembered it, curled up in that barn in Freegate, right after being robbed for the first time, crying and calling for his mother. His real mother.

"Leave her alone, Valen," he said. "She didn't bet, so she doesn't pay. She ain't ruining anybody's time."

Valen stiffened. "What did you just say?"

Ethick snorted. "He said 'ain't.'"

Elora laughed. "Oh, Artus, you *have* been among the peasantry for too long! It's too funny!"

Valen pressed an apple into Artus's hand. "Here. Your turn. How many throws until you can get the old man to beg for mercy? I'm betting six."

Artus let the apple drop. "I don't think this is funny, Valen."

Valen snorted. "Oh, so *you're* passing judgement, too, eh? Artus, I don't think you get it—Michelle over there, she's a nobody—she's just always hanging around. You, though—you are going to be a *somebody*. You *need* to do this, understand?"

Artus scowled. "Why's that?"

All sense of joviality melted away from Valen. It was like he had plucked off a mask. "Look, Artus— I'm doing you a favor, here." He produced a small monocle from a pocket and leaned in close, whispering so the others couldn't hear. "You see this? It's a truthlens—sees right through illusions, understand?"

Artus looked at it, a chill spiking through him. A bluff? He wouldn't dare, would he? That was grounds for a duel. Did they actually *want* to get in a duel with a future prince?

Valen seemed to read his expression. "Oh yes—I know your little secret, Artus of Eddon. I know *what* your mother is, what your *brother* is. I keep secrets for my friends, understand?" He smiled, but it was a cold smile. "But for people who *aren't* my friends? Maybe I'm not so discreet. Maybe I'll tell a few people."

Duel or no duel, this was too low a blow. Did Tyvian expect him to walk away from *this?* Artus found himself growling. "You lousy son of a bitch."

Elora looked horrified. Everyone was quiet.

Michelle picked up an apple. "It's okay, Valen— I'll . . . I'll do it."

Artus clenched a fist. "The hell you will. Put it down, Michelle."

Valen looked at her. "No, Michelle—throw it. Just throw it. Show Artus how things work around here."

Ethick made a mock bow and gestured toward the pillory, his face twisted in a smirk.

Michelle faced the raving old man and the crying boy, her eyes tearing.

"Leave her alone, Valen," Artus said.

"*One* of you has got to play." Valen pointed to the ground. "Don't like it? Then *throw the apple.*"

Artus, scowling, picked up an apple. "This what you want?"

Valen grinned, relaxing. "That's it, Artus—I knew you were all right."

Artus tested the apple's heft in his hand, wound up . . .

. . . and threw it straight into Valen's nose. It exploded in a brown puff of juice and Valen fell, slipping in the mud and going down on his back. "Kroth!" he sputtered.

Artus bent over him. "How's it feel, rich boy?"

Valen surged to his feet and lunged at Artus, trying to grab him by the doublet. Artus took one of Valen's arms and pivoted his momentum into a hip toss that sent Valen sprawling again, this time with his cape up over his head.

"Artus!" Elora shouted. "Stop it! Stop it right now!"

Artus took his eyes off Valen for a second to nod his apologies to Elora. "Elora, I'm sorry, but he was being an arse to Michelle and . . ."

Elora's face was painted with horror. "So *what*? Michelle doesn't *matter*! She should be thankful we even let her into our company! So should *you*!"

Valen was up. "You stinking little poser! You low-born gutter trash!" He advanced on Artus, pulling off his glove. "I'll make you . . . oof!"

Artus jabbed Valen in the nose and then followed up with an uppercut to his solar plexus which knocked the air out of him. He crumpled to the ground. "Stay down, Valen."

Ethick jumped on his back, locking his arm around Artus's throat. This happened to be a move Brana used on him almost every single day, so it was entirely by reflex that he chopped his hand back into Ethick's groin and then threw him off. Ethick, face green, struggled to rise but Artus, still running on reflex, dropped his heel into the side of the squire's head. The move tore his breeches, but it put Ethick down for the count.

Elora screamed at an improbable volume, grabbed her skirts, and fled. Artus looked to follow her, but there was Valen again, blood pouring from his broken nose. He had a knife—a slender stiletto, which might have been a terrifying weapon in the hands of somebody talented, like Tyvian, but in Valen's enraged state, it was more of an insult than anything else. Artus rested in a fighting stance—easier now with his torn pants—and waited for the attack. It was a pretty predictable thrust toward Artus's body. He blocked the knife and, grabbing Valen's wrist, pulled his arm into a lock that forced him to drop the blade. He then kicked him in the knee so he stumbled into the mud and kneed him in the chin so he fell over backward again, spitting teeth.

Valen lay on his back, blind with pain, moaning. Ethick lay in a heap, unconscious. Artus wiped off his hands and crouched over Valen. "What part of *stay down* didn't you understand, you puffy scrub?"

The other young nobles were frozen in shock for a moment, and then hastily began helping Valen to his feet and picking up Ethick. Artus remained where he was, knowing, deep down, that he'd just made a huge mistake. He hung his head.

"That . . . that was the bravest thing I've ever seen." He looked up to see Michelle standing in front of him, tears in her eyes. "Your poor breeches! Are you hurt? Did they hurt you?"

Artus gaped at her. "I . . . honestly I've gotten a lot worse from my brother."

Michelle clutched his hands to her chest. He could feel her heart beating like a bird's, rapid and hard. "You're like a storybook hero. I've never seen anything like that! And for *me*, too! I'm . . . I'm just a nobody! Why did you do it?"

Artus was at a loss for words. He tried to extricate his hands, but could see no polite way of doing so. Michelle was clinging to him. "I just didn't want that kid to get pelted with apples, is all. Being in the stocks is bad enough, right?"

It was like Artus had pushed some kind of button in Michelle. She wrapped her thin arms around his shoulders and pulled him close. "You are the most amazing man I've ever met!"

Then she kissed him. Hard. This time, Artus found he didn't mind the tongue so much.

But he sure as hell was damned confused.

Lady Hool, ravishing and imposing in her shroud, stood in her own parlor facing a semicircle of powder-wigged, rouge-cheeked peers who fluttered fans and stuck their noses in the air with all the gravity of cav-alrymen preparing to charge. Between her and them was Sir Damon, who had both hands up and seemed to be trying to talk everyone down.

This was the scene Artus returned to. He heard it

well before he saw it, too. He had left Michelle behind, running at a sprint across the grounds as soon as he had heard the commotion. "Oh no, oh no, oh no . . ."

A silver-haired gentlemen Artus recognized as Sir Arving, whose mouth looked as though it had been kicked by a horse and whose beard was stained with blood, stepped forward. "I *demand* satisfaction!"

"He keeps saying that—I don't know what he means." Hool smiled, which Artus knew to be a very dangerous sign in a gnoll, but to everyone else probably looked like advanced mental illness.

"Why don't we all *calm down*?" Sir Damon was saying. Nobody seemed to be listening.

Artus's throat was dry. Coming up to Hool, he said, "He means . . . he means he wants to challenge you to a duel."

Hool's eyebrows rose, still grinning. She took a step toward him. "I'll *kill* you, you nasty old—"

Artus and Sir Damon interposed themselves physically, grabbing Hool by the shoulders so she didn't leap across the room and tear out Sir Arving's throat. The assembled nobility, obviously unaware of the mortal danger Hool posed, merely gave her poisonous looks and exchanged rude gossip behind their fans.

"You are *no* lady!" Sir Arving's wife, Lady Sadauer, was fanning herself so fiercely Artus thought she might blow herself away. "You are a violent, brutish creature! We come here as friends, and *this* is how you treat us? And the countess?"

Hool looked like she might breathe fire. "I am a lady! Your Countess is a mean old hag and you are a liar. You said you would put Brana in a cage!"

Sir Arving lunged at Hool. There was a flurry of movement and Arving wound up on the ground somehow with one of Brana's heels digging into his hand and another bruise growing on one cheek.

Arving looked up at Brana. "Someone get this imbecile off me, lest he earn himself a challenge, too!"

"Hey!" Artus pointed at Arving. "Back off, pal—you have no idea what kind of trouble you're getting yourself into!"

Sir Damon grimaced. "Artus, please—let me handle this."

Hool rolled up her lace sleeves, to the gasps of onlookers. "No, Artus, let *me* handle this."

Artus stepped in front of Hool. "No, Hool! You can't kill him, okay! Don't!" He then nudged Brana with his elbow. "Hey, let the old guy up, huh?"

Brana released him, and Arving stepped past Sir Damon and threw a glove at Hool's feet. "You have insulted the honor of my wife, my liege, and myself. You have *struck* me without provocation. I demand satisfaction on the field of honor. To the death."

"Good. I'll kill you right now." Hool growled at a pitch too low to be entirely human. The nobility took a full step back.

Arving, to his credit, stood firm. "As your status as

a lady in Eretheria makes it improper for you to duel a man, I shall expect you to nominate a champion."

Sir Damon stepped forward. "I shall serve, sir."

Hool glared at him. "You will *not!*"

"That is *enough!*" Velia Hesswyn, the Countess of Davram, was standing in the doorway, her bony arm looped through that of one of her vassals. "Lady Hool, this is quite the most egregious display of dishonorable behavior I have ever witnessed! You must apologize at once!"

The whole assembly either bowed or curtsied, as appropriate. All except Hool, of course.

Hool scowled. "I don't bow to anyone. Least of all some little old lady."

Everyone gasped. Even Dame Velia looked shaken. She clutched her escort's arm, what little color there was in her cheeks draining away. "You forget yourself!"

Hool stared straight at the countess—Artus knew that stare. It was the copper-eyed, unblinking gaze of a born predator. It was how Hool looked at something she was considering eating, and let the potential meal know. *If I don't do something*, Artus thought, *things are going to get a lot worse.*

"I accept on her behalf!" he announced, rising from his bow.

"No!" Hool barked.

"Dammit, Hool!" Artus snapped, but then blushed again—a slip. "I mean . . . uhhh . . . *my lady.*"

Sir Arving smiled, showing a new hole in his dental work. "Swords, sir?"

Artus looked at the man—he was a fighter, no mistake. He'd even heard Tyvian mention something about "Ironsides Arving" at some point. No, not swords. "No."

Arving grunted as though this were a reflection upon Artus's character. "Choose your weapons, then."

Artus wanted to say *machete*, but this man wasn't some fop who was looking for a cheap point of honor. This was a professional duelist and a man of significant rank—honor wouldn't be satisfied unless he could come up with something that . . . wait.

Well, it was obvious, really.

He cleared his throat. "I invoke the ancient Illini tradition of t'suul."

Arving blinked. "What . . . a game?"

"Yeah." Artus permitted himself a small grin. "To the death."

Velia Hesswyn nodded, her face grim. "Then it is done. Now, *Lady* Hool, I and my household will take my leave."

Hool glowered at her. "You don't get to leave. I'm kicking you out."

The mood in the room was thick enough to slice and spread with jam. But they all left, and no further duels were issued. As she passed him on the way out, Michelle grabbed Artus's hand and squeezed briefly.

Before he could figure out what to make of it, she caught up her skirts and ran out. He saw no sign of Elora, Ethick, or Valen.

At last, the House of Eddon stood empty.

Artus slumped into a chair. "You know how Tyvian said no duels?"

Hool said nothing. Again, Brana was the only one smiling. "Yeah!"

Artus shrugged. "I . . . I think I'm in two duels."

Hool snorted. "Things were simpler when I was allowed to kill people."

Artus nodded. The gnoll had a point.

Where the hell is Tyvian?

CHAPTER 19

TRUTH AND CONSEQUENCES

The Wheel and Serpent was a guilder place. Everywhere Tyvian looked were tables of bearded men with calluses on their hands talking about tinsmithing or alchemy or some other tedious nonsense. Their wine stores were wholly inadequate, but their bread was hearty and their Galaspiner whisky selection was top-notch. So bread and whisky it was.

But Tyvian found himself without an appetite. "You did *what?*"

Myreon grimaced and she quickly knocked back a tumbler of whisky. "I was trying to help. I couldn't just . . . just *sit* there in that house and do nothing."

Tyvian closed his eyes and shook his head, trying

to get the thousand thoughts rushing around his mind to hold still long enough to form something coherent. "So you taught *peasants* to use sorcery because . . . because you were *bored*?"

Myreon rolled her eyes. "Dammit, Tyvian— don't you care about *anything*? Doesn't it *bother* you that these people are suffering because of what *your brother* did? Because of what *we* failed to prevent? Do you ever even *think* about it?"

Tyvian took a long, deep breath. He pointed to the third person at their table. "Who is that?"

The person in question was a teenage girl who looked as though she'd been kicked in the face by a horse. She had blood all down the front of her dress, her fingernails were chipped, her hands black with filth, and she had the distant stare of somebody who'd recently seen something they had yet to fully process. "This is Bree Newsome," Myreon said. "Say hello, Bree."

Bree looked Tyvian up and down. In his ill-fitting peasant garb, he rather doubted he cut a fine figure. "Are you . . . are you the one who can help us?"

"Who the hell is 'us'?"

"Those people, back at the toll house? Remember them?" Myreon pointed off into space somewhere, evidently in the direction of said toll house. "Those were people like Bree, but *unlike* Bree, they didn't have me to stand up for them. They didn't have me to teach them how to stand up for themselves."

Tyvian looked the wretched girl up and down. "Well, she certainly seems to have benefitted from your guidance."

The girl's hand flashed out and slapped Tyvian across the cheek. "You take that back! You take it back about her! She done more for me and mine than you can know! It's my fault what happened! It's *our* fault!" Tears welled in her eyes. She clutched her dress to her eyes as she began to weep.

Tyvian felt the urge to slap the girl right back, but the ring flared to life and he let his hand lie still. He glared at Myreon. "I suppose you don't think this is your fault either."

Myreon placed a soothing hand on Bree's shoulder. The girl leaned against her, and Myreon embraced her. The mage's own eyes were glassy. "I know what I did. I know what I can do. It's not enough, Tyvian. There are riots in the Ayventry District because of me. Count Andluss is *dead* because of me, and the gods know how many others were murdered today in the riots afterward. And it's only beginning."

"Andluss is dead? Kroth!" Tyvian stared at her, shaking his head. "What in *flying hell* do you want me to say? Good job? Congratulations, Myreon, you've given a pack of undereducated, bloodthirsty laborers the means to vent their social frustrations on any passing man in livery?" Tyvian shook his head even more vehemently. "*Training peasants to use sorcery?* Gods, it's the stupidest crime I can possibly imagine. There isn't even any upside! You probably just got scores of people killed because you felt a pang of conscience and now absolutely *nothing* has changed for the better. Hell, do you know the precautions I'll have to take—that *we'll* have to take now? Every Defender in the city will be out looking for you. This place is probably being watched. Gods, Myreon, it's going to take me all night just to get back home without a tail!"

Myreon kept her arms around Bree, but she didn't look at him—he knew that expression, though. She was wrestling with her own demons. Well good. Tyvian hoped the demons were winning. He sipped his whisky with a sour expression.

"I met with your mother," she said at last.

Tyvian rolled her eyes. "Join the goddamned club. And was *she* sympathetic to your little revolutionary plight?"

"She told me justice isn't real."

"Sounds like her, all right."

Myreon looked at him. Her eyes were sharp and focused again—she'd gotten whatever demon of regret was inside her under lock and key again. "You've been living—*we've* been living in a bubble, Tyvian. Everybody in this damned city is—maybe everyone in the world. Our plans need to change."

Tyvian frowned. "What are you getting at? This sounds suspiciously altruistic."

"I want to prove your mother wrong, Tyvian."

Myreon was watching his expression carefully, reading every line, every twitch.

Tyvian laughed. "That is difficult to do, seeing as she's almost always right."

Myreon leaned forward. "I saw something in you at that toll house. I want *that* Tyvian back. I want *that* Tyvian to do what is needed."

Tyvian sat forward. He could see her game now. "And so you think you can parade this . . ." He gestured toward the ragged Bree. ". . . *person* under my nose and what? Let the ring do the rest?"

Myreon slapped the table in time with her words. "This. City. Is. About. To. *Explode.* Not just one riot, Tyvian—a complete insurrection. Thousands will die." She reached forward and grabbed his wrist. "*You* can stop it."

"How?"

"Become king."

Tyvian scowled. "You and I both know I am not the true heir."

"*Who cares?*" Myreon threw up her hands. Bree still huddled beside her. "Become king in all but name, then—you can do it. You *know* you can do it!"

Tyvian stood up. "I've had just about enough of this! You've lost your mind, Myreon—you and your altruistic little hobbies are going to destroy you." He pointed at Bree. "You can't *save* these people, Myreon—no one can! We were safe in the House of Eddon. Comfortable. Happy. We can go back, if *only* we see my plan through!"

Myreon shook her head, scowling. "You weren't happy. If you were, you wouldn't have moonlighted as a fence. You wouldn't have . . . well, Voth would have never gotten so close."

Tyvian straightened. "Voth again?"

"I wasn't happy, except I *knew* I wasn't. Hool isn't happy. Artus isn't either. Give him enough time to realize what people think of him, and Brana will be just as miserable as the rest of us. The only person who won't get it through his head yet is *you*."

"Look, if you want to live the rest of your life as a fugitive in the sewers, be my bloody guest." Tyvian turned to leave, but looked back at her once more. "If you want to come home, though, I'll be delighted to have you. Ditch the peasant first, though. She'll bring the Defenders down on all of us."

Myreon glared up at him. "Go to hell, you selfish prick."

Tyvian dropped a gold mark on the table, more than covering their tab. "People with blood on their hands don't get to be smug."

He left out the back. Then, with regret, he pried up a sewer entrance and headed for home, his way lit only by the squares of light from the street drains and a smuggler's memory.

It was late, and Tyvian still hadn't returned. Hool had wanted to rage at him, maybe hit him for abandoning them that afternoon, but he hadn't come back. *Something's happened to him*, she thought. *Maybe something even he didn't expect.*

Hool slipped out the window of her bedchamber, her shroud off, intending to find some deserted rooftop on which to brood. Even in this, the human world failed her. The houses in Eretheria were either too far apart to leap quietly or too low to the ground to give her privacy. She was left to choose between crashing atop a rich person's house and waking the entire staff or settling lightly upon the thatch roof of a peasant and being easily visible from the street. So, she found a likely corner on her own estate and sulked there, a mass of golden fur and hurt feelings.

It seemed to her that the past two years—ever since she got this stupid shroud—had been just one awkward and uncomfortable experience after another. Instead of standing tall and proud to face the world, she'd been lurking about in the shadows, her very image a lie. At least before she had become *Lady* Hool, nobody had paid her much mind. Humans might have thought her beautiful, but she was also anonymous. Now? She evidently had a reputation. People wanted to "socialize" with her, which was a fancy way of saying they wanted to embarrass her or make her lie. She had all that money, too. It gave her power, perhaps, but it also curtailed her freedom. It was like a giant, golden chain clipped around her ankle. She ought to have knocked it off and fled into the wilderness ages ago.

Here, though, in the heart of Eretheria, there was barely anything that qualified as wilderness. She was surrounded on all sides by a nearly endless sea of farmland, castles, pastures, and heavily lumbered forests. Even the limestone cliffs and mesas that dotted the southern landscape were riddled with quarries and mines and who knew what else. She was a wild creature trapped by her own safety and wealth. It was enough to make her want to howl. Much to her shame and anger, however, she did not. She didn't want to terrify anyone who didn't deserve it.

If she stayed much longer among humans, she knew Brana would grow to emulate them even more than he did. He hardly ever spent time as his true self anymore. He was only a pup, true, and he had kept his puppy-ish ways, but for how long? How many more parties could they attend before he started acting like Tyvian instead of like her? With every passing day, she felt less and less certain of the future. She felt more and more terrified of what was happening to her and to her family.

Hool sighed and leaned back against a rain barrel, frightening away a stray cat. Above her, the stars twinkled, far away and uncaring. She spotted the various constellations of her people—the Great Worg, the Hunter, Roogor the Leaper. She couldn't see them all, though—only the Greater Constellations had enough power to be seen here, through the polluting light of all the streetlamps everywhere. It was only a little better outside the city—the rolling horizon obscured some of the low-hanging stars, and then to the south there was the ocean, horrific and endless. The very thought of it made her shudder.

What do I do now? she asked herself. She had no answer. Even worse, she had no one else she could ask. She felt alone.

That, she told herself, was the appeal of the shroud. The fake sensation of belonging it gave her—the sense that she was at least part of something. Even if it weren't a gnoll pack, the human race was better than nothing.

Every city Hool had ever been in she hated. Freegate had been filthy and cold, the thin mountain air filled with the foul stench of industry—forges and artifactories, tanneries and alchemical labs. Galaspin had been cramped and ancient—a maze of hard stone walls and hard-faced people with scarcely any room to breathe. Saldor, home of the Arcanostrum and all those magi, had been so crowded that the stench of the people overwhelmed her still, even in memory.

Though not as crowded as Saldor or as filthy as Freegate and certainly not as claustrophobic as Galaspin, Eretheria felt like a city that was hiding something. Everything looked so clean and pretty and neat, but it was all a lie. All those big houses on the big main avenues just hid the run-down houses of the poor that clustered within every block. Those clean streets? They covered rivers of filth that ran just beneath the surface. Even the trees seemed to be in on the deception—pretty, pink-blossomed plants, all designed as a veil for every window, a shroud for every corner. And here was Hool, a wild beast shrouded by the illusion of a beautiful woman, taking part in the endless masquerade. Again, she felt like howling. Again, she refrained.

"Who goes there!" It was a sharp cry from around the corner.

Sir Damon!

Hool fumbled for her shroud.

Sir Damon's eyes squinted against the darkness, his sword out, his buckler high. "I'm armed, sir, and a fair hand at a blade! Come out! Show yourself!"

Hool got the shroud on and came out from behind the rain barrel. She looked at the knight with what she hoped was casual disinterest. "What are you doing here?"

Sir Damon flushed red. "Oh my . . . I thought I saw . . . well . . . I was looking for you, actually. I wanted to see how you were. After . . . you know . . ." He took off his powdered wig. "Uhhh . . . how are you?"

Hool turned away from him and walked toward the house. She really didn't need this right now.

Damon followed, sheathing his sword. "I understand if you're upset with me. I only wanted to apologize, if I could."

"It's the middle of the night," Hool grunted. "Don't you have something better to do?"

Sir Damon searched for an answer. "I . . . well . . . that is . . . no. No I haven't."

Hool stopped and squinted up at him. "Why?"

"I was worried about you, as I said. And I've pledged myself to your service."

"That's it?"

He nodded, looking down at her with his weird brown eyes. "Yes. That's it."

She rolled her eyes and kept walking.

"It has been a difficult day, Lady Hool. Perhaps I could offer some . . . distraction." He pointed toward the stables. "Can I interest you in a ride?"

"No. I hate riding."

"A drink?"

"No."

Sir Damon let out a deflating breath and muttered, "*Dammit, woman.*"

Hool turned on him again. "Do you think I'm stupid? Don't you think I know what you're trying to do?"

Damon's face flooded with color. His shiny head even turned pink. "I . . . I . . . I . . ."

Hool found herself yelling, "You think I'm pretty, don't you? You saw me and you thought I was a pretty lady with money and maybe you could get me to fall in love, right? Maybe you could marry me and not have to pay your debts anymore?"

"My . . . My Lady Hool, no! No, not at all!" He blinked. "I mean, you are certainly beautiful, but

Eretheria has a lot of beautiful women, and . . ." He shook his head. "No, that's not what I mean. I mean . . . I mean . . ."

"You can't even *say* it, can you? You can't even say what you mean! You forgot how!" Hool snorted. "I'm through with you people and your stupid lies and your stupid rules. I'm walking home now. Go away!"

Hool got about five paces away when Damon started after her. "At least let me escort you to the door!"

Hool glared at him. She supposed she could have broken his leg, but he didn't seem to be a bad person. He was just stupid. "Fine. But no talking."

Sir Damon extended his elbow. Hool stared at it. "I can balance on my own. Do you think I'm drunk?"

Damon laughed. "No. But after the day we've had, *I* very well might be. I'd appreciate it if you held me up."

Hool sniffed softly—he did smell like wine. Not a *lot* of wine, but some people it seemed couldn't drink very much before they fell over. Scowling, she grabbed his elbow and held on.

Sir Damon blanched. "Not quite so tightly, please!"

Then they walked, taking the long way across the front lawn. Damon, to his credit, didn't say anything else. He *did* place his free hand over her own on his arm, though. His palms were sweaty, which made her skin crawl, but she let it pass. She could feel him relaxing as they walked, as though just being there with her was soothing. She frowned at this. Was she supposed to be some kind of emotional balm for this man's problems? How stupid was that?

Then again, he *was* a person to talk to. Hadn't she just been wishing she had someone to talk to? "Are you happy?" she asked.

Sir Damon chuckled. "Just now, or in general?"

"In general. I know you're happy right now."

She felt him stiffen at that, but he kept his voice level. "Oh. Well . . . I don't know. I'm not destitute. I'm healthy. My current employer extends to me broad privileges." He gave her a shy smile. "What's there to complain about?"

"Not complaining and being happy aren't the same thing." Hool rolled her eyes. "Say you weren't—say you weren't happy in general. What would you do to fix it?"

Damon thought about this for a while as they reached the portico. "I'm not sure. I suppose I'd figure out what was causing the unhappiness and . . . well . . . change it somehow."

Hool scowled. "That isn't so easy. You make it sound easy."

"I didn't mean to imply that it was," Damon said, sighing. "Change is the hardest of all things, and it's always ugly. Maybe that's why so many people are unhappy—it's easier to stay where you are than risk going somewhere else, even if you'd be better off in the end."

Hool bowed her head. "That's what I thought."

The front door rose up before them. Serving specters opened it for Hool. She patted Sir Damon's hand. "Here I am."

Sir Damon withdrew his arm and bowed to her. "Thank you for steadying me."

Hool snorted. "Good-bye."

Before she left, though, Sir Damon caught her hand. "One last thing, if you don't mind."

"What?"

"Is . . ." Sir Damon paused, took a deep breath, then continued. "Is Waymar really your brother-in-law?"

Hool stiffened. "Of course not."

"Oh." Damon looked lost in thought for a moment, then asked. "Then, are you and he—"

"No!" Hool's mouth slammed shut. "*No!* Never. No." She shuddered at the thought.

Sir Damon brightened. "Oh. Oh, very good then. Well, I'll see you tomorrow."

Hool cocked her head. "Er . . . yes. I guess so."

Sir Damon grinned broadly. "Thank you for a lovely walk, milad . . . errr . . . *Hool.*" Then, with a bow, he skipped off in the direction of the stables.

CHAPTER 20

BELATED EPIPHANIES

After leaving the Wheel and Serpent, it was well past sunset by the time Myreon finally decided they could stop dodging from alley to alley and sit down to rest. The place was a bustling soup kitchen catering to day-laborers—little more than a patched canvas awning set up over a muddy stretch of earth behind a tiny shack containing nothing but a chimney, a cauldron, and an old woman with a ladle. Dinner was a copper—two if you wanted a bit of hard roll to dip in the watery broth. Myreon spent the two for both her and Bree.

There were two long tables set beneath the awning, each with a pair of benches. They were packed with men in functional, filthy clothing who ranged in age from no older than Artus to no younger than her great grandfather. As the only women in the crowd, remaining inconspicuous would have been impossible, were it not for the shroud she had put over both of them. To the men, she looked like a young man of twenty with an honest face and a sturdy frame, and Bree looked like a bent-backed old man. They squeezed themselves into a spot on the bench. The men on either side were gray-bearded and bore more than a few scars on their arms, faces, and hands. They smelled like wet sheep.

"You have a look out, fella," the man to her right said, nudging her. "Press-gang's been by already today."

Myreon managed a shallow smile. "Thanks."

The man to Bree's left spat in his soup for some reason and swished it around a bit before drinking. "Vora men. Just about picked us clean of the strongest backs by now. Next thing they'll be coming for us."

The first man grunted. "Done my time already, Stran. Got the paper what proves it, too."

Stran shrugged, which meant Bree was forced to shrug as well as his arm was so close to hers. "I was there when you got it, Marsh. That battle up in Lake Country, laying siege to Lord Boring Face's keep. Got an arrow through my hand, dammit—think I don't remember? What's it matter, though? That piece of paper don't mean daisies—show it to the press man, and he'll piss on it afore he claps a pot on your head and whips you into ranks."

Myreon frowned. There had been a day when her first instinct would have been to suggest going to the Defenders. Not now, though. Lyrelle Reldamar's voice echoed in her memory: *"The Balance is, and ever has been, the status quo."*

It couldn't be true, though. Justice wasn't a fiction. The Defenders didn't *have* to be the enemy.

Which means you think they're the enemy now? Myreon grimaced at herself. *Was I part of the problem, or was I different?* She liked to think that she had been. With the distance of time and . . . *perspective*, she supposed was the word . . . well, maybe not. Maybe instead of chasing a petty thief like Tyvian all over the West, she might have spent her energies doing something more useful. More just.

"Been talk of the Gray Lady over in the Ayventry District," one man farther down the table said. "Saying she saw to it fat old Andluss got that knife in the eye today."

Stran hushed him. "Where you been talking about that, I wonder? Not near any mirror-man to hear, right? Not near any man a mirror-man has touched either?"

The man waved him off. "Bah—that ain't true!"

Stran pounded the table. "'Tis! A mirror-man can use the ears of any man he's touched—heard it in church, did I. Every man knows you can't tell a lie in church."

The man—he was skinny, young, not yet twenty—

shrugged. "'Tisn't me with the tongue for treason, anyhow. Take that assassin—he talked a good piece afore he got shorter. He yelled something in Akrallian." The man squinted, trying to remember. "More O'Tirran?"

"*Mort aux tyrans,*" Myreon offered before she could stop herself. The men looked at her. She shrugged. "Means 'death to tyrants.' My da was from Camien."

The skinny man nodded. "That was it. Anyway, heard some talk in the crowd. The Gray Lady is with us, they said. They know some underground folk who's with her. Says they know how to beat the nobles' magic and such."

Silence at the table. The next table over was gathered around, too, all listening. Nobody said anything for a long moment. At last, Stran cleared his throat. "Any man here been touched by a mirror-man today?"

Everyone shook their heads.

Stran nodded. "Good." He grabbed the skinny man by the collar and hauled him off his bench. Before the man could protest, Stran pushed him into the mud and kicked him in the backside until the rumormonger got up and ran off. Then Stran came back to the table. "There—all done with. Any man what goes to Dovechurch, Rose Hall, Bramble House, or the like with a pitchfork is dumber than a dead donkey. You all stay home, let these fools get themselves killed, and take all his work the next day. You'll get double pay for a week and a half, is what I think of it."

Men began to mutter among themselves. Myreon looked up at their faces—they looked tired, frightened, and more than a little underfed. Not starving and not hopeless—not yet. They were all men used to a better quality of life, she guessed. A quality of life they remembered no more than a year past, thanks to a plot none of them would ever know about or understand.

She cleared her throat. "He's right, though."

Bree, sullen in her broth, looked up. "What?"

Stran scowled. "Listen here, young feller—have I got to plant my boot in your breeches, too?"

Myreon fixed him with a steady stare. "I've no quarrel with you, old man. And you haven't with me either. Don't fret none about no mirror-men either."

Stran grunted. "And why not?"

Bree chimed in. "Cause she . . . *he's* under her protection."

Silence. Marsh rubbed his beard. "Don't suppose you can prove it, eh?"

Myreon grinned. She worked a quick heat ward on her hand and stuck it into the lantern flame. She left it there, the fire harmlessly licking her fingers. The men gasped. A few made the sign of Hann.

"I'm telling you she's with you. The mirror-men can't stop you."

Stran snorted. "Says a young feller never seen a firepike volley before. *I* saw it." He looked around at his audience. "Men charred and twisted, skin bubbling like lead in a fire. No sense fighting that, Gray Lady or not."

"Sure there is," Bree said. "There's too many of us. They can't shoot us all."

Stran shrugged. "Of course they can. And what they don't shoot, the sell-swords what the highfolk pay will see us dead just the same. Why spill blood just to lose?"

"Why starve just to keep your blood?" Myreon countered, standing up. "You think there'll be a proper harvest this year? How many farmers' fields will lie fallow? How much will the price of bread rise? We can't let the nobles do this to us!"

Marsh nodded slowly. "The young man's got a tongue on him. I'll give him that."

"Tongue or not, we've got no *army*."

Bree snorted. "And what were all you men grousing about no more than a moment ago? Both of you were in the army. Every man *here* was in the army. You all know marching, weapons, the rest. What's to stop you from joining together? What mercenary company will stand against all of you?"

"Your grandfather's right." Marsh flexed his bicep. Myreon had to admit it was pretty impressive. "I did a fair bit of soldierin'. So did half the old men in this city. The levies have been taking them regular for years."

Stran sipped his broth. "I don't like the highfolk any more than anybody else, but you need more than numbers and shovels to make 'em do anything but hang you."

"I know something we got." Myreon looked toward the sound of the voice, and saw a toothless old man raising his hand. "We've got Perwynnon's son."

"That's right!" Marsh slapped the table. "Heard about that today!"

Myreon hid her reflexive scowl. At the mention of Perwynnon, something changed at the table. Men's eyes were alight. Stran was stroking his beard now. "Name's Waymar, I hear. They say he's the spitting image of his father."

"How do you know?"

The toothless man yelled, "I know! I met him!"

"Really?" Myreon stood up.

"He stopped at the Laketown toll and gave a patch of hard-luck farmers a handful of jewels." The old man laughed. "Told them to tell old Wicker-tits Hesswyn that if she had a problem with it, to come look him up!"

Chuckles all around. A man at the back spoke up, "I heard a guildman say they saw him meeting with some mysterious woman this afternoon. Last they saw him he was going into the sewer. Meeting with the Gray Lady, I'd wager."

Someone else nodded. "Heard at the beheading today, a man in armor saved a peasant girl from a whole column of mirror-men! Said he was a handsome feller—charming, too, just like Perwynnon were!"

Marsh and Stran nodded. "Aye. Perwynnon were at that. Marsh and I joined his army back in the war—not more than boys, we were. Never saw action, but I did see Perwynnon." Everyone fell silent, their eyes far away as Stran spoke. "Riding on a white charger, taller than any one of us, armor silver-bright, big smile on his face. He waved to us, got down off his horse, and shook hands." Stran's voice cracked a bit. "Just like a man. Touched me on the head and told me to keep my wits about me, to do him proud."

Marsh nodded, rubbing at the edges of his eyes. "'Tis true. I was there."

The gathering broke down into stories about Perwynnon—about his battles, his duels, his lovers, and his death. They all blamed someone different for the loss of their folk hero, but the supposed perpetrators all had two things in common: they were all members of the peerage, and they were all still alive.

Myreon listened, a feeling building in her. If only Tyvian would agree to help—would agree to lead these men—then big things could change. Justice could come to Eretheria. Lyrelle Reldamar would be proven wrong.

But he'd never agree. He did not embrace the new. Of all the things she had learned about him, this was the lesson she knew best. You could not ask him to change.

You had to *make* him.

For the first time in days, her task became clear.

She tapped Bree on the shoulder. "Stay here.

You'll be safe. The mirror-men don't really want you, anyway."

Bree blinked. "But . . . Magus—what are you doing?"

Stran, sitting next to her, cocked his head. "Magus?"

Myreon stood up and let her shroud drop in full view of anyone who bothered to look. She enchanted her staff to glow, setting her apart even more. "Remember, gentlemen," she said, "the Gray Lady is with you. Your king is with you. Stand ready."

Their eyes could not have gotten any larger. She turned away and walked toward the House of Eddon, not bothering to check if she were being followed.

Because she already knew she was.

Count Andluss's eldest son was a puffy sixteen-year-old who used too much glamour to cover up his atrocious acne. He seldom looked anyone in the eye, not even his servants, and his sword was clearly a decoration—more gold leaf than steel.

Sahand had little trouble explaining to the boy his new reality.

Simply put, that evening at dinner when Count Andluss the Younger sat at the head of the table, Sahand simply stood over him and pointed to the empty seat originally reserved for himself. The boy, pale as chalk, quickly got up and changed seats.

Sahand sat down and put one leg up over the arm rest. He could see a long table of fifteen people, all of them close relatives of the Urweel family, all of them aghast. Sahand grinned.

"Well, don't hold back on my account," he said, gesturing to the magnificent feast arrayed—a feast in honor of their deceased patriarch. "Eat! You will all need your strength for the funeral procession tomorrow. A long trip, as I understand it—the city of Ayventry is so far away."

One of the guests, a viscount of some kind, cleared his throat. "I beg your pardon, Your Highness, but will *you* be joining in the procession?"

Sahand gulped down a glass of wine. "What? Me? No. I think not. I have too much to attend to in the city."

"But . . ." The viscount paused. ". . . I thought your support was being martialed in our own provinces. Won't you be needed to oversee? Especially now that . . ."

"Now that old Andluss got a dagger in his eye?" Sahand chuckled. He'd wished he'd been there to see it—gods, what a lucky stroke! He should have had that sweaty land whale of a Count murdered years ago.

Obviously the table was aghast. Just as obviously, Sahand didn't give a damn. He speared a pheasant from a serving platter with a dagger and plonked it on his plate. "I give you my word that every arrangement I held with the deceased Count of Ayventry will be honored with the current Count of Ayventry. Is that sufficient?"

The viscount nodded, his lips pale. "Thank you, Your Highness."

Sahand sliced off a leg of the pheasant. "What are friends for, eh?"

He laughed, long and hard. Soon, the table was laughing with him, though he doubted they had any idea why.

Later that night, in his chambers, Sahand pulled out his sending stone. It connected him with a chamber deep in the Bastion of Dellor, his castle in the distant north. Taking care to make certain he was not being spied upon, he whispered into the enchanted sphere. "There will be a spirit engine leaving Eretheria City tomorrow bearing the body of Count Andluss and several dozen of his most important retainers. Expect it in Ayventry by early evening."

"What of this spirit engine, My Prince?" a voice whispered back—one of his more trusted lieutenants.

"Inform my forces to intercept and . . ." Sahand grinned. ". . . kill everyone on board."

"Even the women and children?"

"Especially the children." Sahand looked up at the tapestry in his room, depicting the many Urweel Counts and their various progeny. "Yes . . . especially those. The Urweels die tomorrow."

"It will be done, My Prince."

CHAPTER 21

THE MAKEUP

As he predicted, it took Tyvian hours to get back to the House of Eddon in such a way that he felt confident he had not been followed. Much of this involved crawling through the sewers, and his attire was in a state commensurate with such activities. To say he was irritable was a vast, vast understatement.

It was late—well after sunset—and the salon had ended long ago. After ordering a bath drawn, he kicked open Artus's door. The boy sat bolt upright, knife in one hand. *He's learning—I'll give him that.*

Artus blinked at the filthy smuggler in his doorway. "What the hell happened to you?"

"I don't want to talk about it. How did this afternoon go?"

Artus went very still. "Ummm . . . pretty badly."

Tyvian nodded. "How badly?"

"I punched Valen Hesswyn." Artus tried to smile, but it didn't quite work.

Tyvian pinched the bridge of his nose. "Kroth's teeth. You got into a *duel*?"

"Two, actually." Artus looked down at his hands. "That's pretty bad, right?"

Tyvian slammed the door closed. He couldn't deal with this right now. His whole body ached, he stank, and his plans were in shambles. The first two of his problems he could address. In the morning he'd address the third one.

His legs stiff, he dragged his feet up the stairs, one by one. Every step up left a black mark on the red carpeted stairs. Behind him, floating in the air, a serving specter wielded a brush and a bucket of water to clean up after him. He made a note to summon a Rhondian masseuse in the morning in the hopes that his stiff muscles might be hastened to recovery that way. Tyvian disliked massages, as a rule—he felt as though he were a slab of beef being tenderized—but desperate times . . .

The great brass bathtub was piping hot by the time he got to his chambers, staggering along like the living dead. He stripped off the too-large peasant tunic and threw it in the fire—he'd be damned if he'd ever wear that again. He meant to unlace his shirt, too, but his arm cramped up, leaving him unable to do it without flailing around. He might have asked the specters, but they were still busy cleaning up the stains his passing had caused and in that endeavor he did not wish to distract them.

He tried to focus on the bath, but the failure of Artus and Hool that day threatened to overwhelm him. Sure, he'd *wanted* them to fail, but not this much! He felt like the only person he knew who understood the danger they were in and how to solve it. It occurred to him that this was the first time he had felt this alone in a long while. It was strange. There was a time when Tyvian spent literally years by himself, skipping from one plot to another, one step ahead of the Defenders. His life had been a single, unbroken adrenaline rush. He had won big and lost big, and he travelled the world in a fine shirt with nothing more than *Chance* and his wits to defend him. He remembered loving it. Now, the isolation of his princely chambers made him brood.

Tyvian stood, forcing his stiff body to go through a variety of footwork exercises to take his mind off maudlin topics like "being worried about other people." He rested in the en garde position, quickly and precisely advancing and retreating and then lunging at nothing—his recovering muscles obeyed, if reluctantly. He was getting better. He felt a hundred times better each night. One good bath and a good night's sleep, and he'd be his old self again.

Or would he?

Had he, Tyvian Reldamar, *actually* settled down? Myreon talked about all of them living in a bubble, but he'd taken that to mean that they'd let their guard down temporarily, not that he or Artus or Hool had *actually* removed themselves from the "game," as it were. The idea, as it struck him, came as a shock.

But what was even more shocking was this question: *did he prefer it that way?*

Tyvian had just argued with a beautiful woman who wanted to embark on a daring adventure and, instead, he had suggested that staying home and eating good cheese was the better call. He ran a hand through his hair. "Hann's Boots, I'm becoming positively dull."

"Tyvian?" He looked up—Myreon was in the doorway. She'd come back. *Thank the gods.* "What happened to you?"

Tyvian grunted, unwilling to reveal how excited he was to actually see her. After that afternoon, he hadn't had the highest hopes. "Your former colleagues forced me to take a little tour of the sewers— you're familiar with the place, I'm sure."

Myreon seemed to deflate somewhat. "Look . . . I'm sorry. I should have told you what I was doing."

Tyvian ripped off his borrowed shirt and threw it in the fire. "Yes, you bloody well *should have!*" It felt good to yell at her.

She came close to him, her eyes straying to his chest and arms. "I'll . . . we'll talk after you take your bath."

"Kroth take that!" Tyvian spat. "We'll talk *now!*" He unbuckled his belt and threw it on a chair. "But I'm *going* to take a bath now. If your modesty can't handle it, avert your eyes."

Myreon took a deep breath, but didn't avert her eyes as Tyvian stripped nude and slipped into the tub. The water was exactly the right temperature—hot enough to be bracing, but not so hot as to scald. He slipped in up to his neck, his aching body glowing with pleasure.

Myreon took up a bottle of wine from Tyvian's private stores and uncorked it. "I've been angry, Tyvian. I've been very angry for a long time."

Tyvian opened his mouth to say something and she put her finger on his lips. "Just listen, all right?" Myreon poured the wine. A serving specter brought in a second glass. "I grew up poor, understand? My family owned a vineyard and it was destroyed when I was little and most of my family died—bandit raid. This was in the years following the war, when Eretheria was a mess and Galaspin and Saldor's northern domain was still in ruins."

She handed Tyvian the wine and he took a sip. A very good Rhondian white—a Cusaco, maybe a '32. Myreon kept talking. "Anyway, my father was all I had—that and a few aunts who'd married men in Bridgeburg. He was a riverman, and I'd go with him on most voyages. I don't know why he took me along, actually—he could have left me with my aunts, I suppose, but he never did. I don't know if he could let go of me."

Tyvian shook his head. "Myreon, I know—ulp!" Myreon pushed his head underwater.

"I said shut up!" she said when he came up, spluttering. "You don't understand being poor, Tyvian. I never starved, I never froze—nothing as awful as that—but I had a constant understanding of being *worse* than everyone else. You—people like you and your mother—were just *better* than me, and that hurt. My father was a good man, Tyv. He was kind and honest and intelligent and loved me more than your mother ever did you." She leaned in close, speaking softly in his ear. "But he was poor, and that made him *lesser* in the eyes of all the half dukes and guild lords and knights that he ever met. And that hurt."

Myreon placed her fingers on his temples and began to rub. Her deft, sorceress's touch sapped all the tension from his body. He leaned back against the edge of the tub, letting the tiny bit of the Lumen she worked into the massage tingle throughout his body. She kept whispering in his ear. "When I became a Defender, it was because I wanted there to be justice in the world. I worked hard to earn my staff. I worked even harder to do what I thought was right. I was good at my job—my dealings with you excluded. And then, you know what happened?"

Tyvian nodded. "They betrayed you. Framed you. Left you to rot."

"All for money." Myreon's voice got a hard edge. "They ruined everything I was over money. And they could get away with it, because I was just a jumped-up poor girl who no one would miss."

Tyvian leaned back, letting Myreon's arms drape around his neck, feeling the soft warmth of her body behind him. "I missed you."

Myreon looked down from above him, smiling. "That's because you're a lunatic." She reached up with one of her hands and brushed his hair from his brow. "If a handsome one."

Tyvian looked up at her. "I kissed her, Myreon, but that's it. I swear."

"I know." She nodded, sighing. "I believe you."

"You . . . do?"

Myreon kissed him lightly on the forehead. "You're right—you have been more honest with me than I've been with you."

Tyvian grinned. "You were saying about being angry?"

"You know what's the only thing money can't control?"

Tyvian frowned. "Trick question. Money controls everything."

Myreon shook her head. "Not sorcery—not the High Arts. You teach a pauper to cast a spell, and he can cast that spell forever, money or not."

"So you taught paupers to cast spells. Gods, Myreon!"

Now it was Myreon's turn to frown. "And why not? Why shouldn't regular people learn sorcery to make their lives easier? Why shouldn't I teach it to them? Who are the Defenders to say who can and can't learn it?"

Tyvian caught up her hand. "Myreon, my darling, they are the *exact* people who get to say that! That's why they're called 'the Defenders of the Balance'— sorcery is *unbalancing*! Gods, how many times in the last few years have you and I almost seen whole cities destroyed by carefully unbalanced sorcery!"

"The only balance the Defenders maintain is the balance of power—the rich over the poor, the landed over the landless. Your mother made that very clear." She looked down at him. "You know it as well as I do, Tyvian. Probably better. You've been fighting them for ages."

"Yes, but not for the purpose of *demolishing* the status quo! Gods, Myreon—that won't lead anywhere positive! You collected a pack of disgruntled peasants in the sewers and taught them spells and then they turned around and *murdered* a Count!"

"No. They deposed a terrible *man*. A man who deserved it."

He stood up in the tub and wiped the water off his face. "You haven't done those people any favors. You know that, right? You've also . . . you've . . ." He pointed to his burning clothes in the fireplace. "Look at what *I* had to go through tonight!"

Myreon reached out to him, clasping him lightly on the hips. "Tyvian, don't you ever want something *more* than just survival and comfort?" With one hand, she traced a half dozen tight little scars that criss-crossed his taut stomach. "Don't you ever wish you could live without having to go through all *this*?"

Tyvian sighed. "I thought we *had* been doing that—living alone and comfortable, surrounded by friends. It seems I was wrong. It seems that, all that time, you were sneaking away into the city sewers to teach farmers to throw fireballs."

"And you were meeting with smugglers to trade forbidden magecraft. It's the same thing, Tyvian."

Was it the same thing? Had he been unhappy? Of course not! Bored, perhaps—a trifle irritable at times. Unhappy? How could he have been? He had drunk nothing but the finest wine and eaten nothing but the finest food for a year straight, and never once did a Defender try to kick in his door and haul him off. It *should* have been paradise.

Myreon was smiling at him. "There's something endearing about watching this."

"Watching what?"

Myreon shook her head, still grinning. "Watching you figure out something about yourself that the rest of us already knew. It's adorable. You always look like a puppy whose found his tail."

"Puppy?" Tyvian snorted. "A *puppy*?"

She smirked. "A very dangerous, dashing puppy. With a pretty incredible abdomen, if I'm being honest."

Tyvian leaned forward and kissed her gently. "Are we? Being honest?"

Myreon slid her arms around his neck. "I doubt it."

Tyvian and Myreon kissed again, this time a bit longer. When they broke apart, he found himself a little breathless. "I need to hear about you talking to my mother. I need to know exactly what she said."

Myreon kissed him on the neck, nibbling him gently. "Later."

Tyvian ran a hand through her thick, golden hair as she planted kisses on his chest and stomach. "We have a lot of planning to do, you know. The Blue Party is the day after tomorrow, and we need a new way in."

Myreon grabbed him and pulled him up out of the tub. "Later."

Tyvian agreed. Reconciliation required the proper amount of time. It would not be rushed. Or, at least, he desperately hoped not.

CHAPTER 22

THE BREAKING OF THE HOUSE OF EDDON

The Defenders of the Balance hit the House of Eddon with a volley of thunder-orbs first, blowing in the magically sealed doors and shattering all the windows on the east wing. They stormed the entry hall next—nobody was there, so there was hardly anything to stop their progress up the stairs toward Tyvian's chambers.

All of this Tyvian heard while wrapped up in Myreon's arms, half asleep. The booms, the shouts, the pounding of boots on stairs—all of it seemed very important, but was it so important that he had to disentangle himself from the arms of a beautiful, naked woman and put on pants?

Then a man swung a siege maul at the door to his bedchamber hard enough to make the oak buckle, and Myreon was on her feet. "Get up!" she said, scrambling about. She threw *Chance* at his face. "Tyvian! Get bloody up!"

Their bedroom door banged open and, rather than Artus or Brana or Hool, there was a man in mage-glass armor with a kite shield and an arming sword, of all things. Myreon threw a bolt of fire at him that rebounded off the shield's wards. He raised the sword and roared, ready to charge her.

Tyvian tripped him as he tried to round the bed and then jumped on his back. *Chance* was still by his pillow, so he ripped off the man's helmet and raised it to bash in his brains. Just then, *another* Defender, this one helmetless and with a lit firepike, came up behind Tyvian, ready to spit him. Tyvian could feel the heat getting closer to his bare skin, but Myreon blinded him with a sunblast—lighting the bedding on fire in the process—and followed up with another fire bolt that took the oaf in the pelvic region, almost certainly setting some very sensitive things aflame. In the time it took for that to happen, Tyvian had knocked the first man over the head twice with his own helm. He stopped moving.

Myreon had somehow managed to dress in a robe. She pushed *Chance* at him with a spot of telekinesis. "Let's go! I'll cover you!"

A third Defender was in the doorway as Tyvian

was coming out, shield up. Tyvian put *Chance* straight through the shield and straight through the mail-clad stomach of the man behind it without so much as breaking stride.

Tyvian charged into the hall, still without pants. Brana had taken a man down already, but another Defender had him in a headlock from behind and a third was coming at him with a firepike. There were two men trying to beat in Hool's door and another three coming in through the broken windows.

Tyvian darted forward and slashed the man trying to gut Brana in the back of the knee, parting the leather there like gossamer. Blood poured down the back of his leg and the Defender staggered to one knee, screaming.

Another one took a swing at Tyvian's head with a siege maul, which probably would have taken his head clean off were it not for a magical guard that Myreon erected just in time. Instead, the heavy weapon rebounded off a flash of light, knocking the mirror-man off-balance. Tyvian ran him through low—through the kidneys, if his aim was true—and moved on.

Brana slammed his captor back into the wall, loosening the grip for long enough to get out of the choke hold. The two of them still struggled, but Brana was gradually gaining the upper hand. The man threw a punch at Brana's nose, but Brana ducked under it and, in a maneuver impossible for a human, but pretty standard for a gnoll, managed to twist his head and bite down on the man's elbow—not the edge either, but the *whole* elbow. There was a deep, meaty *crack* and the man screamed in a way Tyvian hadn't thought the human voice capable of. At the moment, it gave him a great deal of satisfaction—

Until he was bashed in the face by another damned shield.

Tyvian staggered back until he fell. As he was crashing to the ground, Myreon lit a man's beard on fire and then used a focused telekinetic blast to send him straight out a window, and now Tyvian found himself on his back, rolling to avoid a falling axe. Brana kept growling, at some point Tyvian heard Artus shout out in pain, and the melee became something of a muddle. Just a swirl of knives, fists, swords, axes, and shields. Firepike blasts ripped around at too-close range, lighting the walls on fire. He couldn't remember when, but Myreon must have put up a blade ward that prevented a sword from making his insides his outsides.

Then came Hool.

Tyvian had no idea what had taken her so long, but she was the catapult stone that brought down the wall, as it were. She kicked open the door the Defenders were trying to breach and emerged as her true gnoll self. Her roar was deafening—so much so that, for the briefest instant, everyone in the room stopped moving.

Hool looked angry—very, *very* angry. Her growl

was something almost too deep to hear, but still seemed to cause the room to vibrate. She seethed, her whole body pulsing with enraged breaths, her teeth bared. In her hands was a huge, enchanted mace that writhed with Fey energy so powerful it made the air shimmer—the Fist of Veroth. "Get. *Out!*"

The Defenders did not get out—at least not fast enough.

So Hool began swinging that mace, and the world seemed to explode all around her. Tyvian found himself sailing through the air with an assortment of body parts, stray weapons, and building material. He landed, miraculously, on a couch in the gaming hall.

Hool had blown him through two walls and down a floor.

Tyvian looked up to see a giant crack in the ceiling and the blue sky beyond. "Kroth's teeth!"

Somewhere above, Hool swung the mace again and the entire house shook with the shockwave. One of the great chimneys in the game room rocked back and forth, as though about to fall. Tyvian struggled to crawl out from beneath the debris covering him and actually managed it thanks to a combination of adrenaline and, surprisingly, the ring's influence. He hated to admit it at just that moment, but he had actually missed that feeling of warm, encompassing power flowing up his arms.

Of course, the ring only was giving him that

power because it meant for him to save somebody. That somebody was usually Artus.

There were cracks of lightning coming from the forecourt—the Mage Defender in charge of the raid was getting involved. Tyvian heard Hool roar and a lot of calls to retreat. He ran out of the gaming hall and into the half-ruined corridors of the rest of the house. "Artus! Brana! Myreon! Where are you?"

A Defender popped around a corner and shot a firepike at him, the blazing bolt glancing past Tyvian's ribs, causing the flesh there to blacken and blister. The pain was nearly unbearable, and he staggered against the wall. The Defender raised the pike, ready to fire again.

But Artus stepped out of a doorway and sliced the man's fingers off with a machete and, with his off hand, made a horizontal slash with another machete across the man's face. The guards on his helmet kept him from losing his head, but Artus's blade got through his lips and teeth. Any semblance of fight went out of the man as Artus kept bashing at him. The Defender fled, blood pouring down his chin.

Tyvian staggered to his feet, his ribs screaming. "Good timing."

Artus nodded. "'Bout time I saved *you* from certain death."

Somewhere in the house, the Fist of Veroth struck again. There was an enormous crash, as though one of the House of Eddon's massive chimneys had just been ripped from its foundations and flung across the property—which is probably exactly what happened.

Tyvian and Artus froze, waiting for the roof to cave in. It didn't. "We've got to get the hell out of here."

Artus grinned. "Way ahead of you. Brana's getting the coach. Myreon's creating a diversion."

"What's Hool doing?"

Artus pulled Tyvian by the elbow. "Killing everything, I guess."

They went out the back, into the ill-fated garden from the day before. Here Brana had somehow maneuvered their coach, complete with its team of two horses all harnessed and ready. He grinned widely when he saw them. "I did it! See?"

"Get in! I can't hold this much longer!" Myreon shouted. The thing she was "holding" was some kind of massive sorcerous guard—a shield of rippling Dweomeric force that sealed off the Defenders trying to pierce it from three sides. They had one avenue of escape, and that was straight through the thick hedges at the edge of the garden. Tyvian grimaced—horses, he knew, weren't very keen on running straight through hedges.

They were less excited about fire, though, so he'd bank on that.

Hool leapt down beside them—she had been on the roof, or what was left of it. She had her shroud and an iron key tied around one arm, the deadly enchanted mace in the other. "Let's go."

Tyvian pointed at the hedge. "Clear that first. Hurry!" He looked up, scanning the skies—there. Griffons—two of them—circling, waiting for them to run.

Hool slammed her weapon into the earth, causing a shockwave to uproot trees and rip apart all the hedges inside a twenty-foot radius.

The horses bolted. Brana almost fell off the top of the coach. Had Tyvian not been standing right at the door, he wouldn't have made it on. He looked back. "Myreon! Come on!"

Myreon dropped the guard and feyleapt to the roof of the coach. Behind them, the Defenders formed a firing line and shot after them, but the range was too great and the bolts of fire went wide. They did nothing to calm the horses, though.

Hool leapt atop the coach as it passed as well. A moment later, she passed a pale, exhausted Myreon through the window and then the Fist of Veroth and then herself. They were a jumble of arms and legs and weaponry bouncing around inside. Outside, the Eretherian countryside was ripping past at incredible speed; the coach rattled so fiercely, Tyvian thought the wheels might fall off.

"Brana doesn't know how to do this," Hool observed. "Go and help him."

Tyvian grimaced, wondering briefly if he should point out that he was still completely naked. And injured.

The ring gave him a pinch.

"All right. Fine."

He poked his head out the window only to almost lose it to a passing signpost. Brana was clinging to the reins, tongue lolling out one side of his mouth, and grinning from ear to ear. "Brana," he shouted, "turn us around!"

The gnoll nodded and flicked the reins. Nothing happened, of course—Brana had only told the horses to go faster. A shadow passed over them.

Brana's ears shot up. Tyvian heard it, too—a rough, shrill screech, like that of a falcon only much bigger.

Griffons.

Chance in his teeth, Tyvian climbed onto the roof of the carriage.

He caught a glimpse of something large and black about two hundred feet up and wheeling in their direction. Yanking the reins from Brana, he pulled hard on one side, enough to get the coach turned around and headed back toward the city. They even managed to stop rolling through farmyards and found themselves on a proper road. Ahead of them, people out early leapt aside and flocks of geese and chickens squawked in panic. One oxcart was run straight off the road and into a ditch.

Brana grabbed Tyvian and pushed him down just as something huge swooped low. Tyvian got the barest impression of six-inch talons barely missing his back and then a big gust of wind. Another griffon—a barely missed dive. That rider was a cocky one—lucky he didn't crash.

Tyvian gave the reins to Brana. "Keep them running. Aim for narrow streets. Don't crash."

Brana grinned. "Wheeee!"

Tyvian got up and, keeping one hand on the roof of the coach, crab walked toward the back. He conjured *Chance*'s blade and looked up. The griffon riders were there, a hundred feet above, the creatures' massive wings beating hard to catch up to the speeding coach. He could see the riders had crossbows—probably with enchanted bolts—but there were too many people and houses nearby for them to start firing. If they wanted to stop them, the riders were going to have to get close. Tyvian just needed to narrow down their possible angles of attack.

He caught a glimpse of a signpost. "Brana, turn left!"

Brana pulled on the reins, and they careened to the left, nearly throwing Tyvian off. The tail end of the coach bashed into a rain barrel, breaking it apart in a shower of tepid water. Tyvian held on by wrapping his fingers around the toprail. They were now driving downhill—a broad boulevard called Monument Avenue, so named for the ten-foot statues of Eretherian heroes and Counts that were evenly spaced down the center of the road. It was a straight shot to Lake Elren from here, and in the distance ahead the palace gleamed above the deep blue water.

The statues in the center of the road, the trees on either side, and the high roofs of the manor houses here meant the griffons only had one angle of attack—a dive, straight at them from behind—which was exactly what Tyvian wanted. He got up on two feet, eyes fixed on the flying beasts and saluted the riders with *Chance*. "Come then, gentlemen! Let's see what you're made of."

Tyvian saw one stow his crossbow and take up the lance strapped to his saddle, its purple pennant snapping in the wind. Then, he pressed his guide pole down, forcing the griffon to dive. It tucked its wings and came straight for them.

Tyvian was shocked at how fast the beast moved—it covered the two hundred yards between them in the blink of an eye. Tyvian could see details now—the creature's bright yellow beak, curved and wicked, its sharp orange eyes, the mageglass gauntlets of its rider. Gods, it was almost there . . .

Now!

Tyvian slashed up with *Chance* at the thick, stone arm of a statue of Perwynnon. His whole body shook with the impact, but the mageglass blade proved true, cutting the arm free. The sixty-pound block of stone tumbled into the griffon at the last possible moment, knocking it off-kilter and causing it to tumble and crash into the cobblestones with a shriek of pain.

"Turn again!" Tyvian yelled.

Brana did, again almost tipping the coach.

Tyvian regained his balance and looked up again. The second griffon rider was nowhere to be seen—he was landing. To help his partner. Tyvian grinned. "Good man."

They'd made it.

CHAPTER 23

LOSS OF ALLIES

Tyvian's safe house in Davram Heights was known as the Halfling. It was a solidly built gaming house run by a man whose undying loyalty Tyvian had purchased when he stole back his daughter from Verisi pirates. The fact that Tyvian had been the one to arrange her kidnapping in the first place had, fortunately, not come up. He had every suspicion the ring would have made that encounter . . . awkward.

Gaming houses were quiet affairs during the day, which was exceedingly fortunate, given that Tyvian appeared on the doorstep completely nude and with half his torso blistering from a firepike wound. Myreon was too exhausted from the ordeal to do much tending to it, so he relied upon the generosity of his host, who had a surprisingly large array of high-quality medical supplies. People in his gaming house had a tendency to get stabbed, as it happened.

Of greater concern to Tyvian was not his physical injuries, however. He was getting the full report on the salon the day before—it was worse than he suspected. He pinched the bridge of his nose. "Artus, when I said 'no duels,' how exactly did you interpret that as *all the duels possible?*"

A cool fog had rolled in as the morning progressed, and Artus had stoked the wide fireplace of the private room. Hool and Brana sat at one end of a green-upholstered table used to play chasers—Brana with his shroud, Hool without hers. Myreon sat to Tyvian's right, looking almost as terrible as he did.

Artus looked at his hands. "Sorry."

Tyvian took a deep breath. "Sorry is insufficient."

Hool's ears went back. "You should have been there. This is all *your* fault!"

Tyvian held up three fingers. "I gave you *three* rules—no hitting, no duels, no sniffing the air. Were those *hard* rules? Is there some kind of *challenge* inherent in being a civilized person I'm not aware of? How many of those rules did you break, eh? How *quickly?*"

Hool drew herself up to her full height. "Those were terrible people."

Artus nodded. "That's for sure."

Tyvian pounded the armrest of his chair. "Which

is *why* we needed *not* to offend them to the point where two of them are going to try to kill Artus now. On the same day, no less."

Artus blinked. "Wait . . . what? The same day?"

Tyvian nodded. "Eretherian duels are fought four days following the challenge. Since you got in two fights in one day, you have to fight both duels on the same day."

Artus swallowed hard and looked into the fire. He looked worried, as well he might. Tyvian decided to let him stew.

"I assume this changes your plans," Myreon said, sipping a cup of tea with both hands.

Tyvian closed his eyes—his entire body felt heavy. "This . . . complicates matters. The Hesswyns attended in bad faith—an audacious move, honestly. They couldn't have counted on me not being there." He paused and took another deep breath. "There is just about no way we can expect a respectable invitation to the Blue Party *now*."

"It isn't complicated," Hool said. "We just leave now."

"We *can't* just leave," Myreon shot back. "This heir business will chase Tyvian for the rest of his life."

Hool snorted and pointed a fuzzy finger at Tyvian. "He is being chased by lots of people scarier than these nasty rich people. Who cares?"

"We obviously can't remain here long-term. Not now." Tyvian sighed. "But the fundamentals of the plan remain the same. I renounce tomorrow night at the Blue Party, and *then* we disappear."

"That is the stupidest thing I have ever heard you say," Hool snarled.

Tyvian rubbed his temples—he really didn't need this right now. "Hool, be reasonable."

Hool stood up, her hackles raised. Tyvian distinctly got the sense she was not going to be reasonable. "Brana was almost killed today. The night before last, he was drinking *poison* with Artus. He was sick all the next morning!" She pointed at Artus. "You were supposed to take care of him!"

Artus shrugged. "Hool, he was just hung over—that's it. It's not a big deal. Tell her, Brana."

Brana looked up at his mother, but she stared him into silence. Hool advanced on Artus. "You are bad for my Brana. *All* of you are bad for my Brana."

Artus blinked. "Hool . . . it was . . . it was just *beer*. He'll be fine. He *wanted* to drink it. Right, Brana?"

Brana said nothing. He only stared at the floor, his shoulders slumped.

"Brana is only a *puppy*!" Hool roared. "And you have him pretending to be a man! You have him fighting wizards! You have him giving flowers to human girls! You have him driving coaches and fleeing griffons and who knows what else!"

"To be fair, Hool," Tyvian said, "he *does* seem to enjoy it."

Hool took a deep breath and held it for a moment,

as though physically girding herself for what came next. "We are leaving."

Tyvian shook his head. "You can't go back to the House of Eddon now, Hool. There will still be Defenders going over that place. Best to—"

"No!" Hool faced him. "Not back there. We are *leaving*. We are going home—*real* home. No more assassins. No more poison. No more *humans*."

Artus's mouth dropped open. "Wh . . . what? The Taqar? You can't be serious!"

Hool looked at Artus and, just for a moment, her face drooped a little. "You are a man grown, Artus. You don't need me." Then to Tyvian, she said, "You are only going to get us killed, and you know it. I can see it in how you talk to us. Admit it!"

Tyvian sagged back into his chair. There was a lot of truth to what she said. Too damned much. He licked his lips, took a deep breath. "Go then."

Myreon gasped; Artus stood up, crying, *"What?"*

"This isn't their world, Artus. We've no right to keep them."

"But what about *Brana?*" Artus shouted. "Don't he get to decide? What about him?"

"Brana is only a baby," Hool grunted. "He belongs with his mother. And this place is too crazy for us."

Artus scarcely seemed to find the words. "It . . . it was only one night drinking! That's it! It's just a bloody *hangover*, Hool!"

"How much does my baby need to be hurt because

of you humans? An axe to his chest? Does he need to be drowned in a lake?" Hool showed her teeth. "I am tired of pretending to be a human. I am tired of dealing with humans. I am tired of humans trying to kill me all the time. I have had *enough!*"

Tyvian shook his head. "I can't believe you'd leave us now . . . in my—*our*—hour of need. After all we've been through."

"Maybe you should have thought about that before pretending to be king just so you can surprise everybody by *not* being king or whatever stupid nonsense you are doing this time—I can't keep track of it all." Hool threw a heavy iron key—the key to her vault beneath the House of Eddon—at him, only barely missing some rather sensitive organs. "You needed me when you lived in the wilderness. You needed me when you were all alone. You needed me when you were poor and had no place to go and no one to watch your back except Artus and he was too young. Now you have Myreon and Artus is smarter and you have lots of money. You don't need me. And you don't need Brana either."

Tyvian picked up the key and turned it over in his hands. He could argue with her, he knew. He could tell her some story about how essential she was to his plans or his life or whatever. He didn't, though. He owed her too much for that. "How long before you go?"

"We leave right now."

"No!" Artus pointed an accusing finger at her. "No, it's not fair!"

"I'm sorry, Artus," Hool said, quietly. She enveloped him in a big hug, which the teenager did not return. "I am not your mother, but I love you anyway."

Artus quivered for a moment, his eyes glassy. Then he fled the room.

Tyvian looked up at her. "I'll miss you, Hool."

Hool gave him the same big, furry hug and licked the side of his face. "You are the best human I know. Which is still pretty awful."

Tyvian kissed her on the furry back of her hand. Then the gnoll nodded in the direction of Myreon. "You are in charge of making sense now."

Myreon smiled briefly. "I know."

Hool nodded again and grumbled something toward Brana in gnoll-speak. Glum, the puppy trotted to his mother's side and they left with no further ceremony.

Tyvian and Myreon were alone. She looked at him with a faint smile growing on her face. "Look how far you've come. And in only a few years."

Tyvian scowled. "What are you going on about?"

"You could have lied to her. Tricked her. Manipulated her—you've done it before." The smile remained affixed to Myreon's face. "But you didn't."

"My plans are already going to hell—there seemed little point to dragging Hool and Brana down with me," Tyvian said.

"And that, my dear Tyvian, is my *exact* point."

Tyvian looked at her. He was too damned tired for this. "Stop trying to make me into something I'm not."

"How could I possibly? You still plan on going to the Blue Party, don't you?"

Tyvian nodded. "It's our last chance. Our very last."

"Only if you maintain the same goal," Myreon said, frowning. "If you were to change objectives . . ."

"And what—pretend to actually be king? That's *insane*, Myreon. What possible 'good' could I do as a dead man?"

"What choice do you have, now? If you go to the Blue Party, the Defenders will be everywhere, waiting for you. The only way to keep them from arresting you is to become a head of state—then they *can't*."

Tyvian blinked as the pieces fell into place. "Gods, you set us up, didn't you? You led them straight to us on purpose! That Defender raid was your bloody idea!"

Myreon held up her hands. "I did it under controlled circumstances."

Tyvian stood up. "Controlled bloody circumstances? Me having a sword fight with a Krothing *griffon* on the back of a moving coach is *controlled circumstances*?"

Myreon shrugged. "I had complete faith in you. Now you know what it's like being the victim of one of your ridiculous schemes."

Tyvian pointed to the door through which Hool and Brana had just left. "You're aware that your little plot just cost me one of my . . ." He paused—was he going to say this? *Yes, Hann be damned.* "One of my *best friends* just walked out because of you. And why? Because you want the world to be a better place? *Are you kidding me?*"

"Always about yourself, isn't it?" Myreon stood up. "I've got news for you, Reldamar—not everything's *about* you! I did what I had to do, and now you're boxed in a corner: you can either become king or run away."

"No. I can renounce. I *will* renounce, and then Artus and I will find somewhere else!"

Myreon shook her head. "Until Sahand or the Kalsaaris or the Sorcerous League or the Mute Prophets find you, and then what? You keep running for the rest of your life?"

"*My life is* my *business!*" Tyvian shouted. "I'll not be your pawn or my mother's pawn or Xahlven's pawn or anyone else's. I want peace!"

"And you can have it," Myreon said. "On the throne."

"You're insane." Tyvian threw up his hands. "You've lost your mind—you're some kind of radical lunatic. Last night? That was just a ploy, wasn't it? A plot to get us to this moment, where you'd hoped the memory of your *favors* would be enough to tip me over to your side. Admit it!"

Myreon stiffened. "It wasn't like that. I did what I had to."

"Most whores say much the same."

Myreon slapped him, hard. Tyvian's face glowed with pain and he stumbled back into his chair.

"We're both whores," Myreon hissed. "You know that, right? We both sell parts of ourselves—our pride, our conscience, our better impulses. But you know what the difference is between me and you? I do it for a cause. You do it for yourself."

Tyvian's lips curled back. "And I suppose you're going to tell me that this—your *adoption* of this hopeless cause—has nothing to do with your father dying in some slum while you were off in the Arcanostrum, drinking tea with Lyrelle? Hmmm? That your whole damned life isn't just some haphazard series of events that made you into whoever it is hissing venom at me in *my* bloody safe house?"

Myreon nodded slowly. "We're all of us our fathers' children, Tyvian." She stood up and went to the door. "I only hope you learn who yours is before it's too late."

She went out.

Tyvian sat in the chair, watching the door for a long time.

She did not come back.

CHAPTER 24

DEALS FOR THE DESPERATE

Myreon slipped out of the Halfling just after midnight, when the place was busiest and somebody in a shroud wouldn't be easily noticed. She took care to ward herself against seekwands and to keep wary.

The streets were quiet. Granted, Eretheria wasn't like Saldor or Freegate—it was a city that slept, more or less—but even still, there was a strange hush over the grand, tree-lined avenues and tangled side streets. A troop of mercenaries was on the streets, patrolling in armor, their halberds at their shoulders. This sight gave Myreon pause—for all the prevalence of internecine warfare in this convoluted country, armed soldiers on the streets of the capital city was unusual. The Defenders were there, certainly, but that was different—they were an independent force, owing fealty to no individual house. Even the press-gangs and tax men tended to be small and lightly armed parties of men-at-arms who owed fealty to any number of lesser peers. This group was a world apart from that—these were heavily armed sell-swords in the direct employ of House Davram. They weren't peacekeepers. These men were hired killers.

Myreon stayed well out of their sight.

She turned her steps toward the Ayventry District. She hoped she could find Bree there, or maybe even find a way to link up with her apprentices again. She was going to need their help. Rifling through her satchel, she pulled out some of the most recent items they had given her—things that the Law of Possession might still connect them to. She found the little sewer demon talisman Bree had once hung around her neck. She produced her own seekwand and looped the item around its slender shaft. Then, she let the enchanted tool do its work.

The signs of growing unrest were thick, if one knew where to look. Every pillory was full of offenders. Myreon saw wagons tipped over in the side streets—barricades against intrusion—and out of windows and hanging on doors were flags of royal blue, emblazoned with the white device of a peregrine falcon in a dive. The sigil of Perwyn, the ancient banner of Eretherian royalty—the only Eretherian banner that could fly above those of the five Great Houses.

For all his anger at her, Myreon felt confident her plan had worked. Tyvian would *have* to declare, and once he did, he wouldn't turn his back on these people. She felt more buoyant than she had in months; she actually had some good news for her apprentices, for her people. Their "king" was going to help them, whether he wanted to or not. His ring would see to it.

But then the wand led her to Traitor's Square, and there Myreon's cautious optimism died.

All along the top of the hedges of Dovechurch were planted dozens of pikes. Mounted on these pikes were human heads.

And her wand had led her here. *To Bree.*

"No . . ." Myreon dropped the wand and hurried across the square, forgetting all pretense at stealth—there was no one around, anyway. "No!"

The crows perched atop the grisly trophies took flight as Myreon came close, squinting through the dark of the moonless night. After an afternoon of being picked at by ravens, the heads were difficult to recognize.

But she *did* recognize them. Most of them.

They were her students. All of her students. Including Bree.

Hanging from each pike was a small placard with a single word written in white paint:

TREASON

Tears poured down Myreon's face. She hugged herself against the evening chill and tried not to sob audibly. All her lessons, all her training—it had meant nothing. It had saved no one. They were all dead, and she was the cause.

Argus Androlli stepped from the shadows. "You have been making a lot of work for me lately."

Myreon reinforced her wards by instinct, expecting a black bag over her head from behind or a blast of sorcerous energy taking her off guard, but nothing came. The Mage Defender simply stood in the center of the street, hands clasped around his staff, his chiseled face grim. "I'm alone. For now."

Myreon eyed the shadows anyway. "What do you want, Argus?"

"You know, I wanted to believe you had nothing to do with all of this. I wanted to believe it was a rogue cell of some sort, acting independently. But here you are." Androlli shook his head. "Disgusting."

Myreon snuffled her tears away. "*You're* talking about disgusting? Some of these were children, Argus. You beheaded *children*."

"Spare me." Androlli sighed, pacing around Myreon at a safe distance, his posture loose—he was ready to cast at any moment, ready to react to her every attack. "You know the laws as well as I do. The Defenders have the duty to arrest in Eretheria, but trial and punishment are settled by the local authorities, not Saldor. And when Banric Sahand is the one handing out the punishments . . ."

"Sahand?"

Androlli nodded. "Since your little stunt at the execution, it seems as though Sahand has moved into Ayventry as a kind of *regent*." Androlli scowled. "Do you know how I felt having to *debrief* that beast? Having to shake his damned hand and promise him justice? That's *another* thing I blame you for."

Myreon tried to calm herself, but her heart was racing. They were dead. Bree and the rest of them—all dead. And while the rebellion, the uprising Myreon knew they'd all hoped for, was happening, it was not as she imagined it. And now Sahand was at the center of it. Gods knew what horrible thing he'd fashion from all of this. *This isn't what I wanted*, she thought.

"If you give us the names and locations of all the other cells and other conspirators, I've managed to secure authorization to bring you back to Saldor for trial," Androlli said. "This is a better fate than you deserve, but it is in the service of the Balance. You might recall what that involves."

Others? Myreon watched him cautiously. "If I refuse?"

"Sahand has offered to assist in the investigation." Androlli shrugged. "Frankly, I need the manpower. Your little friends will find themselves squeezed like grapes in a press. I envision a witch hunt—even more heads on pikes, some justly, some not. You could prevent all that here and now. Give them up, and this city is spared a lot of pain."

"They taught other people," Myreon breathed. She smiled faintly. Of course. *Of course* they had! For every spell she taught them, each of her apprentices might have taught two, three, four other people the same little tricks, the same little spells.

Androlli continued to circle her. "I beg your pardon?"

Myreon took a deep breath. "Only blood can wash away the sins of man."

Androlli's dark eyebrows shot up. "Quoting the Book of Hann at me? Ironic."

"If you choose to believe so. The answer, Androlli, is no." With that pronouncement, Myreon tapped her staff to the ground and an eruption of Fey energy shot upward—a geyser of crimson brymmfire. It rebounded off Androlli's and Myreon's wards, but it was enough to scorch the ground and fill the air with smoke. Myreon channeled the Ether next, melding with the shadows and slipping through the darkness like an eel. By the time Androlli had gathered up enough Dweomeric energy to blow away the smoke and pierce the darkness, she was running down an alley.

He wasn't some apprentice, though, and he wasn't far behind. A sun-bright beam of light poured from the sky and illuminated her, melting her Etheric shadow-shield like ice in a skillet. A lode-bolt followed, rebounding off her wards, but knocking her back a few steps. Myreon responded with a stream of fire that blazed down the alley toward where Androlli stood.

He caught it and shaped it into a ball of flame and threw it back. But Myreon was already gone, having feyleapt to the roof of a guild hall. Androlli feyleapt after her. "I BIND YOU!"

Myreon felt the Compulsion come over her, but she pushed back, drawing the Fey from the bottomless reservoir of her anger. When Androlli landed on the roof, she struck it with her staff, causing an explosion of heavy tiles at his feet. Androlli fell backward and toppled off the roof.

At the same time, though, firepike bolts incinerated Myreon's sorcerous guards. Two full squads were in position, one trying to cut off her escape, the other climbing up the side of the guild hall with easy, loping motions—lightfoot charms.

Myreon dropped off the other side of the building. Defenders were there, too. They fired a full volley of firepikes right into her, and it was all she could do to raise a Dweomeric shield strong enough to resist being incinerated.

As if anticipating her defenses, though, a thunder-orb fell at her feet, and the explosion made the world seem to hold still for a second. Everything was weirdly quiet, the street and the sky spinning. *I'm . . . flying through . . . the air . . .* Her thoughts seemed hazy, indistinct.

She hit the cobblestones with a thunderclap impact that brought her back to reality. Her ears still rung, but she was back. She tried to stand.

Defenders stood over her.

Myreon tried to roll away, but one of them stomped on her stomach until she threw up. "Don't you move, rat! You wiggle a whisker and I'll gut you, so help me Hann!"

Myreon tried to breathe, tried to speak a spell, but couldn't manage it.

She wasn't sure it mattered.

Another two Defenders caught up with them. One of them flipped her over and put a knee in the small of her back. The other squatted in front of her and, grabbing Myreon by the hair, bashed her head into the ground a few times. "Where are your Krothing spells now, huh, witch? No more curses for you, eh?"

The venom in his voice—these were men who hated her. Hated what she was and who she fought for. Men who had dragged Bree to the block—just a girl—and watched as she died. The horror came flooding back—it was almost too much to contemplate. *And I used to be one of them. I used to be like Androlli. I was once the monster.*

Myreon spat blood at them.

"Ah!" The squatting one tried to jump back, but fell over instead. "Ah! The arse-face bitch spat blood on me boots!"

The first Defender kicked Myreon in the nose. The world spun and flashed white. "Gimme the 'locks!"

They hoisted her up and pinned her to the wall while one of them worked her hands into casterlocks. She let it happen—any struggle would only earn her more injuries. She wanted to scream, but held her silence.

Of course Androlli set a trap for me. Stupid. So stupid.

The mirror-man with his forearm pressed into her throat hissed in her ear. "I lost some good friends at the House of Eddon, you bloodthirsty bitch. You think petrification is all you got to face, eh?"

They threw her to the ground and loomed over her, setting aside their weapons. One of them cracked his knuckles, grinning. "Magus Androlli said we only needed to bring you in alive. He didn't say nothing about you being in one piece."

"You hear that?" one of them yelled over Myreon's head, as though she were deaf. "Here comes your beating, witch!"

He wasn't lying. The beating came. Or, more accurately, the stomping, as they mostly just used their feet. Boots came down again and again—and once, the butt of a firepike. She lost track of time; the world spun and faded away.

Myreon woke up in total darkness. She thought for a moment maybe she was blind, her eyesight taken by one too many blows to the head. When she felt around, though, she found it wasn't the case. She wasn't in the alley anymore. She heard water dripping from somewhere close by—the flat *spack* of moisture against stone. Beneath her were old bricks covered in moss. The air was stale.

The sewers.

She tried to rise, but she was too hurt and the ceiling too low. Trembling, coughing, she rolled onto all fours and crawled in no particular direction. Around her she felt the sticky, sucking sensation of sewer demons looking to feed. She flinched and knocked them away. How had she gotten here? Was this some kind of cruel joke on the part of the Defenders? "Hello?" she croaked. "Hello?"

She heard a man scream in a way that almost made her water her own breeches. It wasn't a mere scream of pain. Somebody had just died, and terribly. Myreon went perfectly still, a million terrible childhood stories raging through her head of things that lived in the dark and creatures that fed on the souls of the living.

A sickly, thin yellow light shot up—a tongue of flame three feet tall. It spouted from a bloody crack in a severed human head, its eyes white and its face covered in blood. It was the face of one of the Defenders who had beaten her.

Myreon shrieked and recoiled, but there was nowhere to go. The light that poured from the man's head was enough to illuminate her surroundings. It was an older part of the sewers—one she didn't recognize. Here the natural caves had reasserted their dominance over the constructions of mortal man—bricks and mortar lay in damp, uneven piles. Moss and mushrooms grew in abundance, and the walls were slick with moisture. The chamber itself was large—perhaps fifty paces long—and there were placed here a great many slablike tables and mossy wooden benches, all in various stages of rot and decay.

On the tables were bodies or parts of bodies. In the yellow light, the blood looked black. It seemed to coat everything. Myreon screamed again, scrambling backward toward the isolated corner where she had awoken. It was then she realized something: *the casterlocks had been removed.*

"Be not afraid." A voice—a thin, raspy voice, cruel and hard—spoke from the shadows. "You are safe, friend Myreon."

She knew that voice, though she had never heard it in the flesh before.

Myreon could not speak. Her mouth hung open, gasping for air or words or some kind of sense. It could find none. She hoped this was some kind of nightmare.

The speaker stepped into the light, however, and she knew everything that was happening was very real.

He was scarecrow thin and flagpole tall, his eyes

milky white to match his pale flesh, his wisps of white hair. His robe was stained stiff with blood. When he chuckled, his crumbling, rotten teeth were on clear display. "I wouldst think the architect of Count Andluss's murder might have firmer sinew in her belly. Are you a rat, Myreon the Gray Lady, or are you a woman?"

Myreon found her voice, though it sounded very much closer to a rat's than a woman's. "What do you want from me? Why do you talk like that?"

"I speak in the manner of the ancients, as is fitting for a sorcerer. I keep to the old ways, and the old ways keep." The necromancer gestured for Myreon to emerge from her hiding place. "As for you, I wish only your friendship. Come."

Myreon slowly crawled out of the crevice and into the chamber. On the stone slab closest to her, the headless body of the Defender was laid out, his armor set aside and his body split down the center—gutted like a fish. Myreon's gorge rose and she fell to her knees, vomiting.

The necromancer stood over her, looking down—though Myreon could not say how he *saw* anything. The man looked blind. "This Defender, over whom you weep, did beat and scorn you, and would have slain you without remorse. And yet you spill bile for him. Why?"

"What . . . what did you do to him?"

"Speak you of the mindfire?" The necromancer motioned toward the pyre of yellow fire pouring from the crack in the dead man's skull. "The Warlock Kings of old did light their cities with the thoughts and dreams of criminals. A head taken alive from a man's still-living body, its passions and terrors swollen to their zenith, and then lit aflame with sorcerous power. It shall burn for months, consuming his soul in bright fire. So was Ghola, city of Rhadnost the Undying, lit in the darkest winters, a jewel of the world now lost."

Myreon somehow felt even *worse*, now that she knew. "That sorcery is . . . it's forbidden. Has been for ages. It's horrible."

The necromancer reached down with a scarecrow hand, pulled Myreon to her feet. "Horror? *Horror?* You speak without thought or wisdom, Magus. How is this more horrible than a milkmaid beheaded? Than a child doomed to starve for a lord's vanity? Than a father murdered in his own bed for the greed of a landlord?"

Myreon gasped. "How . . . how did you know about my father?"

"Though blind, I see much." The necromancer grinned his horrible, moldy grin. "The eyes of my servants are many places. Through them I am given unblinking sight, unending reach. No one, friend Myreon, evades the gaze of the dead."

Myreon straightened her clothing and tried to shake the vomit and scum off her cloak. "You saved me. How? Why?"

"I have watched your apprentices since you began your tutelage. Moreoever, my esteemed colleagues and I have watched you closely for some years." The necromancer turned and motioned for her to follow. Myreon did, but at a distance. All around her, the awful stench of decay stifled her breath and stung her eyes. She kept her gaze on the ground just behind the necromancer's robe, knowing what she might see on the other tables—during her career as a Defender, she had taken down more than a few necromancers, and their lairs were always a den of nightmares. Her peripheral vision caught glimpses of human bodies in various states of dissection; bowls of blood and viscera, slowly congealing in the damp, foul air; bones cobbled together with sinew and silver pegs; piles of skulls, their teeth gleaming in the sickly mindfire-light. Myreon felt the bile rising again, but she fought it back. *Get a hold of yourself, woman!*

"For too long have the good people of Eretheria been ruled by the vain and greedy," the necromancer was saying. "You understand this better than most. You have journeyed far and wide in this city and in the provinces beyond—I have heard your tales through the ears of dead men; your legend has been spoken to me by the many tongues of the grave. You are the Dark Mage, the Gray Lady—champion of the poor, enemy of the nobility. I salute you."

"That doesn't answer my question." This wasn't a mere hedge wizard or dabbler—being able to use the eyes and ears of dead bodies as spies took real, formal sorcerous training. To her knowledge, there were only a handful of places such knowledge could even be taught: the Kalsaari Empire and the Eastern Archipelago—both half a world away—and the Sorcerous League. It was a secret society of disaffected wizards and sorcerers, opponents to the rigid order and regulation of the Defenders and the Arcanostrum they served. Up until a few years ago, Myreon had thought them a myth. Now she knew different, but this would be only the third member she had met in person.

The necromancer led them through a leaning arch into another chamber, this one larger still—a natural formation into which the light of early dawn poured through some tiny crack far above. The light reflected off dark, cold water and sparkled off quartz deposits scattered about the cave, making the walls seem alive with magic. "I am a creature of utmost gravity, friend Myreon. I sympathize with your cause—the peerage are a corrupt abomination and must be destroyed if any of us are to be free."

Myreon nodded slowly, trying to gauge the ley of the chamber—it was surprisingly balanced, given its location underground. Ideal sorcerous ritual space. "I don't want violence. I've never wanted that."

"The virtuous are at the mercy of the wicked in all things. Think you that the violence has ended? No, no—it has only begun. You wouldst stand by idly

as the slaughter of innocents continues?" The necromancer's chuckle was dusty as old bones. "I think not.
Not you."

Myreon frowned. She wanted to protest, but could
not think of the words. All she could see was Bree's
head on a pole, one pretty eye pecked out, the other
open, searching for her. Believing in her. Hoping
she would be saved. The thought made Myreon feel
sicker than any thousand dissected corpses, than any
million gallons of blood. She had tried to hide, tried
to protect them. She had been so *careful*.

And it had all been for nothing.

The necromancer's blind eyes were turned toward
her, his head cocked. He was . . . listening to her. To
how she breathed, she realized. "It is the common
thought that the art of necromancy is the province
of a wicked heart. It is not true. Though I am cast out
by the realms built by thy enemies and mine own—
the Keeper of the so-called Balance and his wretched
Defenders—I cannot watch the weak starve so that
the mighty might feast. You have my deepest sympa-
thies for the loss of your apprentices."

Myreon took a deep, shuddering breath. How
odd, that his words would make her feel better. It
sharpened her suspicions. She looked at him closely.
"Thank you, sir, but I'm afraid I don't understand
what you want with me. More directly, what does the
League want with me?"

"Well spoken." The necromancer nodded slowly.

"I have been given the weighty honor, Magus Myreon, to once more make you an offer of assistance."

Myreon stopped in her tracks. "Assistance?"

The necromancer had begun to wind his way up the side of the cavern along a narrow track. He stopped. "Yes. Your revolution, if it is to succeed, needs succor."

Myreon frowned. "You . . . . you would help me—help *us*—fight? What does the League get in exchange?"

Now the necromancer laughed—a raspy, dry thing, like leaves in the wind. "Get? Get! Ah, friend Myreon, is it not obvious?"

"Humor me."

The necromancer produced a scroll tube from the sleeve of his robe and passed it to her. "We get *you*."

Myreon carefully slid the contents of the scroll tube into her hand and gingerly unfurled the pages.

It was a contract.

The Sorcerous League—that secret conspiracy of black wizards, necromancers, and wild sorcery—was offering her a membership.

CHAPTER 25

PARTY CRASHERS

On the evening of the Blue Party, the coaches lined up along Crown Avenue for blocks. Everyone—every title-bearing peer, from the lowest of landless hedge knights to the mighty Counts themselves—were dressed in their finest, their masks firmly in place, ready to enjoy this final event before the spring campaigns saw them return to their provincial homes to defend their birthrights against the very people they would be dancing with tonight.

Artus peered out the window of their rented coach, looking at the palace, lit up and shining on the shores of the lake. "You know what I can't believe?"

Tyvian adjusted Artus's ruff and straightened his

doublet. It was of a vibrant royal blue—a message so obvious it would be like a thunderclap. "What is that, Artus?"

Artus jerked a thumb at Sir Damon, who was sitting opposite them both and dressed in a relatively pedestrian doublet, breeches, and powdered wig, a blue armband on one arm and a black one on the other. "So, all this time—after *all that trouble*—all we needed to do to get in this party was to ask *Damon* to invite us?"

Sir Damon raised a hand. "I'd still like to point out that I'm not *technically* permitted to bring guests I'm not married to."

Tyvian nodded. "Which is why I've taken the liberty to draw up documents of marriage." He pulled a pair of scrolls from a pocket in his greatcoat. "Sign here and here, please." Tyvian held out an autoquill.

Sir Damon goggled at the papers. "But . . . but *sir*! We . . . we can't be *married*!"

Tyvian snorted. "And why the hell not? These documents are perfectly in order—I've already had them witnessed by a shepherd of Hann."

Artus looked at them. "How'd you do that, anyway?"

"Your weight in gold marks," Tyvian replied. "I told him that it was for some lovely gentlemen whose names I'd fill in later. He didn't ask too many questions, Hann bless his greedy, open-minded little heart."

Sir Damon took off his wig and dabbed at his sweating head. "But I don't *want* to marry either of you gentlemen—let alone *both*!"

Tyvian snapped his fingers to focus the knight's attention. "Look, Damon, the wards around that palace will not permit uninvited persons to step on the grounds. The *only* reason we're *technically* marrying you is so you can therefore invite us both to the Blue Party and we can get in so that I can get to the throne room and do what must be done. That's it. I promise there will be no actual romance involved."

Sir Damon sighed. "And . . . if I do this, you'll tell me what became of Lady Hool?"

Tyvian nodded, still holding out the quill. "Yes."

"And you're certain she's safe," the knight demanded, looking Tyvian in the eye.

Tyvian didn't waver. "Safer than she is with me and Artus. By a long shot."

Artus grunted and looked back out the window. The boy was still sulking.

Sir Damon sighed and took the autoquill. A few penstrokes later and they were officially polygamists. "How do you know so much about the palace wards, anyway?"

Tyvian shrugged, rolling up the scrolls and slipping them back into his coat. "Last time I infiltrated the Blue Party, I robbed Countess Ousienne of the Star of Rolonne."

Sir Damon's jaw hit the floor. "That was . . . *you*?"

Tyvian nodded, letting his mind drift back. "I pawned it in Tasis for a king's ransom. I bought my flat in Freegate with that money. And a deathcaster, to boot. Damned useful thing . . ." He looked over at Artus. ". . . until *somebody* lost it on an exploding spirit engine."

Artus snorted. "The exploding part was your idea, not mine."

Sir Damon shook his head, his eyes wide. "You fellows have lived *quite* the life, haven't you?"

Artus shrugged. "It ain't as glamourous as it looks. I get stabbed pretty regular. And sometimes have to marry two men."

Tyvian touched where the firepike bolt had singed him. It was still tender. "Risks of the business."

Slowly, the procession of coaches filed through the twenty-foot-tall gates of the palace and rolled along a road through the pastoral gardens that formed the front lawn. The great courtyard of the Peregrine Palace was enclosed on three sides by soaring, buttressed buildings, each a hundred feet high and longer than any single building Artus had ever seen. They were made of gray-white stone with royal blue roofs, and from them rose spires and turrets that flew the banners of all the Great Houses in equal proportion. Ahead of them the gates stood open—thirty feet tall, each door probably weighing multiple tons—and beyond them was a cavernous hall. Pillars of mageglass and silver held aloft a vaulted ceiling of limestone and alabaster, all carved with falcon and raptor motifs—falcons in flight, falcons at rest, falcons standing watch, falcons rampant and passant and every other heraldic posture. Twenty-foot-long banners of pure royal blue hung from poles so high up, only sorcery could have possibly placed them there.

The floor was packed with nobility from every house, all of them wearing some shade of blue—a symbol of unity, of nationhood. They also wore some kind of black, as a sign of mourning for the deceased Count Andluss. Tyvian found both sentiments deeply ironic.

"We made it onto the grounds," Artus said. "So, I guess your marriage thing worked."

"Please, sir," Sir Damon broke in, "I've fulfilled my part of the bargain."

Tyvian nodded. Better to have the limp noodle out of the way, anyway. "Lady Hool and her son Brana have left the city, probably heading north. They left yesterday night."

Sir Damon nodded. "Then, sir, I must take my leave." He held out a hand. "I wish you luck on your quest."

Tyvian took his hand and shook it hard. "And you on yours, sir."

Sir Damon opened the door and set off on foot, walking back toward the palace gates.

Artus frowned. "What was that all about?"

Tyvian shrugged. "I know. And to think we *married* that man."

The coach stopped and a servant opened the door. At most Eretherian parties, there would be another servant with a guest list and a third one to announce their arrival, but the Blue Party was supposed to be more egalitarian than that.

Tyvian slipped his mask into place. "Keep an eye out for Defenders. A fair number of people in here will be shrouded, so expect the unexpected," Tyvian cautioned.

Artus sighed, fiddling with his ruff. "I miss Brana already."

Tyvian slapped Artus's hand away. "Brana is a gnoll, Artus, and a young one, at that. He belongs with his mother and he does not belong here with us. That's enough of your moping. Stay on task. If we do this right, we can end this all *tonight*."

"And then maybe Hool will come back."

"Sure," Tyvian said, shrugging. "You never know."

He did know, though. Hool, he was sure, was already miles outside of the city, headed who knew where, her pup by her side. And good for her, too. Somebody should get out of this mess he called his life in one piece. It sure as hell couldn't be him.

Tyvian got out of the coach and adjusted his own clothing. He had gone for a foreign style—a Saldorian waistcoat and cravat, a long greatcoat over his shoulders, and a tall hat featuring an illusory castle tower with white doves flying about it. The fabric was all done in royal blue as well with periwinkle embroidery. He had a crystal-topped swagger cane, too, just to complete the look of a foreign nobleman. "There. Ready?"

"As I'll ever be," Artus grumbled, looking at the sea of lace and ostrich feathers before them.

And in they went.

There were at least seven hundred guests, not counting all the servants, so just getting inside was a bit of a challenge, as they found themselves pressed against legions of masked peers. Not everybody was going in a uniform direction either, and, given the vagaries of Eretherian etiquette, Tyvian and Artus had to keep bowing and politely waving people past them. Progress through the gallery's atrium into its main hall was agonizingly slow—what should have taken five seconds took ten minutes. It really didn't matter, though. They had been noticed, and word was being passed.

Artus didn't miss it either. "They're talking about us." He nodded toward a group of ladies, whose eyes were locked on them while their fans obscured their mouths—whispering among themselves. There were others, too. Word was spreading.

"How do they know who we are?" Artus asked. "We're wearing masks and hats and wigs and everything."

Tyvian tapped Artus's doublet. "We're wearing royal blue. We're self-identifying."

"Why?" Artus looked down at his clothes. "What's royal blue mean?"

Tyvian sighed. "Think about it for ten seconds, will you?"

A gap opened, and they managed to slip out of the atrium and into the main hall. As the center was given over to dancing, the crowd of people around the edges of the hall was dense—much of it servants, too, who somehow managed to maneuver plates of hors d'oeuvres around each other and all the guests without spilling a thing. One of them paused in front of Artus. "Silver, monsieur?"

On the plate were pieces of silver, beaten wafer-thin and coated in a thin, clear syrup. Artus gaped at it. "To eat?"

Tyvian rolled his eyes. "Stop acting the provincial, Artus. Silver wafers are cheaper than caviar, you know."

"But . . . but . . . it's *money*, not food!"

Tyvian shrugged, scanning the crowd. "These people have so much of both they scarcely pay attention to either one. Now, focus—who do you see?"

Artus nodded toward a high chair halfway down the hall. "There's the Countess of Davram—nasty old bitch."

Tyvian winced. "Artus, we're being watched, remember? These people can all read lips."

Artus stood on his tiptoes. Tyvian realized that, at some point in the recent past, Artus had become noticeably taller than he was. *When the hell did that happen?*

"I think I see Count Duren of Vora . . . and Count Yvert of Camis—they're in the corner over there, sharing some wine."

Tyvian slipped past a few ladies, who curtsied to him as he went. "Any sign of Ousienne of Hadda? Or Sahand?"

"Nope," Artus said, his attention distracted by a beautiful woman in white passing by.

Tyvian nudged Artus. "Try to pay attention, okay? We'd better split up. You remember the plan, correct?"

Artus tore his eyes from the passing beauty. He was blushing. "Find the counts, tell them you're planning to make your claim tonight, hand them your note, then tail them and see what they do."

Tyvian nodded. "And we get out of here before the Defenders crash the party looking for us. Any questions?" Artus shook his head. Tyvian clapped his hands together. "Right—let's go."

Artus slipped into the crowd and disappeared after a few steps—not even Tyvian could pick him out. *Thank the gods the boy has learned something.*

In contrast, Tyvian intended to be conspicuous. The game was a relatively simple one—he needed to renounce tonight. To do that, he needed quorum in the Congress—in the throne room. To get quorum without a patron to drum up support (which had been his initial plan), he needed all of the counts present to have an immediate reason to get to the floor of the Congress, and so he'd written four letters, each of them explaining he was about to do what that count probably didn't want him to. This would cause them to rush into the throne room to stop him, thereby giving him his quorum. Assuming everything went to plan.

"Excuse me, sir." A woman took him by the hand. "Might I have this dance?" Her grip was strong—not the light grip of an Eretherian lady at all. She pulled Tyvian toward her. Between the grip and her slight stature, Tyvian knew exactly who it was he was about to dance with.

Tyvian caught her other arm by the wrist by instinct and kept himself a hand's breadth from her body. "Hello, Adatha."

She was wearing black and silver—going rather overboard on the "mourning" request, only rendered risqué by the plunging neckline and the slit cut up the edge of her gown to above the knee. Hers was not a ball gown at all—it was designed to be moved in. Her mask was a simple black Colombina with a crimson feather attached to one corner and diamonds dotting the edges. The mask had only one eye-socket. "Hello, Tyvian." She tried to press close to him.

Tyvian retreated, and so they began to dance. "Still working for Velia Hesswyn?"

Voth laughed. "Sadly for you, yes."

Tyvian frowned as they spun, but he kept his hand firmly on her wrist. "Why would I be sad? It isn't every day a beautiful woman throws herself at me."

Voth twisted in his grip, so Tyvian spun her and they wound up back where they started. Voth was still grinning. "It's sad because this is to be your last dance, darling."

Tyvian arched his eyebrows, which was no doubt lost beneath the mask. "Really?"

Voth advanced again, and Tyvian retreated, letting her lead. They passed through and between several different couples, also lazily twirling to the music. Voth tried again to get close, but Tyvian turned her momentum into a full extension of her arm, so that they stood connected only by his grip on her wrist. Then he saw it, glinting in the lamp light: a gold ring on her middle finger—a gold ring with a needle extended from its bottom edge.

A poison needle.

Voth spun back into his arms, trying to twist her wrist out of his grip, but Tyvian bent her back and dipped her low, her poison ring still held well away from his body. Voth laughed. "This is going to be fun, isn't it?"

Tyvian grinned, despite himself. "Trying to kill me always is."

CHAPTER 26

LAST DANCE

Artus sighed and straightened his doublet again—the damned thing kept riding up. "Okay, so here it goes—"

Artus dove back into the crowd. His nostrils were assailed by scores of different perfumes, combining to make the dance floor one big olfactory fog. Powdered wigs and masked people, feathers and fans made up the majority of his vision. He stood on tiptoes, just to get a fix on Countess Velia of Davram. There she was, still on the edge, still in her high chair. He pressed forward through the throng, squeezing between dames and knights with a few strategic apologies to keep from being kicked. Every once in a while he stood up on tip-toe to get his bearings again, and then dove back in, making steady progress toward the woman in the high chair—his navigating star.

A person put a hand on his shoulder. "Artus? Is that you?"

Artus turned. It was a girl, but between the wig and the golden, feather-topped mask, he couldn't guess who it was. "Yes?"

She giggled. "I knew it! I'd know those shoulders anywhere!" She leaned in close and whispered in his ear. "It's me—Elora."

"Oh. Uh . . . hi. Nice to see you." He tried to turn away and she pulled him back.

"I'm *so* sorry about the salon. When I heard your house was attacked, I was so worried!" She wrapped her arms around him in a hug, resting her head on his shoulder. "I knew then I had been foolish. I'm so relieved you're safe."

Artus placed his arms lightly on her back. "Umm . . . are you sure you should hug me so close. I mean . . ."

Elora giggled and pressed closer to him. "Don't be silly! It's the Blue Party! Nobody even knows who we *are!*"

"Really? 'Cause I've kinda found almost everybody knows who everybody els—*mmphhfff* . . ." Elora kissed him, pulling him close. Artus felt like he couldn't breathe.

She let him go and smiled up at him. "Can you forgive me? Please?"

"I've really got important things to do, so . . ." Artus tried to pull away, but she kept hold of his hands.

"We could spend the whole night together! The unmasking won't be for hours! Come on, Artus." The eyes behind her mask sparkled with mischief. "We could have a lot of fun, you know."

Artus looked over his shoulder. Countess Velia was no more than five paces away. "Uhhh . . . well . . ."

"Artus!" Another girl—this one willowy and graceful in a lacy gown that tread perilously close to being white, but somehow managed to be sunny yellow, instead—had her hands on her hips in the universal sign of being angry at him. "What are you doing?"

Artus blinked. "I? Me? I was just trying to—"

"Oh please, Michelle!" Elora sneered. "Artus doesn't have time for bony little things like you! If he kissed you, he might choke."

Michelle stiffened and flipped open her fan. Her voice was icy calm. "Funny. He didn't seem to mind at the salon. Did you, Artus?"

"What?" Elora stared at him. "Did you? Is this true?"

Artus's mouth flopped open, but only made a honking sound. "Uhhh . . . see . . . I didn't know that . . . well . . ."

Michelle cut between him and Elora. "He sees right through you, Elora. What, do you think if you hook him, he'll make you princess? Artus isn't like that." She slid an arm through Artus's and smiled up at him. "He'll only marry for true love."

Artus's eyes widened. "True . . . true *what*?"

Michelle leaned against him. "Tell her. Tell her how you and I kissed in the street, beneath the spring sky."

Elora's lower cheeks were turning red. Her mouth was fixed into a firm line. "You *bastard*!"

And she slugged him in the stomach.

Artus, who had spent almost three years being sucker-punched by a gnoll, took the hit well—it barely hurt. It was, however, rather shocking. "What the hell?"

Elora had him by the collar. She was shouting. "You listen to me, Artus from nowhere! You and I are going to be married, understand? *Married!*"

Michelle pushed Elora off him. "Leave him alone! He's too good for a vulture like you!"

For the briefest instant, Artus found himself free of entanglement. He dove into the crowd. *Kroth's teeth!* He ran a hand through his hair. *What was that all about?*

He stopped. He thought about it. What *was* that all about? *Think like Tyvian . . .*

Married, Elora had said—not lovers, *married*. Why would she be so hell-bent on marrying him? He thought back to all their conversations—there had only really been three or four of them, altogether, even though he was pretty certain she had been coming to the House of Eddon for months before she introduced herself on that night . . .

Artus's mouth formed into a perfect O as everything slid into place. *She thinks I'm going to be a prince!* That was it—that was literally all she cared about. Gods, she had talked about it as her *job*—"bring honor to my house." What could be more honorable than marrying a prince? She, Valen, Ethick—they had all tried to play him. Butter him up, make him their pal . . . just so Elora could get her hooks into him. It was all so obvious, he felt like an idiot for not realizing it.

Artus shook his head. There was more to it—there had to be—but he couldn't think about it right now. He needed to get the messages to the counts, and quick, before Tyvian and he wound up with firepikes in their faces. He had already caught a glimpse of a magestaff winding through the crowd—the Defenders were here.

Artus threw caution to the wind and was a bit more forceful heading to Countess Velia's side. He pushed a few people aside, stepped on a few toes, and then he was there. She was in her chair, elevated a half head above Artus, peering through a viewing glass mounted on a copper wire. He bowed. "Your Grace."

Velia cupped her hand and motioned him to rise. "Yes? Who are you?"

"Artus of Eddon." He pulled the letter from the pockets in his cape. "I have a message for you from my uncle, Waymar."

She peered down at it. "Very well—you may present it to me. Though your lack of decorum reflects poorly upon your uncle."

Artus had a few things he wanted to say to that, but couldn't say any of them in public, so he gave her the letter and sought to slip away again. He did not. Instead he ran full tilt into Valen Hesswyn. He knew who he was immediately—he wasn't wearing a mask anymore.

Artus stepped back. Somebody had worked a lot of glamours on Valen's face to hide the bruises Artus had left there, and they hadn't quite pulled it off. The young man's eyes were bloodshot and angry. "Valen," he began, but he didn't get to finish.

Valen slapped him with a glove. "*That* was for my cousin Elora, whom you have dishonored. And *this* . . ." He slapped him again. ". . . is for my friend Ethick, whom you have also dishonored, and *this*—"

He tried to slap Artus again, but Artus ducked. "I get it—we're in a duel, right?"

"The day after tomorrow, swords—first blood. Take off your mask—there should be witnesses," Valen growled.

Behind Valen, his staff poking above the heads of

the crowd, Mage Defender Argus Androlli looked in Artus's direction. He froze. He couldn't take off his mask—not now. "Uhhh . . . in just a second."

Valen looked alarmed. "This . . . this is a matter of *honor*, you foreign dog!"

Androlli cocked his head and headed toward them. "Excuse me? One moment, gentlemen . . ."

Artus nodded, half speaking to both Valen and Androlli. "Oh. Okay." He picked up Valen's glove, weighed it.

Then he turned and ran off with it. Behind him, he heard Valen gasp. "Hey! Hey, you can't do that!"

Tyvian danced with Adatha Voth with as much concentration as he had spent in any duel in his life. He had the viper by the head—let go of her wrist, even for an instant, and he was as good as dead. Draw attention to her, and the Defenders would be here in the blink of an eye. No—he had been lucky to grab her wrist when he had. Now, if she wanted to make the kill, she needed to pretend to dance with him and, if he wanted to escape, he needed to find a way to neutralize her without causing a fuss.

"How long can you keep this up, exactly?" Voth whispered in his ear as he dipped her over one knee again.

"My stamina, my dear, has never been in doubt." Tyvian smiled. "You, however, are in over your head."

Voth laughed. "Short jokes—how original." She flexed her forearm within his grip. "I can't feel my fingers."

They spun, Voth's good hand wrapped around his waist. "That *is* the general idea," Tyvian said. "So, what's Davram's angle, here?"

Voth tried again to press her trapped hand downwards. Tyvian, again, redirected her momentum into a spin. Her gown flared outward as he guided her. One more complicated maneuver, and she was pressed up against him again. Their lips almost touched. "Please, Tyvian—I'm a professional. You understand, I'm sure."

"Actually I don't." Tyvian tried to bend her arm back toward her face, which only pushed her backward. "I've done all my killing recreationally, so far."

When they were right beside the orchestra, Voth let herself fall into a dip and Tyvian was obliged to catch her. One of her legs snaked between his and tried to kick him in the groin, but he snapped his knees together to trap her there. They stayed there for a moment, awkwardly counterbalanced. Grimacing, Tyvian looked up to see he was eyeball-to-eyeball with the concert master. "Maestro."

The man curled his moustache and smiled knowingly. "Signor," he said, "I have just the dance for you and your love." He raised his baton. *"Revien Nu Kassar!"*

The first few bars of the dance were enough to

clear the floor. Tyvian knew the dance, of course—it was probably his favorite. Intense, powerful, passionate, the *Revien Nu Kassar* was the dance of lovers, their bodies pressed closely together, cheek to cheek, heart-to-heart, legs intertwined. Of course, he had hitherto only danced it with a woman he was intending to bed. Not kill.

Voth smiled at him. "Your move, smuggler."

"No doubt." Tyvian grinned back at Voth and, pulling her up, flung her across the dance floor. She spun gracefully, sliding like a top and stopping right on the beat, her shoes clapping to the floor in unison, her arms raised. An open space had formed around them. The eyes of hundreds of Eretherian nobility watched their every move from behind colorful fans and over the rims of goblets.

The strings thrummed with heartbeat intensity as he and Voth came together. At this point in the dance, they were to join. Amateurs who danced the *Revien* simply clasped fingers like children holding hands. A true *Revien* was supposed to be more than that—it was supposed to be sensual, breathtaking in its passion. This one, Tyvian decided, would be no exception.

Voth swung in with her left hand, aiming to scrape his arm or hand. Tyvian saw it coming. He spun his right side away from her—she missed—and then he caught her from behind, his left hand locking down on her left wrist and snaking up to envelop her whole hand. If Voth were a weaker person, he might have been able to crush her hand right there and press the deadly needle against her own palm, but Voth was not weak. She stuck her middle finger straight out, so any attempt to crush or break her hand would have brought his own thumb too close to the needle. She gasped as he pulled her back against him. They were cheek to cheek, with Tyvian behind and her in front. She put her free hand up and rested it against his cheek.

Their audience applauded.

They danced across the floor, their steps mutually trying to trip the other, but without making it *look* like they were trying to trip the other, resulting in what looked a lot like very complicated footwork. When they got to the edge of the crowd, another shift would have to take place. Another chance for Voth to slash him.

The end of the dance floor. Voth flew away from him, trying to get her hand loose, but Tyvian kept control of her arm, sliding his hand down and pushing her away before she could swipe back at him. When she spun around, he was there. He ducked her slash at his face and pulled her toward him, so her arm was sent over his shoulder. She wrapped her hand down, ready to pierce the back of his skull, but Tyvian's hand was there to meet it. He caught her wrist again, this time just next to his left ear, and pulled her so she could get her fingers close enough to scratch his face.

His other hand caught her knee and, with her leg up around his hip, he dragged her across the floor again as the music swelled to its zenith.

He and Voth were eye-to-eye, nose to nose. "Kiss me, Tyvian. One last time before you die."

Tyvian could feel her heart beating—fast and steady, like a hunting cat on the chase. Her lips were there, slightly parted, soft and pink and perfect. He closed his mouth. "Sorry, Adatha," he said. "That first time was a mistake."

She answered with a wry grin, "Your loss, Reldamar."

Around them, the crowd hung on their every movement. Women were fanning themselves, men stood motionless, their eyes burning with envy. There were at least two more passes in the dance. Tyvian's luck was not going to hold out for that long. He had to shift tactics.

At the edge of the dance floor, Tyvian threw Voth off him, raking his right hand across the back of her left as he did. She spun beautifully and stopped, elegant as a bird of prey. Her good eye glowed with anticipation.

They closed again. Tyvian reached for her hand, but she disengaged—a feint!—and spun, much faster than before. Tyvian tried to retreat, tried to block—he couldn't; she was too fast. She slapped him across the cheek, grinning with victory. Her hand clapped against his face like a peal of thunder.

But there was no prick. No blood. Voth held up her hand.

There was no ring.

The orchestra fell silent. Everyone stared as Tyvian straightened from the savage blow, a handprint glowing on his cheek. "Looking for this?" He held up his right hand. There, held between thumb and forefinger, was Voth's poison ring.

Voth looked at him for a long moment. The hall was silent. Then, she laughed—long and hard. "Well played, sir." She curtsied. "Until we meet again."

And that was when the Defenders stormed the dance floor, shouting and pointing firepikes and flashing their armor all over the place. Tyvian stood still, careful not to provoke an attack, and watched Adatha Voth melt into the crowd, people stepping out of the way as she went. "What a woman," he breathed.

CHAPTER 27

MASQUERADE'S END

Tyvian didn't bother trying to escape the cordon of Defenders that was forming around him. There was something familiar about the experience—nostalgic, even. He found himself smiling. It wasn't that he was enjoying it, precisely. He just felt like his old self again.

A troop of Defenders invading an Eretherian party would have been enough to cause a stir at any time. A troop of Defenders invading *this* party was downright scandalous. The assembled peerage was visibly shocked, masks notwithstanding. Indignant protests and theatrical outrage spread through the assembly. The Defenders—who, per regulations, could not be native Eretherians and serve in Eretheria—ignored it all. They stayed focused on Tyvian, their visors down and their firepikes lit.

Argus Androlli was dressed in the uniform gray robes and mageglass helmet of a Mage Defender, his staff held in the crook of one arm. His dimpled grin and fetching five-o'clock shadow was insufficient, however, to hide the Rhondian's unbearable smugness. "Well, well, well—look who we have here."

Tyvian shook his head. "I'm sorry, but do I know you?" The ring gave him a little pinch, but Androlli's smug little grin soured a bit. *Worth it.*

"Don't be coy. Admit you are caught." Androlli flicked his fingers and spoke a word. Tyvian's mask was pulled from his face and dashed on the ground.

Tyvian pointed at the mask's crumbled pieces. "I assume you will pay for that, correct?"

An old man, as wide as he was tall and armored in silver mail, stomped out of an alcove in a pillar. He bore a staff taller than he was and had a white beard that stretched to his knees. "I am the Guardian of Peregrine Palace. None may pass here without my permission! Who disrupts the Blue Party?" He bashed the staff against the floor twice. It made an unusually thunderous booming noise, loud enough to make it seem like the walls should shake. Being mageglass, they did not.

Androlli looked around, as though just realizing what he was in the middle of. He gave the Guardian a stiff, shallow bow. "My apologies, sir. This is Defender business—it will be over shortly."

"No!" The Guardian shouted, "This is a peaceful event! Your invasion is an unspeakable transgression! You must leave at once!"

Androlli's mouth tightened. "We will be on our way, then." He waved to his men. "Take him."

Tyvian rested his hand on the pommel of his sword. "I decline to depart."

The Defenders barely registered his objection, continuing to close in, but with perhaps a bit more caution. Tyvian's reputation preceded him.

The Guardian stepped in front of Tyvian. "If this gentlemen declines to depart, you may not detain him by force."

Androlli rolled his eyes—he'd evidently had enough Eretherian etiquette for one day. He waved his hand and a telekinetic wave shoved the Guardian aside. "And how, exactly, do you propose to stop me?"

The Guardian stood straight, wrapped his thick, hairy fingers around his staff, and pounded against the ground once. From nearby, some women screamed as a ten-foot tall golem of silvered steel stepped out of an alcove, complete with massive, seven-foot sword. "Tread lightly, Mage Defender. I would have words with Master Andair over this."

Androlli frowned. "Then we are at an impasse. If he declines to depart and I may not force *him*, then I decline to depart and you may not force *me*. Is that not correct?"

The Guardian tugged at his white beard, his bushy eyebrows pressed together, but he said nothing. Androlli had him there.

At this point, the counts had found their way to the heart of the ruckus. There was Velia Hesswyn in her sedan chair; Countess Ousienne on the arm of her young husband, Count Duren of Vora, his massive moustache so broad and sharp it could be considered a weapon; and Count Yvert of Camis, a skinny little old man in a wig so large, it looked as though he were being eaten by a llama. It was he who spoke first. "Who is this impostor—this foreigner wearing *le bleu roi?*"

Ignoring Yvert, Duren waved a letter in the air. "What is the meaning of this?" *Good*, Tyvian thought, *Artus found them all.*

Androlli looked at the counts. "This man is a criminal!"

Tyvian *tsked*. "I don't believe that's ever been proven in a court of law."

Androlli rounded on him. "Only because you *set the courtroom on fire!*"

"I set *myself* on fire," Tyvian said, shrugging. "The courtroom was a bonus."

"It matters not what he has or has not done!" the Guardian said. "As a guest, he may not be detained."

Androlli's face darkened. "Per ancient tradition and law, the Defenders of the Balance have jurisdiction to enforce the laws over all the lands of Eretheria, and no man—count or otherwise—may negate that right!"

Tyvian nodded. "Yes, but as we've just established, your attempt to grab me here, in the middle of the Blue Party, is expressly *illegal*. Not to mention rude."

Androlli's face turned the exact same color red as it had when Tyvian had invalidated his testimony in Keeper's Court in Saldor over a year ago. It filled Tyvian with unspeakable joy. Androlli growled, "When they realize who you are, these people won't protect you!"

"Well?" Count Yvert of Camis waved his cane at Tyvian. "*Who* is he?"

A rough and dreadfully familiar voice boomed out from the other side of the hall. "*He* is Tyvian Reldamar—international smuggler, criminal, and killer. And I finally have him right where I want him."

Tyvian felt a chill in the pit of his stomach. "Banric Sahand."

Sahand walked to the front of the crowd, with people fairly leaping to get out of his way. His mask was a full-face Volto of a laughing demon. He cast it aside as he came closer and folded his massive arms. "Now, let's watch you weasel out of *this* one, Reldamar."

The other counts present seemed visibly uncomfortable in Sahand's presence, as did Androlli. Nobody said anything, though. Tyvian decided to fill the void. "You, sir, are on foreign soil in violation of the Treaty of Calassa." He looked at Androlli. "Shouldn't you be arresting *him?*"

"Who do you think told him you'd be here?" Sahand laughed at him. "No, young Argus there knows what he's doing."

Tyvian cocked his head to one side. "So, you were expecting me?"

Sahand spread his hands. "A trap for a trap, wouldn't you agree? You destroy my bid for glory, and now I destroy *yours.*"

Gods, why does everyone think I want to be king?

Everyone stared. It seemed as though the party had been forgotten by now—the courtroom drama playing out around the central dance floor was better entertainment than any celebration of national unity.

Tyvian knew he didn't have long. The Guardian would kick him out *eventually*, and then he was caught. Androlli wasn't stupid either—he'd petrify him straight away, not bothering with a trial—trials were a Saldorian luxury not often extended to other nations. He had a picture in his head of his petrified self, standing there alone in some out of the way corner of Eretheria, and then Sahand coming along, swinging a stone pick and a mallet . . .

A dark, dark end.

There was, to his mind, only one way out of this.

Sahand grinned at Tyvian. "Yes, you see it now, don't you, Reldamar? Two choices—death now or death later. What will it be?"

Androlli cocked his head. "What? What are you talking about?"

Tyvian knew. "I've got to hand it to you, Sahand—this is quite the setup. You could have just sent assassins to my house, you know."

Sahand laughed. "You'd be expecting them. And with those pet monsters of yours? Ha! I'm not stupid. I can appreciate talent, Reldamar, and you are a talented survivor." He stepped forward and spread his arms to encompass the entire hall. "But *this*? The perfect bait—the perfect trap. Just like your mother, you can't resist the finer things, can you? An ego the size of the ocean is easy enough to lead by the nose."

"It was you started the rumors, then?" Tyvian asked.

"A year of very subtle efforts." Sahand gestured to Tyvian, all alone in a ring of firepikes. "It seems to have worked. A year of work well spent, I think. Don't you?"

Part of him thought to just go with Androlli. How bad could petrification be, anyway? And Myreon owed him one—she'd break him back out. Artus would be there for him, too.

Tyvian shook his head. He couldn't. Hool had a point—how much pain was he going to force others to undergo for his own edification? How much could he really expect them to risk?

But was his other option any better?

Dammit. Myreon was right.

Count Duren of Vora grunted. "I, for one, have no idea what they are talking about."

The Guardian grunted. "It seems . . . in the interest of harmony and that the party may go ahead as planned, I—"

"Wait!" Tyvian shouted. "I hereby declare myself heir to the Falcon Throne, rightful descendant by blood of Perwyn the Noble and Perwynnon the Falcon King, my father!"

The world seemed to gasp all at once. Count Duren turned so red that Tyvian thought he might pop like an engorged tick. "What? *What?*" He pointed at Tyvian. "You, sir, need a sponsor! You can't just storm in here, ruin a party, and then . . . then—"

Countess Ousienne raised her fan. "House Hadda supports the heir."

Interesting . . .

Tyvian pointed at the Guardian. "As a declared and supported heir, I am considered your liege lord until my claim can be substantiated, yes?"

The Guardian seemed to crumple beneath his beard. "Well . . . I . . . yes. Milord."

"Then *you* cannot deny me hospitality by law!" Tyvian rounded on Androlli. "And by the laws of the Arcanostrum, no agent of the Keeper of the Balance may detain or hinder a head of state. Correct?"

Androlli looked ill. "That . . . yes, that is correct."

Tyvian snapped his fingers. "Then get these firepikes out of my way!"

Androlli nodded to his men. The mirror-men withdrew their weapons. "This is only a delay, Reldamar," Androlli said. "Everyone knows you aren't the true heir. Everyone."

Tyvian walked up to Androlli and bowed in the most sarcastic way he knew how. "It is the pawn's prerogative to play the game, Magus."

"This is not a formal declaration!" Count Duren roared.

Tyvian spun on his heel. "I'm on my way to the Congress of Peers *right now*, where I will be declaring presently, whether you are there or not! Enjoy the rest of your party, sir."

Tyvian swept out of the hall—something he found he could do because at least one out of every three people there either bowed or curtsied to him as he passed. He assumed his most regal posture and tried to mentally catalogue those who were paying him respect. It was impossible—there were too many, and most of them were masked. *It hardly matters anyway,* he thought, *since at least half of those people kneeling would sink a dagger in my back as soon as they could do it without being caught. And Ousienne of Hadda would be first in line.*

Yet she sponsored me. What's her game?

As he walked past Sahand, the Mad Prince put a heavy hand on his shoulder and squeezed hard enough to make Tyvian's arm feel numb. "This is what I hoped you'd do." He whispered, loud enough for five people to hear. "Now my revenge will be even sweeter."

Tyvian shook Sahand's slablike hand off him

and continued on his way. Artus appeared from the crowd, somebody's glove in his hand. "What the hell are you doing?"

Tyvian whispered out the side of his mouth. "Just smile and act casual."

They escaped the grand hall via a side door which the Guardian held open for them. As soon as they were through it, it boomed shut behind them.

The Guardian frowned at Tyvian. "Will you ascend tonight?"

Tyvian shook his head. "I have a feeling that would be frowned upon."

The man waddled closer. He had big hands, with fingers so thick he may as well have been wearing gloves. "What they want is of no import. If you are king, you will be able to sit on the throne, and nothing they can say will change that."

Tyvian grimaced. "If I am to sit on the throne, sir, I would like to remain there, alive, for quite some time. What the peerage says can change *that*."

The Guardian stiffened at this comment. His big, hairy ears turned bright red. He said nothing, though. "You and your squire will follow me." He led them down another cavernous hallway, though this one with ceilings only seventy-five feet high or so.

Artus followed Tyvian. "Squire?"

"It means you're my stooge," Tyvian whispered back. The Guardian was about ten paces ahead of them, but the huge, empty hall had a way of echoing.

"Oh." Artus shrugged. "So nothing's changed, then."

The Guardian stopped in front of a small side door in the corridor. He glared at them and gestured with one thick arm. "This way, if you please."

They were now passing through a much smaller passage, but still impressive nevertheless. The white and royal blue motif remained in place, but here were stained-glass windows about eight feet tall, each depicting a haloed figure in armor smiting this or that sinister beast or skeletal warlock. They travelled up a grand staircase past more falcon-carvings and beneath more and more elaborate stained-glass windows until the Guardian opened a small door and gestured them to go inside. "This is the royal antechamber. You have a guest."

"Who?" Tyvian asked. "Do you know them?"

The Guardian frowned. "No one dangerous, I assure you. You are both under my protection."

Tyvian pressed his lips into a flat line. "*Who?*"

"The Lady Lyrelle Reldamar, Earless of Glamourvine, former Archmage of the Ether." With that, the Guardian spun smartly on his heel and marched away, staff in hand.

Tyvian froze, staring at the door handle. His mother. It wasn't a coincidence, of course.

"Tyvian? You okay?"

Tyvian steeled himself. "Not dangerous my arse. Come on."

They went in.

CHAPTER 28

FAMILY REUNION

Artus thought the chamber through the door was cozy, or at least cozy in comparison to the cavernous halls through which they had just come. Another vaulted ceiling of polished stone, but only twelve feet high at its center; three stained-glass windows along one wall, one of which was open to reveal a formal garden beyond and admit the sound of crickets chirping in the late evening. A single silver chandelier hung from the ceiling's capstone, casting the soft white glow of illumite through the room. For furniture there were two large chairs situated before an unlit fireplace and a bench placed before the windows, all carved from pale birchwood and affixed with plush cushions of purple, blue, and gold. In one of the chairs sat Lyrelle Reldamar.

Artus had heard so much about the sorceress's existence yet so little about her nature that he expected to see a woman who was cold and calculating, severe, and probably rather ugly. He had fixed in his head the image of an old widower from his village who was known to whip her horses too much and had no patience for children—she had a face like an old, mean hound dog. Artus expected to see somebody like that, except in nicer clothes.

What he saw instead was a beautiful woman with hair like gold falling in waves over one shoulder and eyes of the sharpest blue. She barely looked old enough to be Tyvian's mother at all. When she smiled, her perfect white teeth somehow outshone the jewels hanging from her neck and wrists and fingers and made her silver gown seem drab by comparison. Somehow, Artus felt like she was smiling at *him* alone, and not both of them. He felt a tickle in his stomach and found himself standing up straighter.

Tyvian seemed notably less impressed. "Well, I hope you're proud of yourself, Mother."

"Don't be so dramatic, Tyvian," Lyrelle said with a laugh. "A few years ago, you would have seen this as the greatest opportunity in your life."

Tyvian snorted and threw himself into the chair across from her. "Yes, but a few years ago I could have robbed, cheated, and stabbed my way out of this once it became unprofitable." He waggled his ring hand at her. "But you boxed me out of that option rather neatly, now didn't you?"

Artus frowned. "Wait, what's your mother have to do with the ring?"

Lyrelle turned her dazzling smile on him. "And you must be Artus. Very pleased to meet you at last."

She extended her hand. Artus took it in a handshake, then froze. "Oh, uh . . . sorry." He awkwardly maneuvered her delicate, thin hand so he could kiss the back of it, and felt the heat rising to his cheeks as he did.

The sorceress beamed at him. "Oh Tyvian, he's perfectly adorable. I can see why you love him."

Both Artus and Tyvian stiffened in unison. "What?"

"Calm down, calm down." She rolled her eyes. "May the gods save all men from themselves, I swear."

Tyvian ran a hand through his hair. "Very well then, Mother—you've met Artus. Any other purpose for your visit? Would you like to kill me yourself, right now, and get this over with?"

Lyrelle sighed and looked at Artus. "You see what he thinks of me? No doubt he's told you horror stories. Have you ever met a man who disdains his mother more?"

Artus found himself grinning at her. "No, ma'am, I haven't. He loves complaining, though."

Lyrelle smiled. "He does, doesn't he?"

"Mother," Tyvian snapped, "stop charming the boy and talk to me."

Lyrelle let her smile drop and focused on Tyvian. "You don't have many of the houses on your side, now do you?"

Tyvian grimaced. "Maybe Hadda, probably only to keep Sahand at bay. The rest of them would probably like to see me publicly embarrassed and then dead, in that order. If I sit on the throne, I'm doomed."

Artus raised his hand, and both Reldamars looked at him. "I thought the whole point was to *not* be king!"

"It was." Tyvian sighed. "But then Sahand got me in a corner—either I declared or you and I would have wound up statues."

Artus scowled. "I keep telling you—me and you, just like old times. We pack a bag, we hop a spirit engine, and we're gone!"

Lyrelle raised an eyebrow at her son. "The boy raises a good point, Tyvian. Why *don't* you just run away?"

Tyvian folded his arms and said nothing.

Artus laughed. "You're nuts! We shoulda just ignored the whole thing from the start! Then Hool would be with us, still, and Brana, too!"

Lyrelle looked at her son long and hard, as though trying to read his mind. Eventually, her expression softened. "Myreon has been very good for you, hasn't she?"

"I do not wish to discuss Myreon at this or any other time with *you*."

Lyrelle smiled broadly. "Artus, Tyvian doesn't want to run away. He is only now realizing that he doesn't want to run away because, for the past week, he has been working very hard to convince himself that he did. But now—right now—he's realized that he's failed."

Tyvian's face contorted into a painful scowl. "May you burn in the deepest pits of hell, woman."

Lyrelle was beaming. She looked triumphant, somehow, as though she had just won a long, hard battle. "That's what I thought."

The Guardian arrived. "The peerage has assembled in the Congress and awaits your pleasure. Your rooms are also ready, my lords. If you will follow me."

Tyvian turned away from Lyrelle. "Let's get this over with, Artus, and then let's get some sleep."

Artus followed, but looked back over his shoulder at Lyrelle. She gave him a wink. "Be seeing you, Artus."

Artus waved good-bye just as Tyvian slammed the door behind them.

The Eretherian Congress of Peers met in the Peregrine Palace's Great Throne Room. It was a circular chamber situated just beside the base of the Empty Tower. Its domed roof was fashioned from translucent mageglass and supposedly inlaid with engravings depicting Hannite religious iconography as well as the images of falcons in flight that was the nation's motif. At the moment, looking up from the polished floor toward the midnight sky, it was too dark to see much of anything. Tyvian couldn't help but take it as a sign. *I'm off the map, now.*

The dais stood along the back edge of the room, ten yards to a side and rising ten feet above the floor, an island of white marble atop a sea of azure blue. The throne looked to be about fifteen feet tall by itself, fashioned, predictably enough, into the image of a bird of prey rising from the floor. Tyvian hadn't been in the palace for more than a single night and already the decor was wearing on him. If, by some odd happenstance, he *were* to become king, a complete renovation would be the first of his royal decrees.

Five great doors entered the Congress, but only four were accessible to the peerage. The fifth opened up behind the throne itself and, as that door was reserved for royal use, no one could go through it. This meant that the five Great Houses of Eretheria would, at times, be forced to enter through the same door as members of a different, rival house. In true Eretherian fashion, there were so many books of laws and customs governing who had to enter which door with whom that they could fill their own library. In point of fact, Tyvian was fairly certain that such a library existed and was located somewhere on the palace grounds.

Between the four broad aisles that ran from the

doors to the dais were benches, much in the manner of very comfortable church pews in which the various nobility of Eretheria were ensconced. As this was a meeting of the Congress in the *midst* of the Blue Party itself, the floor was a riotous mob of liveried servants, banner-waving pages, and powder-wigged nobility. They were all in the midst of shouting at each other at once, it seemed. In a room full of self-important rich people, everyone was very keen on being listened to, but not terribly interested in listening to anyone else. Even as Tyvian stood in the doorway, he saw at least three duels being declared.

The Guardian strode into the hall with an exaggerated gait, lifting his knees high and stamping them down as though stepping over tripwires, and then bashed his staff against the floor four times. "The Palace recognizes Tyvian Reldamar of Saldor, Declared Aspirant, who shall address the Congress!"

A uniform hush fell over the assembly. As one, they all turned to stare at him. Fans were raised to lips so that whispers could be spread. Viewing glasses and other such magecraft were stuffed into eye-sockets, all to get a better look at him. Tyvian knew that there were men that would crumple before such scrutiny. Tyvian was no such person. He beamed at them. "Good evening, everyone!"

Tyvian headed down one of the broad aisles that led from the doors to the dais as though he had been doing it all his life, though forcing himself to limp just enough to make himself look vulnerable. As he went, he told himself that the giant, raptor-esque chair at the end wasn't a symbol of impending doom but rather an insignificant piece of furniture one kept in a familiar room—no more notable than an armoire or divan.

All I'd have to do is sit in that chair and, if I wasn't zapped into ash, I'd be king. Just like that. The thought was perverse. It was, he realized, the same thought coursing through the minds of a few hundred peers, earls, viscounts, and counts who watched his every step with white lips—except a great many of them were rooting for the zapping.

Tyvian arrived at the base of the dais, climbed the first stair, then the second, then the third—each step was met with gasps from the assembly. When he was a mere step from the throne, he raised one more foot. He let it hang there, savoring the intake of breath he heard behind him. Then he returned the foot next to its fellow and turned around to find himself with a fine view of all the persons who would plot and conspire to either destroy him or empower him over the next few days.

Tyvian cleared his throat and noted how it echoed—the acoustics in here were good. "Well, let's get this over with, shall we? Standing before a congress of my peers, I formally declare myself, Tyvian Reldamar, the heir to the Falcon Throne and son to Perwynnon, the late King of Eretheria."

"There can be no recognition without ascension!" Count Yvert shouted, to a smattering of applause by the assembled Camis peers.

Tyvian shrugged and jerked a thumb at the throne just behind him. "Would you like me to ascend now, Your Grace?"

Yvert's mouth hung open, then clapped closed, then hovered in an in-between state before he finally said, "If it pleases you, sir. I merely was pointing out an error in protocol."

Countess Ousienne of Hadda fluttered a fan as she rose. Her husband next to her was holding a small dog that yapped in Tyvian's direction. "House Hadda formally endorses the heir's declaration, but asks that he refrain from ascension until the complex matter of his kingdom's administration is discussed."

My, but does that woman know her business. Tyvian bowed to her, but not too deeply. "This seems eminently reasonable. Any present who endorse my declaration are welcome to have a part in such meetings."

Countess Ousienne grinned at his countermove, even as the furor erupted through the great hall. By being the first to sit at his side, Ousienne was positioning her house as having primacy in a theoretical kingdom ruled by Tyvian. By turning the offer around and extending it to everyone, he made it clear that anybody who joined him would be given similar treatment. But, of course, they would be second in line for the spoils.

To their credit, none of the other Counts were really falling over each other to swear their support. Tyvian noted a fairly forceful note of support from some freeholdings, border knights, and lesser peers, but what they wanted had very little to do with what actually happened in Eretheria. Those men had been Perwynnon's strongest supporters as well, and a fat lot of good it had done him.

Velia Hesswyn pointed a closed fan at him. "If you want our fealty, then take the throne!"

Tyvian grinned. "My ladies and lords, I should hesitate to do such a thing without your counsel, especially after the fate of my father. No, no—I would hear your wishes first! If you have no desire for a king, then say so, and I shall leave you in peace. If you wish to raise me up, then speak, and I shall ascend!"

There was muttering among the peerage for a few moments, and then Dame Velia raised her fan. "House Davram supports the heir. Long may he reign."

Tyvian just barely held in a snort—Davram was playing as though he was no longer on the board. Did they have *that* much confidence in Voth? Or the throne itself? Tyvian bowed in the old woman's direction, anyway. "My thanks, Your Grace."

He turned to await the decisions of Vora, Camis, and Ayventry, but before he could, the Guardian entered the hall and smashed his staff on the ground.

"Magus Argus Androlli, Mage Defender of the Balance!"

Androlli was not alone, of course. Two full columns of Defenders followed him into the room, advancing up the central two aisles. Androlli was grinning. "So, Master Reldamar—we meet again!"

Tyvian cocked his head and blinked. "I'm sorry, but do I know you?"

"Oh, ha ha—how very childish, Reldamar," Androlli said. "And since one childish act deserves another, I come bearing a gift, sir."

The peerage murmured. The gifts of magi had bad reputations.

Tyvian frowned. "And what gift is that?"

Androlli spread his arms to encompass the mirror-men in the room. "I present you with a royal guard! Men of good character with no fealty to any Eretherian house to protect you, so that Perwynnon's fate does not also befall his son."

Tyvian did his best not to curse aloud. Fifty Defenders to follow him around and watch his every move. Wonderful. "How very thoughtful, Magus, but I rather doubt—"

"Oh no, sir . . ." Androlli grinned. ". . . I *insist*! And I assure you that, should anyone threaten your life or person, my men will take you into protective custody at once. For your own safety, of course."

Tyvian scowled. "Nevertheless, I believe—"

Count Yvert stood up. "I, for one, think this is an

excellent idea! I move that the Mage Defender's proposal be enshrined in law. Second?"

Count Duren stood up. "Seconded!"

"All in favor?" asked Yvert.

The room thundered with shouts of "Aye! Aye! Protection for the heir!"

The Guardian thumped his staff. "The law passes, with Hann's guidance!"

"As we are making proposals," Countess Velia said, "I propose a recess—this is not an official session of Congress, and any further declarations or proposals ought be postponed until a more amenable time for all. Especially as our cousins of Ayventry have yet to return from the funeral of Count Andluss."

All the remaining Counts seconded *that* one. So much for pinning down anybody else on the question of fealty for tonight. Duren and Yvert were beaming as they evacuated the great hall.

Fine, Tyvian grumbled, *enough's enough*. He walked past Androlli, brushing him roughly with his shoulder as he went. The mage merely laughed. "Going somewhere, Reldamar?"

"Bed," Tyvian snapped. "Want to come? Make sure I don't disappear?"

Androlli shook his head. "Don't worry—you won't be lonely."

And fifty armed Defenders followed Tyvian from the hall.

He was in a cage. A cage he'd voluntarily stepped into. He found his room eventually and slammed the door on the pair of mirror-men posted to "guard" him. He discovered he hadn't curses enough to cover all the people he was angry with.

CHAPTER 29

CAUGHT SLEEPING

The emerald green fields of Eretheria shone beneath a soft rain and hissed lightly as Hool's paws disturbed them. The raindrops were cool on her fur, the air was clean. For the first time in years, she felt free.

Brana wheezed behind her. "Mama. I'm tired."

Hool frowned and slowed her pace. Brana limped to a halt beside her and sat on the ground. She sat down next to him and pulled him into her arms, letting his snout nuzzle up against her chest, just as she had done all those years ago, when he was new and the world was as it should be. "Rest. We will go again soon." She pulled a blanket of pale wool over their heads. It was muddy and filled with sticks, and it would hide them well from casual eyes. She huddled against a rock and let her breathing slow.

They were sitting near the crown of a hill overlooking the Freegate Road and the spirit-engine tracks that paralleled it. She'd been along this road before, though never this far south—it went past the northern spur of the Tarralle Mountains, through Ayventry, then Galaspin, and then to Freegate. Hool didn't intend to go quite that far—once clear of the Tarralles, she and Brana would turn north and head up into the empty, wild territory that separated Dellor from Galaspin. It might not be the Taqar, but it was wide and open and devoid of many humans. It was a place to start. She suspected, at their current rate of speed, the journey would take two or three weeks. She was looking forward to it.

"I miss Artus," Brana whined. "I wanted to go to the big party."

Hool's ears drooped. "Parties are no place for gnolls."

"That's not true," Brana said. "Everybody likes me at parties."

Hool ran a hand through Brana's gold-white mane. "They are just laughing at you. Humans are mean."

Brana whined, but didn't protest further. He nuzzled close to her. "What if Tyvian gets in trouble?"

"Tyvian is always in trouble. That is why we're leaving." She took a deep breath. "Our debt is paid. He understands. We will always love him, but we cannot help him anymore."

Brana opened his mouth, but Hool licked his nose. "Mama!" he yipped, shaking his head.

Hool rumbled a laugh. "Hush, my rabbit. Sleep."

Brana slept. Hool meant to nap as well but found she could not. She was restless—not to move on, not to stay there, but restless anyway. Her mind had things it wanted to discuss with her, apparently, but had not made itself clear yet.

Was she worried about Tyvian? No, of course not. Tyvian, she was convinced, was unkillable. Even if someone did stab him or drop him off a building, that magic ring would probably save him. She wasn't worried about Myreon either—she was smart and knew many tricks. Besides, Hool had never really liked her that much. No, she was mostly worried about Artus.

If Artus weren't a human, Hool would have taken him with her, too. But he was, and life in the Wild Territory was not for him. He was better off with Tyvian.

Probably.

She snorted, shaking off all the visions of danger her mother's brain could concoct for Artus—Artus being poisoned, Artus being shot with an arrow, Artus falling off a horse, Artus falling in love with an evil woman—and focused her senses on Brana, her real child. She breathed in his scent and at the same time tried to remember the scents of all her other pups. Even Api. *Especially* Api.

At night, when she balled her hands into fists,

she could still feel the stiff, dried pelt of her youngest pup there. She could smell her scent, tainted with the scent of death and with horrible chemicals used to clean the skin. She would have nightmares about it—the bloody face of Gallo, Sahand's bodyguard; the darkness of the closet, and the smell. Always the smell. She had never told anyone about these dreams. There was nothing to be said.

Now, she tried to remember Api's scent as it had been in life. She found it very hard to do. She had spent too long trying *not* to remember. The rain intensified, and Hool let her thoughts drift back to Artus, and Artus's mother.

Did she feel the same way that Hool did now? Did she think of her dead sons and could only see their bodies, their living faces lost to her? Is that why she had sent Artus away—to fix him in her memory forever as a living, breathing boy and not a cold, dead corpse? Yes, that had to be it. Hool sighed. She would have done the same thing. Artus's mother must be strong, like a gnoll.

Brana's ear twitched, brushing Hool's cheek. She heard it, too—a wagon coming, its axle creaking. Then hoofbeats—a dozen horses at least, riding at a slow pace heading south, toward Eretheria. Hiding as the gnolls were, far off the road, Hool doubted the people in the approaching caravan would see them. Still, she settled lower down and put her eye to a hole in the blanket to see what was coming.

She saw an armed party, four horses in the van, eight in the rear, a fortified wagon in between. The wagon was pulled by a team of four and loaded heavily with what had to be weapons and armor or other heavy equipment. The men on horseback were wearing black mail with black and silver tabards, a wyvern stitched on their chests. Hool knew the emblem all too well—Sahand's. These men were Delloran soldiers.

Hool had to resist the urge to charge down the hill and kill them all. At this range, they would put crossbow bolts through her before she got halfway. Besides, they weren't her problem anymore. She had gotten revenge for Api, hadn't she? She had killed dozens of men like that, destroyed Sahand's plans, saved her Brana—what more was there to be settled? Even still, she couldn't suppress a low growl as she watched them pass.

Beside her, Brana shivered. "What are *they* doing here, Mama?"

It was a good question, but Hool didn't want to answer it. "Nothing. They are doing human things. We will stay away from them."

"They won't hurt Artus and Tyvian and Myreon, will they?" Brana asked.

Hool snorted. "Don't be silly. Tyvian will kill them if they try. He is much too smart for them. And Myreon has magic."

"Oh," Brana said, pensive.

The two gnolls remained huddled under their

blanket for a while, both awake and alert, even after the Dellorans passed out of hearing. Again, Hool's thoughts were restless ones. Why were Delloran soldiers here? What was Sahand up to? Was he *in* Eretheria? Did it have to do with Tyvian?

Of course it does, Hool snarled at herself. Twelve Dellorans weren't enough to topple a country or invade a city, but it was certainly enough to kill one man. What other single man would Sahand want dead so badly that he marched these men here from the distant north?

"Mama," Brana said, "we should warn Tyvian."

"No. Tyvian is fine." Hool pulled off the wool blanket and rolled it up, but not before dipping it in some mud.

"But—"

"We go north. Forget the stupid soldiers," Hool growled and then started off.

With one last, long look at the road where the soldiers had gone, Brana loped along behind her. His face had lost its characteristic enthusiasm. It looked sad and grim. Much the same as Hool's did, she imagined.

She pressed on through the rain.

The next day they saw more soldiers. This time it was a column of fifty footmen, bearing Sahand's colors and wearing his livery. Hool and Brana hid atop a great flat boulder and watched them march past a toll house without stopping. Sniffing the air,

Hool smelled blood—probably the toll-keeper and his family. She remembered how Sahand worked.

"Where are all the good soldiers?" Brana asked, his ears back. He, too, smelled the blood.

Hool's ears twitched. "Probably in their castles, waiting for the spring campaigns to start. Not here."

Brana said nothing, but Hool knew what he was thinking. She nudged him with her nose. "They can take care of themselves, pup."

Brana said nothing, his ears still plastered back against his head, his hackles raised as he looked at the column.

Hool sighed. "We will sleep here tonight, just to be safe."

Brana let his tongue peek out. "Okay."

They spent the late afternoon catching birds. Hool taught Brana the basics of using a sling, and they caught a half dozen doves, which they ate greedily, not bothering with a cookfire. It was the first wild meat Hool had had in months. She breathed deep, and the air was full of nothing but rain and the scent of pollen.

That night, she and her pup lay on their backs to watch the stars come out, and Hool pointed out the constellations and told the stories that went with them. She found herself gradually shedding the tension she had slept with for too many years—that nagging sense of not fitting in, of having obligations to fulfill, of the human world intruding on her natural state. A knot of muscle between her shoulders that she hadn't known was there relaxed. She rolled on her back in the long grass beside the flat rock—almost like home.

"I love you, Brana," she whispered softly as the crickets sung all around.

Brana licked her on the ear. "I love you, too, Mama."

For the first time in a long time, Hool drifted into peaceful sleep. Deep, dark, and dreamless, Hool lost track of time and space and let her fears slip away. She slept late—well after dawn—and awoke better rested than if she had slept on a thousand feather beds.

Only to find that Brana was gone.

She sat bolt upright, listening to the wind, sniffing the air—where was he? She barked *"Brana!"* Her voice was swallowed by the open pastures.

She found his tracks—he had left them easy to follow. Easy for her to follow.

They went back toward Eretheria. They followed the Dellorans. She cursed like a human.

She followed the tracks.

Tyvian passed a restless night in a huge, circular bed made out of a sorcerous material even Tyvian hadn't heard of. It was like sleeping on water, though without the sloshing. He spent about ten minutes wondering how one made sheets for a circular bed without showing any seams. The rest of the night he spent feeling fundamentally unsafe. The palace, perversely silent given its size, seemed to hide innumerable possible dangers. His personal chambers alone were so huge he couldn't see into the corners in the dark and likely wouldn't hear the door creak open, even assuming the hinges creaked. He didn't even want to think about the thick, heavy carpet laid from one wall to the other. Adatha Voth could skip across that floor and knife him without taking her high heels off. Having a pair of mirror-men at the door did not make him feel any better either.

He found himself wishing Myreon were there. Like it had been at the start, a year ago or so. The two of them, working in concert, trusting each other. Partners.

Maybe it's better this way. He lay with his hands behind his head, *Chance* under his pillow as always. *Sooner or later*, he told himself, *an assassin is going to show up that I can't beat. He . . . or she, I suppose, is going to kill me. If Myreon were with me, they'd kill her, too. In the world I live in, only Carlo diCarlo gets to grow old.*

"I wouldn't worry."

Tyvian flew to his feet, *Chance* drawn in an instant, adrenaline surging like a storm in his veins, narrowing his vision. Someone was there—sitting by the fireplace, clad in black.

The fireplace lit itself, and in the orange light Tyvian could make out his brother, sitting in a comfortable armchair, his staff across his knees. "Xahl-ven!" Tyvian coughed. "Come to finish me?"

Xahlven laughed, his perfect teeth glinting in the firelight. "Well well, you seem to be recovering from bloodroot poisoning quite nicely. Sit down, put the sword away—you know perfectly well it wouldn't do you any good, anyway."

Tyvian did not put his sword away, but he did decide to squat in the chair across from Xahlven, ready to leap if need be. "Mother's here, too, you know. Quite the family reunion."

Xahlven eyed his brother's posture with obvious amusement. "So, how do you like being king?"

"Heir."

Xahlven smirked. "Yes, pardon me—*heir*."

Tyvian felt the hair on the back of his neck rise. There it was again—that infuriating feeling you got with Xahlven that everything you said was according to some script he had plotted months ago. "Is there a reason you are in my bedchamber, Xahlven, or is this just how you make social calls these days?"

Xahlven shrugged. "Pardon me for my excess of caution, but it isn't easy infiltrating this palace, even for me. The Guardian and all those Defenders, well, they can be fooled, but getting past mother is a whole different challenge altogether. I could not contrive a more socially acceptable meeting—I apologize."

Tyvian kept *Chance* pointed at his brother's face. "Well?"

"They're going to kill you."

Tyvian rolled his eyes. "You'll have to be more specific by 'they.'"

"The Great Houses." Xahlven shook his head. "You're playing with precious little latitude—you know this."

"I'm waiting for you to tell me something I don't know."

Xahlven smiled. "I want to help you."

He didn't expect that. "Help? How?"

"By doing what that ring of yours cannot. By seeing to it that your enemies are replaced by less formidable foes."

Tyvian raised an eyebrow. He felt the ring twitch on his finger. "Assassination, Xahlven? Getting your hands dirty like that doesn't sound like you at all."

Xahlven sat forward in his chair, causing Tyvian to extend *Chance* by reflex. The tip floated no more than an inch from his brother's left eye. If he noticed, Xahlven didn't react. "Listen, Tyvian—we are reaching a crucial juncture. Not just for me and my plans, not just for mother and hers, not even for you and your own pointless desires—for the whole of the West. This time—right now—is a tipping point in history. Decisive action must be taken, and if you can't or won't take it, then I will."

Tyvian snorted. At least half of everything Xahlven just said was a lie. The trick was now determining which half. "Ever since this odious ring was affixed to my person, I have been a pawn in everybody else's game, Xahlven, and I am *very* displeased. Starting talking plainly—make your case—and then maybe we'll see if I don't kill you."

Xahlven chuckled. "Brother, you can't kill—"

"Do you notice anything different about my sword, Xahlven?" Tyvian slid off the chair, pressing the tip of the mageglass rapier against Xahlven's robes. The fabric parted cleanly, as though the tear had always existed. Xahlven phased backward through his chair and was then standing behind it, keeping it between him and Tyvian.

"I see nothing different—no."

Tyvian raised an eyebrow. "Interesting. Mother said she altered it, you know." Tyvian watched the corner of Xahlven's eye twitch, just a bit—it was enough. He smiled. "Ah, so you *didn't* know. Mother altered this blade *specifically* to deal with you, Xahlven. You know how prescient she is. She knows you're here—she knows this meeting is taking place. She set it up weeks ago, when she started backing up Sahand's rumors about my parentage."

Xahlven grimaced and came around the chair, gently pushing *Chance* aside. "That, my brother, is what I'm getting at. Inside of a week, Lyrelle will see the culmination of a plan she set in motion more than thirty years ago. You are the fulcrum upon which that plot is levered."

Tyvian scowled. "And you want to make sure her

little plan never happens, is that it? You'd rather I play into *your* plan instead of hers? No thank you." He put up his sword and turned his back on Xahlven, running a hand through his hair. "Get out of here. Skulking around people's bedchambers is beneath you."

Xahlven didn't budge. "Your father *was* Perwynnon, the Falcon King. You *are* the heir."

Tyvian looked back at Xahlven, but did not turn around. "Shut up. I won't hear it—get out."

"Damn your stubborn, stupid eyes, Tyvian!" Xahlven strode across the floor toward Tyvian, his feet making no sound on the plush carpet. "You are *it*, don't you get it? *You* are her grand design—her perfect, ultimate plan. You were birthed, raised, and driven toward this exact moment. She drove you to rebel, drove you to become a survivor, and then she corralled you with that ring. She made Myreon Alafarr into the lure for your passions—teaching her and molding her as a young woman so that she would be an ideal lover for you! She made bloody *Sahand* into a perfect foil, controlling his plots more closely than that violent oaf could ever understand! Don't you get it yet? You are *meant* to be king! She means to make it so, and you would have done it without even asking why, because as far as you understand, it would be your *own bloody idea!*" Xahlven pushed Tyvian from behind, causing him to stagger a pace.

Tyvian came back and punched Xahlven in the nose.

His brother fell flat on his back, eyes watering, blood spurting down his chin. "What about you, Xahlven? What's *your* angle? So you want to help me by eliminating the counts? Why? So I *won't* ascend to the throne? So I can just slip away into obscurity again, and then you can do whatever you please as Eretheria slips into complete chaos? Is that it?"

Xahlven pulled himself to his feet, dabbing at his nose. "Isn't that what you want? Wealth, comfort, and a complete lack of responsibility? The excitement of the vagabond life without any of the petty inconveniences? A pirate ship of your own, to sail and pillage to your black heart's content?"

Tyvian shrugged. "What, no vineyard?"

"You can have it! Just like . . ." Xahlven snapped his fingers. ". . . *that.*"

Tyvian held out his ring hand. "And what about *this*? Can you wave your staff and make *this* disappear? Because so long as I'm wearing it, I'm not going to be pillaging anything! I'll be forced to wander the earth as an idiotic crusader, living in run-down brothels and vanquishing pimps until the end of my ignominious days." He shrugged. "Either that or be miserable."

Xahlven frowned at the ring. "Only the Yldd can remove the ring. I do not know what they are or where they can be found—I have looked, believe me. Mother has as well." He pursed his lips. "I *do* know of someone who knows, though."

"Who?"

"The Oracle of the Vale."

Tyvian laughed. "Kroth's teeth, Xahlven! How stupid do you think I am?"

"She is real, Tyvian." Xahlven was still dabbing at his nose, but his eyes were clear. "I promise you that."

"The Vale, even assuming it exists, is so far away it may as well *not* exist. What a fine way to get me well out of your hair while you execute whatever nefarious plot you have cooking."

"Who says it's nefarious?" Xahlven snapped. "And what do you care anyway? You'll have your damned freedom, won't you? That's all you've ever cared about. Leave the troubles of the world to the people who actually worry about them." Xahlven shook his head. "Heroism doesn't suit you, Tyvian. You are no man's savior."

Tyvian thought about punching his brother again, but also thought he might be ready for it a second time and didn't feel like being hit with some nasty Etheric spell or slamming his fist into a sorcerous guard. "Get out. I want nothing to do with your plots, your lies, or your ugly face."

Xahlven laughed. "Always the contrarian. Fine—I rescind my offer. Die, then. Let's not fool ourselves, though—I'm the handsome one."

"Not with that nose," Tyvian laughed. "Kiss my pale arse, you feather-stuffed gas bag."

But Xahlven was gone.

Neither the Defenders nor the Guardian ever checked on him—they simply never knew Xahlven had been there. He could be dead right now, and none of his supposed "protectors" would have been the wiser. Tyvian threw a pillow over his head. *Great gods, do I ever miss Myreon.*

CHAPTER 30

AN INFORMAL STROLL

The next morning, Artus, Tyvian, and his mother were served in a private dining hall the size of a polo field on plates of mageglass and silver brought to them by a sour-pussed Guardian and his attendant serving specters. They were sitting at a long dining table intended to seat at least twelve in a wing of the palace that few travelled—a wing traditionally maintained for the king and his household, even though nothing of that description had existed for the majority of the palace's existence.

Eddereon was also present, but not as a diner. He stood by Lyrelle's right shoulder, a kind of man-servant in mail—a living example of how the Iron

Ring made one servile and pathetic. Tyvian did not acknowledge his existence. Neither did anyone else.

Lyrelle looked up from a book from the far end of the table. Her voice, however, carried perfectly. "How did you sleep?" she asked, as though such a question were innocent and she were innocent in asking it.

Artus, sitting to Tyvian's right at about the center of the table, piped up. "That bed is *huge*! I got lost trying to crawl out to the privy!"

Lyrelle frowned at him. "Young man, we are at the breakfast table."

Artus blushed. "Oh . . . uhhh . . . sorry."

Tyvian ate his eggs—they were perfectly prepared, of course. He wondered who did the cooking—surely not the Guardian. The cup of karfan he ordered was likewise just as he liked it—lightly sweetened with honey and a dab of cream. The hot liquid was bracing in the coolness of the cavernous hall.

"Talked to Xahlven last night, you know." He mentioned it offhand, dipping a piece of pumpernickel toast into an egg yolk.

Lyrelle sipped tea. The woman seemed to drink enough tea to sink a galleon. "Oh really? Did he visit?"

Tyvian nodded. "He did."

Artus frowned. "Isn't Xahlven your brother? Don't you hate him?"

"*Hate*'s a strong word—but yes."

"Did he mention how he got in?" She flipped a page in her book. It had come from her own library in Glamourvine—he was sure of it. Tyvian knew the exact volume—a book on Eretherian Law, but about three centuries old.

Tyvian glanced over at the Guardian, who was standing nearby. He fumed behind his beard and seemed to be hoping no one would notice. "He probably slipped in while grandfather here was sleeping. Did you need something?"

The Guardian stiffened. "There is a caller at the door—Lady Elora Carran of Davram. Shall I admit her?"

Artus froze. "Kroth!"

Lyrelle glared at him. *"Artus."*

Artus shook his head. "Sorry, sorry." He looked at Tyvian. "So, about the Lady Elora . . ."

Tyvian winced inwardly, but tried to remain outwardly calm. "Yes?"

"I didn't mention it before but . . . I kinda, well . . . I kissed her."

"The Lady Elora?"

Artus turned bright red. "And . . . and another girl, too."

Tyvian nodded. "And her name?"

"Lady Michelle . . . uhhh . . . Orly. I think."

"Also of Davram?"

Artus cocked his head. "Yeah . . . I guess so. Yeah."

Tyvian frowned. Something was tickling his suspicions.

The Guardian cleared his throat. "Lady Elora, sir?"

Tyvian scowled at the old man. "Send her away. Give no explanation."

Artus stood halfway up. "But . . . wait . . ."

Tyvian waved him into his seat. "Shut up and sit down."

They waited until the Guardian had left, and then Tyvian grinned to himself. "This really should have been more obvious to me. That Velia Hesswyn is more dangerous than I thought." He looked at Lyrelle. "You knew about this?"

Lyrelle nodded. "As you said, it was obvious."

Tyvian sipped some karfan, and looked at Artus. "Velia Hesswyn is trying to leverage *you* into being her loyal servant. She's using her grandniece to get her hooks into you, using the duels to scare the life out of you, and then, when the moment is right, she'll show magnanimity and give you an honorable way out. Via marriage, for instance, to this girl."

"I figured that part out myself. Well, mostly," Artus grunted, staring at his breakfast. "But I'm not gonna be king—you are."

"Not if I were assassinated last night at, say, the Blue Party. Then, as my apparent heir, *you* would be king—a stupider, more easily manipulated king. One with marriage ties to Davram. One without any known blood vendettas with Banric Sahand." Tyvian grinned, but he didn't feel it.

Lyrelle nodded. "If they cannot control the man, they will kill the man and control the boy. As you say—simple and quite ingenious."

Artus looked at both of them. "You two know I'm in the room, right?" When Tyvian didn't answer him, he grumbled something about "not being that stupid," and went back to eating his breakfast.

Tyvian watched Artus eat. There was something about how the boy shoveled food in his mouth. The gusto with which he devoted himself—to meals, to t'suul, to, well, *everything*. In that moment, Hool's fears for Brana—which he had always understood intellectually—he suddenly understood on a deeper emotional level. It came over him all at once, making him shiver. *Gods*, he thought, *how much danger have I put this boy in? How different is he than that pathetic peasant girl Myreon was dragging around?*

This thought—so simple, and yet so powerful— seemed to break something open in Tyvian's mind. He took a moment to steady himself, to orient himself in this reality—the one in which he had been living for so long, only never realizing until this moment. He looked at Lyrelle, who was watching him closely, a smile playing around the edges of his mouth. "If I become king, the Great Houses will kill me."

Lyrelle nodded. "That is very likely, though they may keep you around long enough to fight off Sahand."

"If I don't become king, Androlli will snap me up. And I'll also die."

Lyrelle nodded again. "Very possible."

Tyvian frowned at that. "But if I don't become king, Sahand will cement his claim on Ayventry. He will have his path back to power."

"And that is unacceptable," Lyrelle agreed.

Tyvian grimaced. "So I die no matter what . . ."

Artus looked up from his breakfast. "Not if we run away, right now."

Tyvian stared at him. "If I run away . . . then . . . then the worst of everything happens. Androlli will get us. Sahand will win. Civil war will be certain."

Artus paused, midchew. "Since when do you care?"

It was a good question. A damned good question. "I don't know. But we're staying."

"But . . ." Artus struggled for the words, "but then I gotta fight those duels!"

Tyvian shook his head. "Don't be ridiculous. I will be your second and you just won't show up. There— easy. I spit Valen Hesswyn the bully and then best Ironsides Arving at a game he's probably never played before."

Artus's face had toast crumbs all over it. "But . . . I ain't no coward!"

Tyvian found his heart was racing for some reason. "Artus, I don't want you to wind up dead, all right? You're just about the only friend I have left."

Artus folded his arms. "Well, I'll take you as a second, sure, and I'll listen to your advice. But if we're staying, I'm fighting those duels, understand?"

Tyvian stood up. "I forbid it!"

Artus stood up as well. "I might be stupid but I know you ain't king yet, Reldamar!"

Tyvian grimaced. This was it, then—Artus was stubbornly marching off to certain death. And it was all his fault. His appetite vanished. He wanted to cuff Artus over the head and lock him in a closet somewhere. The ring, of course, wouldn't let him. *Fat lot of good you've done me, lately.*

Lyrelle was smiling at him. "I told you."

"Told me what?" Tyvian snapped.

Her eyes sparkled. "You love him."

"Kroth take it!"

He belted on *Chance*. He needed to get out of here. Needed to think things through without his mother or Defenders or the bloody Guardian standing over him. A plan was forming in his mind—a dark, terrible plan. One that required someone's help to execute—someone he could trust implicitly. And how many of those people were left, anyway? His eyes fell upon the big man over Lyrelle's shoulder—his fellow victim of the Iron Ring. "Eddereon, would you care to go for a walk?"

Eddereon looked up from a piece of wood he was whittling. "If you like. But the Defenders won't let you leave the grounds."

Tyvian said nothing. He just motioned for Eddereon to follow him, his mind still racing. He heard Artus say good-bye, but only acknowledged with a nod.

They left the dining hall, Tyvian walking at full speed. There were four Defenders just outside. The sergeant struggled to salute as Tyvian walked right by him. "I'm to escort you today, sir. For your own protection, you are not to leave the palace."

Tyvian nodded, not really listening. He led Eddereon and the squadron of Defenders up narrow servant stairways through hidden bolt-holes in the palace walls—places nobody had seemed to go for ages.

Tyvian counted doors—almost to the fifth floor. "Remember the first time I came to your attention?"

Eddereon nodded, his long legs keeping easy pace with Tyvian's hasty strides. "The Blue Party, about five years ago now. Always wondered how you got in and out without being caught."

They came into a long, carpeted hallway decorated with busts of Perwynnon. Tyvian counted down four doors, until they were about at the corner of the South Wing of the palace. "This is the place."

Tyvian opened the door and motioned for Eddereon to go in. He blocked the way for the Defenders. "My friend and I would like to have a private chat. Is that all right?"

The sergeant's eyes narrowed and he peered into the room. It had a four-poster bed, an armoire, and a balcony overlooking Lake Elren and the Floating Gardens. There were no other doors. "I . . . I suppose it's all right. No funny business, though, Reldamar."

Tyvian cocked his head. "I thought you were calling me 'sir' these days." He slammed the door before the man could answer.

"May I ask why I'm here?" Eddereon said, standing in the middle of the room.

Tyvian threw open the doors to the balcony and then opened the doors to the armoire. Inside it were the disassembled pieces of a ballista—a lightweight Verisi naval model—and a thick coil of rope. "Good—they're still here."

"What are we doing?"

Tyvian began to construct the ballista. "I hid this here when I was planning that robbery at the Blue Party—smuggling it in here was actually the crowning achievement of the operation, frankly—but I didn't end up using it."

Eddereon watched as Tyvian constructed the device with practiced ease. "What is it for?"

Tyvian positioned the ballista on the balcony. "Winch this, will you?"

Eddereon took the hand cranks and winched the ballista back until it was ready to fire. As he did this, Tyvian tied one end of the coil of rope to the four-poster bed and the other to the ballista bolt. "This," Tyvian said, placing the bolt and taking aim, "is an escape route."

THWACK!

The bolt sailed in a clean arc through the clear sky and stuck in a tree at the center of a Floating Garden a bit below them, but two hundred yards distant.

Eddereon smiled. "We just slide down the rope?"

Again without saying anything, Tyvian put *Chance*'s scabbard over the rope and slid into the void. In a minute, he was rolling on the green grass of that Floating Garden, and the Defenders were none the wiser.

Eddereon followed soon after. He was laughing. "Now—what is this all about?"

Tyvian's smile faded. "Come on. We're going to talk about committing suicide."

CHAPTER 31

DARK THOUGHTS

Myreon's knowledge of necromancy was limited to the theoretical. She recalled an old Master of the Lumen explaining that the reasons for its ban were not so much practical as ethical. *"If we are to be stewards of reason,"* he had explained through his bushy white moustache, *"we cannot go about animating the corpses of the people's relations and binding them to servitude."*

There were, of course, the practical concerns as well. The undead were mindless, and so needed constant attention. They were energy intensive—a great deal of Lumenal energy was needed to keep them active. As servants they were merely adequate—

djinns were vastly superior. As soldiers, they were hopelessly inept, winning battles more through dull-witted perseverance and the psychological advantage they had over living soldiers—any disciplined force would easily cut them apart.

That, at any rate, had been the state of the research when necromancy was banned as a practice, some thousand years ago. Myreon's new ally, however, had made significant progress, it seemed.

Myreon looked over a crudely drawn schematic of various Lumenal rituals, each etched into a parchment of human flesh by an undead hand—the blind necromancer could scarcely write for himself. She had managed to control her revulsion for the time being, out of pure curiosity if nothing else. "If I'm understanding this correctly, you are utilizing the same ritual that creates life wards, except applying it to an enchantment rather than a person." She shook her head. "I didn't think that was possible."

"With the Keeper of the Balance holding your chains, there is much that is never attempted." The necromancer showed his ruined teeth. They were standing over the necromancer's workbench in the ritual space, lit by the spear of sunlight coming from the crack in the ceiling and by a few dozen candles flickering about in nooks in the cavern wall.

"How many . . . things could you raise like this?" Myreon looked over the schematics, trying to see any flaws. The work was simply brilliant—and brilliantly simple, she had to admit. The necromancer had a formal style, despite the disgusting materials he used. She wondered if he had been Arcanostrum trained at some point. Many were the apprentices that failed to earn their staff but who left to pursue careers in the High Arts anyway.

The necromancer closed his milky eyes and did some mental calculations. "I, myself, might raise and maintain a hundred, a hundred and fifty such servants this way. With your help . . . with your *vitality* . . . we might raise even more than that. Perhaps four hundred, maybe five hundred."

Myreon frowned—that would take a *lot* of Lumenal energy. "And how would we command such a legion?"

The necromancer motioned toward his work. "Therein lies a schematic for serving specters enslaved to the lattice of the enchantment."

Myreon nodded, flipping through the parchment scrolls and finding the relevant one. "The specters can delegate your authority. Set them with simple commands and they can relay them constantly to the 'troops,' as it were." She felt her mouth hanging open. "This is incredible work."

The necromancer raised up his hands, as though in worship. "Not my work! This one stands upon the shoulders of the Great Masters—King Spidrahk, King Varthold, and Rahdnost the Undying himself."

The names sent a chill down Myreon's spine. "You

think this is how the Warlock Kings managed their undead armies?"

The necromancer merely nodded.

She stepped away from the table, trying to get the goose bumps to fade from her arms and back. "I have no intention of conquering the world, you know. I don't want to be queen or empress or anything. I just want justice for the peasants of Eretheria."

"What kind of justice is it you seek, Magus?" The necromancer stared off into nowhere. "There are many kinds, of this you must be aware. Some my work can see achieved, others still lie beyond all my power."

Myreon took a deep breath, remembering Bree. "The peerage must be punished. All of them. We need to establish a new balance of power. They need to know that what they have done will not be tolerated any longer."

"Vengeance, then." The necromancer turned toward her. "A goodly type of justice, and easily won."

Myreon rubbed her arms. Vengeance sounded wrong to her, but was it? What else could she achieve? How else could she protect the vulnerable? How much of her opinions on vengeance were shaped by her training—her training in the *maintenance* of this oppression. "You will help me do this? The League has no interests other than my . . . my membership?" She looked down at the contract, laid out on the table, as yet unsigned.

The necromancer gave her a shallow bow. "We in the League are scholars. Knowledge is what we seek. Sahand's membership was an exception and a dark mistake. I have consulted with my esteemed colleagues, and they accept my proposal. I shall assist you in your quest, and in exchange you shall share knowledge with us."

"And become a member of the League?"

"Yes."

Myreon hung her head. Joining the League? It would mean betraying everyone she had ever worked with. It would mean walking away from the Arcanostrum forever, from Saldor forever.

But didn't they betray you first? The voice was Tyvian's, summoned up from the depths of her memory. The demon on her shoulder, as always.

She thought of Lyrelle, too—that great woman, her face sad, telling her how justice was a fiction; how the Balance was nothing more than a means of control.

Myreon took a deep breath. *Yes,* she thought, *yes, I can walk away from that.* She took up a quill and signed the contract. "It is done."

The necromancer felt around on the table until he found the contract. "Excellent." He furled it and put it away. "We must discuss tactics, then, and quickly. The peerage shall depart for the countryside soon, and they are scattered all over the city."

Myreon nodded. "They will stay for a few days

more. Tyvian is probably trying to wrangle the sympathy of the houses. I expect the Congress of Peers will be a busy place—lots of nobles, all struggling for position."

"A target ripe for our endeavors, then."

Myreon looked over the sorcerous schematics. "Can the risen dead penetrate the palace wards?"

The necromancer let out a hollow, rasping laugh. "The wards protect against unwanted intrusion by all persons. But these . . ." He motioned to a few corpses, laid out for use. ". . . long ago ceased to be people. When our ritual is complete, the peerage of Eretheria will know terror unlike any they have known before. Come, esteemed colleague—let us begin. The bodies of a half a thousand men do not raise themselves."

The city seethed with anger—Tyvian could hear it in the timbre of the voices around him, he could see it in the set of the people's shoulders. Not just the peasantry either. Columns of foreign mercenaries had their eyes narrowed, their weapons held tight. No men-at-arms were on the street, but rather standing guard at the doors and gates of wealthy mansions and estates. Peasant children moved in sullen little packs, throwing rocks at men in livery when they weren't looking and then scattering like mice. Everywhere Tyvian looked, there were heads on pikes. The little placards read Treason and Killer and Witch.

Tyvian scowled at it all. "Myreon did this. Kroth take her."

Eddereon considered this for a moment. "She did what she felt was right."

Tyvian nodded. "That is exactly the problem."

The tavern they picked had no clear name—just a clay jug with a lot of Xs on it hung from a signpost. It was early, so the place was empty—just a girl behind the bar. Tyvian slapped a gold mark down. "Oggra. A whole bottle."

The gold mark evaporated beneath her wide, white hands. The bottle and two tumblers followed a moment after. Tyvian poured and held his tumbler up in salute. "To good intentions, may they burn in hell."

Eddereon met the toast. They drank. The liquor burned going down. Tyvian coughed. Eddereon drank it smoothly. "Wouldn't have picked you as an oggra man."

"I'm not. I'm getting drunk fast, is all. This way, it will be difficult for me to decide where we are going next."

Eddereon scratched his beard. "And this is important because . . ."

"Because the Defenders will have a harder time scrying where we are going to be if both of us are too drunk to know ourselves."

"You don't need to do this," Eddereon said. "It may be that you could escape this trap before it is sprung. You need not sacrifice yourself."

Tyvian grunted. "And then thousands of poor souls will die in a war that, in the end, will merely sustain the rotten circumstances that got them into this mess. The country will suffer, I will be lucky to survive, and Artus . . ." Tyvian shook his head, looking into his empty glass, "the boy becomes—*is*—a target for my enemies just as much as I am now. I hadn't thought about it clearly before."

"What other options do you have?" Eddereon poured Tyvian another glass full.

Tyvian drank it. The world tilted a little. *Good.* "The *other* option is to do what Myreon wants. Reform. Overthrow the established order. Become a champion of the people."

"Except then the nobility will fight *you*." Eddereon poured himself a glass. "Their peasant armies will be in disarray. And Sahand wins against a divided Eretheria."

Tyvian grimaced. "Scarcely better, is it?"

Eddereon frowned, fiddling with his tumbler. "You should do the right thing."

"What?" Tyvian blinked.

Eddereon held the bottle of oggra out to him. "Do you want to know why I chose you for the ring?"

"My *mother* chose me for the ring," Tyvian said, taking the liquor.

"No, your mother brought you to my attention. I could have refused."

"But she knew you wouldn't, which is the same

thing as your not being able to." Tyvian looked at the bottle. He shrugged—what the hell. Going blind couldn't make his life any worse.

Eddereon shook his head. "You, Tyvian Reldamar, are a good person. You always have been. You spent your childhood defending the weak and when you saw that the suffering of the world did not decrease for your efforts, you grew bitter and jaded. You felt that heroism was a lie—that no one could make a difference—and so you built walls between yourself and the world. You chose apathy over pain, cynicism over misery."

Tyvian took a long drag off the bottle. He felt as though he'd swallowed a campfire. "A . . ." *cough* ". . . a sensible choice, wouldn't you agree?"

"No." Eddereon's dark eyes glittered in the pale light from the windows. "No it is not. Pain should not be avoided. No one ever grew who was comfortable."

"Growth? Who needs it?"

Eddereon took the bottle from him and took a drink himself. "You do. That's why you're here. That's why you saved Myreon from petrification. That's why you stuck with your old partner, Hendrieux, all those years, and why you rescued Artus from the streets, and why you helped Hool and Brana find one another again. You believe in becoming a better self, no matter the struggles you face."

"You aren't listening to me. *Nothing* I do here makes anything better, least of all for me and Artus."

Eddereon nodded. "If nothing you do matters, then you should do the right thing anyway, as the right thing is inherently better than the alternatives. If you fail, then you at least failed for the right reasons."

Tyvian scowled. Why did he bother talking to this man? This stooge of his mother's, who probably was only saying what he was told to say. He took the bottle and knocked back another shot of oggra. The world spun a little more. He steadied himself on the bar. "That is . . ." *cough* ". . . overly simplistic. That's why . . ." *cough cough* ". . . you wound up a gardener for my mother."

"If you didn't want my advice, why are we here?"

"Because you and I are going to talk about a third option."

"Besides controlling the nobles or supporting the peasantry?" Eddereon frowned beneath his beard. "Are you . . . talking about the church or something?"

Tyvian laughed—too loudly. The oggra was working. "Hang the bloody church—useless old men. No. I'm . . . I'm talking 'bout controlling the nobles *and* supporting the peasantry *and* getting Artus away from all of this, all at the once."

Eddereon took a pensive sip of the oggra. "Is . . . is this where the suicide comes in?"

Tyvian yanked the bottle back and pushed it away from Eddereon. He struggled to keep his speech from slurring. "Listen, listen. Listen . . . listen—it's all a setup, right? All a setup. They think I'm a horse in traces."

"Who?"

Tyvian shook his head. "Not important. What *is* important to you, my hairy friend, is how you're going to help me become a martyr."

Eddereon's eyes bugged out. Tyvian laughed.

"First though," Tyvian said, heaving a purse fat with gold on the bar. "You and I are going to be very popular in as many bars as possible."

CHAPTER 32

DUELING DAY

Artus woke up with the sun pouring in the towering windows of his bedroom. He rolled over, expecting to roll out of bed, but found only more bed beneath him. He opened one eye—the vast mattress stretched out before him like a featureless linen plain. It took him four more rolls to reach the edge.

In the corner of the room, the spirit clock chimed the hour—it was ten. "Master Artus." The Guardian was standing just inside his door, dressed as ever in his full regalia, staff and all.

Artus jumped at the sight of the old man. "What? I ain't even dressed!"

"The coach is waiting to take you to your duels, sir."

Artus froze. "Oh Kroth! That's today?"

The Guardian's face remained neutral. "It is in one hour, sir."

"Kroth's teeth!" Artus threw open the doors to his armoire. "I need to get dressed!"

"Shall I have breakfast ready, sir?"

Artus threw off his soiled shirt and began to rifle through a drawer. "I dunno—is Tyvian back yet?"

"The heir is currently not in the palace."

Artus poked his head through the neckline of a shirt. "What? He's not here?"

"No, sir."

Artus stuffed his arms through the shirt. "Are you sure?"

"I have not seen the heir since breakfast yesterday morning."

Artus stood there, a quarter dressed, and stared at the Guardian. "Like . . . at all?"

The Guardian was like a statue. "If I follow your meaning, sir, that is correct."

"I'm on my . . . own?" Artus suddenly felt lighter, as though he were falling through the floor. He grabbed the door of the armoire to steady himself.

The Guardian left without saying anything further. If he had any concerns or reservations about Artus or Tyvian's behaviors, he didn't show it.

On my own. Artus took a deep breath, trying to steady the flutter that was building in his stomach. *I'm going to fight two duels today and Tyvian isn't going to be there.*

Part of him couldn't believe it—for the past few years Tyvian had been the most . . . well . . . most consistent part of his life. Even when he'd been separated from him, even when he'd left, Artus always had the sense he was being watched, being guided. He had always been an integral cog in Tyvian's elaborate plans. It had been . . . *comforting* to know that, even if it had pissed him off.

This felt different. This time, he really did feel alone. *Was it something I said to him yesterday?* It couldn't have been, could it?

As much as he wanted to, there just wasn't enough time to mope about it. Artus pulled on some functional clothing in a Saldorian style—breeches, jacket, shirt, cravat, short wig—emphasizing royal blue and white. He belted on the rapier Tyvian had given him and hastened down to breakfast.

The vast table was laid out with silver trays of bacon, hard-boiled eggs, various rolls and croissants, and an array of jams and steaming pots of karfan and tea. But no Tyvian. No Hool. No Myreon. No Brana. There was only a single place setting—his own. Artus felt that half-dizzy feeling again. He wanted to crawl back under the quilts in his room.

"Good morning, Artus."

Lyrelle Reldamar entered from a different doorway, wearing a striking gown of maroon with thread-of-gold embroidery, the dimensions of which tripled the surface area she occupied. "Well, hurry up and eat something—can't have you dueling on an empty stomach, can we?" She smiled and gestured to his chair. It slid out silently.

Artus sat down, and Lyrelle sat across from him. "You know about my duels?"

Lyrelle smiled. "I'm sorry there is nobody here for you, Artus. This past week has been trying on everyone."

Artus grabbed a hard-boiled egg. He had it halfway to his mouth when he realized he ought to have used the serving spoon to retrieve it. He found himself blushing in front of Tyvian's mother. "Oh . . . uhhh . . . sorry."

"No, no—eat. I remember when Tyvian was your age, he would eat five eggs at a sitting." She made a sharp inhaling noise. "Just suck them right down."

Artus frowned at her as he took a bite from his egg. He didn't feel like eating five of anything just then—he felt almost ill. He didn't want to be alone, but he wasn't sure he wanted to talk with Tyvian's mother either. "Is there something you wanted?"

Lyrelle smiled. "Of course there is. But eat first. You need your energy."

All of Tyvian's warnings about his mother started creeping into the back of Artus's mind as he sat there, eating his egg and then a second egg (he really *was* hungry, it turned out, or maybe it was nerves). She was up to something, sure. But her warm smile and her, well, her *motherly* way about her was nice. He hadn't known her for too long, but she seemed to like him. To be honest, he kinda liked her, too. "Are you . . . are you gonna come to see me duel?"

Lyrelle reached out and took his hand. Her fingers were cool and strong as they squeezed his gently. "I'll be there. I'll be watching your back, Artus—that I promise. Eat more. You're still hungry, I can tell."

Artus helped himself to some bacon. He was beginning to feel a bit better. With Lyrelle there for him, he felt less worried about that skunk Valen pulling some kind of underhanded trick. He ate the bacon quickly. "So, what do you want?"

Lyrelle leaned over the table and, when she spoke, it was as though she were whispering in his ear. "*I want you to lose the first duel.*"

Artus jumped. "What? No! No way!"

Lyrelle still had his hand. She held on to it—with a much stronger grip than he would have thought. "Artus, Artus—I need you to listen to me: Valen Hesswyn is a spoiled bully. He's the same kind of nasty young man *my* son spent his teenage years vanquishing in Saldorian alleys, and I'm certain you would love nothing more than to stab him in the eye."

Artus grunted a laugh. "I'll say."

"But you *can't*, Artus. You can't. Valen is the grandson of the Countess of House Davram. Tyvian needs her as an ally if he is going to succeed as heir, and right now she is only technically backing Tyvian's claim. Stabbing her grandson will not improve matters."

Artus blinked. "But . . . but *getting stabbed* don't seem like it would work out well for me."

She pointed at the dish of grapes. "Eat some fruit." As Artus ate, she went on. "You have to trust me, Artus. I know Tyvian doesn't, and I know he's said some terrible things about me to you over the years, but believe me when I say this: I want nothing more than the safety and happiness of my son and his friends."

Artus looked her in the eyes—those bright, hard blue eyes, so much like Tyvian's—and, dammit, he believed her. What had she ever really done to Tyvian, anyway, except tell him what to do? That's what mothers were supposed to do anyway, right? "So . . . like, if you want me to lose and all, do I need to make it look good or something? I don't know if I can do that. And then what about the second duel?"

Lyrelle smiled at him—that incredibly bright, warm smile—and patted his hand. "Don't you worry about that—you are sending a message to House Davram. You will willingly offer yourself to injury by Valen, and then you will play to win against Sir Arving. If you win, honor will be satisfied between House Davram and Tyvian's household. You will have helped everyone a great deal."

Artus frowned—letting himself get stabbed by Valen didn't sound appealing at all. "Helped everyone do what, exactly?"

"Avoid civil war," Lyrelle said gravely. "That's

right, Artus. I'm asking you to risk your life to save the lives of countless others. Can you do that for me?"

Artus drank some apple juice. "So, I'll come off looking *good* here? Not like some coward or idiot?"

Lyrelle chuckled lightly. "Oh Artus—everyone will *love* it."

Artus remembered Michelle telling him he was like a knight from the stories, and the press of her lips against his. His stomach fluttered. He grinned. "Okay, sure—let's do it."

Lyrelle motioned to the exit. "Your coach awaits. Bring a croissant with you—they're fresh."

The Floating Gardens were filled with spectators, both noble and common. Somehow word had gotten out about the Young Prince (as Artus seemed to be known) and his two duels. It was a damp morning after a late night rain and the sky was speckled with gray clouds through which the sun would sometimes blast with great strength, lighting up the wet grass of the gardens and sparkling on the pure blue of the lake.

Artus and Lyrelle were announced by a herald, and the crowds parted as they emerged from the coach. On either side, ladies with parasols and lords in broad feathered hats watched him pass, some of them favoring him with a bright smile and a warm hello. Lyrelle whispered that he ought to go and meet them, and so Artus did, shaking hands and nodding politely to a few dozen people whose names he forgot as promptly as he learned them.

There were also the commoners—peasants in ragged clothing and simple woolen cloaks, smoking pipes and carrying children on their shoulders. These cheered as he passed by, the men bellowing as loud as they could, the children shrieking, and the women blowing kisses. Lyrelle told him to go and meet them, too. And so he did. Daisy chains were looped over his head. Babies were thrust into his arms to be kissed. Men took off their crumpled hats and knelt to him. "I knew your grandfather," the older ones often said. "You look just like him, milord."

Artus knew of nothing to say to this—to any of this. So he just nodded and smiled at everyone and said "thank you." He did his best not to blush. The whole thing seemed surreal. As he ascended the mageglass walkways from floating garden to floating garden, it seemed that he, too, was rising out of himself. He was watching himself as though from a distance, wondering who it was they all thought they were talking to. Surely not him. There must be some mistake.

Lyrelle steered him by his elbow, whispering in his ear from time to time. *"These are lesser peers from House Ayventry—they aren't your friends in this. Those four are cousins to Sir Arving—don't shake their hands. These people are shepherds from the nearby countryside, probably Camis vassals. Smile. Good job. Don't walk too fast. You are doing so very well, Artus."*

Then, at last, they found themselves at the highest floating island of the gardens—Falcon's Perch. It was only about thirty paces across, connected by a single mageglass arch to the next lowest island, which rested thirty feet below. The island itself was two hundred and fifty feet above the surface of Lake Elren, and beneath it could be seen the entire elaborate chain of Floating Gardens going down, down, down to the great gardens that encircled the lake. The view was dizzying.

At the center of the island was a life-size statue of a king in a throne, a falcon perched on one arm, his long beard reaching to his toes—Perwyn the Noble, founder of Eretheria, and Tyvian's alleged ancestor. About twenty people were here as spectators—most of them House Davram vassals. Countess Velia was there, perched on her sedan chair, holding a truthlens to her eye and looking Artus up and down.

Valen was dressed in a tight doublet fitted for dueling, a vibrant hunter green with gold piping, a boar device embroidered into the breast. He stood in the ready position, side pointed to Artus. Behind him had been set up a canopy beneath which was a small table and some chairs—the site of the day's *second* duel. It had all been arranged. Everyone stared at Artus as he arrived, their faces grave. Artus was wrenched back to earth. *Gods*, he thought, *this is really happening.*

Artus looked at Lyrelle, who was still on his arm. "How do I know they won't cheat?"

"It's about time, Reldamar!" Valen yelled. It took Artus a moment before he realized that Valen was talking to *him*. "We were beginning to think you wouldn't show."

Lyrelle extricated her hand from his elbow and gave him a kiss on the cheek. Before she pulled away, though, she whispered one last thing. *"Artus, they are* certainly *going to cheat."*

Artus felt his stomach sink at that. *What in hell have I gotten myself into?*

"No second, scrub?" Valen growled.

Artus squared his shoulders. He'd be damned if he let that dandy priss intimidate him, cheating or no cheating. "Well, I was gonna ask your mom, but she had to leave early."

Whispers spread across the little garden. Out of the corner of his eye, Artus spotted a kid run down the bridge to the next garden. *They're spreading what I say. Everybody is going to know what happens here.* He knew that was important. He knew that, somehow, Lyrelle had counted on this event being so public.

And he was just realizing that he had absolutely no idea why that really was.

CHAPTER 33

THE MANY ADVANTAGES OF BEING STABBED

Artus faced Valen across ten paces of marble flagstones beside the old statue of Perwyn the Noble. Valen had a rapier and a parrying dagger, which he was whirling around in a display of athletic prowess. Artus tested the balance of his own blade—it was very good, as Tyvian insisted on only the best, but it still felt strange in his hands. Artus had always preferred a knife to a sword. He preferred a machete to both of them.

But it didn't matter anyway since he was about to get himself stabbed on purpose. Right? That still was the plan, right? He wanted to look at Lyrelle, to perhaps glean some sign from her, but the witness was stepping forward and calling them both over.

He was a tall, thin man with ears that stuck out far beyond his wig. Between that and his long nose, he looked a bit like a ferret, but his manners were genteel as he bowed to both Valen and himself. "Please, sirs, if I may be allowed to inspect the weapons."

Artus surrendered his first, keeping his eyes on Valen. The young nobleman had a vein sticking out from the side of his temple that was visibly pulsing with rage. "You are going to pay, you common-born brat. I'm going to make you weep for *your* mother."

Artus glared at him, thinking of a dozen hurtful things he might say, but found himself holding his tongue. He clenched and unclenched his sword hand—oh how he *ached* to prick this miserable jerk. To paint his blood across the flagstones in front of his whole damned family—oh, the embarrassment would be just *perfect*. Then, finally, that sneering jackass would shut the hell up forever.

The witness returned his sword. "This is a fine blade, young man." The witness gave him a tight smile. Artus noted his colors—House Vora. Neutral, then. Theoretically.

Valen surrendered his weapons and began to pace back and forth like a mad dog in a cage. "Will you hurry it up?" he snapped. "Let's get this over with."

Artus cocked his head. It was more than just anger here. It was fear. When Valen's hands weren't wrapped around the hilt of a blade, they were shaking. He was breathing hard already. A sheen of perspiration coated his forehead. *He's scared of me!*

And why wouldn't he be? Artus had beaten him senseless the other day, and without any trouble whatsoever. Valen had no idea how good Artus was with a sword—he might be assuming that Artus was just as deadly with a blade as with his fists, but he was here to fight anyway, as a point of honor. Perhaps his family wouldn't let him back out. Come to think of it, backing out of a duel was just not done by noble types. He had to go through with this every bit much as Artus had to.

Valen was returned his weapons and the two young men took their positions, ten paces apart. The witness stood between them, holding up his hands for silence. "In accordance with the ancient laws of Eretheria, Artus of Eddon did declare a duel upon Sir Valen Hesswyn of Davram when he laid his hands unlawfully upon him four days ago in Davram Heights. Sir Valen has chosen swords as the weapon of honor. The duel is to be fought until one of the combatants draws blood from the other, and not a stroke or thrust more. Then honor shall be satisfied, and the two men shall live in peace with one another with Hann as their guide."

With Hann as my guide, Artus thought, bowing his head. A priest stepped forward and blessed them both—it was almost time.

Artus knew he ought to be focusing on what he was going to do when someone shouted *"Allez."* He couldn't shake the revelation of Valen's terror, though. He thought back to that first night, at the brewery. Ethick and Valen had been deliberately trying to egg him on, he felt, but Artus hadn't risen to the bait. And then at the stocks, when he'd beaten them both up—that had been a setup, too. They *wanted* him to get into a duel. It was a trap, right from the beginning. Now Valen was here, terrified he was going to get another whooping, this time in front of his family and peers.

The witness waved a handkerchief. "Quarter is to be given if asked. If a man is disarmed, the other will withdraw to give his opponent opportunity to retrieve. Understood?"

"Let's just get on with it!" Valen barked.

Artus nodded. "I'm ready."

"En garde, messieurs!"

Artus fell into the en garde position, his mind still racing. It didn't *matter* who had put Valen up to it and why. The fact was this entire thing was a farce, disgusting and pointless. He knew what he had to do. He knew what was right.

"Allez!"

Valen advanced carefully, weapons out. Artus threw down his weapon. "Valen . . ." He took a deep breath. "Valen, I'm sorry."

Valen snorted. "You're what?"

Artus put up his hands. "I shouldn't have hit you,

okay? You were being a jackass and I was angry, so I smacked you around, and that wasn't right. I'm sorry."

Valen jabbered through a few half-baked responses before he hit on something intelligible. "You think this is going to save you or something? Pick up that sword, you gutter-born commoner!"

Artus took another deep breath. This was going to be harder than it looked. "I was mad, okay? I'm sorry, like I said."

Whispers from the audience were so loud they were like the wind in the trees. People were trotting up and down the bridge, carrying news to the spectators below.

"You're *sorry*?" Valen's mouth hung open. "Do you think that undoes your dishonorable behavior? Do you think you can just *apologize* and get away with that? You . . . you *handled* me like . . . like . . ."

Artus shrugged. "Yeah. Sorry, like I said."

"I'm going to stab you anyway!" Valen shouted, advancing close enough to lunge.

Artus kept his right shoulder toward Valen. "I get that. So . . . just . . . just go ahead. Stab me."

"I want a proper duel!" Valen shouted. "Pick up that sword! This isn't fair!"

Artus looked up at the sky and sighed. "Look, Valen, I've got two duels today, all right? I don't really feel like wearing myself out, and, besides, you're right—I shouldn't have messed you up. Just give me a stab, okay, and we can put this behind us."

Valen glanced at the crowd. They were all watching, whispering among themselves behind fans or cups of wine. Most people were looking at Artus. When Valen looked back, his face was screwed up into a vicious leer. "Fine."

He lunged, putting his rapier into Artus's stomach and straight through the other side just above Artus's pelvis. Artus felt suddenly cold and, when the blade withdrew, the pain hit him all at once. He crumpled to the ground, clutching the wound. "Kroth," he swore, "you . . . you nasty little shit . . . ohhhh . . ."

Valen tried to summon up phlegm, but apparently his mouth was too dry. He spat at Artus anyway. "Apology accepted."

Then Artus was crowded with people. Faces, most of them strangers, clustered over him. Something soft was put under his head. A girl grabbed him by the cheeks—Michelle! "Oh, Artus! Don't die! Don't die! I won't be able to stand it! Oh!"

The witness's face replaced hers. "Sir, can you hear me?"

Artus groaned. "Of course I can Krothing hear you—you're right in my goddamned face!"

The witness looked up at people he couldn't see. "You there! Help me get him to my tent!" Artus tried to sit up, but he felt blood bubble from his stomach and a tearing pain that made him fall back down again. The witness put a hand on his shoulder. "Don't be a hero, son—I'll take care of you."

But there was Ironsides Arving, dressed in black with a green and gold cape, standing over both of them. He looked down at Artus over his hooked nose. "He seems quite fit to me."

The witness scowled up at him. "Sir Arving, this young man may be in grave danger. I have not yet had the opportunity to diagnose his wounds. There could be serious bleeding. The intestinal humors may have escaped. His kidneys may have been scratched. If I might—"

"This man and I have a matter of true honor to settle—not that foolishness we were just made to watch. He must answer for his mother's crimes against me, and I will not have this duel forestalled, Sir Michial." Arving fixed the witness with a hard look.

Sir Michial, the witness, looked down at Artus. "How do you feel, sir?"

Artus blinked. "Like I been stabbed in the guts!"

Sir Arving grinned, but it wasn't the happy kind of grin. "There, see? If it had been the kidneys he'd be unconscious by now—much more blood. Surely he's well enough to play a silly tavern game."

Sir Michial, the witness, stood up. "I am bound by duty to protest! This young man is gravely injured—your duel must be delayed to allow him to recover!"

Sir Arving put out his hand and somebody slapped a scroll into it. Unfurling it, he began to read. Even from the ground, Artus could see the fat seal of the

Congress of Peers at the bottom. "In matters of duels to the death that are not to be settled in a physical contest, defined as . . . etcetera, etcetera, the health of the participants shall not be sufficient reason to forestall the restoration of honor by the wronged party." Sir Arving grunted and extended the scroll to Sir Michial. "Voted through Congress just this morning. There was quorum, as you can see."

Artus grunted, which hurt rather a lot. "You sneaky bastard. You're awful eager to kill me, aren't you?"

Arving looked down on him as though Artus were a bug that had just invaded his picnic. "I kill quite a lot of people, boy. Don't imagine you are significant."

So this was what Lyrelle meant—they'd set him up to duel while injured, and legally, too. Cheating, essentially, but somehow cheating while using the rules. It was a new level of underhandedness Artus was only just becoming aware of.

He pushed himself up on his elbows. It hurt like hell and the world spun a bit. "Just patch me up, okay. I've played t'suul drunk plenty of times—this can't be much worse."

Sir Michial looked from Artus to Arving and back. All around him, the grim faces of House Davram vassals looked on—not a terribly friendly crowd. Nearby, three little girls—Arving's granddaughters, Lyrelle had said—held each other's hands, their eyes shining with worry. Michial sighed. "Very well. But I wash my hands of it, understand? I'm not responsible."

Arving nodded. "When the boy is dead in fifteen minutes, it won't matter anyway."

Artus shuddered as two men helped him to his feet and guided him to his chair beneath the canopy. In the crowd, he spotted Lyrelle, fanning herself lightly and laughing with a man in Davram livery. The nature of her angle was becoming clear to Artus, now. She'd *known* Valen would stab him deep instead of giving him a nick. She'd *known* Arving had manipulated the law to make the next duel inevitable. The crowds had gathered, had cheered his name, and now they were going to watch him die at the hands of this dour, stuffy old man. And then what would happen?

He'd be a damned martyr, that's what.

Lyrelle had set him up to die.

"Artus!" Artus felt a pair of cold hands on his shoulders and then grasping his hand. It was Elora, dressed in green and royal blue (the color combination struck Artus as odd—was that some new house he didn't know?). Elora kissed the back of his hand. "I've just spoken with my great-aunt. This can't go on! You *can't* duel Sir Arving, my love!"

Artus tried to blink away the pain. "My love?"

"Yes! Yes!" Elora's eyes looked wild, her cheeks flushed. "Countess Velia agrees to forfeit the duel in your favor—in your *favor*—if you only agree."

Artus frowned. That sounded a bit too good to be true. "What's the catch?"

"Oh, it's no catch at all!" Elora kissed his hand

again. "We need only be married! That sounds nice, doesn't it? I'm so very sorry about the other night! I'm so, so sorry! Michelle is right about you—you're a good person. A good man. Please, Artus! Agree! For my sake—for *your* sake!"

Sir Michial and Sir Arving were watching him, waiting on his decision, apparently. Marry Elora? Gods! *Getting their hooks into him* was the phrase Tyvian had used. Marriage was the hook; Elora was the bait.

Artus pulled back his hand from Elora's white-knuckled grip. He looked at Arving. "Let's do this."

"*No!*" Elora shrieked. Artus elected to ignore her, keeping his eyes on Arving.

Someone came from the crowd and grabbed Elora by the hand to escort her away. Before she left, though, she leaned back to whisper in Artus's ear. "You selfish twit! I hope you die!"

Artus grimaced. "Miss you, too, my *love*."

The crowd grumbled at the drama.

Sir Michial tried to offer Artus a bloodpatch elixir, but Sir Arving denounced it, saying it might "skew the contest," so Artus had to settle for his jacket being stripped off and a regular old bandage being wrapped around his midsection beneath his shirt. A screen was set up for his privacy, but in the chair across from Arving he stayed.

The t'suul table was a square eighteen inches on a side, its top upholstered in firm black felt. At the center of the table was the sakkidio. Artus felt a little light-headed as he looked at it, but he chalked it up to blood loss. He was a good t'suul player—he rarely lost at the House of Eddon. He could do this. He looked at Arving. "Ever played before?"

Arving sat in his chair blade straight. "On campaign. A way to improve morale among my levies."

"Well, this ain't a morale-boosting exercise anymore. This is serious."

Arving nodded once, but didn't rise to the barb. Artus reminded himself that it wasn't Valen he was facing here. Sir Arving was a famous duelist, a professional killer—he wasn't going to be thrown off by small talk. His mouth felt dry—he thought to ask for water, but decided against it. He'd be damned if he let Arving see him sweat.

The witness for *this* duel was about as far from Sir Michial as it was possible to go and still remain within the confines of the human race. She was a dark-skinned Rhondian sailor, her wiry arms a net of black, risqué tattoos—mostly of certain sensitive parts of the male anatomy. Someone had stuffed this woman in a simple dress, but the way she wore her kerchief over her bald head and sauntered to the edge of the table like a sword-wearing bravo implied that dresses were not her normal attire. Unlike Sir Michial's somber and official demeanor, this woman was smiling from ear to ear, her gold tooth sparkling in the intermittent sunlight. "Well now, my lords—here it is: t'suul be the game, as played in the dark corners of Illin. Not for gold, no sirs, but for blood." She produced two vials with a flourish and slapped them down on the table with good dailiki. "Venom of the reed serpent—thins the blood so as you bleed from the inside out, understand?"

Sir Arving moved to pick up his vial, but the sailor woman slapped his hand. "Fie, my lord! When you raise it, you raise it together. You drink together—one last between enemies, eh?" She laughed and pulled a pouch from her belt and dumped the contents on the table. It was a pile of dried, thin yellow leaves. "Khoos-leaf—antidote. Gotta eat all this to live, my lords—not one leaf less."

She pressed her hand into the exact center of the little pile of antidote leaves and spread it apart into two groups of about eight or nine leaves—one half she pushed toward Artus, the other toward Arving. "Your wagers, my lords. Take the other man's fortune and live. Fail and die."

Arving frowned. "What if we pass out before we can win?"

The woman grinned. "Play fast. Good dailiki."

Artus had a half dozen questions of his own—did it matter that he was bleeding from his insides *already*? What about the fact that Arving was bigger than he was? How could they know both vials were poisoned?

Arving seemed to read his mind. "How am I to know if both vials are poisoned?"

The sailor laughed again, this time loud and long, her head thrown back. "Maybe they are not—maybe this duel ends with both dead or neither. Such is fate, my lords. Such is the price of honor in the Dreaming City."

Arving scowled and straightened his wig. He didn't like being laughed at, did he?

Artus nodded toward the vials. "Which one do you want?"

Arving picked the vial closest to Artus and, together, they drank. The poison sizzled on the tongue, hot and bitter, and slid down like a drop of hot lead into Artus's injured guts. Arving scowled at the flavor and held the vial out to the sailor. She looked at each and nodded—they had both drunk. She then poured the sakkidio out and took the count—a balanced set—even on all colors except gray, which was one tile heavy.

With a sweep of an arm, the sailor put the tiles back in the sakkidio and Artus and Arving took turns drawing tiles for their initial clutch. The game had begun.

T'suul began with the Heart—a tile of each of the five primary colors being placed on the board in an X pattern, the gray at the center. Atop these was a leaf apiece from Artus and Arving's piles, though the central gray tile remained naked. Each player took turns placing a tile from their clutch adjacent to another tile. If the tiles were opposed (black with white, red with blue), they would duel—the player would get to collect both tiles (and both antidote leaves).

Artus, being the instigator of this whole affair, slapped a black tile with one leaf atop it adjacent to the white on the board—a duel. He tried to sense if the poison was working yet, if he felt faint or if any more blood was running from his wound, soaking his bandage. He couldn't tell.

Arving's immediate response was to stack another black atop Artus's black, his with two leaves. An aggressive move—there were only seven black tiles in the set, and right now three of them were visible on the board and Artus had one more in his clutch. The remaining three might be in the sakkidio still, or might be in Arving's clutch—too early to tell. He elected to let the duel go Arving's way—the old duelist slid all the tiles into his hand and added the leaves to his own pile.

Play to Artus again. He slapped a gray between the red and black tiles on the board. His clutch now consisted of a black tile and a red. He was betting that Arving, like a true fencer, would press his current black-white tile advantage, guessing the odds that Artus had a stack of black tiles in his clutch would be slim now.

Arving, his face a mask of concentration, carefully laid a white tile beside the gray Artus just played, setting up a bridge between the black and white tiles on the board. Another duel, this time involving both the black tile and the gray one—higher stakes. Also a stupid move.

Artus couldn't help but smirk as he pulled out his last black tile and slapped it hard beside the blue tile on the opposite side of the Heart—another bridge, this encompassing two grays, a black, *and* Arving's white. This was called "burning the stack." It was the t'suul equivalent of stabbing a man in the back. But it netted Artus three tiles, one of which was Arving's. Around them, the spectators gasped.

Arving grimaced, a little rivulet of blood running out of one nostril. "You, sir, have no honor."

"Says the guy who made it legal to kill a kid with a sword wound in his guts." Artus started to laugh, but it turned into a cough that produced some blood in his palms.

Artus collected his tiles—he was now at a one-tile advantage. The remaining blue and red tiles on the board were cleared by each of them in turn—Arving had a blue, Artus had a red. Had they been playing for money, he would have been pleased by the clutch. Playing for his life had a totally different feeling. *I'm not playing fast enough*. His heart was beating double time, even though he was only sitting there. He took a deep steadying breath and tried to calm himself, but the eyes of everyone around him kept him tense.

The board cleared, the next clutch was dealt and a new Heart placed. With two players, the clutches would be short and knowledge of what his opponent was hiding would be limited—this game would be decided by chance as much as skill. In a four-player game, it was easier to know what was in play and what wasn't by cataloguing the moves of the players. Here, Artus could be walking into a trap and never realize it until it was too late. He remembered Tyvian explaining this to him, once—*t'suul is a metaphor for how the Illini see life: harsh, short, and unfair. But, with a little bit of guts and cunning, you can still come out a winner.*

The question was, then, did Artus have the guts . . . especially seeing as how some of them were seeping out of him as they sat there?

He played the next two clutches quickly, slapping down tiles almost the moment Arving made his play, *shaming* Arving into increasing his pace. The old duelist still dallied, though, still placed his tiles carefully and gently on the felt. He was playing for time, but his pride was at risk.

Artus felt the blood seeping through his bandages, through his shirt. He felt faint, ill—the world seemed to revolve slowly. Still, he slapped the tiles down, even as his life leaked out. He kept his eyes fixed on Arving, making his stern face the anchor of his world. He slapped another tile down, grinning. He could feel blood pooling in his gums, so he spat it aside.

He was beginning to really understand what dailiki was all about. Why it was so important in Illin. The sign of a true man, perhaps—grinning at the approach of death, daring his opponent to do the same.

Arving's cropped goatee was fringed with blood by the fourth clutch and his hands trembled. Despite Artus's bravado, he was trailing the old man by three leaves. Artus was shivering by now, blood pooling in the seat cushion beneath him as it ran out of his deep wounds. His heart hammered in his ears.

Another Heart. They drew their clutches and Artus could barely suppress a gasp—five grays. The worst possible clutch in the game—he could initiate no duels, burn no stacks. The smart move would have been to forfeit—grant Arving his ante of two and try for another hand. But that would leave him with only three leaves, and after another two for the next clutch's ante, and he'd be without enough bet to play. He would die.

There was only one way to win—a rare thing, a hard thing to manage. He had to make the Serpent—connect all four colors without letting a duel resolve. It was a stupid thing to play for—nobody ever did it unless they were drunk—but it could pay off. A man who made the serpent claimed all tiles on the board as his own, along with all the ante placed atop those tiles.

Arving, his lips red with blood spilling over them, his eyes dripping red, slapped a gray tile between the black and red in the Heart. Artus grabbed the side of the board to keep from tipping over. *He's trying to draw me out! He's trying to end it now!*

Artus slapped a gray between the black and the

blue, setting up a bridge across the Heart from red to blue. Arving grinned, expecting this apparently. "Ha." He breathed and slapped red tile atop the dueled red. "Burn that. I dare you."

He must have most of the blues. Artus thought. But it didn't matter—he placed his second gray between black and white, unifying the whole board. The Serpent was made.

Arving blinked. "What? What?"

Artus collected his tiles. Net gain of seven. The score had gone from eleven and five to four and twelve. A devastating lead. Artus shook his head and spat more blood. "Shouldn't have played that gray. Got . . ." He coughed, and blood leaked from his nose. ". . . got greedy."

Arving was panting; his posture had crumpled into a slouch, his mouth hanging slightly open as blood dribbled out. "You . . . you should be dead by now."

Artus nodded. He could scarcely move well enough to let the sailor woman collect his tiles. "Giv . . . giving up, old man?"

The Heart was placed again. Artus didn't even look at his clutch—he slapped down an opening duel of blue against red. "Your . . . your move."

Arving, his elbow loose, arm quavering, threw a blue tile atop his and brushed two leaves in his direction—the end of Arving's pile of antidote.

Artus could scarcely see at this point. The world

seemed drained of color to the point where he barely knew which tile was blue. He found it though and, with the last of his strength, he slapped it atop the stack, adding three more leaves. "Mine. I . . . I win."

Arving slumped back in his seat, his head back, mouth open. Artus heard a cheer go up, but it was a distant one. Arving's little granddaughters rushed to the old man's side. They were weeping.

Artus tried to call to them. "I'm . . . I'm sorry . . ."

But then he was falling. The pit, whatever it was, was dark. And all too deep.

CHAPTER 34

MAN-EATER, HEARTBREAKER

When they were about a day's march outside the city of Eretheria, the Delloran soldiers moved off the roads, avoiding the toll booths, and bivouacked on large pastures or commandeered farmhouses and barns. Hool moved quickly after dark, scouting their positions, trying to find Brana's trail again, but the pup was clever enough to hide evidence of his passing—the Dellorans were alert, with fast horses they used to run down anybody who came across them. The bodies were hidden. Many flocks would go untended this spring, their shepherds and their families buried in shallow graves.

Hool hid beneath her cloak and watched from a

distance, counting cook fires in the early morning. There had to be almost a thousand Delloran soldiers closing in on the city, all in the guise of mercenary companies. From a distance, they might look like sell-swords hoping to get a fat contract just before the campaigns began. But they weren't. The way the men prepared their weapons, the way they slept in their armor, the way the officers conferred with one another over maps late at night proved it.

They were here to invade.

Maybe Brana had been right. Maybe Tyvian needed the warning. Hool had trouble imagining him being caught off guard, though. Tyvian seemed to know everything just before it happened. Humans just didn't surprise him.

Hool dozed a bit once the sun was up, always alert for the jingle of armor or the heavy tread of hooves. None approached. The Delloran scouts were beyond her hiding place—she had slipped through their pickets in the twilight of dawn, and they would never think to look for her so close. Besides, they were expecting nosy peasants and foolish travellers, not a gnoll.

She awoke just before noon to the sound of shouting. Three horses were approaching the camp, very close to where Hool had hidden, in a crevice of earth beside the edge of a big boulder. Two Dellorans had a horse between them and a man strung over the saddle. The man was wearing finery not suited to the road, but it had been through a difficult time—he was sodden, mud covered, and bleeding from an arrow wound in the shoulder. He was also making unreasonable demands of his captors. "Release me at once! You have no right to treat me this way! This . . . this is banditry!"

The man was Sir Damon Pirenne.

Hool's ears perked up and focused on the men as they passed. The Dellorans weren't saying anything except the occasional whisper to their horses as they approached the camp. One of them was riding close to Sir Damon and holding his horse's reins. The other had a short bow out and an arrow nocked, ready to shoot the knight if he tried anything funny.

Hool knew what would happen next. The men would bring him to their captain, who would ask Sir Damon questions to satisfy himself that nobody else knew they were there. Then he would cut Sir Damon's throat and throw him into the open grave they were maintaining for just this purpose. Already three people, two of them children, were occupying the bottom of that pit.

Hool felt her hackles rise.

The horses stopped just beyond the closest cook fire. This particular camp had about a hundred and fifty men in it, their pikes steepled all over the rolling pasture and men sitting around sharpening blades and roasting mutton on spits—the former flock of the people at the bottom of the open grave.

A man in black mail with the wyvern tabard of Sahand came forward to chat with the men on the horses, ignoring how Sir Damon struggled against his bonds. The man—the captain—rested his hand on the pommel of his broadsword with the ease of someone used to wearing it. He had a thin cigarillo hanging from his mouth beneath a long black moustache. Hool could smell the foul odor of it from here.

There must be a way to stop them. No, it was a bad idea—they'd shoot her before she got close. Their guard was up, they were too wary. Damon Pirenne just had to die . . .

But I don't want him to.

She growled to herself and laid her ears back against her skull. She hadn't done anything to save the poor shepherd and his two boys—why should she do something to save Sir Damon?

Hool didn't have any answer to that. As she thought about him and his bald head and his kind voice, however, she did find herself with something else instead—a plan. She reached into her satchel and drew out her shroud.

Seconds later, she was wearing it as she walked toward the encampment, her hands raised, her illusory auburn locks fluttering in the breeze. Sir Damon by this point was off his horse and kneeling on the ground before the captain, who had drawn his blade and was resting its point on the knight's shoulder.

When she was spotted, the cry went out and

men's heads began to turn. A few of them whistled and made lewd suggestions. All of them stared. The scent of arousal coming off the camp was stifling, but Hool kept coming forward.

When they were in earshot for their stunted hearing, Hool called out. "Do not kill him! He is my husband!"

The captain laughed and lifted the sword from Sir Damon's shoulder. "Well, well, well—I *thought* he wasn't alone, but I didn't think he'd be travelling with something like this!"

He barked a few harsh words over his shoulder at his men—mostly about shoddy scouting and letting a girl slip through the pickets—and then fixed a grin on his face and sauntered forward to meet her.

"You keep your greasy hands off her, you ugly—*oof.*" Sir Damon struggled to stand, but earned himself an axe handle in his face as a reward. He fell backward, blood pouring from his temple. "Run, Lady! Leave me! Run!"

Hool kept coming forward, keeping her hands up. She spotted three men with bows or crossbows at the ready, all clustered more or less in front of her. Good. "I will do anything you want if you will not kill my husband!"

The captain shot a look over his shoulder at his men, which caused them all to burst out laughing. He was probably winking at them or something else juvenile. *Let him.*

When the man was three paces away, he stopped. His broadsword, still drawn, rested flat against his armored shoulder. His posture was relaxed. He extended a hand. "You must be the loveliest flower in this valley, milady."

"I want to bargain for my husband's life," she said, hands still raised, her eyes fixed on his feet in what she hoped looked like submission. She took a step closer to him.

He did not draw back. "What exactly have you got to bargain with, my beauty?" The captain's leer was blatant, even for Hool's tastes.

Hool took another step closer. Only four steps away now. "Would you take me, instead?"

He laughed and stuck his broadsword point-down in the earth. "I'd take you right here, right now. I'll even let your man go." He licked his lips, letting his eyes ride up and down her body. "I'll even let him watch, if he likes."

Hool took two more steps. He was close now—so close Hool could see the creases at the corners of his eyes, the faded scar along his chin. She bared her teeth, which to the captain must have looked like a bright, toothy grin. "I am sure he will want to see this."

Hool grabbed the captain by the sideburns, and pulled him close. He was grinning . . . until she opened her mouth and tore off his jaw.

The captain couldn't exactly scream, but he gurgled at an impressive volume for a second as the blood poured out of his face and down his throat. He passed out immediately after that. Hool picked him up around the waist and started running toward the camp and Sir Damon.

It took the Dellorans about two seconds to realize what they were witnessing was not a particularly violent courting episode but, rather, a frontal assault. In those two seconds, Hool covered half the distance to Sir Damon. She felt the captain's body jerk three times—the men had fired their crossbows and their leader, in his role as shield, had absorbed the damage.

The crossbows would take a few seconds to reload. The archer got off two more shots—one wide, one feathering his captain's calf, before Hool threw the body at him.

The man with the axe who had hit Sir Damon swung at her and she darted aside into a crouch and drove the blade of her hand into the side of the man's knee. With all her strength behind it, it was enough to crack bone and cause him to stumble. She then picked him up by arm and leg and swung him around and into the next two men coming at her.

A Delloran threw an axe at her. She caught it out of midair and threw it back, hitting him in the hip. She grabbed Damon by the baldric and threw him over one shoulder. Four Dellorans surrounded her, brandishing broadswords and hatchets. They moved with caution this time.

Hool didn't want to fight, though. She wanted to

escape. She leapt at one of them—a stunning eight-foot horizontal leap that caused him to stumble over the captain's body in his haste to retreat. It was enough of an opening to throw Sir Damon into the saddle of one of the horses and leap up behind him. *"Ride!"* she roared in the knight's ear.

He set spurs to the horse and off it shot, through a rank of Dellorans still trying to understand what was happening. Hool clipped a man on the side of the head as they went past, knocking him sprawling.

And then they were away, galloping at full speed toward Eretheria.

"How did you . . . what was . . ." Sir Damon stammered, even as they rode.

"Shut up!" Hool snarled and tapped his arm. "Go that way."

They rode perhaps a mile over a hill and through a small copse of trees that Hool knew would hide them from any pursuers. She had them dismount from the horse into a tree and hoisted Sir Damon up into it with one arm. Then she roared at the horse so it kept galloping as fast as it could.

Sir Damon's eyes looked likely to fall out of his head. "My lady! Are you enchanted in some way?"

Hool sighed. "No. I'm just strong."

Sir Damon tried to more gracefully wedge himself between two tree branches, but was doing a poor job of it. "You—damn—you were throwing men about like scarecrows!"

"Stop moving so much!" she hissed. "You're shaking the tree!"

"I'm sorry—I mean, *thank you*, but I—"

"Stop talking, stupid!" She slapped a hand across his mouth and held it there.

There was a distant thunder of hooves, which grew louder and louder until a party of eight Dellorans on horseback rode through the wood. The man at the lead had his eyes fixed on the ground, following their trail. Hool hoped they were moving too quickly to notice something like the horse getting lighter as they hopped off. They were—they kept right on riding after barely a moment's pause. When at last the hoofbeats had faded, she released Sir Damon's mouth.

Weirdly, he was smiling at her. "I feel as though there is a great deal more to you than I have realized."

"Why are you out here?" Hool leapt down from the tree. She then turned to offer Sir Damon a hand.

He insisted on sliding down the trunk himself. With his injured shoulder, the descent was awkward and ended with the knight falling onto his back and groaning as he hit the ground. He was panting. "I . . . well . . . I . . . I was looking . . . for you . . ."

Hool frowned. "Why?"

Sir Damon rolled gingerly onto his feet and slowly rose, clutching the tree trunk to keep himself steady. "I am still technically in your service, milady."

Hool tried to parse out the meaning of this. "You are released from my service."

Sir Damon chuckled through his pain. "Then, as a knight errant, I choose to seek you anyway."

Hool cocked her head. This made very little sense to her. "But *why*?"

Sir Damon sighed and, with visible discomfort, got down on one knee. He took up her hand and held it tightly. "Lady Hool of Eddon . . . I . . . well, it's becoming very clear that I know very little about you or your friends or really, well, *anything*. I do know this, though: you are the most beautiful, most incredible, most admirable woman I have ever met . . ." He looked up into her face, his eyes glassy. ". . . and I love you very much."

Hool yanked her hand back.

Sir Damon put up his hands. "And even if you do not return this love, milady, it is my intention to stand by your side in your service for as long as you will have me." He clasped his hands together in pleading. "Please, Hool—have me."

Hool looked down at him. She couldn't decide if she should laugh or scowl or cheer. Laughing, she decided, would be too mean. So would scowling.

She didn't feel much like cheering either.

"There is something I think you should know," she said at last. "Get up."

Sir Damon rose painfully. "What is it? Are you a criminal? I honestly surmised that for myself. I really don't care if you are, and—"

Hool took off the shroud, and Sir Damon's voice

died in his throat. She stood there before him, clad only in her satchel, the Fist of Veroth in a sleeve between her shoulders. She towered over the knight, broader than him by half and taller than him by several hands. She waited to see what he would do.

"It's . . . you . . . you're a . . . a . . . what? What?"

Hool's ears drooped a little. "I'm a gnoll. From the Taqar."

Sir Damon looked down at the enchanted belt on the ground. "A . . . a shroud? But why? All this time? Why?"

"People don't get to pick their packs. We all have to do what we can to live." Hool sighed. "Do you still mean all that stuff you said before?"

Sir Damon was still staring at her, from foot to ears and back again. "I, well, I'm a man of my word, and—"

"No." Hool stopped him. "You will not stay with me because you said stupid words. If you stay with me, you will because you want to. We will never be lovers, Damon, but you are a kind man and a good one and I like you. If you want to stay, say so. If you don't, then go away."

Sir Damon sat on a fallen log and ran his good hand across his balding pate. "Damn . . . damn, what a fool I must look. Confessing my love to you?" He shook his head. "Story of my life, eh? Always signing up for the wrong commitments. Here I am, almost forty-two, and no land, no family, no money. But I

was respected at least. Tolerated in good company."
He laughed. "And I throw it all away for a beautiful
lady . . ." He motioned toward Hool. ". . . and look
what happens."

"It isn't my fault you're stupid. And I don't like
being insulted."

"No, no, milady . . . Hool. That's not what I meant."
He shook his head and then smiled at her. "I'm in."

"You are in my service?" Hool's ears climbed up.
"Really?"

Sir Damon sighed. "It's like some kind of fairy tale
in reverse but, dammit, you have no idea how boring
my life was before I met you."

Hool grunted. "If you think this is exciting, you
have no idea what you're getting into."

He smiled at her again, from his chin all the way
to his eyes. "Well, milady, perhaps that's why I'm getting into it."

Hool snorted a laugh. "I will get that arrow out. It
will hurt." She took off her satchel and started rummaging around for the pliers.

CHAPTER 35

ALL YOU CAN WISH AND MORE

Tyvian woke up on the palace grounds, beneath a lovely cherry tree in blossom, a cool wind tossing its branches. It had rained at some point early in the morning—Tyvian was soaked through—and as the branches shifted, more droplets of rain spattered on his face. That was probably what woke him.

He immediately started cursing at the tree. He tried to get up, but only made it onto his side before vomiting among the roots. His head felt like an anvil in use. The morning sunlight was a dagger in each eye.

He managed to squint and look around. The Guardian was standing nearby, at attention and clad in his ceremonial mail, as usual. "Good morning, sir."

"Go straight to hell." Tyvian rolled onto all fours, puked again, and then managed to pull himself to his feet using the tree. "How the hell did I get here?"

"You arrived after midnight in the company of some peasants. You insisted I pay them a gold mark apiece for being your 'stewards' and then subjected me to verbal abuse for about half an hour before you wandered out here to 'clear your head.' You are fortunate the Defenders still seek you in the city, otherwise they would have found some pretense to arrest you."

Tyvian closed his eyes, trying to recall any of it. All that was there was a giant, oggra-shaped hole where his memory should have been. "Kroth. Draw me a bath, will you? I need to become presentable for those stupid duels."

The Guardian's expression was entirely neutral. "I beg your pardon, sir, but *which* duels?"

"Artus's duels, obviously. Gods, man." Tyvian began to walk back toward the palace itself, his legs stiff as oars.

"The duels were fought yesterday. It is currently the morning of the twelfth, not the eleventh."

Tyvian froze and, for a moment, thought he might vomit again. "Wh . . . what? I lost a whole bloody *day*?"

"I was quite concerned," the Guardian said, with no outward indication of any such concern.

Tyvian touched his temples with his index fingers and rubbed gently. They felt like warhammers. He'd missed the duels. Artus needed him, and he'd been out drinking and plotting. He'd been so . . . so miserable for himself, for the world, he had left Artus alone to face death—the express thing he sought to avoid. The ring quaked to life, pricking him, but it needn't have bothered. Tyvian felt horrible enough as it was. He knew the question he had to ask next, but he was afraid to ask it. "And . . . and Artus? Is he . . . well . . . did he . . ."

"The Young Prince is alive, sir, but grievously hurt. Valen Hesswyn ran him through, and that, coupled with the poison—"

"Where?"

"In his chambers."

Tyvian funneled as much energy as he had left and ran to Artus's room. Well, he *intended* to run. He mostly staggered, tripped, and fell his way upstairs and down stately corridors. He arrived on Artus's doorstep, hands on his knees, dry-heaving into a chamber pot he'd snatched up along the way. He tried the knob—it was open.

Inside, Artus was beneath the heavy quilts of his massive bed, his face gray, his eyes closed. Tyvian stumbled to the bedside and reached for Artus's hand. He was cold as ice, but alive. "Oh gods. Artus . . . Artus, I'm sorry."

Artus said nothing. He barely moved. He barely seemed to breathe.

Tyvian's discussions with Eddereon came back to

him in full clarity. "I . . . I had a plan. It seems so stupid now . . . now that you're . . ."

"He is going to be all right, Tyvian."

Tyvian turned. His mother was sitting in a chair by the windows that overlooked the gardens along the lakeshore. It was thrown open, to let in the light and fresh air. To Tyvian's hangover, it was like gazing into the mouth of hell.

He was too exhausted, too sick to yell at her. "What happened?"

Lyrelle was wearing a relatively simple dress of royal blue, cut for riding, with a small white hat bearing a lace veil. She looked like she was about to go observe a hunt or possibly a battle. "What happened is that House Davram's honor is preserved—they lost a lesser vassal, but Valen Hesswyn was vindicated. Meanwhile, your young man there demonstrated remarkable grit and poise. There isn't a person in this city that isn't speaking of him with admiration right now. And at least four fifths of those people now loathe Davram."

"You used him, in other words." Tyvian climbed to his feet. "You made him into a martyr. You drove the wedge deeper between the nobles and the peasants. Why?"

"Tyvian, you talk as if the wedge between peasants and nobles was not already acute. Need I remind you of what has been happening in the streets of this city?"

"Myreon drove them to it."

"She merely lit the kindling. The hearth was already set, long ago." Lyrelle came away from the window and around the bed. "Now she has fallen in with the Sorcerous League."

Tyvian blinked. "She's *what*?"

"Myreon's frustration and anger has driven her to it, as the League knew it would. They want a war—that has always been their plan, and so they will give the world the Gray Lady. I want peace, so I gave Eretheria *you*."

"I'm *not* king." Tyvian's voice was weak, though. His plan—perverse, final—loomed over him.

Lyrelle pointed to the city beyond the gardens—picturesque from this distance, a city of broad streets and beautiful mansions, of church steeples and domes. "There are blocks full of people out there who think you are. Who *need* to believe in you. Without you, they believe they have nothing—no hope, no future that they can see. Those people will tear this city apart without you, and the peerage will drive them to it."

"And if I placate the masses, I will destroy the peerage! That isn't better!" Tyvian threw himself into a chair and covered his face. His head pounded—he wasn't up for this. He'd thought this all out already. It seemed inexorable, now—there was no other solution.

Lyrelle knelt before him and took up one of his hands. "All your life you've been afraid of what I asked of you. I understand that, Tyvian—I truly do. I knew your life was never going to be easy. Your brother casts a long shadow and your name would always follow you and I . . ."

She paused. Tyvian looked at her, searching for the lie. Gods, she was a magnificent actress—the way she bit the edge of her lip, the way she could get her eyes to be so large and so warm somehow. The softness of her touch, so nostalgic—of a world long dead, where he was a boy who loved his mother.

He pulled his hand away. His voice was bitter with irony. "Save it. Go dupe another boy into almost dying for you."

Lyrelle slapped him.

It was jarring to say the least—Tyvian nearly fell out of his chair. He stared at his mother, and saw that Lyrelle's eyes were heavy with tears. "That boy over there *loves you*, Tyvian! He is, in all this wide and horrible world, the only person who would follow you to certain death and smile. Do you really think I would take him away from you? He is alive because of *me*. Because I stuffed his face with food enchanted to absorb much of the poison *before* he could be poisoned."

"You let him get *stabbed* beforehand!"

"*Every* augury I could cast had that boy being run through by Valen Hesswyn—*this way* he got stabbed without exerting himself. He got stabbed in a way that made him a hero." Lyrelle wiped a tear from her eye. "I kept him alive, no thanks to you. *You* were too busy drowning your sorrows over the fact that the world is full of fools hell-bent on their own destruction."

"And you'd have me be king of them."

"Who else better to tell fools how to manage their affairs, than a man who's made his profession out of manipulating them?"

"If that's all it takes, then why don't *you* rule them?"

"*I am not a man, Tyvian!*" Lyrelle shouted, the steel flashing behind her eyes. "Goddammit, boy! What do you think I've been trying to do *my entire life?*" Lyrelle swept her arm around, indicating the fullness of the world. "Do you know what the most important things in the world are? I will tell you." She held up four fingers. "Peace, food, home, and children—that is *all*. Every damned other thing mankind has ever devised is *worthless*."

"I'm reasonably attached to wine."

"Don't be glib with me. I am not in the mood just now." Lyrelle was pacing. A frantic, nervous energy seemed to be spilling out of her and she could not stem the tide. If this was an act, it was beyond good—it was supernatural.

Gods, he thought, straightening in his seat, *I might actually be hearing the truth.*

"Human beings are imbeciles," Lyrelle said. "They all want the same things I just mentioned, and they use all the wrong means to achieve them.

How do they seek peace? Why, they invade other nations that look threatening. How do they seek justice? They imprison some and murder others. How do they make their homes? By stealing them from the original owners. It goes on and on and on, across cultures, nations, continents—it is all the bloody same, everywhere. I decided a very long time ago that the only reasonable way to get people to behave themselves was to *lie* to them. Tell them fairy stories. Get them to believe in miracles."

Tyvian frowned. "And this is where I come in, eh?"

"The fools in this kingdom want a demagogue, and either *you* will be it, or Sahand will. The people *believe* in you, Tyvian."

"The people are idiots, as you say."

"*So what?*" Lyrelle pointed in a direction that Tyvian imagined was north. "Sahand will step into any vacuum you allow him to. Eretheria is wide open—he is probably already marching on Ayventry as we speak. Without you, in a year he will own this kingdom, thanks to those idealistic fools Myreon courted in the sewers. Gods, by the time Sahand gets here, their families will probably join him willingly."

"I doubt that."

"Don't. Sahand is a fool in many respects, but he knows what people want to hear. He is a master at channeling the worst in people and forging it into an awful weapon. He'll do it here just as he did it in

Dellor. Just as he would have done in Galaspin and Saldor had I not stopped him thirty years ago."

"Gods . . ." Tyvian looked around for a glass of water. He needed a glass of water. "You . . . Xahlven . . . Xahlven was *right!*" Tyvian staggered to his feet. The room seemed to spin. She knew his plan—she had to. She had driven him here, to this very pass, just as she had done with all those others. "You *made* me into this! I'm your greatest tool!"

Lyrelle stood up slowly. "Tyvian, you have controlled your destiny—"

"No!" Tyvian snapped, backing away. "I don't want to hear it! Shut up!"

Lyrelle shouted over his objections. "You have controlled your destiny your entire life! I have only nudged you here and there. I've only seen the path ahead of you and cleared away obstacles! What mother would do any less?"

"Leave me alone!" Tyvian tried to find the door, but before he could get to it, his mother had grabbed him from behind. He struggled—was she attacking him? And then he recognized the gesture. She was . . . she was hugging him.

"I'm sorry," she whispered into his back. "I'm so sorry."

Tyvian pushed her away and turned around. Tears were streaking down her cheeks. Her, Lyrelle Reldamar, the Queen of Poise. "What the hell is the matter with you?"

Lyrelle remembered herself suddenly. She wiped away the tears with a handkerchief that materialized in her hand. "This will be the last time I speak with you."

Tyvian's heart leapt into his throat. "Nonsense."

She took a deep breath. "I'm quite sure of it."

He shook his head. What wasn't she saying? Where was the trick? "Why should I believe you? You have never spoken a true word to me in all your life."

Lyrelle dabbed under her eyes with the handkerchief. "I have spoken eight."

Tyvian's eyebrows rose.

"I am your mother, and I love you."

With that, she vanished from the room.

Tyvian stared where she had been for a long time. Only the sound of Artus breathing and the faint rustle of the curtains in the breeze could be heard. He ran a hand through his hair—it had sticks in it. "Fine," he muttered to no one. "If I'm to die, then fine. Let's get on with it, then."

The Congress of Peers was in an uproar. What to do about the overreach of Saldorian power into the Congress—of Defenders in the actual chamber—was in hot dispute, even as the Defenders stood there, pikes in hand, waiting. Camis wanted a headsman. Vora wanted them drawn and quartered. Hadda would have simply settled for banishment. Ayventry—or what was left of it—wanted an investigation into Eretheria Tower, claiming that this couldn't have happened without the Master declaring Argus Androlli Magus Errant. There were shouts and oaths, duels declared, and angry faces all around.

Then the great doors swung open. The Guardian entered and bashed his staff upon the ground. The peerage counted the strikes: once meant a commoner or foreigner, twice meant a knight or viscount, thrice meant an earl or count, and four times meant . . .

"The palace recognizes Tyvian Reldamar of Saldor, Declared Aspirant, who shall address the congress!"

The heir stood in the aisle. He was filthy—his hair mussed, his eyes bloodshot, stains covering his clothing. Black grime was caked under his fingernails. Only his sword looked clean.

He walked toward the dais, his eyes fixed only there, at the far end of the room. He hadn't gone three paces before the Congress began to shout his name. Tyvian couldn't make out what everyone said, but he knew what they wanted—his endorsement, his plan, him to use his clout with the peasantry to get them into line. A few hundred highborn men and women, all shrieking for attention like so many children. And from him—a man who looked like he'd been dragged through the gutter and hadn't even the decency to bathe before appearing before them.

The Defenders came alive. Androlli started barking commands, moving his men to cut Tyvian off, readying spells. House Hadda's own sorcerers— themselves former Acanostrum apprentices—raised wards to shield Tyvian from Androlli's compulsions or spells of binding.

Tyvian kept walking, looking neither right nor left. When he passed the Davram box, Countess Velia hailed him. "Sir, House Davram stands loyal to you! We are so pleased you are unharmed!"

Reldamar said nothing. He passed them right by. Right past the benches and to the stairs up the dais. Where he should have stopped, like he did before. Where he ought to have turned around and addressed them.

Except he didn't slow down.

He didn't stop.

The entire Congress fell silent at once, their eyes riveted to Tyvian Reldamar. The smuggler. The criminal. The swindler.

As he climbed the stairs and threw himself into the Falcon Throne.

The world froze. Countess Velia's mouth fell open. No one spoke or moved or did anything. Even Tyvian waited for the sorcerous retribution for his presumption, his arrogance, his *blasphemy*.

It did not come.

Tyvian slowly let out a breath he hadn't realized he'd been holding. *I'm not dead. This didn't kill me. Not yet.* Tyvian felt himself relax. His spontaneous act of suicide had just made his *eventual*, expected suicide much easier.

He leaned back in the throne and threw one leg over the armrest. "There. Now that's settled, you miserable sons of bitches are going to listen to what I say and, when I'm done, I want to hear a good hearty 'yes, Your Majesty' or you're all going to see how nasty I can be with a hangover. Is that understood?"

The only sound was the heavy sigh of Countess Velia as she fainted dead away.

CHAPTER 36

TYVIAN THE FIRST

Tyvian had always been comfortable in front of crowds—a side effect of his large ego—but sitting on that hard throne in front of that array of wealthy peers, Tyvian felt more than comfortable. He felt transcendent. He hadn't been king for thirty seconds and already he could see what the fuss was about.

His head still throbbed, his throat was still parched and, if he stood up, he was fairly certain his whole body would be trembling. Still, he managed a smile. "First things first." He pointed at Androlli. "As the King of Eretheria and all its provinces, I hereby banish you and your representatives from the Peregrine Palace."

Androlli's mouth flapped. "But . . . I was only . . ."

Tyvian slapped his hand against the armrest. "You heard me—get the hell out!"

The Guardian tapped his staff and a pair of armored golems standing in alcoves along the wall came to life, their giant swords gleaming.

Androlli froze, weighing his options, and then quickly ordered a retreat. "This isn't over, Reldamar," he said over his shoulder before leaving the hall, although it didn't really have quite the effect he probably hoped, as he was walking rather fast in the face of the golems. A hearty applause rose up from the assembly as he disappeared.

Tyvian snapped his fingers. "Not so fast!" He pointed at House Davram. Countess Velia was only just regaining consciousness. "By royal decree, House Davram and all its vassals are hereby forbidden from the floor of the Congress until further notice."

Old Countess Velia looked likely to faint again. "Wh . . . Your Grace . . . by what *right*?"

"You may address me as 'Your Majesty' and I'm the damned king, that's by what right—get out of here. Think you can poison and nearly kill my boy and not face the consequences! Go!"

Again, the golems flexed their sorcerous muscle. House Davram, their collected faces ranging somewhere from mute outrage to numb shock, filed out of the hall. When they had gone, Tyvian rubbed his hands together. "There—now that such unpleasantness is over, let's get down to business." He gestured to the remaining lords and ladies. "You people have a very serious problem. In your haste to steal land from one another to escape your monumental debts, you have earned the enmity of almost everyone who serves you."

The peerage looked sullen at this. Countess Ousienne opened her mouth to speak and Tyvian took great delight in shushing her. "Not just yet, Your Grace—your king is speaking."

A murmur of indignation arose from the Hadda section of the Congress, but it died down when Tyvian kept talking. "Let's not mince words—a pauper with a few spells didn't stick a knife in Count Andluss because everything's fine. Something is very conclusively amiss, and yet since that attack, the only thing you lot have bothered discussing is how and to what extent the rest of you might exploit Ayventry's lack of a leader to your own gain. Nobody—not one of you—has given more than a few moments' thought to *why* it happened."

Silence. Nobody seemed willing to meet Tyvian's eye. Fine.

"Well, I'm going to tell you what happened: you've been taking your people for granted. For centuries the peasantry of Eretheria have, more or less, happily gone along with your pointless little provincial wars with only the occasional uprising. And, it should be noted, that about a hundred years or so back, possibly a bit longer, the spring campaigns didn't happen *every* spring. I know, because I looked at the history—a subject your tutors could do a better job of, I should note—and while the spring campaigns date back to Perwyn's founding of the kingdom, the past hundred years has seen the number of actual battles go up by one-hundred and sixty-six percent. That, my friends, is a lot of dead people. What's worse, after my . . ."

Tyvian's voice caught on the next words. He had to take a moment to clear his throat, take a deep breath. "After my *father* . . ." He looked at the throne and around the massive chamber. "Gods, he really was my father, wasn't he?" He shook his head. "Anyway, the point is, after Perwynnon unified you against Sahand, he reinstituted the custom of popular conscription. And you people loved it so much that, after the war ended, you kept on doing it. Saved you a ton of money, and money was the thing you needed to wage war, and war was what you needed to make more money, and on and on and on."

Tyvian sighed. "You got so caught up in that vicious cycle, you forgot that the quality of life in your little fiefdoms was going down. Far too many households bereft of their primary earner. Taxes that climbed every year. And now, after the Saldorian Crash, it's worse than it's ever been. And none of you seem to care."

Count Yvert brandished his cane. "And what of it? This is the world! You cannot change it by waving your hands! You cannot issue a royal decree and make it vanish! If I stop taxing my vassals, if I order them to countermand their levies, my cousins . . ." He pointed to the other houses. ". . . will pounce upon me. I will lose everything. That is not reasonable."

Seeing an opening, Count Duren hopped in. "Just so! And even if you command us to do it *collectively*, all it would take is one of us to go back on their word and . . . and . . . well, it would be chaos!"

"Not to mention," Countess Ousienne added, "that it would make us weak in the face of Sahand, who is clearly influencing Ayventry's decisions. He may even have troops in Ayventry city as we speak."

This caused an uproar among the Ayventry folk—as much of an uproar as could be caused by their dwindling contingent, Tyvian noted. Many of them must have quit the capital already.

Tyvian raised his hand to silence them. To his complete surprise, it actually worked. He imagined this was due mostly to the novelty of it. He doubted it would last long. "Nothing can undo the damage you have already wrought among your subjects—on that, I totally agree. But you are going to need to make amends." The Congress bristled and Tyvian had to head off an uproar with that wave of the hand trick—which again, surprisingly, worked. "I know, I know—your pride would be crushed and your authority undermined. But that's why you aren't going to do it—*I* am." He cleared his throat. "I hereby decree two things: First, that the spring campaigns are hereby *cancelled* and all peasant levies be released to return home."

There were shrieks of alarm from the gallery. People came to their feet, gaping at him.

Tyvian pressed on, "Second is this: all persons of Eretherian birth, be they of high or low estate, are hereby invited to my coronation, set to take place this very evening."

Then the uproar came in full force.

The whole Congress came to its feet, shouting at him all at once. The wall of human noise was so absolute that he couldn't pick out individual words at all. He got the meaning well enough, though. These people were terrified and the only way they could express it was with anger.

But he had diverted that anger now—toward him, and not toward the people. He wondered whether Myreon would approve of the gesture or not. *It'll make it harder for her to start a war, at any rate.*

When it became clear that no one in the Congress was willing to hear another word he said, Tyvian rose and, rather than leave the direction he had come, elected to exit via the fifth door—the King's Door. The door that hadn't been used in nearly thirty years.

It opened easily, on counterweighted hinges, and when he closed it behind him, the furor of the Congress of Peers was wholly blotted out. Tyvian sagged against the doors for a moment, closing his eyes. He was trembling.

My father was Perwynnon, the Falcon King. Even as he said it to himself, it didn't seem real. Perhaps his mother had tampered with the enchantment upon the throne. Maybe this was all some elaborate dream of his, and he was still drunk and dozing beneath that cherry tree in the gardens.

But no. *I always knew your life would be difficult.* His mother's words. What had he been like? Had she loved him, or was he just another pawn in her massive, decades long game to . . . to do what? Prevent a civil war that Xahlven would only seek to cause almost forty years after Tyvian's birth? It made no sense. His whole life was just a jigsaw puzzle of his mother's incomprehensible plots.

He opened his eyes.

The chamber before him was vast—far larger than the Congress and also far, far older. A perfect circle about a hundred yards across, the floor of polished marble. The ceiling . . . was not there, or if it was, it was so far away that Tyvian's eyes could not resolve it from the filtered sunlight that streamed down from a thousand tiny windows. He realized that he was gazing up the central bole of the Empty Tower itself, the hornlike white spire of the Peregrine Palace, visible for miles and miles in every direction. Seven hundred feet tall and all of it hollow. He heard the coo of doves and the twitter of starlings roosted in the windows high, high above.

At the center of the room, beneath a pure beam of

soft sunlight, was a bier. On it, still lying in state, was the body of Perwynnon, Falcon King of Eretheria, dead these twenty-seven years. Tyvian could see the runes etched into the floor—a ritual of stasis erected around the body. Within that circle, no time would pass. Perwynnon would look exactly as he did at the moment of his death, or whenever it was that he was laid here.

Tyvian walked closer, shielding his eyes against the light, his soft boots making no sound on the smooth floor. His heart was pounding.

Perwynnon had Tyvian's red hair, bound in a long braid that ran over his left shoulder. He would have been a tall man, but lean. His chin was Tyvian's, there could be no doubt, but his nose was rather larger and more hawklike. He wore a short goatee with no hint of gray. On his chest he clutched his famous broadsword, *Justice*. He wore mageglass plate of staggering quality, and lay among a sea of white carnations and blue roses. Tyvian looked on him in silence.

Tyvian had been ten years old when this man died. Ten. For all those years—both before and after—he had asked for his father, over and over again, and his mother had never told him. To think he might have met the man, perhaps even remembered him. Had he? He tried to throw his mind back that far, but all he got was the impression of a thousand social events, him standing next to Xahlven in a starched ruff, bowing to men and women whose names he could never hope to recall. He knew he had always been on the lookout for a man who might be his father. Perhaps their affair was a secret one. Perhaps Perwynnon hadn't even known he existed.

The thoughts were a kind of pain he had never experienced. Tyvian felt hollowed out, like the very tower he now stood in.

The Guardian entered and knelt. "Your Majesty."

Tyvian tore his eyes away. "What?"

The Guardian remained on his knees. "Your Majesty, with so many people inside the palace, I will be unable to afford you my fullest protection."

Tyvian frowned—a threat or simple honesty? It scarcely mattered. "I am not the person you need to worry about protecting, sir."

"If I may, Your Majesty, who *is*?"

Tyvian sighed. "The peasantry. Or possibly the peerage. Depending."

"I don't understand," the Guardian said, still staring at the floor.

Tyvian remembered that he had to bid him rise, and so he did with a little wave of the hand. "When I was a boy and I would fight with my brother, my mother's solution was often to lock us in a room together and demand that we reach an accord before we were allowed to leave."

The Guardian, for the first time since Tyvian had known him, exhibited a facial expression. It was one of complete shock. "So, you plan to . . ."

Tyvian grimaced. "Your task is to make sure no blood is spilled, never you mind what I intend to do. Now, if you will excuse me, I am overdue for a bath." He brushed past the Guardian and, casting one last look over his shoulder at the man who was his father, began the long, long trek back to his bedroom.

CHAPTER 37

CORONATION

Artus woke up when the light of the setting sun rested upon his face. Late afternoon. He was alive. In his room in the palace. "Tyvian?" Artus murmured.

"His Majesty is . . . he's busy." Michelle sat by the side of the bed. She was dressed in a spring green gown that highlighted freckles in her thin cheeks. She looked very pale.

"Since when do you have freckles?" Artus asked.

Michelle laughed and each laugh was accompanied with a little snort. Then she blushed. "Oh, I'm sorry. I didn't mean to laugh! Please forgive me!"

Artus tried to sit up, but the room spun and his stomach blazed with pain. He rested back into the pillow with a groan. "Michelle, I'm not gonna stop talking to you just 'cause you laugh at something I say. I'm not like those jerks you hang around with."

Michelle's eyes grew wide and she nodded. "I know. Gods, I know you're not. That's why I'm here. I had to say I'm sorry."

"You didn't do anything," Artus said, smiling at her. "You got nothing to apologize for."

Michelle sighed. "I hung around with Elora because she was a climber . . . and I guess I was, too. I always figured, when she became a great lady, I could become her handmaiden or some such. Maybe even marry one of her husband's squires."

Artus reached out to take her hand, but of course the bed was too enormous, so Michelle had to sit on the edge and reach back. Her fingers were hot. "You listen here, okay: Elora Carran is never gonna be as great a lady as you."

Michelle blushed. "I should go. The king has banished all of House Davram from the palace. I shouldn't even be here." She stood up and gathered up a parasol.

Artus blinked. "Wait . . . king? What king . . . Tyvian?"

Michelle nodded. "He's being coronated tonight. People have been filing into the palace all day, common and noble alike."

Artus gaped at her. "Kroth's teeth! That . . . that idiot!"

Michelle blushed at his profanity. She pointed to the bedside table. "He left a letter for you. I hadn't noticed it before, but he's really very regal, isn't he?"

Artus had no answer for that. He reached for the letter and Michelle handed it to him. With weak, trembling hands, Artus cracked the wax seal and began to read:

Artus,

    First you must allow me to apologize for placing you in the situation you now find yourself. There is no excuse for it. I have made a mess of many things in my life, but your life was never intended to be among them. I have taken you for granted. I am very sorry. Tonight, I plan to set many things aright. Do not try to find me because where I go, you are forbidden to follow. The death of a king is no small thing, and it would be best if you were well away from here before it comes to that. In the ultimately likely event a speedy and surreptitious escape is required, I've rigged the corner room on the top floor of the south wing so that you can pull a Galaspin (remember?) and get away. Please live a long, happy life somewhere far from here.

    Your friend, forever and always,

Tyvian Reldamar, King of Eretheria and all its Counties, etc, etc.

P.S.: Put the funds to good use. I trust your judgement.

In the envelope was the heavy iron key—the key to Hool's vault beneath the House of Eddon. Artus looked up from the letter at Michelle, who was halfway out the door. "Wait!"

She looked back at him. "What?"

"Help me up!" He held out his hands.

Michelle ran to his side and tried to press him back into bed. "You shouldn't be up! You're gravely hurt!"

"You don't understand!" Artus yelled, "Tyvian—the *king*! He's going to let them kill him! You've gotta help me!"

Michelle chewed her lower lip for a second and then nodded. "Okay. What do I need to do?"

Artus pointed to the armoire. "First, get my pants."

The great necromantic ritual was completed with the last rays of the sun to fuel it. Myreon had never experienced such power before. The ritual space in the ancient cavern glowed with sun-bright radiance, and the magic circle—the veta—was but a column of pure white energy. Lightning arced from it, striking corpse after corpse that Myreon and the necromancer had so painstakingly arrayed over the last two days—all of them lying in perfectly ordered rows, stretching down the path that led to the veta and into the sewers beyond. Soft green light came to life in their hollow eye sockets. Slowly, the bodies began to rise.

They were soldiers, mostly—taken from cata-

coombs and mass graves from ancient Eretherian bat-
tlefields, amassed here by the necromancer for years.
Once Myreon got past the horror of seeing the dead
walk, she could see the poetry in it. Many of these
poor souls had been levies as well, or poor men-at-
arms or mercenaries, all of whom had died for some
noble house or another and had nothing to show for
it. They had died for the vanity of their so-called betters, and now, after long ages, they would have their
revenge.

The necromancer waved his hands gingerly
over the glowing Lumenal script that powered the
ritual. The focusing medium was a great block of
quartz at the center of the veta, and it was so full of
power Myreon could not look at it. The necromancer
nodded, his blind eyes oblivious to the glare. "The
animation construct is holding. Five hundred and
two score risen dead await our bidding."

Myreon caught up her staff. "I will lead them
into the palace via the sewers. You will maintain the
ritual?"

The blind old sorcerer laughed. "No. I would join
you. I would see this thing done."

Myreon snorted a laugh. "You're blind, old man."

"Permit a blind man his metaphors. You are certain the palace wards shall not hinder us?"

"No wards will hold me back. Not tonight."

The necromancer grinned. "Then sound the advance."

Myreon nodded and thrust her staff forward. As one, her undead legion took one faltering step forward, then another, then another. They were on the move.

Myreon was officially a necromancer.

She only hoped she was a good one.

The night of Tyvian's coronation was cloudy but warm, with a stiff breeze blowing up from the south. A new throne—one more comfortable and personable—had been set up at one end of the grand ballroom, beneath the massive portrait of Perwynnon, lest anybody forget who exactly Tyvian was and why he was here.

The nobility arrived early, the rows of stately carriages stretching the full length of the palace's vast front courtyard. As there were no traditions associated with coronations, per se, and particularly not for ones requested on such short notice, royal blue was in evidence on most everyone's attire—something that typically would have been a faux pas. They knew this and wore it anyway—an act of defiance. *You do not rule us*, it said.

Tyvian tried not to read into it.

The peerage was, as Tyvian had predicted, accompanied by a vast array of professional duelists, hard-faced sell-swords, and hired goons. They were dressed well, of course (being accompanied by a poorly dressed bodyguard just wasn't done), but their bearing made them stick out like bears in a henhouse. Tyvian's ingrained threat senses were in a state of high alert, as everywhere he looked were men who had the physique and confidence of trained warriors and killers. The vast majority, he couldn't help but note, weren't Eretherian at all. They were Galaspiners, Ihynishmen, dour Illinis, sharp-eyed Verisis, and even the occasional stiff-backed Eddoner. Some were even more exotic than that, hailing from the Deep South, beyond Kalsaar, or from the distant Eastern Islands.

He mingled freely with them all, dragging the Guardian along into indefensible positions— surrounded by Ousienne's sell-swords at one moment, accepting drinks from Yvert and Duren the next. He felt wild, almost out of control, even though this ought to have been the safest of environments, watched as he was on all sides by teams of rivals eager for his favor and flanked by armed men. He knew better, though.

Tonight was the night he died.

The common folk showed up just before sundown, after the day's work was done. They came in family groups or in little clusters of twos and threes. They were dressed in their feast-day best, which was several orders of magnitude less impressive than even the most humbly dressed palace servant. Still they came, and Tyvian had left standing orders that they were to be made welcome by the Guardian and his golems. Whether the Guardian did it or not was on his conscience. It was abundantly obvious that, as much as Tyvian would have liked to control every aspect of this harebrained scheme of his, it was quite beyond any control at all. He was merely the man who spiked the dam. The encroaching torrent was truly beyond him.

But it *was* exciting.

He threw himself among the commoners next. They knelt in his presence, they laid kisses upon the hem of his ermine robes, they held their children on their shoulders. There were those, he noted, who drew away, who scowled—but they were the minority. He touched heads and spoke quiet words of encouragement—empty as they were insincere, he felt—but they worked anyway. He left women trembling. He made old men weep.

I can't believe it, he thought as he wound through the press of hands and faces and bodies, *these people really think I can save them. I could say the word, and they would die for me.*

Then the Guardian touched him on the shoulder. "It is almost time to begin."

Tyvian nodded and extricated himself from the crowd. He retreated to his chambers, where his formal robes of office had been laid out, along with an orb and scepter. Here, alone, he would prepare himself for his formal crowning, just as Perwynnon had done, and emerge on the ballroom floor as the first announced to take his seat and prepare to formally receive the title of King.

And so Tyvian, clad in regal robes, was installed on the throne and the nobility were paraded before him, each being introduced by the Guardian with the proper number of thumps from his staff. Two hours later, Tyvian sat back as the last of them did their curtsies and bows. Two of the last hours of his life wasted being introduced to people. Gods.

The peerage had arrayed itself along the walls of the ballroom and, beyond the doors at the other end, a press of peasantry peered from behind a length of velvet rope. In the vast empty aisle of blue and white tile that stretched out before him, standing at perhaps the center of the room, his mother held a crown on a cushion. She was serene, beautiful—a sorceress from a storybook, wearing her black robes and bearing a long staff.

Tyvian was surprised to see her, though of course it made sense—the magi had been crowning the kings of the West for over a thousand years and, retired or not, Lyrelle Reldamar was the ranking mage present. Whispers coursed among the crowd. Tyvian knew what they said; he didn't need to hear. *There is Perwynnon's lover. Behold her bastard son. Can you believe it?*

Tyvian stood, adjusting the long cape of ermine that draped over his shoulders. He took a deep breath, and recited the lies he had written just hours before. "I wish to welcome you all to the palace of my father, and of his ancestors before him. I know you are all afraid of what is about to happen—I am afraid, too. But I also know that the noble peers and good people of Eretheria can overcome this fear. That we can all start anew, amend our faults, and join together. I stand ready."

The ring, interestingly enough, remained silent.

Lyrelle nodded deeply—approval? Impossible to say. She started toward him, moving at a stately pace, the crown held high for all to see.

This was it. Tyvian marveled at the madness of it all. He saw the crown approaching as though in a dream—he wondered whether if he tried to flee, his feet would find purchase on the ground or not.

The shouts of alarm, when they came, caused him to crash back to reality. Oddly, with the beginning of his death, he found he could breathe again.

All heads were turned toward the doors. Shoving through the press of the peasantry was a tall man, balding—Sir Damon. With him was Hool.

Tyvian frowned—*this* he had not expected.

"My liege!" Sir Damon yelled, panting. "The hosts of Dellor are at the edge of the city! They march upon us as we speak! To arms! To arms, Eretheria!"

Cries of dismay and roars of anger rose up from the mob. Tyvian sighed as he heard them—he had been hoping for a few more hours, at least. Just a few more.

Hool was by his side. "It is Sahand. He has come."

Tyvian shook his head. "Sahand can't hold the city—never in a thousand years. He must know this."

Hool snorted. "He isn't here for the city, stupid. "He is here for *you*."

CHAPTER 38

ULTIMATUMS

The Delloran army, masquerading as mercenaries, marched in neat blocks up the grand avenues that led from the edge of the city to the palace and lake at its center. They came up the Freegate Road from the northeast and along the Old Coast Road from both west and east. From the pillars of smoke arising from the north, Tyvian guessed that Sahand had spiked the spirit-engine tracks. Anyone who sought to impede them was impaled on the foot-long tips of their pikes and left to bleed out in the gutters. There was no apparent escape.

Tyvian stood atop one of the few flat turrets of the old palace and watched them approach, his face grim.

Hool was with him. "I can't believe I didn't see this coming. Gods, Sahand must have been placing these men in position for months. This was his endgame all along. Not conquest of Eretheria, just . . . just petty revenge." Tyvian cursed—he'd been distracted, too self-involved in his own personal nonsense to see this simplest, most obvious of plots. Gods, what a dunce he'd been!

Hool didn't seem to care for his self-pity. "Everyone is running around like scared rabbits. You need to tell them what to do."

"I've got five warring factions down there and a giant crowd of unarmed civilians. Does it really matter if they die running around like idiots or while standing in neat little rows like idiots?" The ring gave him a twinge, though. Yes, he supposed it was his duty. Even if he hadn't been technically crowned yet. He sighed. "Fine. But don't blame me when this goes sideways."

"Everything with you goes sideways," Hool said.

Fair enough.

The Guardian, through his golems, tried to spread word that everyone should gather on the floor of the congress. It had partially worked, and the majority of the nobility and some quarter of the peasantry had crammed into the vast chamber. The five great doors stood open, meaning people could cluster in the wide halls beyond and still be able to hear. The great vaulted ceilings echoed with panicked cries and angry shouts. That many people made the air stale and hot. Yet when Tyvian entered through a secret door the Guardian revealed to him, the mob grew quiet.

Tyvian didn't have time to balk at the enormity of the danger or the absurdity of his command of it—he had expected chaos, just not of this kind. Fine. He would improvise even his own demise, it seemed. "Ladies and gentlemen, Banric Sahand and his army will be at the gates of the palace in less than half an hour, at a maximum."

Somewhere a woman howled in terror.

Tyvian shook his head. "This great palace, in Perwyn's wisdom, was not built for defense, but rather for diplomacy—Sahand will not besiege us, he will simply assault. The wards upon this place will keep his men out, but they won't stop him from bombarding this place and reducing it to rubble."

Tyvian took a deep breath. *Time to lie.* "The good news is, we outnumber him—with the collected might of the mercenaries brought here by the peerage and the patriotism of the people, we can throw him . . . *ow* . . . back." The ring gave his finger an awful wrench, so hard he had to sit down. He pressed on. "Together, just as in my father's time, we can overcome the Mad Prince."

The crowd immediately began arguing with itself, an oceanic uproar of finger pointing and order shouting. Tyvian retreated to an alcove and waved for the

Guardian to follow him. The unflappable old man was a rock of evident calm in a sea of panic. "The golem stand ready for your command, sire."

"How many golem are there?"

"Functional, or altogether?"

"Hann's Boots, man, does it look like we're going to *repair* any golem in the next fifteen minutes? *Functional*, for the love of all the gods!"

"Ten."

Tyvian blinked. "There have to be at least thirty on the grounds! Only ten work?"

The Guardian shrugged. "Well, sire, there usually isn't that much here for them to protect. Ten always seemed a reasonable number."

Tyvian scowled. He was, in a perverse way, glad that he had expected to die here tonight. It made everything a bit less stressful. "Keep them in reserve. Wait to see where Sahand plans to break through and then deploy them there."

The Guardian bowed his head. "As you command."

Tyvian gave him a terse nod and emerged from the alcove into the chaos of the Congress. There were about a thousand metaphorical fires he ought to put out—he needed to secure Ayventry's loyalty, to unify Hadda and Davram, to prop up the panicky Houses of Camis and Vora.

He didn't do any of this.

Instead, he walked through the screaming masses

of peers, nodding regally to certain important persons, and then through the pleading throngs of peasants, all of them begging for salvation, and went to the balcony overlooking Ayventry Lawn—the palace's front door.

Across two hundred yards of stately gardens and carefully pruned trees was an iron fence, fifteen feet high, that comprised the only defensive fortification the palace possessed. The stone pillars that anchored the fence every fifty feet or so all bore the wards that kept uninvited persons out, but Tyvian rather doubted those would hold for long. Beyond the iron bars, the city seemed quiet, or perhaps was just in hiding. He could hear the beat of drums in the distance, growing ever closer.

On the lawn, a variety of mercenaries from numerous companies were seeking to arrange themselves into some kind of cohesive fighting force. Their efforts were going rather well, Tyvian thought, but their numbers only just reached into the several hundred. It wouldn't be enough at all. Not by half.

He was joined on the balcony by the Counts Duren and Yvert and the Countess Ousienne, plus their champions. All of them gazed outward, awaiting the approach of the Delloran army.

Count Yvert was wringing his hands. "Join together? Is this the extent of your plan, *monsieur*? You can't be serious! You must do something!"

Tyvian spared him a hard look. "If you can't work

together to survive this, *monsieur*, then you deserve what comes. You lot have put a lot of labor into destroying my father and making me superfluous—this turn of events is out of my hands."

On the lawn below, troops of peasants, armed with improvised weaponry torn from the fixtures of the palace, were forming crude ranks to bolster the mercenaries. He watched men hug their wives and kiss their children before joining the defense. Many, he noted, turned to salute him as they slapped a pot on their head and entered ranks. The ring squeezed hard, and Tyvian blinked away tears from the pain.

At last, the enemy appeared.

The Delloran soldiers marched in perfect unison, a wall of glittering iron beneath a forest of pikes. As they deployed on the other side of the great plaza before the garden's main entrance, Tyvian felt as though he were watching some kind of complicated machine unfolding for use—efficient, organized, and remorseless. The drums beat steady time, drowned out only by the sound of hundreds of hard boots on cobbles stamping in unison. Tyvian felt his stomach shrink.

The Countess Ousienne leaned on her husband's arm. "What do you suppose his terms will be?"

"Terms?" Tyvian laughed. "This is Sahand, isn't it? He won't offer terms until half of us are dead."

Ousienne glared at him. "Then why isn't he coming across the plaza? Why isn't he shooting?"

The drums stopped and there was a rapid call of a short horn. As one, the legions of Dellor planted their pikes butt-down on the cobbles. The front rank knelt behind shields that the third rank passed up and planted in front of them. Some kind of defensive formation. Then silence.

"Hold steady!" Tyvian yelled to the defenders below, but couldn't see the point. Not a man in his rag-tag force was about to set foot beyond the enchanted borders of the palace—not for him and not for anybody. If Sahand didn't come to them, they would happily stand here and starve to death.

The quiet stretched out. "What are they waiting for?" Count Duren hissed.

Tyvian felt something—a change in air pressure, perhaps a down draft. It made him look up. Something was coming—something *big*.

It swept over the palace defenders, too high to see clearly, but low enough to get a sense of its scope—a forty-foot wingspan of purest black, darker than the sky itself, with a slender body like a serpent, a pair of huge, horse-snatching talons pulled up underneath its body. Tyvian felt his mouth fall open. "Oh . . . oh sweet merciful Hann . . ."

Below, a mercenary officer's horse began to panic and he struggled to control it. Countess Ousienne put a hand to her mouth. "A wyvern? An actual *wyvern*?"

The beast did a lazy circle over the battlefield and at last landed on the roof of a Saldorian trading house across the plaza, behind the ranks of Delloran steel. It folded its wings like a parrot and dipped its head low, its talons clutching the ridge of the roof tightly enough to make the shingles buckle. There, seated in an elaborate saddle just in front of the wings, was a man in black plate wielding a huge scepter. There was only one person it could have been.

Count Duren muttered aloud what they all knew. "Banric Sahand."

Tyvian grimaced. That pass alone had probably lost them twenty men who now fled back across the gardens toward the palace itself. He yelled down at them again, "Hold the line, dammit!"

The orders echoed through the air. It didn't look like anybody was bothering to listen.

Sahand's voice, boosted by sorcery, boomed across the plaza, loud enough for all to hear. It began with a laugh, hard and vicious—a bully mocking his victim. *"You all know me. You know my reputation. You know the reputation of my men."*

Sahand let that sink in for a moment. Tyvian's heart was pounding. He knew him all right. He felt tingles running up and down his body—a little voice was telling him to run, but he knew well enough that there was no such option.

"This time," Sahand boomed, *"There is no Perwynnon that will save you. No Finn Cadogan to stop me. No Conrad Varner to bring you victory. There is only my army and yours."*

"We're all going to die," Count Yvert muttered, pale. "Sweet merciful Hann, he'll kill us all!"

"All the more reason to stick together, then!" Tyvian snapped at him.

"*But I have good news,*" Sahand said, laughing, "*I am not interested in you and your miserable little country. I have no need to spill Delloran blood to teach you a lesson. All of you may yet live, if I have my way. All I ask is very simple: bring me Tyvian Reldamar, the son of Perwynnon, your so-called king. Bring him to me, throw him out of his own gates, lay down your arms, and know my mercy. Or . . .*"

A shot of adrenaline bolted up Tyvian's spine. He shouted down to the gardens, "Get down! Everyone get down!"

But it was too late.

The wyvern's long neck bulged for a moment and then its snout opened. A jet of sticky liquid arced across the plaza and struck the palace gates and those standing immediately behind it. The caustic slime sizzled at the silver metal and burned through the flesh and bone of those it struck. Men screamed as their clothing burned away. Tyvian caught a whiff of some horrid chemical—it made his eyes water. The ranks of peasants behind the gates fell back, some noble souls dragging their still-burning comrades away.

Then the arrows began to fall. Not crossbows bolts, with their flat trajectories—these were longbowmen, hidden somewhere in the rear of the Delloran column. Yard-long arrows fell across the lawn, mostly at random. Peasants went down left and right—they had no shields, no armor, no way of protecting themselves. Even the mercenaries, dressed for a party, were ill suited to weather the barrage. The whole Eretherian "army," such as it was, retreated twenty paces from the palace border. The grass before them was littered with a few dozen dead and injured.

"That was but a gentle caress, Eretheria," Sahand said. Tyvian could somehow *hear* his smile. *"Next time, the rain of death does not cease. Bring me Reldamar. You have ten minutes."*

Tyvian looked at the nobles surrounding him, at the terror on their faces. He saw the champions reaching for their swords. "I'd like to say, for the record, that handing me over to that man would be a mistake."

Duren smoothed his thick moustache and nodded to his champion. "Go on, then—seize him."

Tyvian backed away, sword drawn.

Ousienne was somewhat less restrained than Duren. She screeched, "Get him! Get him—a thousand marks for Reldamar!"

It was at about this time that the living dead showed up.

CHAPTER 39

IT'S ALL FUN AND GAMES UNTIL THE DEAD WALK

Artus was just about dressed and ready to go. Michelle, blushing the whole while, was helping him lace up his shirt. Outside, there was some manner of commotion—he could hear people running, people screaming. "Something's going on." He grimaced, trying to see how easily he could move. He nearly fainted, and Michelle had to hold him up. "Kroth."

"Artus," Michelle gasped, "language, please!"

With all that was going on in his life, he almost laughed at the absurdity of it all. Before he could, though, the door was kicked in and on the other side was a . . . a thing. A rotting corpse, dusty from the grave, wearing a torn and ancient tabard so filthy that its heraldry was forever obscured. In its hand was a rusty axe, dripping with blood. Behind it, reaching out with skeletal fingers, were more of the same.

Michelle literally jumped into Artus's arms. *"Kroth's teeth!"*

Artus, completely unable to support her weight, fell down right away.

The animated corpse stomped slowly toward them.

Michelle screamed and threw a pillow at it. The creature did not seem to notice. It raised its axe and staggered forward, swinging wildly.

Artus rolled to his knees and struggled to his feet. "Michelle . . . a little help . . ."

The girl put an arm under his and hauled him up, still shrieking.

Artus pushed a chair in the thing's way. The risen dead smashed it apart. Artus and Michelle found themselves backed into a corner of the room. Artus tried to think where he had put his weapons—in the armoire!

The armoire on the other side of the room.

"Do something!" Michelle screamed.

"I'm open to suggestions."

And that's when Brana arrived, swinging a war-hammer. The undead were little match for the young gnoll's gleeful ferocity—they were crushed utterly. The one with the axe barely had time to turn around before Brana smashed it into pulp. He kept smashing it, too, even as the body twitched and tried to rise.

Artus grinned at him. "Good timing."

Brana wiggled his rear end. "Found you, brother!"

Michelle fainted dead away.

It was then that Artus realized Brana wasn't wearing his shroud.

"Brana, help her up, okay? What the hell is going on out there?"

Brana closed his mouth and eyes, searching for the words. "Everything" is what he came up with.

He wasn't wrong. In the corridors, men in fancy clothes dueled with swords, some yelling "Perwynnon and the King" and others yelling various other things that Artus couldn't bother to figure out. Mercenaries hacked at legions of the living dead who smelled of wet earth and rust. Common people ran to and fro, looting what they could carry while others searched for safety that was not to be found.

In one gallery, a ten-foot golem of silvery steel crushed four wriggling corpses with its massive hammer even as a half dozen more swarmed on its back. A Defender shot at them with his firepike before being run through from behind by mercenary, who took the weapon and started shooting at *other* corpse-things. The madness of it boggled Artus's mind. "We have *got* to get out of here."

Brana nodded.

Hool found them, with Sir Damon by her side, his

sword drawn and blooded. He had a look on his face of near-permanent panic. Artus thought maybe his eyebrows were going to climb all the way to the top of his head.

"Mama!" Brana rushed to leap into his mother's arms.

Hool batted him away. "Hurry up! There are soldiers and monsters and walking dead people all over this place!"

"We hadn't noticed," Artus said.

"You sound like Tyvian now. Let's go."

Artus tried to put some power behind his strides, but he felt as though . . . well, he felt as though all his blood had been recently drained out. But she brought up a good point. Artus pointed to Michelle, still passed out. "Get Michelle, Hool. I need to find Tyvian."

Hool laid her ears back. "No. Nobody is finding anybody. We are getting out of here right now."

"I really must concur, Sir Artus!" Sir Damon said, even as he turned to face a small party of animated skeletons seeking to clamber up the stairs.

"No!" Artus staggered to a pillar, trying to stay standing. "I won't leave without him."

Brana barked his support. "I stay, too, Mama."

Hool bared her teeth. "Tyvian is fine. Tyvian is always fine. If we stay, one of us might die . . ." She pointed at Michelle, who was only just coming to. ". . . probably her. Do you want her to die?"

Artus looked at Michelle long and hard, his jaw clenched. Finally, he shook his head. "No."

"Then let's go." Hool turned to head down the hall, but Artus stopped her with a shout.

"No," he said, "I know another way."

With Brana's help, Artus led them up the stairs and down another corridor and up more stairs. Everywhere he went he saw people in need of help, in need of rescue, in need of comfort—old men, cowering in corners. Children crying over the bodies of their parents, both commoner and noble alike. Each of these sights was like another sword in Artus's stomach. He wanted to pick them all up, carry them on his shoulders. But he couldn't—he didn't have the strength.

"Leave me . . . ." Michelle howled as they stopped to rest for a moment. Behind them, Hool was tearing apart a pair of mercenaries who had shouted for them to halt.

Artus blinked at her, shocked at the echo of his own thoughts. "What?"

Michelle wiped the tears from her face. "Save someone else, Artus. Some of the children. Some of the innocents. I'm just dead weight."

Not totally knowing what he was doing, Artus pulled her into an embrace with one arm and kissed her on the lips. "You're coming with me, understand? I'm not leaving you. Not ever."

Hool poked him in the back with a helmet. It was coated with blood. "Stop kissing her and put this thing on. We are running out of time—the Dellorans will be in the palace soon."

"Dellorans?"

Hool sighed. "You have no idea what is even going on, do you?"

Artus staggered to a window and looked out at the front lawn. He saw the scattered lines of peasant soldiers and sell-swords tasked with holding back the Delloran assault crumpling beneath arrows that fell like rain. Sahand himself, atop a monstrous wyvern, soared over the battlefield like a shadow, raining fire and poison on those below. From his scepter leapt bolts of crimson lightning that shattered the great stone pillars that held together the fence. "He's destroying the wards," Artus breathed. He looked at the others. "Come on—we're almost there."

He got to the bedroom Tyvian had described to him in the letter. Inside, just as described, was a ballista of Verisi construction—a lightweight naval weapon, designed for easy transport—mounted just inside, overlooking a balcony.

"What are we doing?" Hool asked, ears back.

"Remember Galaspin?"

"Yes."

Artus opened the doors to the balcony. "We're doing that."

"That's a bad idea."

Artus shrugged. "You got a better one?"

The balcony was broad and long, running about

fifteen feet to the other door at the opposite end of the room. Rain was beginning to fall in thick, heavy drops and it was the tail end of dusk—visibility was poor. Artus squinted into the growing dark, trying to make out the silhouettes of the Floating Gardens against the dim lamplight of the rest of the city. Behind him, he heard Hool winding the ballista.

There was a pounding on the doors, too rhythmic to be the living—the dead, then. Sir Damon rushed to bar them by slipping his scabbard through the door handles. "We have company!"

They had bigger problems, though—literally. A massive shape swooped past the balcony and the city lights were obscured for a moment, it was so close, Artus felt the breeze. He squinted into the darkness. "Sahand's out there."

Hool stopped what she was doing. "On his flying lizard thing?"

Michelle, sitting with her knees to her face, rocked back and forth in her chair. "We're all going to die."

Hool shrugged. "Probably."

"No!" Artus shook his head. An idea was forming—a crazy, electrifying idea. A *Tyvian* idea. "No we aren't—we're going to do the opposite of die. We're going to win!" He smiled. "In fact, we're going to save the day!"

Sir Damon frowned. "I . . . I beg your pardon?"

"What do you need to take down a wyvern, huh?"

Sir Damon laughed. "You need your own wyvern, or sorcery, or . . . siege equipment."

Artus pointed at the ballista. "Courtesy of Tyvian Reldamar."

They all exchanged glances. Hool looked grim, Sir Damon was incredulous, Brana was terrified. Artus put out his hand. "Let's be heroes tonight, huh?"

Sir Damon was the first to put his hand atop his. "If I have gone mad, let it never be said that I did it halfway."

Brana was next. "Let's get him."

Hool was last. "This is a bad idea. You'll see."

Michelle's face was streaked with tears. "Wh . . . what can I do?"

Artus nodded to the door. "Just make sure the dead don't get in, okay?"

Brana snorted. "She gets the easy job. Hmph."

Artus scowled at him. "Just help me get it into position, dog boy. He should be making another pass soon."

CHAPTER 40

THE BATTLE OF THE EMPTY TOWER

Lyrelle Reldamar stood over the body of Perwynnon, forever in stasis, in a room too quiet for all the chaos taking place around it. Part of her wanted desperately to touch the cheek of the dead king, but the stasis spell there prevented it. She could only look at him, forever young, forever the man she knew and nothing else.

Her simulacra around the palace gave her the same reports—blood in the halls, battle in the gardens, the dead rising. The vicious, violent climax of a social trend she had struggled and failed to control. In her heart, she wept for the people of Eretheria. She wept for the people Perwynnon had loved so fiercely.

But she was not done yet. There were still a few more plots in process. A few more things Xahlven could not predict.

"Magus Reldamar," a thin, raspy voice hissed from the door. Lyrelle didn't bother looking—she knew what she'd see. A gaunt, storybook necromancer—rotting teeth and blind eyes and all—there to draw attention. She considered dispelling the ruse, but then she would give away that she knew it to be a ruse. She gathered her power instead, and waited. The world trembled with her effort, as though reality itself might crack beneath her displeasure.

"Ahhh . . ." the "necromancer" laughed, "I feel that I am in the presence of true power. At last."

Lyrelle still didn't look at him—she didn't need to. In this room, at the juncture of the Trondor and Saldor ley lines, space and time were concepts she could grasp in the palm of her hand. "Must you be escorted by *those*?"

The necromancer nodded to the two undead stewards who flanked him. "Wait outside. Let no one disturb us, understand?"

The undead hobbled to the great doors and vanished through them. They closed with a heavy boom, and then Lyrelle was alone.

With Xahlven.

The necromancer image faded away at once, and there he was—the sitting Archmage of the Ether, staff in hand, robes intact. His golden face was fixed into a hard frown. "I warned you the price of interfering with me again would be severe."

Lyrelle faced him and let a bit of the Lumen leak into her voice, giving it strength and vitality she did not actually possess. "I am your mother, Xahlven, and I will meddle with you as I see fit."

"Something Tyvian and I have in common, then." Xahlven began to circle her. His own wards and guards shimmered with power, seamless and absolute. Breaking through them was impossible—Xahlven knew this, too, since he walked without care, looking down at Perwynnon and sneering. "I can see how he was a tempting prize, Mother. Shame he betrayed you as he did, but he never was very smart, was he?"

"You have become terribly free with your speech in my presence, young man. Continue and you will face my displeasure."

"Ha!" Xahlven shook his head. "We are far beyond the day where your displeasure gives me pause, *Lyrelle*. My presence here should be evidence enough of that."

"You always were a good student, Xahlven." Lyrelle moved her left hand just enough to prod at the edges of Xahlven's defenses—strong, smooth, the work of a master. But even the greatest fortress was not immune to certain vermin. She laid a soft, barely perceptible enchantment upon the edge of her son's wards—an Etheric curse that would slowly nibble away at the structure of those defenses, so that they would eventually shatter.

Xahlven smirked. "I see what you're doing—stalling for time? Hoping for rescue? Surely you have scryed this battle a hundred times by now. What does it tell you of its outcome?"

Lyrelle said nothing. There was no point in feeding Xahlven his own answers. Xahlven was entirely the image of his father—haughty, delighted at his own intellect. Blind to his own failures.

"No matter. Tonight, I become an orphan," Xahlven said at last, and lashed out with a series of death-bolts that crackled across the circular chamber like black lightning.

Lyrelle conjured a shield of mageglass that dispersed the attack and then she hurled the razor-sharp disc at him. She struck only smoke, though—Xahlven had displaced across the room, this time launching a barrage of lode-bolts at her.

Lyrelle caught them in midair—drawing them all to her hand like moths to a flame—and then fashioned them into one gigantic globe of deep cold. When she threw it at Xahlven, his wards took the hit. He staggered backward. Then he grinned. "How much more of that do you have in you, Mother?"

Lyrelle said nothing, answering instead by summoning up a host of fiery fey-sprites and setting them after Xahlven. He responded by forming a colossus of mageglass armor around himself and stomping on the little things, one after another, while he reached out for her with giant, three-fingered talons.

Lyrelle made herself insubstantial and levitated right inside the colossus. One burst of force and the giant war construct shattered, spilling Xahlven onto his back on the floor. Lyrelle remained airborne, floating above her son, invisible winds of power loosening her golden hair and making it dance. "You will find, boy, that there are few replacements for experience."

This time it was Xahlven who said nothing, striking back with the Fey—a wave of crackling energy, oven hot. Lyrelle reflected it back. He blanketed the room in shadow; Lyrelle called down the light. Explosions of the raw energies of creation rocked the tower to its foundations, and Lyrelle remained a half step ahead of her eldest son, her mastery of the arcane arts just barely enough to keep the younger man at bay.

But she knew it couldn't last.

With every spell, Lyrelle felt her body grow weaker. Xahlven was a clever opponent, forcing Lyrelle to use the Fey to defend herself and forcing her to channel the Dweomer when attacking, more often than not. For a woman of her advanced age, her endurance for those physically taxing energies was limited. Her body ached, her hands trembled. Still, she fought on.

Xahlven appeared as thirteen simulacra of himself, each of them throwing bolts of pure Dweomer at her—bolts that would paralyze or transform or even imprison. Lyrelle's wards flashed with fiery Fey energy as the Dweomer was dispersed, but the toll was becoming noticeable. She was sweating, staggering beneath the onslaught.

"You were once mighty, Mother, but your time is past, and your plans are of a bygone era." Xahlven's simulacra grinned as they pressed their attack. "Surrender—you cannot kill me. Even if I were at your mercy, you would spare my life. Why put yourself through such pain?"

Lyrelle bent her knees and, with them, bent space and time for the barest instant. When she rose, the fabric of the world snapped back, sending a ripple of invisible force that obliterated Xahlven's simulacra and knocked the true one on his backside. "This is not pain, Xahlven. You took nineteen hours to be born—*that* was pain. To that, this is but exercise."

Xahlven rolled to his feet. "You cannot win. You must know this."

Lyrelle smiled at him, noting that her curse had eaten away almost half of Xahlven's wards by now. *Ah*, she thought, *but I do not have to win to have my victory.*

Xahlven, face red, called down all the fires of heaven upon his mother. Lyrelle, still and serene, raised the choirs of hell to hold it back. And so the battle continued.

Once the undead entered the equation, things began to click for Tyvian. He watched as they terrorized peasant and noble alike and knew that this wasn't Myreon's work alone—not at all.

It was Xahlven's. It had always been Xahlven.

It wasn't difficult to find his brother—Tyvian now knew with a kind of chemical certainty what Xahlven's endgame was. He had to admit that he'd basically known it since his brother slipped into his room that night and tried to enlist him in his little game. This wasn't about Tyvian and never had been. Xahlven had always looked at Tyvian as a pawn, anyway—he couldn't imagine a circumstance where Tyvian would manage even a minor disruption to his plans. In Xahlven's eyes, Tyvian had never been a threat. No, this whole thing—this massive, chaotic bloodbath—was designed to destroy the one person who Xahlven actively feared: Their mother.

So, Tyvian just dodged the packs of people trying to kill him and followed the sound of apocalyptic sorcerous battle until, at length, he arrived in the Congress of Peers. The great doors behind the throne boomed and buckled as rainbow light flashed behind them.

Myreon was standing on the dais beside the throne, flanked by a half dozen animated corpses, still dusty from the grave. She looked up—her face was pale, her eyes bloodshot. "Tyvian. You shouldn't be here."

Tyvian advanced on her. "Have you lost your Kroth-spawned mind?"

Myreon threw a buffet of force at him that knocked him off his feet. "I am not here to *debate* with you, Tyvian! This is happening! For all your and your mother's attempts to prevent it, this is happening!"

Tyvian scrambled to his feet. "Innocent people are dying! Those *things* . . ." Tyvian gestured toward the undead. ". . . are murdering people as we speak! This is your justice?"

Myreon scowled. "We are doing the best we can—the undead are proving harder to manage than we thought. It wasn't *my* idea to fill the palace with innocent commoners!"

"The nobility are innocent, too!" Tyvian shook his head. "You can't believe that because somebody was born with a title, that makes them deserving of death, can you?"

Myreon's lips curled back. "That's a comforting thing to say if you're born with a title."

Tyvian shook his head again. He had an urge to pace, but the room was too damned big and the gesture would get swallowed by the architecture. "You were a Defender, Myreon! You're working with the League? Am I going mad?"

"Calm down. You've worked with less savory persons, and you know it." Myreon folded her arms. "This is for a cause, Tyvian. It's still me you're talking to."

"Yes, but who *is* that, exactly?" Tyvian threw up his hands. "First you're teaching peasants to rebel, now you're leading an army of the dead to . . . to . . . to what? I don't even know what you hope to accomplish here!"

Myreon's tone was cold. "It's very simple, Tyvian—I'm ending the peerage, here and now. This system must be destroyed and, unlike you, I'm actually doing something about it."

"It's war, Myreon. It's dead bodies and burned homes and weeping children." Tyvian sighed. "I can't ever justify that."

"Why? Because there's no profit in it?" Myreon's voice was hard.

Tyvian frowned and turned to face her. "This . . . this isn't about that. You're right, you know—this isn't about *me*. It's about *you*. About what you've become."

"And what exactly is that?"

Tyvian searched for the words, but couldn't find any but the simplest ones. "A madwoman. A fanatic."

Myreon nodded slowly. "Fine. If I'm a fanatic for justice, I gladly bear that title."

In that moment, he marveled at what a perfect tool Xahlven had made of her. He could have told her, maybe—told her that whoever she thought was fighting Lyrelle on the other side of that door, it was, in fact, the person she loathed more than any other. But he couldn't. Not only because she wouldn't believe him, but because, even if she did, it would wound her more than any dagger. Besides, there was another way to get her to step aside.

Tyvian pointed at the doors behind the throne. "I'm going in that room, Myreon. I won't let you stop me."

Myreon moved to bar his path. "How do you propose to get past me?"

Tyvian took a deep breath. "By pointing out that, at this moment, Banric Sahand has an army of Delloran soldiers ready to put this city to the torch and there is no one—absolutely no one—there to stop him."

Myreon paused. She worked a quick spell, and then her eyes went wide. "Oh gods!"

"I might have been able to do something about it myself—*might* have." Tyvian motioned to the ruins of the Congress, its benches knocked over in panic, the sounds of battle echoing up the corridors. "But you made sure I couldn't. It's up to you now."

Myreon nodded. "This conversation isn't over."

Tyvian looked at her, trying to see the woman he admired. She was still there. It was still her. Just on a different path. A path he couldn't follow. "Yes . . . it is."

Myreon stepped out of his way, wary. "Take care of yourself, Reldamar."

"Good-bye, Myreon. I wish . . ."

But she was gone.

". . . I wish it could have been different."

Tyvian took a long, slow breath, dusted off his doublet, and headed for the doors. It was time for a family reunion.

CHAPTER 41

A BLOW TOO FAR

Sahand's tactical plan seemed to work on the justifiable assumption that the peasants that lived within the tangled neighborhoods of Eretheria's districts wouldn't stick their necks out to have them chopped off by Delloran steel. From what Myreon could observe with her sorcery, Sahand had tasked a brigade of heavily armored troops with besieging Eretheria Tower and keeping the Defenders bottled up inside, but otherwise had only light skirmishers protecting his flanks and rear—men on horseback with sabers, riding back and forth, setting fire to houses and cutting down any person who crossed their path. It was certainly a sufficient deterrent for any rabble. Myreon could see families huddled in their homes, hiding under haystacks in barns, and hugging each other close in root cellars.

Once the palace was secured, however, Myreon knew Sahand would put the city to the torch. That was how Sahand operated—sheer terror was his best defense. Though not an accomplished military tactician, even Myreon could tell Sahand was overextended. Getting his army here had to have been a logistical nightmare, and retreating back to Dellor now that their presence was known was risky. Reducing the capital city to ash with minimal casualties would act as a good deterrent against any army of conscripts that might wish to confront him. He was counting on the audacity of the horror he was creating to give him time.

He was not, however, counting on Myreon.

She aimed for the largest collections of peasants she could—people huddling in churches, in guild halls, in taverns. Feyleaping from roof to roof, block to block, she presented herself glamoured to appear taller, more imposing, more inspiring than she knew she could look. The people of the Ayventry District saw the Gray Lady, golden hair streaming, her gray cloak flowing like gossamer, her eyes alight with power. Her message was simple and her plan easy. *"Be not afraid!"* she called to them, working just a little bit of Compulsion into the words. "Together, we can save the city from Sahand. Spread the word."

When there was resistance—and at times there

was—Myreon thought back to that evening on the bench with those commoners, the way their eyes glowed at the memory of Perwynnon. "You served the Falcon King, did you not? Now, I ask you to serve his son, through me. Gather what weapons you can, muster what able-bodied men are willing to die to save their children. Bring them here." With one hand, she formed a globe of pure Lumen, bright as the sun and warm as daylight. She smiled. "I have a plan that no one will be expecting."

In under an hour they had assembled a few hundred men. It would have to be enough.

Rain was coming down in sheets now—it spattered against Artus's face hard, like little slaps. In the distance, thunder boomed. "Get ready!" he yelled, sighting along the ballista bolt.

Sir Damon and Brana cranked the arms back at lightning speed. The wind gusted hard, blowing the doors half closed. Artus struggled to push them open again—they couldn't afford to miss their shot. He looked up at Hool, perched on the ridge of the roof like a bird of prey. "See him yet?"

"Almost!" Hool shouted down. "Get ready!"

Artus stared hard into the darkness. The rain obscured almost all visibility—he only got impressions of shadows against the swirling water and wind. He licked his lips as water poured off the end of his nose.

"Here he comes!" Hool shouted. "Off to your left, a bit low!"

From somewhere in the room behind him, Artus heard Michelle weeping as she dragged the armoire in front of the door—the dead were still out there, clawing to get in. He clenched his teeth, trying to block out all distractions.

"There!" Sir Damon yelled, right next to Artus's ear, pointing. "There!"

Artus followed the gesture—yes! A serpentine shadow, slicing through the windy sky. Artus moved to position the ballista, but Brana was already there. He swung it to point at Sahand. "Got him!"

"Brana, wait!" Artus yelled, but the gnoll pulled the trigger. The bolt rocketed through the night, lost immediately in the rain.

Sahand swooped past, unhurt.

Artus punched Brana in the arm. "Dammit, you idiot! We missed him!"

"You came close!" Hool said. "Wait longer next time—it went in front of the monster's face!"

Brana punched Artus back—it hurt more. His tongue lolled out. "Almost, see? Next time!"

"If there *is* a next time." His stomach felt cold. He remembered being Sahand's prisoner in Dellor, remembered the man's utter, callous ruthlessness. His sadism. Part of him wanted to hide and wait for it all to blow over. *But that wouldn't solve anything.* He took a deep breath. Tyvian had been right about that much.

Artus searched for another bolt—there was one more, but only one. They reloaded and waited. They waited longer this time, though. Much longer. The lightning arced over the palace, striking the Empty Tower. The rain pooled around their feet on the balcony. "What's taking so long?" Artus yelled up to Hool.

Hool didn't answer. In a flash of lightning, he could see her ears up and rigid, her posture crouched. She was looking the opposite way.

"What is it?" Artus yelled up.

Hool leapt behind a chimney. "HE'S COMING THE OTHER WAY! HE SAW US—"

Before Artus could react, the roof disintegrated above him in an ear-splitting explosion of fire and red lightning. Artus was blown over the balcony railing—he barely caught the edge, his poison-weakened fingers slipping on the slick surface. He realized he couldn't hear—the world buzzed and moved slowly, as though moments had become minutes.

The wyvern skimmed low over the rooftop. He saw its huge talons lash out at something and then it was gone. Artus was losing his grip. He was going to fall.

The world snapped back into focus as Sir Damon grabbed him by the wrist and hauled him up. The first sound that came back was the echoed shouts of the knight. *"Are you all right? Artus! Artus, can you hear me?"*

Then came the sound of wailing—Michelle, terrified beyond all measure.

Then came the sound of Brana, whining softly . . . but nowhere in sight.

Artus pushed Sir Damon out of his way and dove into a pile of rubble. He pulled heavy stones aside, tearing his fingers and burning his skin against the hot and jagged edges, but he didn't feel the pain. "Brana! *Brana!*"

Hool was next to him in a second, throwing stones the size of her head aside. Digging with all her feet faster than Artus thought possible. And there was Brana.

His fur smoked from the heat of Sahand's spell. His face was broken, one eye lost. Blood poured from his mouth and nostrils. His arm was crumpled into a bloody mash. His breathing was labored. Weak.

Artus trembled as he laid a hand on his friend . . . his brother's fur. His eyes were blinded by tears. "Brana? No . . . no . . . you can't . . ."

"Mama?" Brana whined in gnoll-speak, barely audible.

Hool pulled her pup from the rubble and took him into her arms, cradling his long body, resting her head against his face. She howled a soft, haunting melody. "Shhh . . . shhhh . . . *all is well*," she purred in gnoll-speak. *"All is well, my love."*

Artus, Sir Damon, even Michelle cleared out of her way as Hool laid Brana's broken body on the bed.

No one spoke. No scrabble of the undead disturbed them. Even the thunder fell quiet.

Hool leaned down and licked Brana on the nose.

He had stopped breathing.

When Hool stood up, when she turned around, Artus staggered back from the look on her face. The mother gnoll he had come to love was gone. What he saw was a monster from the darkest tales of his youth.

She reached up and drew the Fist of Veroth from its sheath. Saying nothing, she leapt off the balcony and into the storm. Artus rushed to the railing to see where she had gone. In a flash of lightning, he saw her, climbing a turret, coming to stand atop its flat head. The enchanted mace burned with a bright orange fire—Artus swore he could feel the heat from here. And then Hool roared. One word:

"SAHAND!"

"Merciful Hann," Sir Damon breathed. "He'll kill her."

The black wyvern of Sahand swooped once more over their now-ruined perch and glided toward Hool, its talons outstretched.

"The ballista!" Artus shouted . . . but the machine was destroyed. They had to stand there and watch. They could do nothing else.

Hool held her weapon high, howling into the gale. Sahand cast bolts of fiery energy at her, but the Fist of Veroth absorbed them, growing brighter and hotter with every blast. The wyvern was almost upon her—it would snatch her from the battlements like a bird on a branch. She'd never get close enough to use the mighty mace. Never, unless she . . .

Hool leapt into the void, a suicidal jump—twenty feet into nothingness, an abyss of two hundred feet beneath her. It was madness.

But Sahand hadn't expected it. Who *could have* expected it?

She landed atop the wyvern's right wing. Artus could barely see Sahand twist in his saddle before the Fist of Veroth struck down. Not on him.

The wyvern exploded in a fireball of black scales and yellow-black viscera. One wing was blown off, the other caught fire. All of them—beast, gnoll, and Mad Prince—plummeted from the sky.

Sahand's soldiers were breaching the palace even as their Prince fell. Blocks of disciplined pikemen, blooded in a dozen battles against the barbarians of the harsh wilderness of Dellor, moved through the mismatched ranks of mercenaries and peasants like a scythe through stalks of grass. The palace's human defenders broke and ran or tried to surrender . . . and were killed where they knelt.

Then the pikemen met the golems.

Five of the armored constructs, moving with inhuman coordination, struck one flank of Sahand's army, crushing men beneath their five-ton feet and slaughtering them on the edges of seven-foot blades. For a moment, the battle seemed to turn.

Even golems, however, have their weaknesses. Myreon never knew what exactly had happened, but she imagined someone somewhere inside the palace had found the Guardian and realized what he was. And then they slipped a knife between his ribs.

The golems froze in place, one with its sword raised. The Dellorans, falling back, rallied and, when the sorcerous constructs didn't advance any farther, resumed their attack.

This is when Myreon struck. Using the storm, she called lightning down on the Delloran flank—the longbowmen, held in reserve, who were making a sport of shooting down anybody fleeing the palace on foot. Each blast killed two or three men and knocked another dozen sprawling; she followed it up with fireballs thrown as far as she could manage, lighting supply wagons ablaze, killing the skirmishers.

It didn't take them long to figure out where Myreon was—deep in the winding neighborhoods of Ayventry District, standing on a church steeple, making a nuisance of herself. A brigade of Sahand's troops were recalled from the palace assault—two hundred men in ranks, pikes ready—to make a foray and put the troublesome mage to the sword. The drums called the advance, and in they came.

Just where Myreon wanted them.

Pikes were a fine weapon for the open battlefield—deadly to cavalry and infantry alike, lightweight and durable, able to be used with minimal training. In the claustrophobic streets of an Eretherian peasant neighborhood, however, they were a liability. As the pikemen marched in columns down the narrow lanes, Myreon's hastily mustered peasant militia struck from the alleys and houses on either side. Men with hatchets and barrel-top shields struck the flanks of Delloran formations. Men with hunting bows shot from rooftops, picking off officers (a task they referred to as "pulling a Cadogan").

And there was Myreon, bolstering the attack—blade-warding this peasant here, blasting apart that Delloran there. She seemed everywhere, running on adrenaline so heady that she lost track of time.

They didn't exactly win the battle—the Dellorans quickly ditched their pikes and resorted to arming sword and shield, which, combined with their mail and their battle experience, made them potent enemies—but neither could the Dellorans advance. They had to withdraw and muster in a small square. They had to call for reinforcements.

Which is when Myreon did the same. Leaping to other neighborhoods, working her magic on other downtrodden commoners. She needed only to invoke Perwynnon's name and the name of his son, Tyvian Reldamar, and they came.

They came by the hundreds. By the thousands,

perhaps. Even as the palace burned, even as the peerage of Eretheria fled or died upon Delloran pikes.

The peasantry might not be able to drive Sahand
out of the city entirely, but Myreon knew, by the time
the palace clock tower struck midnight, that Eretheria would never be Sahand's to burn.

CHAPTER 42

A GOOD DEATH

It took some time getting the doors to the mausoleum open—Tyvian had to resort to swinging a golem's gigantic sword until, eventually, he'd hacked enough of it away to pry it open with *Chance*. He entered just as there was a massive explosion of frigid air that froze the walls and coated the floor in ice. Xahlven floated in the air above Lyrelle, who crumpled to the ground, her body smoking from the energies she had channeled. Xahlven raised his hands, calling together a black orb of foul-smelling energy—pure Ether, the stuff of death itself.

"Xahlven!" Tyvian shouted.

Xahlven pivoted and threw the orb of oblivion at him.

Stupid, stupid, stupid . . .

Tyvian rolled out of the way as it splashed against the mighty doors and disintegrated them into dust. He caught up his boot knife and threw it underhand, just trying to nick Xahlven in the leg enough to interrupt his concentration. It sailed wide, but only barely.

Xahlven laughed. "So, little brother. It's come to this at last, has it?"

"Is this your primary occupation, now? Toppling governments? Sowing misery?" Tyvian slid carefully along the icy ground toward the edge of the room, where a slender staircase wound up the bole of the huge tower.

"Don't presume to lecture me, Tyvian—you haven't the slightest idea what my plans are. Besides, not more than three years ago, you would have toppled governments and sown misery as recreation." Xahlven continued to float in place, his black robes flowing and crackling with visible energy. That was, itself, unusual—only poorly made or damaged enchantments manifested themselves so visibly. Lyrelle, it seemed, had given her son as good as she got.

Tyvian started up the stairs, *Chance* pointing up at Xahlven. "So, what now? You kill Mother and then me, too? Seems cold-blooded, and that's coming from me."

"I take little pleasure in it," Xahlven said with a shrug, "but sacrifices must be made." He cast a spell at Tyvian—something devious, no doubt. He didn't take time to identify it—he merely dove for cover. The black lightning, though, arced as it came and sought him out, striking him all over his body. Tyvian braced for the pain.

It didn't come. The spell winked out with a *whupp* of rushing air.

Both Tyvian and Xahlven blinked at one another for a moment. Then Tyvian noticed *Chance*, dark with absorbed energy. *Of course.* He smiled. *This is what she meant!*

Tyvian thrust *Chance* in Xahlven's direction and released the spell back at him. His brother vanished and reappeared on the stairs above him. "Interesting. Mother's design, I presume? I'd recognize her handiwork anywhere." He looked over his shoulder at the unconscious Lyrelle. "The old bitch is defeated and still she interferes."

Tyvian charged up the stairs and lunged at Xahlven, but he was suddenly four steps higher up. *Chance* dug itself into the stone of the stairs and was stuck there. "Kroth!"

Xahlven tapped his staff and the stairs beneath Tyvian's feet collapsed into dust. He wound up dangling from the hilt of his own sword, fifteen feet over the hard marble floor. Xahlven came to stand over him. "Even if I can't blast you directly, what exactly do you hope to accomplish, here?" He pressed his staff down on Tyvian's hands, putting all his weight on it. Tyvian's knuckles screamed beneath the pressure.

Xahlven shook his head. "Pity. All those wasted years studying swordplay, and look where it's gotten you."

Tyvian grinned. "It's gotten me awfully close to *you*, I'd say."

"Wha—"

Tyvian reached up with his ring hand and grabbed Xahlven's staff. The ring's power bloomed inside him and with the barest pull of his sword arm, he leapt up into Xahlven's chest, knocking his brother sprawling. Still with his hand on the staff, he ripped it away and broke it in half over his knee.

Xahlven scrambled backward to get back to his feet and Tyvian took the moment to rip *Chance* free from its stone prison. Tyvian's shoulder screamed with pain, but he felt alive, glowing with energy. He came en garde. "I hope that's not your best trick."

Xahlven rolled his eyes. With a snap of his fingers, a long rapier of blackened mageglass appeared in his hand. Another snap of his fingers and a simulacrum of Xahlven appeared behind Tyvian with the same mageglass rapier. "Adequate enough for you?"

Tyvian grinned and turned sideways so he could see both of them. From a sleeve he drew a dagger and flicked a switch to extend a pair of spring-mounted parrying tines. "You know me—I'm never satisfied."

Both Xahlvens came at him at once. Tyvian bound one blade with the dagger and beat the second blade out of line and followed up with a quick thrust aimed at the upper arm. But Xahlven wasn't there—he was five inches to his right, his displaced image vanishing as Tyvian cut through it. Then the Xahlven on his dagger side pressed him hard, but Tyvian had the higher step and he kicked the simulacrum in the face, knocking it back.

Xahlven was back at him again, sending a flurry of fast thrusts and cuts his way that Tyvian could barely parry—Xahlven had never been this good, not before. He was boosting his reflexes with Astral energy, slowing down time for himself while things remained the same for Tyvian.

The simulacrum stabbed Tyvian through the back of his thigh in a suicidal lunge that earned it the parrying dagger in the eye. It vanished in a puff of Ether, but the damage had been done. Tyvian crumpled backward.

Xahlven pursued his advantage, trying to drive his blade down through Tyvian's shoulder and into his heart. Tyvian brought both his weapons in an X over his head and diverted the thrust, then locked the blade and twisted it from Xahlven's hand.

But Xahlven already had another one, appearing in his offhand with a flash. Tyvian thrust at his brother's stomach, but Xahlven parried. He was on the defensive, though—it was Tyvian's turn to press the advantage, staggering to his feet and driving his brother back with the years of fighting experience no Astral enchantment could match. He used his two weapons to Xahlven's one to draw his brother into feints and binds that would have ended him, but for his brother's unnatural speed.

So they went up and up and up, each man fighting for his life as they wound higher and higher up the Empty Tower. For all his skill, Tyvian could not score a touch on Xahlven, whose illusions and enchantments were almost impossible to see through. He, however, was struck several times—a cut across his left arm, a slash across the cheek, a shallow thrust into his chest that wedged in a rib.

Finally they locked blades and Tyvian dropped the dagger to catch Xahlven's wrist. He then pivoted and, using his body as a fulcrum, catapulted Xahlven out one of the narrow windows of the tower. Tyvian followed him, not so foolish as to think a throw from a window would be enough to do in an archmage.

It hadn't been. Xahlven floated down to the ridge of the highest roof in the palace—that of the palace chapel. Powering through the pain in his leg and relying on the ring to propel him, Tyvian followed, leaping across the void and landing with a crash right in front of his brother.

Xahlven was out of breath, which Tyvian took as a great compliment. "What do you hope to gain here, brother?" The archmage spread his arms. "You court your death only! Look!"

Around the palace, Tyvian could see the ranks of Dellorans assaulting the palace. Fire leapt from the towers and belched from broken windows. In a flash of lighting, he could see how the bodies of peasants and noblemen alike littered the gardens, staining the puddles crimson. Further still, he caught glimpses of fire and mayhem in the streets beyond—fighting in the alleys, in the neighborhoods, house to house.

"You've lost!" Xahlven yelled over the boom of thunder. "Eretheria will be plunged into civil war. Myreon Alafarr will lead a rebel army that will plague the five counties for decades! Sahand will invade! There is nothing you can do to stop it now!"

Five more Xahlvens, each with his deadly blade of mageglass, came into being around Tyvian. He ran his options—none of them looked good. He wasn't making it off this roof alive.

Tyvian shook his head. "*Why?* Dammit, Xahlven— why *do* this?"

"I do not reveal my plans to my enemies," Xahlven said.

"I'm your *brother*, not your enemy! Dammit, Xahlven—I spent my whole childhood trying to convince you of that! What the hell did I ever *do* to you?"

Xahlven blinked—for the first time in Tyvian's memory, he had said something to his brother that he hadn't expected. Finally he said, "It wasn't some-

thing you ever did, Tyvian. It was who you were."
He pointed back at the tower. "You were *hers*—so
clearly, so obviously her favorite, her protégé. The
little boy she had *abandoned my father* to make and,
when he grew angry about it, you were the boy that
my mother murdered my father to protect." Xahlven spat. "My brother? Ha! I was never your brother,
Tyvian, just as I never was her son. I was never anything more than a political convenience—a child
borne to snare my father into loving a treasonous,
hateful witch."

As Xahlven talked, Tyvian palmed the poison ring
he'd gotten from Voth. "So you decided to destroy
the world out of revenge?"

Xahlven laughed and his simulacra closed in, their
blades raised. "This is not about destroying the world,
Tyvian. It's about saving it—it always has been!"

"You're about to kill me anyway—just tell me. I
know you're dying to!" Tyvian put his free hand to
his leg wound and made a show of rubbing it, but he
was actually pressing the ring's needle into his thigh.
It burned like white fire and then got deathly cold.
Tyvian's heart began to race even faster than before.

Xahlven laughed. "You're just wasting time,
but fine—if it means so much to you, I'll tell you.
The Balance—the forces that hold our universe together—is becoming more and more volatile. It has
been ever since the Illini Wars. I know this—I studied
it underneath Master Vodran in the Arcanostrum. If

we continue as we have been, we will trigger a cataclysm that will wipe out everything—all life will end."

Red tinged the edges of his vision. Tyvian shivered. The world began to spin. "That . . . that sounds like . . . like you believe in Kroth the Devourer."

"It's a fable rooted in truth—too much sorcery will upend the Balance and destroy the world." Xahlven laughed once more, a bit ruefully this time. "I can't believe I'm telling you this."

Tyvian shook his head, trying to stay cogent for a few moments longer, at least. "So your solution is . . . is to *destroy civilization* to save the world? Am I understanding this right?"

Xahlven sighed. "Enough talk—let's finish this."

The poison in his bloodstream was enough that Tyvian could barely follow what happened next. He only knew he needed to get to the back of the chapel, where the roof overlooked the lake—*everyone* needed to see him fall, commoner and nobleman alike. A spectacular, public death—his only remaining weapon.

So he ran, unevenly, sliding and slipping across the steeply angled roof. One of the Xahlvens stabbed him in the back as he went. And another. And another. Tyvian didn't bother trying to defend himself—it was either too late or it wasn't. Besides, with the poison, he barely felt the blades.

He saw the edge of the chapel and the darkness of

the lake beyond, both at the end of a tunnel somehow
darker and brighter at the same time. He felt himself
falling.

He felt nothing more.

All according to plan.

EPILOGUE

Sahand dragged himself from the lake, his life ward pulsing cold against his flesh, preserving him from death. Gods and devils, that had been close! Breathing hard, he rolled to his back and stared up at the night sky, rippling with lightning. He tried to breathe, but only coughed up more lake water. "That infernal beast. That Kroth-spawned animal . . ."

Staggering to his feet, he cast about for a weapon, keeping one eye on the water where, impossibly, his wyvern still managed to burn. Steam rose from the surface of the lake. The she-gnoll still lived, he knew. She and he had struggled in the depths for gods knew how long. Long enough for him to drown, that much was certain. Long enough for her to . . .

He reached up to find a mangle of flesh where his right cheek should have been—the thing had torn off part of his face, exposing his teeth. Blood poured over his jaw and down his throat. He gagged on it.

"*Kroth!*"

Sahand threw a bolt of fire into the water, and another, and another—they hissed and were gone. He struggled to channel the Dweomer so he could freeze the lake solid, but he was too wild, too angry. The gnoll, though, was somewhere out there in the dark, in the lake. Perhaps swimming off to lick its wounds before it came back again. He roared into the night, "*I'll be waiting, beast! You hear? I'll. Be. Waiting!*"

Armored footsteps behind him. Sahand created a ball of fire in his hand and whirled, ready to throw. One of his lieutenants dropped to his knees. "Sire!" He held up a rapier of pure mageglass—Sahand recognized the weapon, if only vaguely. He looked at the lieutenant, who continued, "The palace is ours, sire. The king is dead."

Sahand frowned to the extent that his ruined face allowed. "You're certain?"

"I saw him fall with my own eyes, sire. He landed in the lake, grievously wounded. I posted men to watch for some time—he did not emerge."

Sahand grunted—*good enough for now.* "Hostages?"

"A good number, sire, as you requested." The lieutenant looked up. "Also, there is something else."

Sahand saw the grin working to burst from the man's face. Some of his rage dimmed. "Tell me."

Lyrelle awoke to find herself on her knees, an iron collar clapped around her neck connected to a chain that bound her to at least a dozen other women in ruined gowns. Her head spun; she tried to figure out where she was—somewhere in the palace. She heard Northron being spoken, but in the Delloran dialect. Sahand had won then. *No!* She hadn't planned for that. She'd known she would lose, but . . . not like this.

She drew a deep breath. She needed to remain calm. Needed her wits.

A door opened and a broad man marched through, his mail coated in blood and ash, his boots soggy. His iron circlet was gone and his face was a ruin of blood and bone, but Lyrelle would know Banric Sahand anywhere. Around her, the other captives cowered, some weeping, others throwing themselves on their faces. Lyrelle tried to stand.

She was struck from behind with something heavy and knocked to all fours, her breath coming in ragged gasps.

"Pull her to her knees," Sahand barked, his voice wet with the blood in his mouth. He was missing a cheek, his teeth exposed in a permanent half grin, dripping red.

Lyrelle was dragged by the collar back to her knees. She struggled to channel a spell, but she couldn't— Xahlven had taken too much out of her. There was nothing left. She could only kneel and look her captor in the eye as she kept her posture as straight and defiant as possible, given the circumstances.

Sahand said nothing. He smiled his blood smile and unbuckled his belt. Around her, the women shrieked. Lyrelle forced herself to remain calm. Serene.

Sahand removed his manhood from beneath his armor and, shaking it at her for a moment, let loose a stream of urine that struck Lyrelle in the chest. It was hot, pungent. Lyrelle's nostrils flared, but she kept herself still, never looking away from Sahand's ruined face. He never looked away either. He kept grinning until he was done. "There." He spat blood on her face. "You're mine now."

She opened her mouth to reply, but Sahand spoke over her. "Take her thumbs. If she speaks a word, take her tongue, too."

Sahand crouched in front of Lyrelle, his hard eyes so close she could spit in them, but she chose not to. "This wasn't part of your plans, was it?"

Behind her, a man grabbed her wrist and tore it loose from her bonds. He bent her arm back. She felt the bite of a knife in the webbing between her thumb and forefinger. Then a white-hot pain and the sound of her voice screaming, as though from a long distance.

Sahand rose. "Pack them up," he bellowed to his men. "We withdraw at dawn."

Hool laid a wreath of wildflowers upon the cairn. She had spent the whole day preparing it. Artus didn't think she had eaten in three days.

The cairn stood on a hillside a few miles outside of the city. The smoke from the fires was still thick in the air, even at this distance. A black smudge smeared across the western horizon. Artus couldn't bring himself to look at it.

Hool stepped back from the grave of her pup; her great golden mane seemed limp in the humid air. Beside her, Sir Damon took her hand and held it. To Artus's great surprise, she did not draw away.

Myreon was beside him, dressed in mail, her staff replaced with a poleaxe inscribed with all manner of runes. Her face was hard. "Should we say a few words?"

"Leave your stupid gods out of this," Hool growled. It was the first sentence she had uttered in hours.

Myreon didn't flinch. "We have all lost people, Hool. But we can make their deaths have meaning."

Hool turned to face her. "You mean join your stupid army? Fight your stupid war?"

"Justice, Hool," Myreon said, her eyes flashing. "Justice is never stupid."

Hool shook her head. "Yes it is. It's stupid right now." She looked back at the cairn. "Go and die for your stupid justice. Leave me out of it."

Artus came forward and hugged the big gnoll. He felt her great body sag against him for a moment and then return the hug. "I'll miss you, Hool. I . . . I love you."

Hool held him by the shoulders. "When Sahand is dead, I will find you again. I swear it."

Artus felt a tear swell up in his eye. "Can't I go with you?"

"I will not have the blood of any more pups on my hands," Hool said softly. "It will be Sahand or me who will die next. No one else."

Sir Damon cleared his throat. "I may have something to say about that, my lady."

Hool looked at him for a moment, her ears back, and then nodded. "That is true. Sir Damon might die first."

In spite of himself, Artus smiled. He reached up and ruffled the fur behind Hool's ear. "He was my brother. I'll never forget."

"Neither will he," Hool said, licking Artus's hand. Then she and Sir Damon started away, heading north. Artus watched them go for a long while. Before they crested the next hill, Sir Damon paused on horseback to salute them. Then he was gone.

Myreon put her hand on Artus's shoulder. "The milita leaders will be mustered by now. We should get back. Besides, Michelle is waiting."

Artus sighed.

"Cheer up, Artus." Myreon climbed onto her horse. "Turns out you're quite good at being a convincing crown prince. Tyvian would have been proud."

"I know. Can't wait to tell him all about it."

"You're going to win this war for us. You're not going to die, Artus."

Artus laughed. "That's not what I meant."

"Then what?"

Artus shook his head and patted the letter Michelle had found. Just it's being there gave him a sense of comfort.

"Tyvian ain't dead."

ACKNOWLEDGMENTS

First and foremost, I'd like to thank my agent, Joshua, without whom this book may never have seen the light of day. Also big thanks to my editor, David, whose efforts made this book sparkle. A big thank you also goes to my beta-readers (Brandon, Katie, and Jason) as well as all my readers, past, present, and future. Finally, and most importantly, I'd like to thank my wife for all her support and her endless willingness to let me lock myself in my office and wander the green fields of Eretheria for hours on end, even if there were chores to do.

ABOUT THE AUTHOR

On the day **AUSTON HABERSHAW** was born, Skylab fell from the heavens. This foretold two possible fates: supervillain or sci-fi/fantasy author. Fortunately he chose the latter and spends his time imagining the could-be and the never-was rather than disintegrating the moon with his volcano laser. Auston is a winner of the Writers of the Future Contest and has had work published in *Analog*, *F&SF*, and *Escape Pod*, among other places. He lives and works in Boston, Massachusetts. Find him online at aahabershaw.com, on Facebook at www.facebook.com/aahabershaw, or follow him on Twitter @AustonHab.

Discover great authors, exclusive offers, and more at hc.com.